THE RISING OF KEDTAIR

THE RISING OF KEDTAIR

THE ENCHANTER'S WEB BOOK III

M. Turville Heitz

Copyright © 2025 by M. Turville Heitz
979-8-9918853-5-5

First Edition

For information address Oakland Hills at P.O. Box 531, Cambridge, WI 53523
Oaklandhillsfarm.com

Cover art and design by Ingrid Kallick https://ikallick.com/

For David who wanted to see this in print and didn't, and for Morgan who will.

Acknowledgements

Thanks to all those who provided feedback and insight as this work took its long journey from a college writing thesis to novel. Special thanks for in-depth review by Jay Clayton, Kandis Eliott, Hal Gillam, Kathleen Massie-Ferch, Steven Rogers, Fred Schepartz and Morgan Turville-Heitz.

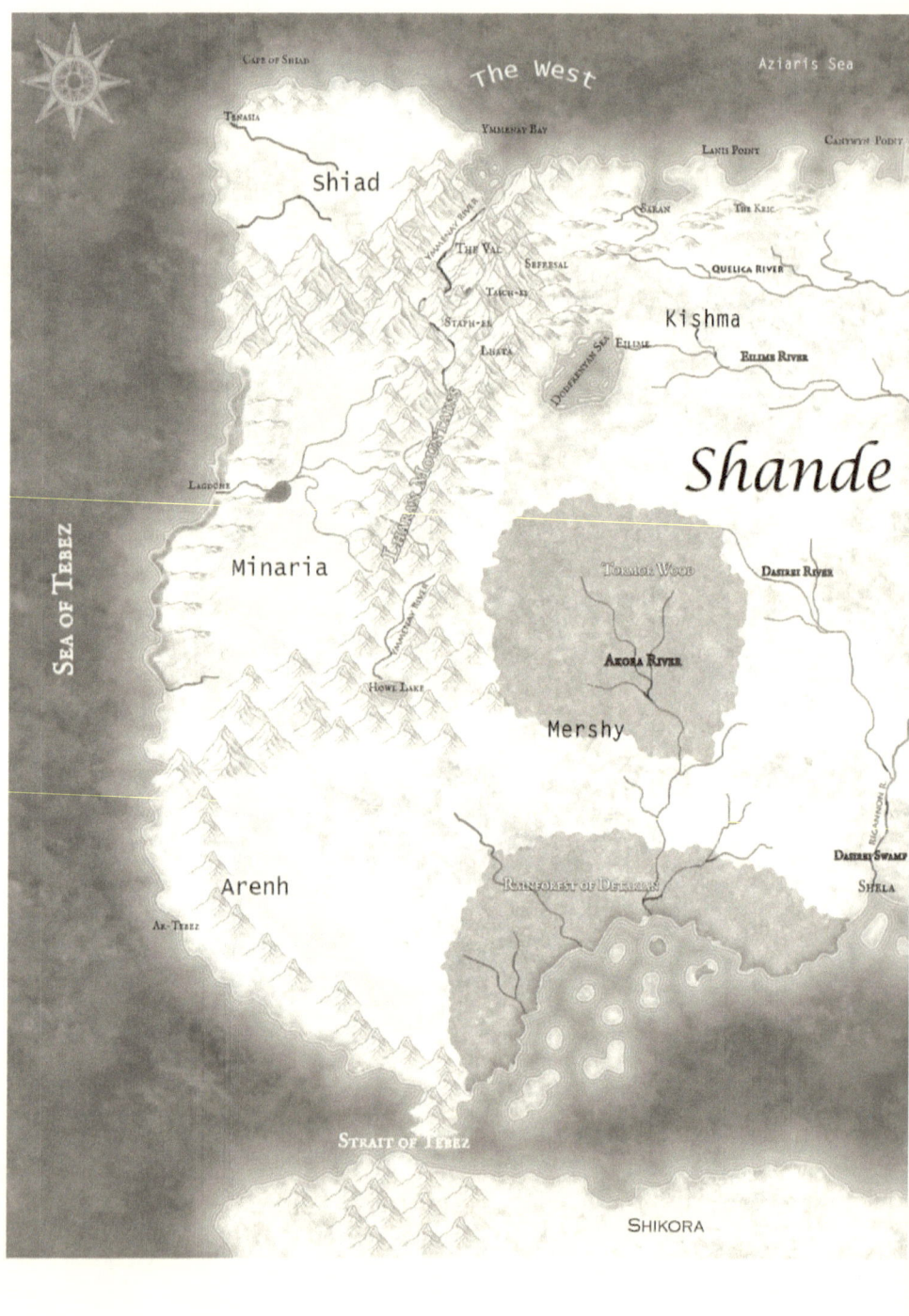

Part 1. Revival

1: From the Dead

Someone pounding on the door of his tiny shack brought Ramel to his feet. Likely a neighbor child buzzed around again, looking for him to perform some sleight of hand. Certainly not his purpose on Ea, to entertain imps, but it seemed little else occupied his time these days. If he ignored it, perhaps the child would leave. He glared at the door less than a pace from him, silently daring the child to knock again.

The entire shack – four walls, packed-sand floor, and a flat roof – barely held his narrow bed, a stool, a few shelves crammed with oddments and a wash basin. He needed nothing more than this portable abode that moved with the village. He had no desire to live in the flimsy, impersonal tents others called home.

The knock again shook his walls; a jar shimmied toward the lip of a shelf. He resettled it and yanked the door open, prepared to send the imp running with his testiest growl. The sunlight glared off the sand, burning his eyes as it flooded his dim shack.

"Ramel!" urged a silhouette in the doorway. "We found a dead man in the dunes."

"What do I care for dead men?" he said with a growl, forcing his bushy eyebrows up into a sinister slant that usually sent visitors away. He made a shooing motion with his hand, preparing to shut the door again.

The distraught man dared grab the sleeve of Ramel's white robes. Ramel stiffened.

"Shawnsi," the man insisted.

"Who?" Ramel demanded. The man shrugged, motioning Ramel to follow.

"We wanted the finer sands the storm left for a special glass order from Loch Asmodiel up in Sihmad Shal," the man explained as Ramel pulled his hood up to shield the top of his sparsely covered head from the sun. "My boy found some strange dried plants, started poking around, and there he was."

"Lost on the road," Ramel said.

"No, a good hour south of it and a half a day west of here. Maybe he lost his way in the storm and wandered off the track."

Unlikely, Ramel thought. The road, like Hainad, lay on one side of a rift valley cutting through the Jashiho Desert, thus protected from the shifting dunes and sheltered from the wind. While in this location Hainad used a natural spring that fed a few trees and grasses, the wells the length of the road at past sites where the mobile village had stood drew from a river hidden beneath the valley. One couldn't wander up the valley sides unwitting, even in a sand storm.

The man led Ramel to a wagon filled with buckets of sand of varying quality, color and consistency. The body lay tossed across the top like so much baggage.

"Don't know how long he's been dead," the man said, biting into a hunk of bread. "Didn't feel stiff." The man continued to chew his bread as he hefted the body over the wagon side like a sack of feed.

"That is because he is not dead."

"No lifebeat, no breath."

"He is not dead." Ramel glared at the man to silence him. "Help me get him inside."

They lugged the body to the little bed in Ramel's shack, Ramel studying the man like a hawk on prey. The stranger bore the white hair of an older man, thick and curled about a face that appeared ashen despite the sunburn and wind-chafe deep enough that sections of his cheeks and brow had scabbed. Sand clung to the scabs. The sinewy muscles of intense labor and lean rations clung to his bones.

2

"No scepter, no crown. How does he convince them?" Ramel muttered to himself. Then the left hand fell open to reveal a large opal embedded in the palm. "Ah, Cree, you remembered."

Ramel chuckled to himself as he lifted the head and pressed water to unresponsive lips. The Hainadan sand collector stared at Ramel as if he looked on a crazed mourner.

Fever burned like a furnace in the shawnsi. Ramel gestured at the sand collector. "He came to see Zel, best call him."

One look at Ramel's favorite stern visage sent the sand collector running the short distance to Hainad in search of the Joffan ruler.

"Well?" the voice registered impatience. "Weeks we've waited. Why do I let you keep calling me here, Seer? I have better things to –"

"His fever broke, Zel." A patient tone.

"So? A week ago, you wanted me excited that you drew him from his hideyhole with that demonstar chant. Then the talk you dragged from him with your seer's potions. What torture have you concocted for the dead now?" Sarcasm lay heavy on a tongue thick with Joffan accent.

"You have learned a great deal from my 'seer's potions.'" A deference tinged with danger permeated the words.

"Pshaw." A dismissal.

"He may never wake."

"Then what good is this vigil, Ramel? You keep telling me he's so necessary. The moon hasn't come crashing from the sky without him. The sun doesn't hesitate to rise. On what do you base this certainty? On a kingdom lost, on the tally of failures you claim he's recited? You regale me with these. I think it's all in your imagination. He sleeps. That's all, taking up my time and your bed. If he speaks, why don't you make him speak when I'm here? Or maybe you just imagine your potions brought out this fanciful story."

"My osfothye mixtures never fail to work."

The voices continued, growing louder, an irritating buzz to match the horrible throb in his head.

Arshal opened his eyes to the searing pain of muted light

striking them. The bleariness of long sleep blurred his vision. Voices in heated argument. Over him! He reached for his sword, but found empty air. Had they captured him? Had he stumbled on a mountain raiding party? Perhaps Khoti stalked them, hoping to save their king. King! He must escape! He flew upright, the stone in his hand blazing.

"Do not use it!" A voice shrieked from the blurry light around him.

He saw then an old man who grabbed for Arshal's hand to turn the blaze of the stone aside. With a bellow that shook the walls, the old man flew back with a gasp, cradling his hand. The stench of burned flesh filled Arshal's tiny world. The old man leaned against the wall and fought for breath.

"Arshaldon!" he screeched, at last drawing Arshal's foggy mind to quench the light.

The old man fell onto a stool, still clutching his hand. "It is Terremar's gift. No lesser god could burn me," he muttered as he cradled his hand.

"What are you babbling about, Ramel?" a tall shawnsi demanded, a man who felt familiar.

"Cree?" Arshal asked, staring at the old man who, though garbed in the white robes of the desert and gold sash of Prince Euzzeldir's house, could be the twin of Arshal's old tutor.

"Fool, what would he be doing here?" the old man retorted, still cradling his arm. "Only you would be so foolish as to wander through the desert alone. Where is your counselor?"

"In Sihma Harbor," Arshal muttered then shook his head. He tried to erase the bleariness. He lay back again on the bed. "Not Cree, no. He's dead."

Ramel sagged. "I thought I felt him pass home." He reached for Arshal's hand. "But he did this first. Terremar's gift would be too powerful for even a Visionary to hold in his head!"

"What are you talking about?" If the tall shawnsi would just move out of the shadows, Arshal thought he'd recognize Euzzeldir.

Ramel gave the Joffan an impatient glance. "I can be killed, but I cannot be injured so easily. Only one of the greater gods, Fyraer perhaps, or Terremar could harm me so. Any mortal's weapon that draws my blood would do so at his peril."

"You said these godly powers can be turned to evil. Perhaps Fyraer struck you, Seer."

He moved out of the shadow, eyes still gathering the dark of Ramel's shack. Wavy black hair hung in braids wrapped with gold. His thick brows met; his forehead furrowed in a deep crease. Arshal had a memory of the man's face, younger, dark and imperious beside the pale northerners of Sihmad Shal. The prince's household had disdained the city to camp outside the walls.

"You would know evil if it assaulted us. Terremar grants this gift to aid us. It could kill lesser deities such as myself, and mow down mortal warriors with barely an effort." He stared at Arshal with bright eyes that reminded Arshal of threatening visions. "And you were strong enough to put it in the stone to manage it."

Arshal shook his head, an action that made an ache throb over his eyes. "I almost died."

"But Terremar saved you, in the form of a healer, Khoti –"

"How do you know that? Who are you and what games are you playing?" Arshal demanded, sitting up again. Though he'd balled his hand in a fist, light leaked out around his fingers.

"Do not use it. You know it weakens you," Ramel ordered.

"How do you know? Where is this place?"

"You're in Hainad, King," Euzzeldir said. The way he emphasized the title revealed his skepticism. "I'm sure you've surmised Ramel is a Visionary, though I've seen little that's awesome about him. I keep him around because he and his kind have provided good advice since the days of Dynfearn. I remember you as a brash boy always racing off to trouble with Zopher don Saran. You came to see me."

Arshal fell back to the bed, for the first time feeling the pain in his leg, the weakness that first flare from the stone had brought. "How do you know?"

"You talked in your sleep," Ramel soothed.

"Don't lie to him!" Euzzeldir gave Ramel a sidelong glance, his words filled with his disgust. "Ramel gave you some potion to make you talk. We know all about your journey. Ramel, you're like a child with a new toy. But the game's not amusing and the toy's a king, no matter what his abilities."

Arshal struggled against the weight of his eyelids. He felt so tired, drifting toward that room in his mind.

"Cree taught you too well," Ramel said. The old man gripped Arshal's shoulder roughly and shook him alert. "It is too easy and dangerous for you to slip away. Few have the skill to call you back. And your journey is not over yet. I see the purpose now. You are not ready – not strong enough or wise enough to use it."

"Zel?" Arshal tried to force his eyes open. "You must help. We need you."

"What?" the prince scoffed. "You can't even gain the support of our most oppressed peoples. If Shela turns away –"

"But Arenh, Shiad, Han –"

"Insignificant for your lofty goals."

Arshal forced himself to one elbow, fighting the weariness and a nausea that made his head throb, his stomach rumble. If only Khoti stood by to give him strength, healing, merely his presence. He stared at the stone, which glowed royal blue in his palm. "I must convince you."

"You are weak yet," Ramel said, pushing Arshal down. "If you over-exert yourself, you will again be near death. There is so much you have yet to learn. You have been a-bed for weeks."

"Weeks! How long?"

"It is better than a week into the last moon."

"Last moon!" Arshal tried to swing his legs from the bed and rise. Stabs of pain reminded him of a dream where the bone protruded from his flesh. "Oh gods, I've broken it," he groaned, falling back on the bed a moment before again trying to rise.

"Don't be a fool, King," Euzzeldir said. "You can't walk. You're too sick to do much of anything."

"Thousands will die if I fail! I must reach Shikora, Otayr. There isn't time."

"Well, it's a fact you have to wait to mend."

"No, send for Khoti in Mershy. He can help," Arshal demanded, desperate as he tried to find some way to salvage all the plans hinging on one man. Such fools they'd been.

"This Khoti's with Habdelion?" Euzzeldir asked. "That's weeks distant. By the time he arrived you'd be hale."

"So much time!" Arshal wailed. He knotted his hand in his

hair, pulling with frustration, letting the sting of it help him think. "I'll fail and Shande will be lost forever."

"You place great confidence in yourself, King," Euzzeldir said with a wry twist of his mouth. "A young man, untested, crawls to me to claim he's Shande's salvation because he can burn a Visionary's flesh."

"I wouldn't need to come if you hadn't driven my messengers away! They risked their lives to carry my words and you laughed in their faces. You forced me to come here! It's not my fault I couldn't imagine all possible outcomes."

"If you risked your life just to meet with me, then you're a fool twice. You place too much stock in me."

"No," regal dignity crept into his tone. "I placed on you only the expectations of being served by one who pledged fealty to the House of Dyndevas."

Euzzeldir straightened. Even Arshal heard it. Something in his words made Euzzeldir emit a small gasp of wonderment. From Ramel it drew a broad and knowing grin, an expression Arshal couldn't have imagined on a face so like Cree's.

"We need every Shandean, not just those who find it convenient," Arshal went on. "Are you so much better than the rest of us? Have you had no deaths in Joffa? Are none of your people forced to labor with little to survive on, merely to sate some alien god? You live in hiding. But if it's more convenient for you to cower like the other fools of Shande –"

"You dare to call me a coward!" Euzzeldir reached for his dagger. It rested there like a challenge.

"Yes! What else do you call it when a man refuses to serve his king in defense of his country?"

"Wisdom."

"Oh, it's so wise to let the Minarians rape Shande," Arshal said around a sneer, gasping for breath.

"No, it's wise to not rely on an upstart king who hasn't proved himself. Even you admit you weren't prepared."

"What's proof?"

"Do not use it," Ramel warned again. Arshal had forgotten the seer who watched the exchange with an intense fascination, like Nali had when he heard Cree's tale of the beginning.

"What's proof?" Arshal repeated. "Sure, we lost Sihmad Shal.

But a bunch of fishers and farmers held for two weeks against a trained army. I helped lead hundreds across the country, helped make a home in an inhospitable valley for thousands of refugees, crossed this country alone, drafted plans that this moment move ahead without me."

"That's nothing," Euzzeldir said. "So, you wandered about the country and failed at everything you tried, lost the city, your people exiles. Ramel said you spoke of a healing warrior. His rumor came with messengers and scouts. The Minarians ask after this great Verdaen. Now if this man had come, declaring his feats, there I believe is a man who could lead us."

"And he's one of mine, King's Champion, Sword of Shande," Arshal returned. "Do you suggest such a warrior would have blind faith? I had to earn it." Arshal glanced at Ramel. "He called me back from death with the plea for Kedtair. And while he called, Terremar passed through him."

"How would you know that!" a bitten-off laugh snorted through the prince's nose.

"I know Terremar. He came to me in an osfothye vision. I'd know him in anything."

Arshal took a deep breath, wishing he could again feel the comfort of Khoti's spirits. Weariness threatened to pull him under. "When Kedtair rises is when we'll be strongest. Then I must face Ghyldus to defeat him or die in the effort."

"And how would you accomplish that!" Euzzeldir almost laughed in his sovereign's face, but caught himself. "You look nothing like a warrior. I wonder at what skill you might have, being raised as a soft son of Ebon in Sihma Harbor. You've yet to show great wisdom in your travels."

"No, Zel," Ramel said. "He has shown wisdom. He listened to his visions and went in search of the missing arts of his gift. He could keep sending messengers, but who would believe a faceless promise? They had nothing to believe but the rumor. If he rode into occupied Shande, a shawnsi among a troop of warriors, how far could he have traveled? How many battles would he have fought, risking death to stay one step ahead of the Eidhalt? The hard road, alone, shows dedication to his people, himself and the gods. He had to learn to wield a deadly power, rely on his instincts and become one with himself, trust himself and those guiding him. And this accumulation of wisdom is not complete," Ramel was watching Arshal, his eyes taking on an odd and speculative gleam.

"Admit it to him, Zel," Ramel went on. "You marveled at the tale. Said his were worthy feats. Now you deride him. What skill he has for battle? You already heard it. In his voice, the power to move you to his orders, a skill, a command no king's possessed in generations. You sense power emanating from him, even weak and ill, the feeling of a threat and strength cunningly concealed. You have seen it." Ramel tapped the stone glowing in Arshal's palm. "Right there. Terremar's gift safe in a stone like Dynfearn's, a power of the ancients."

"But what is it?" Euzzeldir demanded. "A bright stone –"

"Look at my hand!" Ramel held out his arm. The skin of his hand already sloughed away to leave a bright red slash, blisters all around. "And he only meant to stun us as he did the animals in the forest. If he had thought instead to explode a pond wall? I would be dead. To break a sword? My arm would have shattered. It is with this power that he will face Ghyldus."

"Then why not just go now to Lagdche instead of racing about the world gathering armies?"

"Ramel may not have the powers to defend himself against this but Ghyldus does," Arshal explained. "He has Fyraer. It's always been an even contest between Terremar and Fyraer. We need to force a confrontation when we're ready, when we're strongest. We must strike a blow so hard Fyraer can't simply set up another godhead, can't find an ear on Ea to hear his claims."

Ramel nodded. "Cree taught you well."

"Cree preached caution," Arshal retorted. "He near killed me, and never forgave himself. It's Nali's counsel I follow."

"Your counselor tried to kill you?" Euzzeldir blinked.

"He couldn't call me back. Tried to bleed me." The humming in Arshal's ears had become a chorus.

"Cree could not call you but your warrior could? I knew Cree weakened. This Khoti I must meet."

Arshal struggled against his mind's urge to find the peace inside and forget all these trials. "I need your help, Zel." He fought with the words. "And I need to reach Shikora and Otayr to beg the same. The longer I wait, the bleaker our hopes for success. We just can't afford more delays. We have one hope, and that's a final blow under Kedtair. Please, trust me, honor your pledge."

Euzzeldir's dark eyes gathered shadows in Ramel's gloomy shack. "Let me think about it." He turned to leave, but paused, glancing back to study Arshal, his dark eyebrows arching. "I remember you with fair hair, not white."

Arshal held up the stone. "It takes life. Even if I defeat Ghyldus, I likely won't survive it."

Euzzeldir grasped the door latch. "I'll think about it," he whispered, sounding less certain of his convictions.

As he opened the door, a blaze of light flared in Arshal's palm, stabbing out to strike the sand beyond the stoop, fusing it into a glassy surface. Euzzeldir stared at the melted fragment of stone. A glassmaker knew what it took to make such a substance. He glanced at the sweat-soaked king, then slipped out, closing the door softly behind.

Ramel had to lean over him to peer in his face. "That was a stupid thing to do."

Arshal's small smile seemed to stun the seer. "You sound so much like Cree. As annoying as he was to have around, it's nice to meet a Visionary again."

As weariness at last won and he sank into sleep, he wondered if he truly played the fool to think he could ever meet the timetable to which he called all of Ea.

The fever returned when he used the stone, as Ramel feared. After weeks of illness, he just didn't have the strength to battle the poisons in his infected leg. Ramel's herbal poultices weren't rife with spirits like Khoti's medicine. The sour humors and pain remained. Ramel muttered about removing the limb to speed him to health. Arshal couldn't let that happen. It would take too long to heal. Nor could he travel across the country or do battle with only one leg holding him in his saddle. He certainly didn't need to offer Ghyldus any more advantages.

He rose from the deep dreams of the fevered to feel a damp cloth that sent shivers through him. He tried to swipe at the hand washing his face, but the hand merely brushed his aside like a bothersome insect.

The wet cloth pressed to his forehead; another lay across his neck. Then the insistent hands bathed his chest. A violent shiver took him. He tried to pull the blanket up to cover him, but again the hands pushed his away. Struggling to open his eyes, he needed to see why Ramel tended him so patiently rather than grumbling at him for the trouble he caused. Perhaps he'd grown worse. He needed to read his fate in the seer's face.

At last, he managed to lift his lids then blinked several times to clear his eyes. He smiled a little; it made his cheeks ache and his head buzz.

"Ramel, you look better each day."

"Oh, go on, Lord," the woman's voice returned. "You're too sick to tease."

"Have I died then? Is this what comes after?" His smile widened as he took in more of the woman's face. Long waves of auburn hair – sun-tinged light chestnut in places and bound back with a gold scarf – framed sun-coppered features. Beneath the arch of thick, dark brows glittered eyes that swirled brown, green and gold. If not for the mark at her temple, he might not have known her for shawnsi. Her face appeared like a vision hanging in the midst of the blur.

"I don't think you're half as sick as you pretend, King." She laughed, dipping a rag in a bucket of water chilled by the Hainad spring, then dropping it on his chest.

As the water ran down his sides, he again shivered, pressing eyes shut against the trembling and again tugging at the blanket.

"This will cool the fever," she said as she pushed the blanket back.

Eyes still closed, Arshal nodded. His teeth chattered. "It's working. Where's Ramel?"

"Trying to convince my father to do what you ask, Lord," she said, her tone as cool as the water. "I'm charged to tend you when Ramel's away." She again moistened the rags on his forehead, neck and chest. "Now be quiet and rest."

"Zel's your father?" Arshal asked as sleep closed on him.

"Is that a problem?"

Her image faded, becoming the tatter of some old memory he knew had been a vision. He concentrated on the image, trying to remember if it had been an osfothye vision or one of his odd dreams. A woman walked away from him. A great beast smashed ships to flotsam. The face he'd come to know as Ghyldus glared after him, determined, its evil chuckle filling him with fear and doubt. He'd fail. He'd wither under the mighty god's stare and like the vainglorious braggart he was, he'd be sent running, shame-faced and maligned through the ages for leading his people to their deaths.

Familiar voices drew him from his dreams.

"Don't be foolish! It's too much risk. If someone sees your face –" she said.

"That's my risk to take, Dynresa."

Arshal tried to force his eyes open to see what confrontation took place in the cramped shack. But he could only lie still, listening, the words flitting in and out of his dreams of failure.

"But for what? He'll probably die."

"He'll live; he has to. Too much depends –"

"You've never been one to give in, Father. Why now? What makes you weaken that you'd risk the safety of our people on this martyr's mission?"

"It's not weakness, Resa. It's wisdom. I may have doubts, but there's times a ruler must take risks like this. What if he falters because he tried to gain my help and nearly died for it? We'd be doomed to this occupation. The morale of the people he's convinced: shattered."

"But if you go and he fails anyway? If you lose your life, risk your people's safety and he still fails?"

"If I don't go, he will fail. We must have their support."

"Ramel put you up to this." Her tone bit, a scathing accusation. "He has his own purposes for this king."

"Perhaps." Euzzeldir sighed. "Just give me his ring and let's be done with it."

"Then he'll charge you with stealing as well."

"I need a marker. They'll believe me if I tell them I trust him."

"Do you really believe he can do what he claims?"

"Have you looked out the door? He turned sand to glass."

"Some trick of Ramel's."

"None like that."

The shack's silence lasted so long Arshal thought he'd fallen asleep again.

"There's little risk, Resa," Euzzeldir said suddenly, startling Arshal's straining ears. "It's open country. The Minarians seldom come this way, and only by road. You know that."

"And if you return safely, what then?"

"Then we do as he's asked."

"You'll all die!" She almost shrieked her reply.

"We will sooner or later anyway! When they finally control the country, they'll venture here. There's an awful lot of missing shawnsi on their lists, Resa. They'll find us. And what of the children taken away? How do we explain to their parents that we refused to do anything? When will these work quotas exceed what we can bear? Then the Minarians will set up an outpost to ensure it. Then the remaining children will be found, the shawnsi, derna, and all the others they've named undesirable. Consider your own mother!" His breath came in a swift gasp. "How many more of our people will die? Don't you think I've thought of all the drawbacks? His plans have merit, Resa. They could work. But he needs all of us. I'll not have it said that the Prince of Joffa doomed Shande."

"Prince of Joffa. A glorified title. You couldn't be farther from any throne. You rule sand and glass and are just as much a puppet of the king as ever. It should be Shande that you rule."

"What kind of nonsense is this? You still rankle over your ancestry? I should never have let Ramel fill your head with this talk. It's past history. Dynfearn didn't return. The closest in his line didn't step forward. That isn't the fault of the Regent, or the House of Dyndevas, but the choice of an ancestor who wanted life as a happy recluse in Joffa."

"So, you're left with an empty title."

"It means a lot, Resa. The claim is recognized."

"Then keep his ring. Be King. None will contest it. He could well die here."

"I can't believe I hear this! His family holds the title now! Of what would I be king? An occupied country I'm no better prepared to rule than he? Where's my stone with which to battle Ghyldus?"

"Take it!"

"It's not mine to take!" His voice roared out so loud it seemed to shake the shack's walls. "The gods bestowed it. Likely the power to wield it comes from him. I don't have that power."

"You could try."

"I'll hear no more! I can't believe this from my own child! What so jaded, so twisted you to even think it? All for just another empty title!" Euzzeldir's voice grew louder as he neared. Something tugged at Arshal's shrunken finger. "I don't even know if I can trust you here, Resa. Perhaps I should warn Ramel that you're more a risk to the king's health than any injury."

"I wouldn't stoop so low! How could you say that?"

"If you'd take a kingdom by deceit you'd also murder. If you'd refuse a plea from your country then you'd also betray it. My only offspring is twisted by sickness. To not be able to trust you ..." His words came slow and heavy as with pain. The shack's door wrenched open with such force it shook the walls, threatening to collapse the little shack. "Ramel has charge in my absence. I will not return until I have a satisfactory reply."

Dynresa stared after her father, not wanting to admit the tears of frustration, fear, guilt that threatened to spill. The king shifted on Ramel's bed, his fingers searching for the missing ring. She hated him. She pitied him. Looking on him brought fear. And hope. His family's rule caused all their woes, brought war and took her mother. Now the King in Exile sent her father into danger.

Yet this same demon promised deliverance, promised to undo Ebon's wrongs. He held an authority she must honor. His presence exuded something ... and somehow this soft northerner survived Jashiho, though to look on him he appeared stronger than she would imagine. The gods gave him power, Ramel claimed.

She took up the calloused hand in which seers had embedded the gemstone. The gem appeared dark and murky, the true light of an opal absent. As she bent closer to peer at it, it suddenly flared, its hues shifting to a blazing royal blue. Gasping, she looked up to find the king watching her.

His gaze searched hers a moment before the hand clenched into a fist. The opal's light leaked through his fingers as he yanked his hand away from her with a strength she thought lost in the desert. The lines around his mouth had grown hard. Gray eyes regarded her with such depth and contemplation she felt certain he read her thoughts.

"I merely meant to look, Lord. Just curiosity." She reached for his shoulder. He pulled from her conciliatory touch.

"Curious to see how easily it could be removed?"

She shrugged, inclining her head a little. "That's fair. You heard. So, what are you going to do, King?" She smiled a little. "What can you do? You're at our mercy."

He rolled to lean on one elbow. He studied the white mark where his ring had been. "How the princess of a people suffering under Minarian conquest, someone so tender in treating the ill, how such a woman could be so wicked and scheming ..." He shook his head. "I don't understand. All for dreams of power."

"I've no such desires."

"Really?" One brow punctuated his skepticism. "You've concocted a dream of yourself as Queen of Shande. You've let it twist you so it overrides your better wisdom. You might cut the gem from my hand," he admitted. "But it's vested by me, part of me, about as useful to you as any other limb you cut from my body. Without it I'm maimed. With it you gain nothing. I made it with the power of the gods placed in me. It can only be wielded by my thoughts." He looked up from his contemplation of his ringless finger and looked through her with those gray eyes.

"Do you think it great fun to turn sand to glass with a flick of the palm, an aim of the stone?" he queried with a cynical smile. "Or to strike enemies with but a thought? The wielder of such powers pays. It takes life each time I use it. It saps my strength, my will. While the weakness passes, the life spirit I expend never returns. It draws from within. In the end I'll probably fall inside myself so far no one can call me. Then someone like Ramel will slit my throat to bleed me and that will be that. Some gift."

His bitterness made her wince. He pointed at a scar on his neck.

"The cut will be here. No blood will flow because the life will have been long gone."

"You misjudge me, Lord," Dynresa whispered.

"Do I? Isn't that the tenor of what you begged your father do? 'Take it,' you said. 'He could well die here.'"

15

Her ears grew hot. Sweat spread across her forehead. He'd heard all of it.

"Why do this if you know it could kill you?"

"Ask the same of your father," he returned softly. "I could say, 'I don't choose to do this because I don't want to.' But I pledged a marriage to Shande when I became King in Exile, not just to the land, but to the people. As between lifemates, a king has obligations of respect, trust, communication, and a promise to stand firm no matter what the future holds. I took that pledge in some of Shande's darkest days as I mourned, and my people mourned. I must trust the people of Shande to help me help them overcome the occupation. I'll save myself to meet that obligation but I'm willing to die to achieve it."

Dynresa stared at him. Perhaps his mission was no different than when her father risked his life to save Dynresa's mother from the Minarians. Her father failed but a greater failure would be not trying. Now the Prince of Joffa rode into danger, out of fealty to Shande and this king as if to rescue his lifemate. The view felt so alien. To sacrifice oneself for an idea ...

"This must be a difficult burden to bear, King, all these lifemates you have." She couldn't keep the sarcasm out of her tone.

"It is," he replied, serious. "And often I've wished I could divorce myself and just live the simple life I always dreamed. I never wanted this title, much less this role. I've always hated it. I've heard the arguments from the people that we don't need kings of Shande. Maybe not. No one else has come forward and the gods designed this for me, this is what they expect." The king again studied the white mark on his hand. "Fate thrust it on me at my birth, and I'll honor it. I knew that when I took the ring from my father's dead hand."

Dynresa turned away, finding something startling and unnerving in his admission, as if she'd become privy to a secret best held inside, unrevealed, forever.

The king grabbed her by the arm and yanked her around to face him. "So, tell me," he commanded in a tone that made her pale, something about him making her feel small and petty. "Where did Zel go and why has he taken my ring?"

Dynresa placed a hand on his clammy forehead. His fever had

broken. "He went to Shikora to plead his king's case. He took the ring as token, though he knows they'll receive him." She didn't care if she appeared sullen. "He didn't want you to foul your schedule. So, he's carried on your fool mission, a shawnsi wandering the world like a plains deer browsing before Otayran hounds in the blood moon."

The king lay back and pulled the blanket to his chin. "Where are my clothes?" he demanded.

Dynresa gave him a facetious smile. "Why should you care now, Lord?" Her words dripped spring sap. "Tailors mend them. Do you feel vulnerable without them?"

The king didn't smile nor blaze out at her in anger. "I've always felt vulnerable. I want to leave and have no intention of doing so without clothing."

"Don't be stupid ... King." She added the courtesy as an afterthought. She knew better, but she couldn't stop herself. "You're nowhere near hale. All you'll do is foul your leg worse and we'll be stuck with you even longer."

"Just bring my clothes and sword!" Again, something in his tone, some command made her heart skip like no rebuke of Ramel's could.

As she slipped out, uncertain what trouble she'd brought herself in challenging the King of Shande, the king already tested his weakness, working his muscles with a determination she couldn't understand.

2: Hainad

A few days later, Arshal leaned heavily on the back of the sturdy chair in Ramel's shack, sweaty and weak. Already they closed on the new year, almost three weeks into the last moon, and he couldn't even place weight on his leg. Likely another week would flee before he could pull on the buckskin breeches he'd worn. His tunic hung to mid-thigh where it revealed the rough splints and ugly wound, the mere sight of which brought flickers up in front of his eyes. In just over a year, Kedtair would rise and here he remained too weak to fully dress himself with half of Ea yet to travel.

Everything seemed so clear now. Whether he'd somehow purged the doubts that tormented him, or if he'd at last passed some waymeet allowing him to view the road ahead, but for the first time he felt certain he'd made the right choices when he left the Val. He had to.

The door slammed open, shivering with the force as it bounced back from the flimsy wall. Glaring sunlight blazed at him as he looked up at the silhouette in the doorway.

"We have to get you out of here!" Fear tinged Dynresa's urgency.

"Why?" he demanded, embarrassed to be caught bare-legged and sweating his pain in a moment of weakness.

"Minarians. Coming up the road. They'll be here soon."

"Where do your children and shawnsi hide?" Arshal almost stood on the unhealed leg. Had they finally caught up to him? Would people now die because of him?

"We scatter: in the dunes, in the valley, wherever we can, then move around if we need to. You're a different matter." She sounded annoyed. She pointed at his leg. "You can't move far or fast. We'll all die if we're caught with you."

"Your sudden concern is touching." Arshal sneered as he hopped to the bed to retrieve his sword belt. "I didn't know you cared."

Dynresa looked out into the bright street outside. "I'll not have my father risk his life for nothing. And it's true. If they find one shawnsi they'll look for more and punish our people for harboring you. Please." Her tone softened. "We don't have much time."

He straightened and leaned on her as she put an awkward arm around him. She stumbled on the stoop and almost tangled herself in his weak leg.

"This won't work," Arshal muttered. "Where's Ramel?"

"Already gone."

"I'm a popular person. Everyone should be saddled with a one-legged king in a time of crisis."

As she again took his weight, she looked up at him and let out a nervous laugh.

"Not your retinue of choice?" she asked as they exited and hobbled toward the steep valley wall towering over Ramel's shack and the high dune at the base of it.

"A healing warrior would be better than someone who hates me with such passion."

They had just reached the dune at the base of the protective valley, Arshal barely able to absorb his surroundings for the pain in his leg and their urgency, when they heard horses in the valley gorge behind them. With a last frenzied effort, in which Arshal had to support himself on his bad leg to gain the last pace, they at last crested the dune, and threw themselves down in the narrow gap between it and the cliff face. Arshal panted as he lay in sand that clung to his sweaty clothes.

The fall of the wind down the slope had sculpted a trench between the dune and the rocky wall of the valley. A short distance away the gap narrowed, deepened, a few chunks of the cliff fallen into the trench.

Arshal pointed at the bottom. Half sliding, they reached the bottom of the slope where Arshal studied the rim of sky. He felt too exposed, their prints too easily leading the pursuit to them.

Grasping Dynresa with one arm and clinging to the rock with the other, he hobbled to the shelter of a slab of stone, at last sinking in its shadow.

He couldn't stop the tremble when he heard again the mournful and isolated sound of the sand shifting and settling around them. Dynresa felt his forehead.

"You're shivering. No fever. Afraid?"

Arshal glanced at her from the corner of his eye. What sour thing worked in her? "I thought I would never hear it again."

"Hear what?" she asked with that challenging smile.

"The sound of the sand covering me, suffocating me." He gazed into her multi-hued eyes. "It can be a very lonely sound."

Her mouth opened, but she didn't say anything. She looked away as if she couldn't find the appropriate counter-assault for his honesty. She couldn't hurt him when he already bore, self-inflicted, the wounds she would give him.

Arshal tensed at the sound of voices on the lee side of the dune. He drew his sword. Little chance would he have in battle, and an archer could easily pick them off.

"There's more tents than people," Dynresa whispered. "That's why they raid us. They don't stay long. Too harsh and dangerous out here."

Arshal clamped a hand over her mouth, motioning his head toward the rim of the dune just to their right. When he took his hand away, he tried to push her farther behind, but the jagged stone already pressed against their backs. Silhouetted against the sky he recognized the distinctive shape of a Minarian helmet as it bobbed, bodiless, along the opposite rim of the dune. Tassels dangled from the helm's crest. Eidhalt wouldn't bother with a village with too many tents. At last, the head and neck appeared then shoulders and torso. Soon the man stood a dark smudge against the dune, hands on hips as he peered into the narrow crevice.

Arshal pressed against the rock, praying the shadow concealed them. The Minarian looked over his shoulder then descended the slope in giant step-slides that brought him to the bottom with a cascade of sand. Arshal lost sight of him, but heard his slow passage along the bottom of the trench.

"We left tracks," Dynresa breathed in Arshal's ear.

He nodded, tightened his grip on the sword, and shifted so he crouched on one bent knee, his game leg wedged out to the side for balance and throbbing its protest. The tension pulsed in him so hard he barely thought about the numbing ache. The footsteps closed on them, boots crunching grit.

"How many?" Arshal mouthed.

She shrugged then held up both hands, displaying all fingers, then shrugged again.

The Minarian halted, likely noting the churned sand of their passage. The soft slide of a sword in its leather scabbard made Arshal's skin crawl. He gripped his sword tighter as the Minarian slowly rounded the corner of the crag they hid behind.

Arshal shoved Dynresa behind him and at the same instant sprung. He struck the Minarian in the lower chest and again felt that odd sense of otherness as his sword pierced the mail coat and sank into the man's body. The force of Arshal's momentum slammed them to the ground with a jolt that set Arshal's leg afire. Everything darkened around him. He gasped as he shoved his hand into the soldier's mouth to stifle a shout and jammed his elbow against the Eidhalt's throat until the man went limp.

Glancing up at the rim, he motioned for Dynresa to drag the man out of sight and cover him with sand. Fighting down the desire to faint, Arshal still struggled to regain his wind when Dynresa returned from her grisly task, the Minarian's sword in her hand.

"He wore a breastplate."

"They came for me. Eidhalt, Ghyldus's elite henchmen," Arshal rasped as he clenched his teeth and pressed his eyes shut against dizziness.

She touched a drop of moisture escaping from his eye. "It hurts, huh?" she said.

Arshal took a deep breath and gave her a weak smile. "Just a little."

"Why didn't you use that?" she asked, pointing at the stone glowing faint in his palm.

"You don't listen well. I don't want to use it unless I must."

"And banging up your leg's helped you any?"

"Flesh and bone will heal. This draws from the spirit."

"But you stunned animals in the forest."

"With little enough effort and just enough to survive."

She opened her mouth to protest. He made a slashing motion with his hand.

"I'm done hearing it," Arshal whispered with menace, a commanding tone in his voice that even he noticed. Something to ponder when this ended. She choked on her words, her expression turning to resentment. She helped him to his feet so they could move down the gap to another hiding place.

"Now the rest of them will come in search of him," Arshal said. "Can you use that?" He pointed at the Minarian sword.

She levelled her icy gaze on him then nodded.

"Good, because it's going to be nasty." He glanced at her sidelong. "Unless, of course, you have a better idea."

"With that kind of attitude, I should have just left you at Ramel's."

He didn't mean his words to convey as much sourness as they did. Despite the argument he'd overheard, he didn't want to believe ill of her. She'd come to help him, hadn't she? He didn't have to like her.

"If we could only use your sarcasm against them, we'd have the better odds," Arshal said as he studied the rim in search of danger. "You could ride before an army, yell curses and insults at the enemy and drive them from the field. Shande's secret weapon: a tongue so sharp it cuts to the quick, no mercy and certain victory."

Dynresa stared up at him a moment as if uncertain whether he jested. She giggled then clapped her hands over her mouth as the giggles grew uncontrollable.

"I'm sorry," she gasped. "I can just see it."

One corner of Arshal's mouth lifted. "I know. Everyone deals with their fear differently." He gazed at her, his smile becoming a grin. "You can be so dazzling when you laugh. Too bad you ruin it with that streak of meanness."

She turned away, the giggles ceasing as if a spigot closed.

They didn't have long to wait before soldiers came seeking the missing Eidhalt. Two Minarians crested the dune and looked down into the gap. Arshal entertained a glimmer of hope when he saw neither wore Eidhalt markers. After scanning the gap, they crouched, working their way down the slope with swords drawn.

Arshal tapped Dynresa, signing for her to move a short distance away to flank. When she stared at him in confusion, not recognizing the signs Khoti had taught him, he breathed the instructions into her ear. As she crawled to her position, he again wedged his bad leg out and crouched on his knee.

When the Minarians stopped to examine the tracks in the sand they paused, only a few paces from Arshal. This time, instead of flying outward to fall on the nearest man and risk jarring his leg, he hopped forward from beneath the ledge and balanced on one leg. Bringing his sword around in a sweeping arc, he struck his foe in the face. Just then, Dynresa dashed out to stab the other before he could cry an alarm. With both hands, she drove her sword into the man's chest. The weapon shattered on his chain mail.

She stared at the useless weapon for a moment. Her mouth fell open as the Minarian swung at her. When she jumped back, she fell in the loose sand. The Minarian grinned at her, a lecherous grin that made Arshal's throat constrict. An instant's image of Resala stood out in his thoughts. The Minarian turned from Dynresa to Arshal, ignoring the broken blade to which Dynresa still clung. Arshal parried the Minarian's blows. With both hands he brought his sword down onto the man's head. The weapon crushed the man's helmet into his skull.

At that moment, a giant cat-like beast, black and toothy leapt from the ground a pace away. Claws ripped at Arshal as he stabbed the sword into its belly to tear it to sparks and a puff of ash. A glint caught his eye. He turned to find an Eidhalt clutching Dynresa's throwing dagger where it protruded from his throat. The Eidhalt's next conjuration remained only half emerged from the ground, its grotesque viper's head so large it would have towered above the king, well beyond sword's reach.

Arshal fell to the ground beside where Dynresa huddled cross-legged beside the dead Minarian, her arms held over her stomach and her gaze distant and startled. With a rueful smile, he picked up the shard of her broken blade.

"The men of Staph-el are too efficient," he said. "And here I taunted a woman so handy with a throwing knife."

He expected some retort. She appeared not to have heard. Her face still held that uncertain startled expression.

"What is it?" he asked, tapping her arm to get her attention. His fingers came away bloody.

The arms folded over her stomach held back a seep of blood spreading down the front of the flowing white tunic she wore belted at the waist. Arshal gently pulled her arms from the wound. The Minarian's sword had severed the belt and become tangled in the loose layers of cloth. Through the large rip in her tunic, he could see a long gaping gash that bled its length.

"Is it bad?" she breathed, not looking.

"It should be sewn. It isn't serious. Ramel can fix you up with a poultice and in a few weeks, you'll be as good as new." He peered at her. "How do you feel?"

"Stunned, I guess. It doesn't hurt much, just stings a little."

"Give it a day or two. It'll hurt." He looked up at the rim again. "This just isn't going to work. Aren't there others here with weapons? We can't take them all on alone. I'm just not strong enough and we can't rely on the Minarian swords."

"Maybe if we just hide."

"While they seek their dead? Even if they leave, they'd only come back with more men. They want me!"

"But the creatures –" She motioned at the eroding conjuration that lost its menace as it became scale and ash and dust.

"It's only an illusion –" He faltered as her finger traced the deep cut from a claw on his forearm. "Still illusion, defeatable if we recognize it in time." Arshal studied the rocks above. "Can we get up there?" He pointed to a small ledge.

"What for?"

He gestured at the spilled quiver of arrows and bow in which one of the dead soldiers had tangled.

"You can't make it with your leg. And I'm not feeling all that well, kind of dizzy."

Arshal tried to suppress a smile, ready with a biting reply but refraining. As if sensing it, she turned away as if he had hurt her.

"Help me move them out of sight. Then you hide under the ledge."

"And do what?"

"Nothing. You have your daggers. I'll leave you my sword."

With an effort that left him again sweating and light-headed, they concealed the bodies. Then, slinging the quiver and bow at his back and clinging to the rock for support, he clambered over the loose sand and fall of stone until he reached the back of the huge block hiding Dynresa. He braced his back against the cliff wall, using his good leg and hands to shimmy upward. By the time he reached the niche he'd sought in the back of the rock he felt so worn he could only sprawl on the rock and pant. After several minutes, he hid behind an outcrop with an open shooting lane down the gap and up the side of the dune. Their survival relied on archery skills Khoti had found lacking.

When the next Minarian crested the rim and slid down the slope, Arshal let the man reach bottom and follow the trail toward Dynresa before releasing an arrow. The man's hands came up to clutch the arrow embedded in his neck. Dynresa darted out, stabbed him then towed the body from sight before returning to the cover of the ledge.

When six soldiers stormed the gap, Arshal thought certain his end had come. He expected an army of illusory creatures, each more treacherous than the last, to march at them from the magics of six medallions held toward the sun. But ordinary soldiers approached cautiously. Four came over the rim in front of him. The other two came in from either side. Arshal waited until all scrambled down the loose dune before shooting. In moments, three had fallen, a fourth scrambled back up over the rim to escape while the remaining two aimed at Arshal. Arrows skipped off the stone around him, one grazing the top of his hand. He struck a fifth man in the throat. The sixth escaped with a minor wound, scurrying to safety. Out of arrows, Arshal could only watch helplessly as the two fled.

He let his heart slow before easing himself down to the base of the rock to hobble to Dynresa. He sat beneath the ledge, good knee pulled up to hold his bowed head. He knit his fingers in his hair. The arrow slice on his hand bled freely to mingle with the gash from the magical cat. He ignored these minor wounds, too disappointed in himself to care.

"Well, I've failed again, Lady," Arshal muttered. He looked up at her from bowed head. "What, no comments? No victory riposte of how I've proven myself inept?"

Silently, she handed him his sword, then huddled with arms locked around her knees, shivering in the heat of the desert's afternoon.

"What would I say?" she asked, her voice hollow as he tucked the blade in his scabbard. "That injured and weak, you took on eleven, and two got away? It's not a minor feat –"

"It isn't major. I don't like killing. I'm not very good at it and prefer to leave it to others. I shouldn't have taken on one if the chance existed any could go for help. Facing them all only increased the risk to both of us, and that many more men they'll send. That deserves your derision."

"You had to fight or be captured," she protested.

"I shouldn't have been here to be caught."

"You could rationalize all the way back to the day you were born and find fault."

Arshal chuckled, a contagious kind of laugh that made Dynresa stare at him with a quizzical half smile as if certain the joke would make her laugh too.

"I do find fault with the day I was born," he said with a snort, no longer smiling. "The burden was given me then and I've since managed it terribly."

"You deride yourself more often and more efficiently than I could. You can talk at me about responsibilities and how I shouldn't criticize you. Yet you dismiss every accomplishment you have." Her eyes grew wide. "I think you hate yourself."

"That's foolish!"

"Is it?" She leaned back against the stone, pale, a fine sheen of sweat on her forehead. "You said you wish to be someone you're not. You have a death wish, saying this power will kill you, ensuring it does. If your attitude improved maybe you wouldn't get in so much trouble. Everything you've said to me is rich with your self-hatred. You wear your role like a shroud."

Arshal stared at her then closed his eyes and let his head again fall on his knee.

"It is a shroud. I'm walking death. My family's blood is on my hands. Thousands died in Sihmad Shal and the Harbor because I chose war, not conciliation. Dozens died in exile while others took injuries for me. In the next year, thousands more will die because I lead them to their deaths. Now the Minarians seek me here, likely to hurt or kill more people because I dared them to find me, dared them to come for me! In the end we may hold Shande but what will it be without all those who've died?" He shrugged. "So, I live for this one goal. Maybe you're right. Maybe I want to fulfill that death. I guess I'm just thinking of a place of peace when it's over, where I don't need to deal with the pains and hardships that'll come before me when we try to put this country back together."

"You talk at me about duty. Then you turn around and say you'd give it up for your own peace of mind before the task's done. Some king we've got ourselves. He discards his people when it's convenient."

"Deserved."

He took a deep breath, a glance revealing that blood continued to seep from her wound.

"Using the stone makes me feel destitute inside. It grows. You rail at me as if I weren't the king." He gave her a cynical smile. "I am your king, you know, deserving of a certain amount of respect, and detraction only from my council. But see, I don't seem a king. Thus, you test me. I don't feel like a king to myself. I once did, felt it go through me like stepping into destiny. Now I grow emptier by the day, grow toward that goal of becoming just another man of no special import. Soon I'll pass that and be nothing."

Dynresa touched the wounded hand with the stone embedded in its palm and the white band on its ring finger. Her hand bounced back, as if charged by his presence.

"Not if you struggle against it," she said. "Certainly, the gods knew the effects. Do you think they find you so invaluable they'd let you destroy yourself?"

Arshal scowled. "At times I do think that. Who knows what they want? We haggle in council, assume the gifts have a purpose. Some think the gods use us as tools to repair errors they made in their war with Fyraer, just weapons in their arsenal, nothing more. We try to interpret vague and distorted visions. Then when a prophecy comes true, we don't know if the visions intended to warn us from that path, or guide us to it. I knew my father would die if I led him into the mountains and he did. Why? Perhaps the gods warned against –"

"Maybe it was so you could step forward?"

"I already performed his role! He died an unnecessary death. These gifts the gods dole out are unpleasant, Lady. Foresight? Power? Too strong for us. The gods torture Khoti, a legendary warrior. They gave him compassion and the tools to use it. But a warrior sees many friends fall in battle. What a burden to live with, determining who may live or die! See, Princess, power has an ugly aspect. It can drive you mad."

When he looked up, he found her eyes moist, her expression dismayed.

"You tease that I could fight a war with insults. You inflict more wounds with your honesty. It frightens me to hear from the king such dismal projections, such doubt. Just listening to you erases any hope at all." Her voice had lost its challenging edge. Trembling, she rocked as she glared into the bright sand. "Why did you tell me these things? Couldn't the doubts of your council have been left there? If I have to rely on a king, why couldn't he be a warrior, or someone who at least emanates assurance?" Arshal put his arm around her. She turned her head against his chest. "I want to hate you," she mumbled into him. "I want to hurt you for all the pain and fear you've brought."

"I know." Arshal rested his chin on the top of her head. "I'm an awful person for wrecking everyone's lives like this."

"You're teasing," she slapped at his wounded arm as he reached for her hand. She wiped her eyes, trying to pull away. "You laugh at me because you've won. My words can't hurt you."

"But they do," he said, not releasing her. "Because they touch the truth and make me think about things I'd like to forget. I wouldn't laugh at you. You're hurt, not alert. Otherwise, you'd have certainly sunk a few more barbs in me."

"You're such a comfort. Is that how I seem? Like some predator waiting for a moment to strike?" When Arshal didn't answer, she tilted her head to look up at him. "I can't believe I'm here sobbing on the King of Shande."

"Ah, now you recognize me as king. This is progress. But of what shall I be king? That title, too, is empty. I'm just another man with an empty title."

He gazed down at her, smiling when her eyes flared at the rebuke. He would not let her forget.

"Tell me my father's not risking everything for nothing. Promise me?"

"I can't promise." Arshal sighed. "I can't read the future. For all I know I'll die here when they come back. The answer is not to give up without a fight."

She turned into him again, as if to hide from his uncertainty. He felt her breath on his chest, the sticky touch of her blood soaking his clothing. Her hair hinted of cloves, the touch of it on the skin of his arm soft and assuring. He'd been lonely and alone for so long even this battle-blooded opponent gave him comfort, filled him when all inside had grown empty.

They sat in silence, not daring to return to Hainad until they knew for certain the enemy had gone. The sun fell low. The cold evening flowed at them intermittently with warm gusts from the heated sands. Shivering, they huddled closer.

Suddenly waking from a doze at the hint of danger, Arshal grabbed for his sword and shoved Dynresa aside. Ramel peered out of the darkness of night at them.

"Here you are." The old man gave Arshal a disapproving look.

"No thanks to you," Arshal returned as Dynresa tried to shake herself alert.

"No time. And an old man like me could help you?"

"Some old man. I knew Cree all my life. You've more strength than you want to admit. So, why leave the princess to support me when you could have carried me and run as if toting no burden?"

Ramel glowered at him a moment then inclined his head.

"I admit my error. I thought first of my own skin, forgetting I had other responsibilities. I am capable of errors. I am sure you realize I am no longer a god. I could not reach you in time anyway." Ramel nodded his head toward the bodies in the gap. "You appear to have survived."

"At what cost? Dynresa was injured. The two that escaped likely gather reinforcements."

"I know that. We have spent the last hours gathering everyone up to move into hiding."

"Because of me."

Ramel gestured at Dynresa. "Can she move? We must depart before the night ends."

"We've plenty of time. The soldiers can't bring help that soon."

"We can leave no trace. That takes time to hide. They may have acted as vanguard to a larger patrol." Ramel peered into the gloom at Dynresa. "Let me see it." He turned to Arshal with a glint in his eye. "I need light." Ramel examined her wound by the light of Arshal's stone.

"Should you be doing that?" Dynresa asked. "If you grow weaker ..."

Arshal could only gape at the blood soaking her clothing.

"The wound is not serious but the blood loss is," Ramel said as he stood. The light in Arshal's hand faded. "I will carry her to Hainad, and send someone back for you." He easily lifted her in his arms.

As Ramel carried Dynresa away, she stared back at him. He couldn't read her expression, perhaps fear. He felt so drained, as if having someone to protect had kept him alert and filled him with purpose. Now he could let the tension fade to exhaustion. The room in the back of his mind beckoned.

Distantly he knew two Hainadans had come for him. He heard their calls as they searched for him but he couldn't answer. Deep within, the king drew closer to the locked door in his mind behind which none would find him. Khoti came there once but Khoti was far away. Ramel took him from the threshold. He just wanted comfort, that feeling of fullness he missed, a place to hide from everything. He rattled the lock, and turned the key. As he opened the door he paused, standing on the threshold, debating to which will he would succumb. He listened first to the argument of responsibility, and next the argument that he would likely fail anyway and might as well seek this comfort – after all he deserved it.

Then he heard a call that made him turn and look back the way he had come. When he turned his back on the door it swung shut with a loud slam, the key turning in the lock on its own. He gazed at it with longing for a moment. Then with a weary sigh, he began the long walk back to answer the urgent plea for Kedtair.

3: Fealty

Arshal had a vague memory of Ramel's grave expression after again calling the king back from the room Cree had taught him too well. He'd had no time to recover before Ramel had him placed in the back of a bouncing wagon, each jolt stabbing through his knitting bones and torn muscles so that they ached for days after the three-day journey east.

The glassworks, equipment and pigments, remained behind, but the rest of Hainad picked up and moved. Here the valley walls drew wide and low. The winds didn't push the sand over the rim. Though still desert dry, tough plants and scrub held the rocky soil in place and succulents grew sturdy in the dew rising from marshes they had dwelled beside for four days now.

They weren't any safer. They could flee in need to the brown hills east near the Otayr border, where the fresh water that fed the marshes flowed and game and scrub pine provided food and shelter. But Otayran hill tribes lived there and remained secure by killing on sight rather than hearing any plea for help.

Now, another week delayed on his journey, Arshal studied Ramel from his perch on the only chair in Ramel's tiny shack, transplanted to New Hainad, his leg propped on the bed.

"How can you have no weapons here?" Arshal asked of the Visionary sitting so calmly on the bed.

"What purpose would weapons serve?" Ramel replied.

"Protection?"

The Visionary smiled with a pleasant nonchalance. "From what? Swords and arrows cannot hold back sand and wind."

"What about food? Don't you hunt?"

"Same story, sand and rock and wind. Nothing to hunt. Zel

has his weaponry. His ancestors kept it, Resa trained in it. A few members of his house ride south to the savannas to hunt now and then for a plains deer that feeds on the valley scrub. Most of us carry daggers against poisonous snakes or other predators. But we have always traded off our glass, with which we purchase Kalilian meats and vegetables, and cured seafood from Shela. Some areas support a little grain and a hardy wine grape. East there are these marshes for the wild rices and spices, birds and eggs. That is how we have fed ourselves for generations. We have never needed weapons."

"But when the Minarians began rationing –"

"We got less food and went more often to the marshes and savanna."

Arshal groaned with frustration. Ramel's air of detachment felt contrived. "There must be something we can do. How can you sit passive when you know what could happen? Do four hundred lives mean so little to you?"

A perilous light gleamed behind Ramel's eyes. "I did not remain on Ea because I have no concern for her people. And I have not lived in this desert with the Princes of Joffa because I dislike their company." He shrugged, the dangerous feeling about him fading as quickly as it appeared. "Worrying about it serves no good. We have no weapons and no hope of any mysteriously arriving. Who will help us? The Joffan herdsmen dwell far north of here. What can they do? They have no weapons. The rainforest tribes south of here cannot be reached easily and likely made no better preparations for occupation than did Hainad." Ramel gave him a paternal smile. "See, Arshal, worrying does no good. If it happens, we are lost."

"A coward's approach, Ramel. You encourage the same complacency that got us into this."

A figure moved in front of the open doorway. Arshal peered into the bright square, blinking at the sun glaring off white robes.

"Are you baiting our sovereign again, Ramel?" Dynresa called as she entered the cramped shack.

With a smile, she set a cup of wine and bowl of steaming rice tossed in a spicy sauce beside Arshal's chair. The whiff he caught of the rice made his eyes water. He grimaced; certainly, she ordered the spiciest foods only to watch him suffer through his meal, consuming flagons of water and wine to quench the fire in his stomach.

"It surprises me, Ramel," she continued. "I'd think a Visionary would find the King of Shande an intriguing subject, someone you'd want to assist, not hinder." She gave the seer a disapproving glance. "I thought Visionaries wanted to help Ea. Wouldn't a king empowered by the gods be such providence?"

Ramel's disarming smile stunned Arshal. The expression came to this old man like it had never come to Cree. Though almost child-like in its innocence, it seemed somehow ethereal.

"And you have never been one to test, challenge, or push Resa?" Ramel asked, chuckling, a sound like wind chimes in the windows of Sihmad Shal. "He expects me to magically produce weapons and a defense plan I do not have."

"What kind of test is this?" she challenged. "You lie to him for what purpose?"

Ramel made a silencing motion.

"What lies?" Arshal demanded. "What are you keeping from me, Ramel?"

Ramel crossed his arms and remained silent.

Dynresa smiled triumphantly. "He tells you we have no weapons or defense, and you believe him? Maybe this is your lesson in gullibility and misplaced trust."

"Perhaps." Arshal clenched his fists, his glare stealing the smile from her face. "I should remember the traitors I've encountered. Most damaging. The ones I've known are dead now. Perhaps I'm too 'gullible' believing traitors wouldn't be found among shawnsi and Visionaries, the people with the most to lose."

Ramel continued to study him with that irritating scholar's speculation.

"So, Ramel, have you turned to Fyraer? Is he your master? Why would you lie to me? Perhaps you'd like to see me caught, even betray me. It would explain the Minarians seeking me here so soon and your lame excuse for your absence during the raid. So, what's your purpose?"

Ramel straightened, his arms dropping to his sides. He seemed to fill the shack with his presence as he glared down at the king. Arshal dropped his leg to the floor and shakily stood to face the seer. In an instant he'd drawn his sword.

"Stop it!" Dynresa shrieked.

She pushed between them, throwing Arshal off balance so he thunked down on the chair.

"You're both fools!" She glared at Ramel. "You, old man, know better. What's your game? He has a right to know." She turned on Arshal. "What makes you so hot for battle, King? Isn't it enough you're already weak? We're supposed to trust in someone who risks it all for heroics? If Ramel wanted to harm you, he could have when you were brought here for dead."

As she stood between them, panting for breath, she alternately glared from one to the other then clutched her stomach where Ramel had sewn her wound.

"Sit down, Resa," Ramel said with a quiet authority that brought her automatic response. The seer's scrutiny made Arshal's skin prickle. "You can put your sword away, King. I would not fight the king on whom we count. What strength have I to match yours?" He gestured at Arshal's hand where a bandage only partially concealed the flaring stone. "At least you went for the sword, not the stone. You are learning your limitations. And you do have them." Ramel sat on the bed beside Dynresa, leaning forward to peer at him.

"Why lie to me?"

"To test you, of course. I do not know what Cree accomplished with you or how he prepared you. Already, I hear the power to compel in your voice, the command I have that allows me to force even strong-willed Dynresa to act at my word." He took her hand and patted it, a fatherly gesture Cree would never have admitted. "Even your presence hints of your gifts. You fill a room with foreboding. The air around you charges with concealed power. I feel it! Your new advisor has counseled you well but he cannot guide you as Cree or another Visionary could. This Nali understands the power no better than you." He took a deep breath and leaned back. "Clearly, you have not learned to rely on your instincts yet. You lean on others and your gem. That is a fool's way to die, King. During the raid, and just now, you relied on yourself. But you have much yet to learn, things I can teach. I commanded you use your stone to give me light to reveal Resa's wound. You should have overcome the command and ignored it. You worried over Resa. You must protect yourself and only yourself, or you will end up so far inside that hiding place of yours not even your champion can bring you back."

A wry smile lifted one corner of Ramel's mouth. "Cree and I teach by different methods. Evidence might be found in Dynresa's cynicism and refusal to trust even what her own eyes show her." He squeezed the hand he still held. "I do not know what Cree taught, but he certainly did not bring you to think of yourself first and trust yourself. We cannot afford to lose our only hope. So yes, I want to show you what you gain from gullibility and unquestioning trust: Nothing. You must independently verify everything, doubt everyone. I want to see you prove you can think when you are angry. One thing you can believe: I have never considered honoring Fyraer. I had the option once, long ago. I chose against it as all the wise did."

"Is it fair to ply your tests on me when I'm still recovering from illness and fever?" Arshal asked in a surly tone.

"Certainly!" Ramel said, stunned by the question. "When else are you most vulnerable? Besides, you are better now. You cannot claim illness as an excuse. Now we have a lot of work to do. We must develop the power of your voice for you to succeed. You may need it to assure the frightened. You still need to find in yourself, or in others, the elements to make your power whole. You are not ready for Ghyldus. He has Fyraer's power behind him, you Terremar's. If you do not steal a little of Fyraer, you will have a stalemate. You need those elements, too, to make you strong. You must know him. He cannot know you. The thing possessing him is too consuming for Terremar's passions."

Ramel told him things Cree never had. Had Ramel been that much stronger than Cree, or had Cree misremembered, or misjudged, or merely not thought him ready to know this?

"So, there are weapons?" Arshal probed.

Ramel inclined his head. "When your messengers arrived with the call to arms, we acquired what we did not have."

"So, you listened to at least one courier. What should I have learned by not knowing?"

Ramel held out his hands in a gesture of open debate. "Perhaps this confrontation is what you learned: that someone would dare lie to a king. I establish the circumstances. You must discern the lesson." Ramel stood. "More important things need my attention than playing nursemaid to a king who would be hale if he had learned his lessons properly."

The bright daylight beyond the door swallowed the seer.

Arshal and Dynresa sat in silence, neither looking at the other. At last, Arshal took up the dish of rice, sniffed, and grimaced.

"Is this a test, Dynresa?" he asked with a wry smile. "You want to see how long I will subject myself to these spices before I beg for mercy?"

"Maybe a little heavy on the Otayran threespice," she mumbled. Her dark brows creased, features contorted with the confusion he seemed to generate in her. He remembered the feel of her face pressed against his chest.

"So why did you do it?" she asked. "You used your stone when you knew you shouldn't. My wound wasn't fatal."

"The way you bled –"

"But you risked your life! You'd just finished telling me how it emptied you, then you recklessly risk yourself."

Arshal recognized the point in yet another of Ramel's tests. "I must relearn a lot. Cree and my parents taught me to serve my people, to think of their interests before my own. They considered me reckless for spending my time gaming in the Harbor and drinking with local folk instead of in court. I figured I needed to understand and care about the people I would lead. Besides, I had more fun holding court in Harbor inns. When I asked the people to defend Sihmad Shal, I called on friends, not faceless subjects. Many of those friends died. I hold an awesome power over people with names and faces, who I might have shared a drink with or a game of dice or even pinned in a wrestling match. Selfishness just isn't in me. Self-pity maybe." He smiled shyly. "When I think of the people I think of the individual as well as the whole. I just haven't arrived at that medium between selfishness and selflessness."

"I don't think I could do it," Dynresa admitted.

Arshal sat back, a grin splitting his face. "Now there's something I didn't think I'd ever hear."

"How have you gotten this far?" She shook her head with a

laugh. "With so much weight on your shoulders it's a wonder you didn't sink to the bottom of Simiriel."

"Princess, are you making light of your king's concerns?"

She looked away. "I don't think I can anymore."

"Don't tell me that Minarian sword bled all the sourness from you." Arshal's chuckle faltered at her wounded expression. He leaned forward and touched the hands she had knotted in her lap. "You said you hate me and want to hurt me, that I frighten you. Is that why you keep returning with your spicy food and acid tongue?"

Dynresa straightened, pulling her hands from his. She wiped her palms on her tunic. "I just haven't figured you out yet."

"As much as I've told you?"

"I studied with Ramel. He taught me to doubt everything until independently proven."

Arshal leaned back in his chair again, crossing his arms over his chest as he smiled. "And what have you learned?"

"That you're hardly fit to be a king. You're too soft, too gullible, too possessed by all the conflicts in your head. I hold little hope for you as a sovereign. I think you'll drive yourself mad. I'll need more proof to be certain."

"You're probably right," he muttered as she stood to leave. He held out the untouched bowl of rice.

She stared at the bowl. "You need to eat to regain your strength so we can be rid of you." She lightly pushed the bowl toward him.

"I'd sooner starve to death then be subjected to this again."

Jaw clenched with an anger that always seemed to simmer in her, she wrenched the bowl from his hand, turned and strode from the little shack. He threw his cup of wine against the wall of Ramel's shack but it made him feel no better. As she joined the bright square of outside, Arshal decided he would be well rid of these trials. He had never met such a frustrating person.

Yet, he wondered when she would return.

As the last moon passed into the first and another Evenday approached, Arshal slowly regained his strength. Ramel fashioned a more flexible splint for his stiff leg, allowing him more freedom to explore the transplanted village, and to move into a tent near the village's center. Though the poison that almost destroyed the limb faded, his long illness left him gaunt. When he hobbled, stiff-legged, among the cluster of tents, families drew him to their cookfires, urging him to stuff himself with dishes laced with so much Otayran threespice he coughed, sneezed and sweat through each meal. Soon the hollowed cheeks and deep shadows around his eyes filled out a bit and he no longer sneezed at Otayran threespice. Though he still appeared emaciated, in time his shoulder muscles again strained the seams of his light Joffan tunic.

He knew Dynresa avoided him by the way she altered her path to not cross his. As the weeks lengthened to a month since her father's departure, she grew wan, her features empty without smile or sneer.

Needing to do something to shorten the drag of days until he could depart, the king took an interest in the village's defenses. An arsenal of heavy glass balls could be flung from slingshots with deadly force. Families had jealously guarded bows, swords and spears each time the Minarians raided Hainad but knew little of the weapons' use. Stepping back into the role of military leader he had assumed in Sihmad Shal, Arshal called competitions, setting up targets for archers and making reed-filled dummies to spar. This time he had the benefit of experience and Khoti's lessons to make the training more effective. Almost without realizing it, he found himself thinking like a warrior. With Ramel's help, he directed the erection of a rock barricade across the valley. Overlooking a steady decline toward the west, the rampart gave the defenders the advantage of altitude and range. He assigned other villagers to cut a crude path to the valley rim where they could flank an enemy attack.

Though he doubted the small arsenal could dent a determined attack, the work gave purpose to those days when Ramel didn't needle him with his oblique lessons. Activity diverted him from worries about the next leg of his journey and what went forward in the world. It couldn't expel Dynresa's image from his dreams. He looked forward to each chance meeting, only to be left frustrated and impatient to escape her scathing judgments. She fascinated him. Fiery and unreachable, she refused the rapport he developed with Ramel and the other Hainadans. And he couldn't purge her from his thoughts.

On a hot first moon day a few days shy of Evenday, Arshal stood atop the barricade protecting the village. He noted a small speck emerging from the wavery heat of the desert. About to raise an alarm, better sense told him Minarian scouts would not return so boldly and alone.

The speck grew as the rider's horse picked its way along the valley bottom in search of the firm ground. Arshal discerned the white robes and loose hood of a Joffan familiar with desert travel. From the man's size and carriage, he grew certain Euzzeldir sought his missing home. Arshal hailed a sentry. As the man ran for Ramel, Arshal studied the approaching prince, troubled by the way Euzzeldir sat his mount.

A few moments later, Dynresa reached Arshal's side. Her labored breath told him she had run. Hands cupped around her eyes, she peered into the late sun to verify the rider's identity. She sobbed then, an exhalation of five weeks of worry. Arshal put his arm around her.

"See, Princess? He returns without my promise."

Dynresa turned her face into his shoulder. A comforting feeling of fullness came with her touch. A hot wind tossed her hair into his eyes.

"You'll only drive him off again. I have no one but my father. Everyone else is dead or captured or far away. I don't want to be alone."

"You aren't alone," he soothed. "A family's what you make it, a place you feel at home and comforted, people to whom you can turn."

She gazed up at him with a quizzical expression. "No matter how cruelly I treat you, you still try to console me."

Arshal laughed, the chuckle coming from deep inside him. "As much as you hate me, you still come to my aid."

"It's not personal," she admitted. "I just can't stand what your presence here means, the way you've disturbed my world, what you represent."

"I represent Shande, Lady." He gave her an easy smile. "Have you finished your research then? Have you come to some conclusion about who I am?"

"You're hopeless. A lost cause, but I guess you'll have to do. No one else appears ready to take on your burdens."

Arshal opened his mouth to laugh, but when he glanced down at the approaching rider, the chuckle died inside him. Euzzeldir had sagged in his saddle. Pushing Dynresa aside, Arshal shouted for help, then clambered down the rock barricade and in a limping-stride, ran to meet the prince.

When Arshal reached Euzzeldir, the prince fell into Arshal's arms. Despite the ache of Euzzeldir's weight on his limbs, Arshal hefted the ill prince to his shoulder and stumbled up the stony slope to the rampart. Villagers rushed up, only to stop and stare at their fallen leader.

Ramel barked orders, then shooed a paled and unsteady Dynresa away as the king approached, guarding his burden from offers of help. Shande continued to bleed and die for him.

Ramel waited in his little shack, readying his bed for the prince. As they removed Euzzeldir's tunic, Dynresa sidled up to the shack's doorway. She gasped when they revealed the ugly wounds striping Euzzeldir's chest.

"Cat," Arshal said as he examined the deep slashes.

Ramel nodded. "They master the rainforest."

Arshal's breath caught in his lungs a moment. How many nights had he spent weak and ill and at the forest's mercy? Dynresa pushed forward, trying to reach her father. Ramel tried unsuccessfully to hold her back.

"Get her out of here!" Ramel growled at Arshal.

When Arshal turned to oblige, Euzzeldir's hand grasped the king's arm.

"Liege," Euzzeldir rasped. "Accept my apology."

Stunned, Arshal turned to look on the prince. He pushed Dynresa toward the door. She stumbled in a sprawl on the stony ground outside, cursing. Kneeling beside Euzzeldir, the king shook his head.

"What could you possibly apologize for?"

"I doubted you. I was wrong," he said through dry lips.

"We'll talk when you've rested. Let Ramel help you. Your news can wait a few more hours." Arshal rose with an effort. Euzzeldir again reached out, pressing something in Arshal's palm before allowing Ramel to minister him.

When Arshal stepped into the bright sunshine where Dynresa sat on the ground, head in hands, he found his ring glowing in his palm. He clenched his fist, feeling the warmth of the gold as he helped Dynresa up. She clung to him on unsteady feet. He studied the fading white mark on his ring finger a moment before again sliding the gold band on his hand.

He flexed his fingers as he led Dynresa away. The gold flashed. As if he picked up a destiny lost somewhere in his wanderings, the mere sight of the ring on his hand made him feel stronger.

Dynresa tripped. Arshal caught her before she could fall. He pulled her close and held her for a moment. He shouldn't savor this feeling he took from her. "He'll be fine," he offered. "Feisty Dynresa so upset about a few small scratches? He's home. No matter what, remember you aren't alone."

Her fingers dug into the skin of his neck as a sob shook her. He couldn't leave her, not like this. He led her to the rush mat in his tent and as afternoon wore to evening watched over her as she fell into the deep sleep of a warrior exhausted with battle.

Dynresa reached for the blanket to ward off the chill of night beside the damp marshes. As she groped, other hands pulled the blanket to her chin and tucked it around her. Her eyes flew wide open to find the king looming over her. He didn't notice her watching him as he adjusted the blanket and arranged the rush pillow beneath her head. Then, he settled back near the tent wall, knees tucked up to his chest in his silent vigil.

"What are you doing?" she asked. She sat up to stare at his faint image silhouetted by the moon shining on the white walls of the tent.

His teeth flashed in a smile. "Being that awful version of nice you hate. I didn't want you to wake alone."

"My father?"

"Is resting in Ramel's shack. Though the old man's grumbling a bit over losing his bed again. He should survive the seer's ranting."

"Then he's –"

"He'll be fine, Lady," Arshal said in a tone that silenced her next question, leaving her staring, open-mouthed, at the silhouette emanating so much strength toward her. "He's merely exhausted. A little weak. You can see him in the morning."

"I made such a fool of myself." Dynresa turned away, feeling the heat of shame rush through her.

The king scooted to her side. Brushing the hair from her face, he sought a damp cloth that had fallen from her forehead. "It was your turn. I've done it often enough. But then, you know I'm not perfect."

"Don't tease me. I'm sure you've enjoyed a good laugh at my expense."

She turned to throw him an angry glare, but in the spare light she could see his serious expression.

Arshal tucked a few strands of hair behind her ear. "I couldn't laugh at you for perfectly natural emotions." He pulled the blanket up to cover her shoulders as she shivered.

"You have an answer for everything."

"You just haven't found the right questions."

"People will talk if you keep me in your tent this way."

"You're free to leave. I wouldn't want to be accused of forcing a distraught woman to put up with my gullible, protective instincts."

His smile faded as he continued to stare at her. He reached out and touched her cheek. He jerked his hand away as if angry for his impulse.

"I'd prefer if you stayed."

"The way we argue?"

He studied his hands where his thumb twisted the signet ring on his finger. He shrugged. "My council, the people I call family, are far away. I guess sometimes it's just nice to not feel so isolated."

"Ah, but you're never alone."

"But I am." He tapped his chest. "Inside. It won't end soon."

She touched the ring gleaming in the soft light from the opal. "Only because you think it. You should find heart in how your family lightens your burdens. Even my father joined your ranks. Your family grows, King. Soon it'll be all of Shande, perhaps even beyond." Her breath quickened as she caught the way muted moonlight glimmered in his white hair, his gray eyes.

She sensed some battle inside him. Tension trembled in the hand brushing hair over her shoulder, a light touch charged with subdued power.

"You fill that empty place. Your touch makes me feel whole." He pressed his face into her hair. She held him then, letting him soothe the chill in her. Closing her eyes, she wondered at her ease with this king she worked so hard to hurt. His shoulders quivered with a tearless grief she would never fully understand, a pain there long before her. Stroking the knot his shoulders made, she assured him he, too, must release the things inside. Finally, she accepted the things he had told her, and thought no less of him for his weakness.

Propped up in Ramel's bed, shoulder and chest loosely wrapped, the Joffan prince picked at a plate of food in his lap as Arshal and Ramel waited for his tale to emerge. It had only been a few days, but already the man had shaken his fever and weakness. Something akin to adanan existed in the Joffan line.

"They expected you, Lord," Euzzeldir said. "You needed no hard convincing there."

"They expected me? Even Arenh, when told the king called, thought of my father."

Euzzeldir smiled, a warm expression. "Your word goes before you, my King." He uttered the title with reverence. "They honored me for bearing your marker. Shikora and Arenh continue trade illicitly with Detarian despite the Minarians." The prince gazed at Arshal with bright eyes, near breathless with excitement, as he told the king what had happened in the world since Arshal left Tormor, detailing news of Khoti in Detarian, Arenh's providence and children freed from labor camps. "Shikora expects to be blockaded, soon, both east and west. King Azren pleaded your case most ardently. All of Ea comes to your call!"

Arshal clasped his hands, afraid to entertain the glimmer of hope growing deep inside. He sensed Dynresa's presence behind him in the doorway, a faint scent like cloves. Did she know what this meant?

"They awed me, filled me with hope at their promise of aid." His mouth took a wry turn. "So euphoric I wasn't alert." He touched the bandaged shoulder. "With so many heeding your call, I had to rush home to apologize. I shouldn't have treated you so ill. You are sovereign. You are my king. I had no right to doubt you without cause. Then there's the matter of your ring –"

"I understand," Arshal said. "Better that you didn't wait to ask me for it. Time's already short."

"There's other news," Euzzeldir hedged.

"Do not tell him," Ramel said.

"It's his right to know!"

Arshal straightened. "What's this news you're so loathe to tell me?"

"It's confirmed. Prince Peshal leapt from a Minarian ship in the Sea of Tebez rather than submit to a sacrificial rite."

Arshal clenched his fists to conceal the flare of the stone in his palm. He felt the blood draining from him, all the strength he'd gathered from news of Khoti and Shikora.

"I dreamt of it," he said through clenched teeth. "How did you learn this?"

"Via your sister."

"Resala!" An instant's hope tingled through him, but Euzzeldir shook his head.

"King Azren told King Wyeff Shikora that Princess Resala has been made ... courtesan to Ghyldus."

Arshal's hands turned to ice. A ragged breath stuck in his throat. He wanted to scream, to keen and mourn her. Yet, she lived. Had Ghyldus broken her? He imagined that toss of hair as she turned her eyes on him so dark and deep like the waters of Sihma Harbor.

He nodded stiffly. "Thank you for your sacrifice."

He turned and strode from the shack, pushing by Dynresa into the cool desert evening of the first full day of spring.

Dynresa stared after him. The shroud he'd wrapped around his soul seemed to have tightened into something that made his movements slow and stiff.

"I told you not to tell him," Ramel told Dynresa's father. "He needs no excuse to give up. He already resists his lessons. It is no easy thing possessing powers larger than yourself and having a whole country's fate on your conscience."

"It'll make him tough," Euzzeldir returned. "More determined to avenge the wrongs against his family. He deserves that hatred, must savor it, as I savor my mourning for my lifemate."

"He has not learned those elements yet. They must become a part of him, slowly, so they do not overpower him in a destructive rage. You do not know him. I witnessed the markers of his birth. He was not made to kill with malice. Remember the prophecy of Kedtair: To great good or evil? I doubt he can even entertain that kind of hate. He would sooner destroy himself than go against the teachings of Terremar."

"He fought for Hainad, for Sihmad Shal and proved himself capable enough then."

"Self-defense is one thing, Zel. Wanting to kill for the act itself, the pleasure in vengeance? It will not appease him, only confuse him more. The gods bestowed a gift of awesome power on a man possessed of guilt and passion and sympathy. He serves on Ea in Terremar's stead, warmed by Terremar's compassion and fidelity. He must learn the other elements to defeat Ghyldus, but slowly, so those more intense and alien passions do not dominate. He is not ready."

"The young prince I heard of wasn't so simpering, Ramel. I heard stories of brawls and defiance and a penchant for gambling in Sihma Harbor," Euzzeldir said with stubborn chin set.

"You heard of a young prince, untouched by experience, and still no warrior. Brawls and a few drinks in a tavern do not resemble war. They tend to be good-natured and followed-up-by-an-ale-for-the-victor affairs. This king gambles now with Shande's fate. His derna counselor tempered his hopes with pessimism and taught him to think deeply on his actions. Arshal will be a just and sympathetic king, if he lives to achieve it."

As the two continued their debate, Dynresa backed from the little shack, turning to run for Arshal's non-descript tent. Empty. She ran among the clusters of tents glimmering in the dusk, then recognized his silhouette high up on the barricade. He stared west down the valley.

He startled at her touch. In an instant he had folded her into his arms, his eyes closed, head tilted upward with some silent entreaty.

"Your heart goes out to her," Dynresa whispered. "She'll know that. It'll give her strength to survive."

The king looked down at her, his features so stark and lost. "You sound so certain."

"She must know. You share the same blood. You told me so much about this strong martyr. Do you think her less capable of inner strength? You must be so proud of her sacrifice for Shande." She shook her head. "Look at me, defending a selfless act. She only fills that mission assigned her, as you do. Ramel didn't want you to know. He claims you'll become despondent because you're incapable of hatred. He fears you'll destroy yourself if you turn from the principles of Terremar to avenge the wrongs against your family."

"Perhaps he's right." Arshal held her tighter. "She did it for me ... What if I thought wrong and Pesh died for nothing and Sal –" He buried his head in her neck. "I am truly alone."

"She's not dead."

"Certainly she wishes she were."

"Is this self-defeat a trait of the Dyndevas family?"

"Ah, the comfort of my Dynresa returns –"

"Your Dynresa?" Had he said that?

"I'm alone when you're away. You make me strong."

"You rely on me too much, King." She pulled away from him. "You have a country to regain. You have to find your own strength. I can't give it to you." She took a step back, shaking her head. Why must they rely on Terremar when they needed Fyraer? The thought made her heart skip. Without looking back, she fled.

4: Command

For long hours Arshal regarded the stone in his palm, recalling Dynresa's touch, so fleeting and fickle, how his flesh went cold when she ran, and his heart seemed to have tugged from him and followed. His need for her rankled. He had a mission for which he must remain strong and alone. He didn't need such distractions!

A slight noise made Arshal look up. He dropped flat on the rampart. A half moon broke from the hills behind him. Far distant down the funnel of valley he thought he spied movement. His eyes strained at the dark. When the moon at last shed a few rays onto the light gravel of the valley floor, he discerned the black-caped silhouettes of men leading horses. He slid down the slope of the barricade, and loped to Ramel's little shack.

In minutes the village sprang to life. By the time Arshal returned to the rampart, silent Joffan shadows climbed the crude stair to the valley rim. He found Euzzeldir standing in the midst of milling Hainadans behind the barricade, a sword strapped at his side.

"You're in no condition to fight," Arshal told the prince.

"My sword arm's fine, Lord, the other I don't need." He gestured at Arshal's leg. "King, you are the one I worry about. Your agility –"

"I did fine when my leg held no weight at all."

"You must protect yourself. Resa could lead you to the other side of the marshes where you'd be safe. We can't afford unnecessary risks to you."

"I'm not going to cower while people die because of me." He glared at Euzzeldir, who merely inclined his head in deference,

47

as Arshal recognized with a sense of wonder how his voice had resonated, powerful, something both alien and natural.

In moments, the men and women of Hainad, whom Arshal had drilled with such painstaking patience, had settled into positions that overlooked the moonlit gorge below.

As if some current passed the vast distance between Sihmad Shal and the barren lands of Joffa, Arshal sensed Nali beside him and had the instant's vision of Dyndevas pennants flying from Sihmad Shal's towers. He turned, expecting to see his counselor's face. But the moment fled and he found only frightened Joffans lining the rampart.

An ominous silence closed on the valley. Even the wind ceased as the moon rose overhead, its rays like an omen. They gleamed from a clear sky to reflect from the light rock of the valley with piercing intensity. The black shapes moved against this background with dream-like slowness, presenting easy targets. Arshal glanced up at the rim where the furtive passage of Hainadan marksmen went unnoted by the enemy below. He gasped, caught by his second sight.

Euzzeldir turned to stare at him. "Lord, Arshaldon?" He reached for Arshal's arm.

"It's from a vision," Arshal whispered. "In the dream, we lost ... everything. We must call them back, hide. We'll all be destroyed –"

"There's only but a hundred of them."

Ramel crept up beside them.

"Convince him, Ramel," Arshal insisted. "We must pull back. I dreamed this, a defeat so terrible none lived to tell of it."

Ramel laid his hand on Arshal's trembling shoulder, a calming, strengthening weight. "Have all your visions read accurate?"

"Most, but the risk –"

"And the visions that came true, not a detail varied?"

"My father died as I dreamt it."

"Exactly?" Ramel turned to him with an expectant gaze.

"Only minor differences. It's too dangerous to risk! In my dream I had to dig in the snow to find him. In reality he lay face down, not fully buried."

"That is an important distinction," Ramel returned with

patience, as if they rested on a bench along the Harbor boardwalk. "Visions can be symbolic or realistic. Or they might not come true at all because of some change in fortune. Or they may hold true only in part because of altered routes to the result. You cannot base your decisions on them."

"Others have been true!"

"Lord, if you're worried, find Resa as I said and have her lead you to safety," Euzzeldir urged.

"You're determined to fight?"

Euzzeldir pointed down the gorge. "We're already committed."

Arshal followed Euzzeldir's gaze to where the Minarians neared the long slope leading to the barricade. While to this point the enemy had appeared unconcerned by the barrier thrown across their path, they now rushed it as Hainadans sent to flank them on the valley rims flung glass balls and arrows.

"Hurry, King, there's time for you to escape yet!" Euzzeldir cried.

Arshal didn't move. Euzzeldir stared at him a moment as if seeing a moonlit apparition.

"Please," Euzzeldir begged.

"It's too late. They come up the barricade, and your daughter's on the other end ready to do battle."

Euzzeldir scanned the other side of the valley where Arshal had picked out Dynresa's figure among the many lining the rampart.

The Minarians left their horses and darted up the loose rock of the rampart, at last recognizing the silhouettes of heads peering down at them. Behind, a dozen Minarians lay dead. Others, wounded, stumbled on as more arrows and glass shot pelted them. A volley of arrows from the rampart dropped the lead ranks of Minarians nearing the top. As they fell, they tumbled and slid down the slope, knocking comrades from their feet. Most merely jumped aside and continued their headlong rush up the slope. A few more fell as pikes reached out to stab from a man's length and spears impaled soft targets.

A cluster of Minarians loomed up before Arshal. Euzzeldir took on a burly soldier who struck from the prince's left, Euzzeldir unable to wield his sword two-handed or shift hands to defend himself. On the other side of Arshal, Ramel displayed his ancient prowess, driving his enemy backward. It all seemed so like one of his dreams. Arshal momentarily froze, waiting for the terrible doom to fall. Ramel's words echoed in his head in Nali's voice. He had an image of Khoti admonishing him that all concerns but fighting must be wiped from a warrior's mind.

Arshal brought up his sword to parry the sudden onslaught of two Minarian soldiers. As they charged him, he strove to keep his footing. If he lost his balance or favored his leg they could use it to their advantage. He watched for the flashes of metal in the moonlight that warned that one or the other weapon came at him. Grasping his sword with both hands, he swung indiscriminately, ignoring the metallic snap as one of the weapons shattered on his sword, the other pushed away.

The Minarian whose sword broke lunged at him, drawing a dagger. Arshal jumped beyond his reach, coming down hard on his weak leg. He stumbled as his knee gave way, falling into the rough stones, rolling over the jagged edges to leap up just beyond his attacker's reach. With a sweeping arc, Arshal brought his sword down on the man's helm. The otherness in him toppled the man. As his opponent rolled down the slope behind him, Arshal gasped for breath. His second attacker had turned to Ramel and fouled the seer's otherwise uncontested control of a stretch of the rampart. From behind, Arshal drove his sword through the Minarian's mail, the fine weapon shearing the chain away to penetrate flesh fattened on Shande. Ramel nodded his thanks without looking up.

Euzzeldir still struggled with his initial foe with the skill of an accomplished swordsman. He tired fast. Arshal maneuvered to come to the prince's aid, but from the corner of his eye he spied a breach in the barricade. Several Minarians slipped down the slope and ran for the cluster of tents where ancient and infant awaited the outcome of the battle. Arshal shouted to archers, who trained their sights on the fleeing enemy. But the enemy zig-zagged to foul their aim and soon disappeared among the tents. Arshal scrambled down, then loped toward the point he had last seen the Minarians, the handful of archers following.

Screams told him where to go. He slashed open a tent to reveal two Minarians sidling around an old man fending them off with barrel staves. Half a dozen elders and a few children huddled at the tent's rear. Before the first Minarian knew his danger, Arshal felled him. The other spun to face the king, the old Joffan's barrel staves not enough to harm the soldier through his sturdy helm, though irritating him enough to swing one arm back to strike the man while he brought his sword up to face Arshal with the other. The distraction gave Arshal his moment. He lunged, trying to make his moves automatic so that he never relied on his weak leg. The Minarian spun. Arshal's blow struck him in the arm, peeling away a chunk of unprotected flesh.

The soldier's blood splattered their witnesses. The Minarian lunged. Arshal stumbled backward to tangle in the tent flap. A sword arced toward Arshal's neck. He brought his blade up to parry, but the power behind the blow drove Arshal's own sword into his flesh. Using both hands to push the Minarian weapon away, Arshal twisted his blade with a finesse Khoti taught him, ripping the man's weapon from his grip. His foe stumbled to his knees, reaching for the sword lying just beyond him. The old Joffan kicked it away. Discarding his staves, the elder scooped up the dead Minarian's sword and drove the blade into the Minarian's upturned face. Before the Joffans could look up Arshal had already moved on.

As Arshal came around the corner of a row of tents, he felt the air shift as something flew at him. He turned to block the dagger aimed for his chest. It instead struck his arm brought up to ward off the blow, the tip of the weapon driving on to glance across his forehead and scalp. Before the attacker regained his balance, Arshal stabbed without thinking. He hurried on to leave his foe bleeding into the parched soils of the Jashiho.

The din of battle faded. Fewer cries carried to him and only occasionally did he hear the clash of weapons. Had they overwhelmed the Joffans? He'd sent thirty up on the valley rims. One hundred and fifty lined the barricade. Another two hundred noncombatants remained in their tents. At least one hundred Minarians, better trained and armed, faced them. On the barricade, some fifty Joffans had only bow, useless in close battle, and others had only spears. Alone he accounted for five of the enemy. Ramel took on several. Perhaps Euzzeldir still struggled against his first. As he searched among the tents, his thoughts went to Dynresa and the sight of her peering down the gorge, sword in hand, a brace of throwing daggers in her belt.

Arshal slowed. His leg ached. He reached up to wipe the sweat from his eyes, to find blood. When he noted it, he at last felt the sting of the gashes on his neck, head and arm. The deepest wound, on his arm, throbbed as the quick beat of his heart pumped out his strength. He paused and leaned on his thighs to catch his breath. He hadn't used the stone, hadn't even considered it.

Taking a deep breath, he wiped the blood from his eyes with his forearm. He went from tent to tent, pulling back the flaps in search of Minarians. In one, he found a child sprawled. The mother, her bow abandoned, keened over the body. He remembered the child's giggling delight at the opal changing colors in the king's palm as they sat beside the family cookfire one cool evening. He went on, a hard knot swelling in his chest.

He peered at a deep shadow thrown by two tents. The gleam of moonlight off the ground fired two red pinpoints of light. Something bitter made his lip curl, building in him as he thought of the death he had brought to peaceful Hainad. An image of Resala, tossing her fair hair in defiance, filled his thoughts, of Esthen with arms crossed over his thick chest, of Peshal's stony gaze as he related his struggle to return to Sihmad Shal. Arshal tried to breathe deeply, to control himself, uncertain if strange creatures might leap from the ground beside him any moment. Thumping in his ears, his heart kept pace with the strange otherness in him, a sensation that gave him both fear and elation. He couldn't give in to recklessness. Already he'd given blood to this battle. Too much rode on his survival.

Suddenly, the red lights shifted. A Minarian leapt from hiding to strike the king in his chest. Thrown to the ground, Arshal lost his grip on his sword. The Minarian's dagger struck stone instead of Arshal and the man lost his grip, the weapon bounding away from him. Arshal rolled to pin the struggling Minarian beneath him. He smiled. Doubtless the Harbor's wrestling champion could pin a Minarian hindered by mail and helm.

Arshal sat on the man's chest. For each feeble strike of the

Minarian's fists, Arshal struck twice with hard, fast blows that soon knocked the man senseless. Arshal leaned his weight on the man's throat. The man's face darkened in the moonlight, eyes bulging as he struggled for breath. Dynresa's words haunted him. Did he kill with malice? Was this hatred he felt? He stopped pressing. The man choked and gasped. Arshal retrieved his sword and examined its bloody blade as he stood over the Minarian. Survivors would only call for more troops to put down the recalcitrant Hainadans. With a dispassionate thrust, he slashed the man's throat. The blood coated the medallion glowing in the dirt beside his neck.

Arshal looked up at a sound then crouched, bringing up his sword.

"Arshal," Ramel called.

He lowered his sword. "Is it over?" He leaned on his weapon as he caught his breath, his ribs aching where he'd rolled in the stones on the rampart, or perhaps from this man who had struck him full in the chest with his weight.

"Mostly. Just rooting out a few like this one." Ramel pointed at the dead man at Arshal's feet as he detached himself from the shadows.

"How many dead?" Arshal demanded, staring into the blood-soaked sand.

Ramel shrugged. "Some." The Visionary peered up at Arshal's blood-smeared face. "I hope you do not intend to take up space in my bed again." He examined the flowing wound on Arshal's neck where the king's own sword had cut him.

Arshal shook his head. "I was thinking I have to be going soon anyway."

"Soon enough," Ramel admitted, nodding. "Not quite yet. I will be certain of your health and skills before you leave. There will be much to do here."

"I don't know how many got among the tents. There's a dead child down there."

"Not the only."

"Zel? Dynresa?"

Ramel shrugged again. "Zel is fine. I have not seen Resa." Ramel leveled a penetrating gaze on the king. His dark eyes glittered in the moonlight. "You are not meant to think of Resa,

King. There are other concerns to take your time."

"Have I expressed such an interest?"

"It is written in your face. Such thoughts hinder –"

"And you are, of course, the expert in such matters as kings meeting birthrights and fighting Ghyldus."

"Already Resa's sarcasm rubs off on you." Ramel pointed at the body between them. "Why did you pause in your fight? What made you decide to use your sword?"

"You told Dynresa I couldn't accept hate."

"And I was right?"

Arshal smiled, laying a bloody hand on Ramel's shoulder. "Not yet, Ramel. It's there. We'll see how I handle it."

Arshal turned and strode away, leaving the Visionary to stare after him as he wandered among the tents in search of the enemy while survivors identified the dead, tended the wounded, gathered Minarian horses and stripped Minarian bodies of weapons and armor.

When he neared his own tent, the call of his rush-filled mat doused the heat of war and in moments he slept.

He still slept when Dynresa found him at Ramel's request.

She never thought to look for him in his own tent so soon after battle, while all others in camp gathered yet to assess damages. She held up her lantern to find him sprawled, prone, face buried in one arm while the other still gripped a bloody sword. She shook his shoulder. Her fingers came away sticky. With an effort, she rolled him over. She gasped and went chill at the bloody mess she found. The wound on his arm had coated his face, as had the cut running from his forehead across his scalp. A long gash on his neck seeped. The wounded arm had already swollen. In places his blood-reddened hair stuck to his scalp. When she glanced at his hand, lying palm open beside him, she noted even the opal had been sheathed in it.

"King," she urged. "Wake up." She shook him, insistent, until he blinked his eyes open, only to squint them shut again.

"Put out that lamp, Sal."

He rolled over again with a groan. He released his grip on the sword, bringing his hands up to shield his eyes.

"You're hurt. How bad is it?"

"How should I know? I'm sleeping." He opened his eyes again, at last recognizing her. He sat up, grasping her hand. "Are you all right?"

"I twisted my ankle in the rocks. No battle scars for me." She said the last with a laugh that didn't hide the fear in her voice.

Arshal sighed. "I worried for you. I meant to find you but I guess I fell asleep. Not the act of a thoughtful king."

"Arshal, you're injured. I'm trying to find out how badly," she pressed.

"Arshal it is now. Once it was King –" He stopped when she didn't smile. He tried to pull her to him but she twisted away.

"You're all bloody."

He looked down at the cut on his arm. "That's no matter."

She gestured at his blood-sheathed face.

"Nothing serious," he said as he explored the cut on his head and neck with blood-caked fingers. "Just messy." Dynresa bit her lip as she watched him examine the cuts. "I repulse you now, do I?" he asked with a laugh. "A little blood and you look at me as if you saw some demon –" Before he could finish, she'd fled in search of Ramel.

It didn't take long to find the Visionary, and in moments light flooded Arshal's small tent. Dynresa hung back as the one-time god plied his herblore.

"Well, you will not be leaving as you planned," Ramel muttered as he bathed the gashes.

The king glanced at her. She turned away.

"I can't wait any longer," Arshal said, his gaze still on her.

Ramel frowned. "As much as I want you to move on – your mind should be on your mission, not your heart – you need to wait. We cannot risk you falling into a fever again."

"I feel fine." Arshal pushed away Ramel's hand and sat up.

"In a sour humor, King?" Ramel sneered. "Perhaps hate is not a passion to your liking?"

Arshal grabbed the Visionary's arm, pulling Ramel so close they were near eye-to-eye. "I'm not in the mood."

The command in the king's voice had grown strong, heightened, compelling. Dynresa heard it, gasped a little at the way Ramel blanched.

"What have we wrought?" Ramel whispered. "Perhaps you are not strong enough to control so much power. What wrong-headed fates gave a mortal flawed with shal blood the power of gods?"

Dynresa knew what Ramel didn't postulate: could the king become power corrupted?

Ramel shook off Arshal's grasp. "I will not let you leave until I am certain you can travel. You lost a lot of blood. There is likely poison in the wound."

"You'd stop an army." Arshal flopped back onto his mat. Dynresa let out her breath.

"There is too much at stake," Ramel said, again tending the wounds. "I would be a fool to let you risk it. I wish Zel could spare men to ride with you to the edge of Jashiho. He will need all to protect us from future attacks. We lost thirty, another fifty injured –"

"And you're wasting your efforts on my minor cuts?" Arshal bellowed. He pushed Ramel so that the seer fell back hard. "Go to them! When you're finished you can come back!"

"Your health is paramount –"

Dynresa's mouth hung open. Ramel faced a creature with a millisecond's experience compared to his long life. The king pushed, commanded, one who had once been a god!

"That's an order, Ramel. Do not defy me." Arshal's voice held such menace, his eyes flickering with such anger that Ramel rushed from the tent with only a brief backward glance. What power compelled Ramel to obey a man, not a god?

"Anger doesn't become you," Dynresa said in a small voice as Ramel's steps receded.

Arshal buried his face in his hands, the exhaustion weighing his limbs. "I won't have more deaths on my hands. I bear so many already."

"You didn't tell me you planned to leave."

"I decided tonight."

"When?"

Arshal stared at her, unblinking. "After you ran away. Life will be easier for everyone when I'm gone."

"Oh, the poor-lonely-me thing again."

Arshal rolled away from her, facing the bare wall of the tent.

"Just leave me alone. I don't feel like playing this game with you again."

He heard her rise, felt her passage as she went to push aside the flap.

"Resa?" The tent flap dropped. He rolled to see she stared at him with hands clenched at her sides. He held out his hand. She took a step then stopped. "Please," he called. "Don't leave." He closed his eyes when he felt her hand in his. She held it a moment, the glimmer of the stone that sapped his energy shining through her fingers.

"This can't go on."

"What can't?"

"You're relying on me when you should be relying on yourself."

Arshal opened his eyes to find the stubborn set of her features. He tried to pull her down beside him, but she resisted. "You torment me, Princess Dynresa. Let me just hold you."

"Ramel says I distract you. I guess he's right. You count on me for too much!"

"Ramel says this. Ramel says that. I'm tired of Ramel. What does Dynresa think? Haven't you a mind of your own?" She appeared to hesitate. "You ran away from me tonight. You didn't say why. I worried about you and wanted to apologize for whatever I did to hurt you."

"You didn't hurt me." She knelt beside him with her hand still locked in his. "Don't you see? This has gone too far. For some twisted reason you turn to me for comfort. What'll you do when you're far from Hainad and you have no one but yourself?"

"Think of how nice it was when I was here."

"Oh, there you go with an answer to everything, King. You keep looking to others to make you strong. We should be looking to you for our strength."

"Resa, I made it this far without you. Believe me, there's plenty of things to brood about when waiting for Simiriel's wind. But for some unknown reason I've grown fond of you. Maybe I like being abused. Who knows? When I feel hopeless, I'll think of you, even if it's just a memory. When my journey's done?" Arshal shrugged. "Maybe your attacks won't hurt so much."

"You make more of this than there is," she warned, turning

from his challenging stare.

"Do I? Maybe you make less of it. Maybe you don't know your own mind."

She stood abruptly, yanking her hand from his. She grabbed the lantern and left before he could say another word. Arshal rolled over with a groan, pounding his fist against the rough ground beneath his tent. Staring into the darkness, he felt every ache nagging at him, sleep far away. Thinking of Dynresa, yet trying not to, then considering the 'otherness' he'd welcomed in the battle just fought, he could only toss, feeling wider awake by the moment.

Hours later, he still lay awake, staring up at the tent's ceiling. When he heard the tent flap lift, he froze. He reached for his sword, which made a metallic scrape against the ground as he pulled it close enough to grip the hilt.

"Arshal?"

His sigh ripped the dark tent, followed by the clank of the sword dropping back onto the stony floor.

"I didn't mean to startle you. I thought you'd be asleep," Dynresa whispered.

"People will talk if they know you're here." Why must he so easily conjure a picture of her and her multi-hued eyes, how her forehead furrowed in the dark?

She knelt beside him, her hand searching for his forehead. She bumped his nose before finding it.

"What are you doing?"

"I just worried you might fall sick again."

"Your concern is touching. I know you're anxious to see me gone, but couldn't it have waited until morning?"

"My, some people sure are grumpy when they wake up."

"I wasn't asleep." He sensed her staring at him in the darkness. "So, any fever?"

"No. I couldn't sleep either. That's why I came to check now," she said with nonchalance.

"I kept you awake?" Arshal let sarcasm creep into his tone.

"Just a lot of things."

"I was one of them? Well, I'll admit thoughts of you keep me from getting a much-deserved rest." He reached toward the darker shadow where she knelt, searching for her hand and finding it twisted in his blanket. "Why are you so afraid of me?"

She stiffened. "You think I'm afraid?"

"I know so. I doubt you fear I'd harm you. I figure you're afraid of feeling anything for me because you think I'll fail."

"I don't think you'll fail!" Her vehemence startled him. "I believe you can succeed if you want to, and survive. I just –" Hands knotted his blanket.

"Just what?"

"I don't want to hurt you. That sounds funny, I'm sure. You have enough problems. I just don't want to be another of them."

"You already are." Her hands stopped working the cloth. "Resa, don't deny you care."

"I don't."

"Then what brings you here in the middle of the night?" He chuckled at the absurdity of his own feelings. "See, you might as well admit it."

"What good would it do?"

"There's later."

"Is there? You the king, and so determined to die." She took a deep breath, almost a gasp. Arshal reached up to feel the heat in her face, moisture on her cheek.

"You're the one who doesn't want to be hurt. I'm such a bother to have around. You a strong woman who can face battle, and I make you cry. Another burden."

"Don't tease."

"I'm not. Though you deserve teasing for eternity the way you dole it out. This funny-looking man who's king but shouldn't be, with his white hair and bothersome stone and all the problems he carries like a shroud and you've found in all that some redeeming quality."

"Gods, but you reek of self-pity! Any king would have duties."

"But I'm not the appropriate sovereign so they come harder to me. I have a good excuse to feel bad."

"All right, I'll grant you that. But funny-looking? So, you have a gem in your hand. Some tribes wear gems in their lips. That isn't an excuse."

"This gem is powerful."

"But if you're connecting it to appearance, it isn't odd. And so you have white hair, many do. And so it waves strangely around your face. We'll braid it and it won't curl that way. Actually, I think some might say you were even attractive. Not me, though. And as for shouldn't be king? What's a king supposed to be like? I've only met one. So, if I had misconceptions I'm excused. You could be saner than most or madder than most. I wouldn't know."

"You're turning the subject."

"No, I'm not." She giggled.

"So, you think I make a fine king, might be attractive, may have a reason to feel picked on. So, why do you fight me?"

It was a long moment before she cleared her throat.

"I just don't want to care for someone who wants to die."

"How can you stop yourself from caring?" He brushed his hand against her cheek and let it fall to her neck. "I wish I could."

She shook her head and pulled away from his hand. "If you're determined to die, I'll find a way to not care."

He pulled her close until her hair fell over his face, surrounding him with the scent of cloves. He peered up into the shadow of her features. "Then I guess maybe I'll have to be careful." He looped his arm over her neck and kissed her.

She pulled away, bracing herself with her hands. "You shouldn't do that. If something happens to you ... and you a king, carrying on this way."

"Ah, but how should a king act?" He chuckled. "On what have you based your perceptions? If I'm the only you've met, this must be perfectly acceptable. Aggravating, isn't it?" He drew deep of the clove scent in her hair.

"Only a moment." She sighed, snuggling against him. "Think of the scandal." She nestled her head in his chest. He pulled the blanket to cover her. In moments, both slept.

When the tent flap whipped open to admit glaring day, Dynresa's eyes flew open. Euzzeldir peered at her, his anger a burning coal in his gut.

"Resa!" he bellowed.

Dynresa sat up, struggling to untangle herself from the king. He slept on his stomach, his left arm across her. "It's not what you think."

Euzzeldir took in Arshal's bare, bruised back, the tangle of blanket, Dynresa's sleep-creased features. "I won't hear lies!"

"Arshal!" She shook the king, continuing to call when he failed to respond. Panicking, she shrieked his name. Finally, he rolled over with a groan, revealing blood-caked wounds. Euzzeldir felt the fire in him sputter out at the sight of cuts and bruises on the king's face, the purpling marks on his side. She kept calling him. At last, the king's eyes flew open. His hand went for his sword and brought it up as he sat up, his face drawn.

"No!" Dynresa pushed his sword away. "My father ... tell him there's nothing –"

Arshal started to laugh, but stopped to clutch his bruised ribs with an arm swollen and purple from a deep and gaping wound that seeped around darkened blood.

"I feel like I've been buried in an avalanche." He pulled away the blanket. "See, Zel, clothed," he said with acid in his tone. "If you're even suggesting anything you aren't questioning her honor, but mine. Do you imply the king would risk your allegiance for personal passions? I've heard enough battles over the honor of nobles' daughters. I won't let them continue to divide allegiances. It's foolishness."

"You are grumpy in the morning," Dynresa said, her tone high and shrill as she emitted a nervous giggle.

"Leave, Resa," Euzzeldir ordered. He waited until she had scrambled up and hurried from the tent. "You place me in a dilemma, Lord. I respect you as my king. Yet my daughter's future is precious to me. If you were any other man –"

Arshal gave him a wry grin. "Appearances aren't what they seem."

"Dynresa's almost twenty-five. She should have been betrothed long ago, but no suitors long abide her attitude. Now this rumor –"

"You exaggerate the damage."

"It's more than the rumor. You've other duties, King, Arshal. I won't have it said this daughter of Joffa kept the king from his own, that she turned your thoughts from Shande's need to –"

"Zel, I never stop thinking of Shande. You echo the excuses

Eithur gave Khoti. Clearly, if the Lady Asteria accompanied him to Detarian as a warrior then the ways of the past are over and we must think in terms of survival and expedience, of carrying on with life whenever and however we can. Not think of Resa? I haven't stopped thinking of her since the day you two fought over me in Ramel's shack."

"You heard that and you'd still want anything to do with her?"

"She's a challenge. Call me a fool for abuse."

Euzzeldir took a deep breath, trying to ignore all the nagging emotions of a father then peered at the king. "You look terrible. Ramel's angry that you wouldn't let him stitch you."

"I feel lousy."

"How did this start? Who instigated this tryst?"

"It happened. Nothing more serious than other suitor's stolen kisses."

"She didn't spend the night with them!"

"I'm glad to hear that."

Euzzeldir was forced to chuckle at Arshal's raking grin. He couldn't find it in him to stay angry at a man he'd disdained unjustly. When Arshal staggered up, Euzzeldir gasped, reaching for the king. It appeared buckets of blood had been tossed on him. The king reached for his stained shirt lying in a heap in the tent's corner, but his legs collapsed beneath him. He grabbed for support, almost bringing the tent down with him as he sprawled on the stony ground. Euzzeldir bellowed for Ramel as he struggled to lift the king.

Another week passed before Ramel allowed the king to speak of leaving. Blood loss weakened him to such extent he couldn't protest the Visionary's decision to post a guard outside his tent to ensure Arshal didn't leave his bed.

But when ten days had passed and the first moon drew to a close, Ramel could no longer find excuses to keep Arshal from his journey. The old seer had given all the wisdom he had, but whether it helped remained to be seen. Much of what Arshal needed had to be discovered from within. Already the power to compel strengthened in his voice. At last, he trusted himself.

At their parting, Ramel muttered an entreaty to his brethren to watch over the young king and provide him the stamina to survive, not that Ramel's tone gave any expectation that the gods heard him or would act on the king's behalf. The time had come for Arshal to leave, whether on a headlong flight into death or a calculated journey toward victory even the gods didn't know.

Arshal still ached from many of the bruises that had jarred his bones, and his leg remained weak. He had much to accomplish before two more Evendays passed.

As the king sat astride the horse Euzzeldir had ridden to Shikora he felt like a different man. Dynresa had wound his white hair in Joffan braids bound with gold and Euzzeldir had him dressed in Minarian mail and a white Joffan tunic and cloak. His saddlebags bulged with provisions that gave off the odor of Otayran threespice and crude maps peeked from his bag. Lean, scarred and purged, he sat erect in the high-backed Joffan saddle with its archer's stirrups. His leg ached with the horse's every shift. Could he have even left the Val knowing the discomforts and danger he'd face? And the road ahead looked no better.

The village turned out to bid him goodbye. In the long years of Ebon's rule, the king never came to Joffa. King Arshal would know their needs and understand their troubles. He fought for them and survived in their world. If they only knew a rumor, they might have hesitated to support him. But as Arshal prepared to depart, Euzzeldir's messengers raced in search of other Joffan tribes to come to Euzzeldir's call to arms.

After drinking a parting toast with Euzzeldir and Ramel, Arshal turned north, seeking Dynresa among the crowd but not finding her. He urged his mount to a trot, trying to ignore the pain the jolting gait brought as he left behind the dusty Hainadan village with more reservation than he thought he could hold for anything in this barren land, as if he left his family.

Arshal paused at the rim of the valley to look back at the nest of tents below and the marshy green slash pushing against the brown desert. When he turned, he found a white-clad figure before him, her hair streaming loose from a gold scarf.

"Well, you did it," she said when he stopped beside her. Looking up at him, she squinted against the sun. "You made me go and start worrying about you."

Arshal dismounted and pulled her to him, squeezing the breath from her. He buried himself in her hair, cherished the whip of it in his face. He leaned back, holding her in the loop of his arms to memorize each curve of her face.

"Keep your mind on your business, King," she said as she peered up at him. His stone-bearing palm raised a chill on her flesh. She pushed away to rap on his mailed chest. "You've grown thick-skinned. So, maybe I've helped a little." She laughed, tugging a braid so that his mouth formed an 'O' of feigned pain.

"Come to Sihmad Shal after Kedtair," he begged. "If you don't come that'll be your answer." He grinned at her. "I'm sure you'll do what pleases you and not think of me."

Her mouth opened then closed, as she shook her head.

"You wouldn't want to be courted by a king?"

"Just be careful. Remember your promise. You have a land to regain. Take no unnecessary risks."

"So demanding! Perhaps I don't know what I'm getting into when I think of a future with you –"

She slapped his chest then shook out her hand from the sting of meeting metal. "You'll find some soft Kalilian girl easier to mold to your needs who won't challenge you. Then you'll forget Dynresa and her barren desert." She turned from him to hide the thoughts she wore so openly on her face.

"Ah, but the challenge is the fun." He stroked her hair, trying to memorize the sensation. "It would be impossible to forget you. Just don't go dying for me."

He mounted his horse before he lost his resolve. Goading it to a gallop, he didn't dare look back.

5: On the Edge

As the greening moon gave way to the blossom moon and late spring, Shande gasped. The king who rode from the barren reaches of Hainad couldn't see how the world trembled around him, on the verge of certain collapse.

In Minaria, the Pladde rebellion crumbled, its ranks decimated and efforts enfeebled as Ghyldus dispatched thousands to crush it. Within the Enchanter's web, Princess Resala teetered on the edge of despair – each day closer to falling under Ghyldus's spell. Daily, Verdred remembered less of himself. So little remained, Verdred doubted his name had once been Zopher, could not recall why he felt pride for the tattoo at the base of his neck, and what cruel trick made him bear the shawnsi birthmark in the employ of one dedicated to the destruction of the shawnsi.

In the Lharan mountains the tribes holding Sefresal, the mines, and the Val could barely maintain their ruse of occupation as increased demands for weaponry and metals for Minaria had them laboring dawn to dusk. The Shandean soldiers holding Sefresal cringed as Imperial Couriers came and went. The Minarian inspectors, suspicious and wary, no longer gossiped with the impersonators of Minarian officers and held to themselves information about what passed in the world and in Ghyldus's halls.

Near Eilime, Eithurdon, struggled to build an army from downtrodden fishers and farmers so destroyed by Ghyldus's reprisals and destructive edicts that before they could be trained, he first had to feed and rest them to strength. Even their fear of the enemy that had so terrorized them made the duke wonder if the new recruits could even fight.

The fractious tribes training in the rainforest of Detarian no longer remained insulated from the occupation by the treacherous forest. Under Sedaik, practice for the army often meant rooting out Minarians that attempted to expand control over the region. With each Detarian assault came even more Minarian troops.

After the Tachi raid on the Minarian lumber camps in Tormor Wood, nearly five hundred Minarians came up the Akora River. The reprisals threatened to force Tedwa and Habdelion's army into the open.

While Euzzeldir gathered his people, Shela, the largest of Shande's southern cities, suffered more and more reprisals for the other provinces' actions, burdened by more than two thousand Minarian soldiers. The people who had spurned their king both blamed him for their woes, and prayed he would return and give them another chance.

To the north, the Harbor Gnats, under Nali, Jan, and Pedr's leadership, had become so numerous Peshal's Tunnel beneath the city could no longer house them. When he learned his city verged on rebellion Loch Asmodiel tightened his reign. Reprisals for Gnat raids became more severe. Curfews and restrictions threatened Nali's entire operation. For the first time, easterners starved to death as Loch Asmodiel initiated many of the policies that had so destroyed Eilime's people.

So, as the greening moon passed into the bright blossom moon, Shande groaned. The people of Shande witnessed the nation's darkest days since the Great War of the Gods so many centuries before had taken the lives of hundreds of thousands and darkened the world for generations.

The rich soils of the Saran River region could not produce osfothye at the rate Minaria demanded. Soon the north winds lifted the soil to rain it in large muddy drops on Quelican pastureland. Kishman wheat fields choked on weeds with no tools sufficient to uproot them. Fallow fields forced into production yielded stubby and pest-ridden grains. Fields of vegetables sprouted few blossoms, the bees not even bothering with such haggard blooms. Minarians culled the stock of Kalilian horse herds until the few animals left strained bloodlines. Few laborers yet lived around Shela who could tend the rice and fruits. No saplings replaced lumbered tracts of forest, the bare swaths giving way to scrub. Rivers ran brown with wasted soils, sweeping away fisheries and choking the bays into which they flowed. In just two years of occupation the rape of Shande turned a lush land poor. Shandeans trembled in fear of the day they could no longer sate Ghyldus's desires.

Throughout the country rumors brought both hope and despair to a people seeking anything from which to draw strength. Tales arose of a white-haired god, wielding lightning in his hand. Others said the god fell in battle. Some said One called him home. Legends arose of a green-eyed mountain man – a shackle on his wrist and fangs tattooed on his shoulder – who single-handedly destroyed entire armies and saved thousands of captives. Other stories spoke of a pair of giant sea beasts that ravaged Minarian ships like Maura of old. Many doubted the tale. Legend claimed Maura took to the seas alone, where even her lover Aziaris could not join her.

Some stories suggested the Westlands evaded Minarian control because the king had come there. Others pointed out how the list of missing royal family members had shrunk to only the crown prince. Some rumors claimed that Princess Resala had become Ghyldus's consort and helped him direct attacks against Shande. More claimed she led the Pladde resistance. Most considered all tales of Resala too fanciful to believe.

In isolated hamlets and hidden cottages derna secretly read omens for the coming Year of Kedtair and retold the tales of the gods to the communities sheltering them, finding a sudden significance in the legends and rumors coming in advance of such an important time. Desperate for the glimmer of hope derna gave them, the people guarded their seers and storytellers against discovery from Minarian patrols, slipping them scraps of food in exchange for renewed faith in gods who had largely been forgotten. A fervency gone for thousands of years reemerged as more and more turned their thoughts to the hope and dread the prophets gave the Rising of Kedtair.

So as spring of the second year of the occupation wore toward summer, the destitute people clung to storytellers and rumors, legends and auguries for the hope to survive another day in occupied Shande. Yet, even as hope sank deep roots, power corrupted the conquerors as Ghyldus's prophecies appeared to become reality for them: the Hogde arose throughout Ea as the true tribe of god. Sheer brutality left many Shandeans too stunned to rebel as their conquerors discarded concern for how other countries perceived them. More and more, traitors were born in Shande's darkest hours yet. Despite the armies forming in far corners of Shande – armies that must eat from lands grown barren – the King in Exile's plans grew more precarious with each day as Shande held its collective breath. Too much depended on too few.

6: Assassins

Nali and Jan stood in the Fearnia market square, their faces concealed by hoods pulled low against a drizzle coming in off the sea this cold, light moon day. The executioner shoved Pedr onto the platform, the Reve's face so battered they barely recognized him. Nali and Jan had heard each blow fall, their flesh twitching in sympathy as Pedr's cries carried from the dungeons to the storerooms beyond the hidden doorway.

"The man who sold him will die so horrible a death he'll beg us to speed his passing," Nali said.

"Even if it's Aron?" Jan asked.

"Moreso for ever trusting him."

Jan nodded, his eyes black beneath his hood.

The drone of the executioner's oratory couldn't penetrate the absolute silence as thousands of supporters poured into the square to witness the execution of Reve Pedr the Drayman.

Minarian ranks who watched the demise of a man they assumed led local resistance might have fled in fear to realize that among the thousands witnessing this execution, at least five thousand attended as Gnats. Hundreds of Gnat sympathizers – who slipped information to the Gnats, or supplied them, or created diversions to hide Gnat activities – lined the alleys, walls and rooftops to witness Pedr's death. From Sihmad Shal and the Harbor stretching south to Whittea and east and west as far as Eithira Point and Mania Point, the region supported more than two hundred thousand Shandeans. At least half of them openly supported the Gnats. Yet even though the square emanated a hostility Nali could taste, one that made the executioner sweat on this cool day, made the Minarians in the square tense up, rebellion would not erupt just yet. Too many Minarians, too brutal, well-armed, and swift patrolled the region. Shande's tens of thousands had no weaponry or armor, or were too old or feeble. Among the young and hale many feared doing more than congratulate others' efforts. And the time Nali awaited hadn't come.

Thus, as a Minarian executioner ordered Pedr's neck bared, and soldiers forced the Harbor man over the block, the brooding silence became deafening. Pedr stared back with a wry smile in a broken face, his gaze marking the place where Jan and Nali stood. When the executioner raised his deadly tool of Ghyldus, the crowd took a deep breath almost as one, seeming to pull the wind from the sky. Pedr's smile broadened to a defiant grin.

As the blade raced down toward his neck, Pedr roared the gods' curse on Ghyldus in a bellow so loud it carried beyond that silent borough and into the alleys below. With a sickening crunch and snap that ripped Nali's heart from him, the executioner severed Pedr's head from his body, blood splattering to strike those in the front rows. As one the assembly turned backs to the scene and hung heads in silent mourning.

The unified reaction of so many thousands brought the Minarian troops to nervous attention. But Pedr's witnesses passed from the borough in silence. A few Minarians dared boast, in catcalls and the taunts of the powerful, that the presumed icon of freedom who had dared flaunt Ghyldus's rule was but a bloody heap of flesh. Nali couldn't even gloat at their ignorance, that even the Minarian's spies and ledgermen, in their confidence, failed to note the number of people drifting by the two hooded figures, nodding as they passed as if paying tribute. Too raw in Nali's throat lay his need to avenge Pedr. When at last he and Jan filed from the square, only Jan's restraining arm kept Nali from drawing his sword and silencing a jeering soldier.

When Jan and Nali joined the crowd of Gnat officers in the cavern beneath the city, an ominous silence settled in as gazes drifted to the empty chair to Nali's left.

Nali scanned his officers, just these leaders cramming a cavern that once housed their entire army.

"Our purpose here today is two-fold." Nali's forefinger tapped a slow beat on the table. He tried to keep the tremble out of his voice, an emotion not quite grief, but hard and bitter like the poisoned pit of sweet fruit. "First, you must elect a replacement for Pedr. It's hard to think of any man filling Pedr's place, but the Gnats have worked best with a trio of leaders, each having an equal voice and representing all views. You know how Jan and I stood on various decisions. You must elect someone who will represent the kind of caution Pedr championed."

Bertal collected ballots that represented the consensus of the squads the officers led. Jan and Nali waited in silence, their stares a challenge as Cookie, tallied the vote. When Bertal handed his father the results, Nali allowed a slight smile.

"A wise decision," he said. "I doubt anyone better represents Pedr's views. Tel, take your place." As Olna's stunned cousin eased himself onto the edge of Pedr's chair, Nali cleared his throat to quiet the assembly. "We'd like to put a proposal before you. Because we were only two when we made this decision, we'll give Tel the opportunity for rebuttal or comment." Nali glanced at Jan, taking a deep breath. "We propose retaliation for reprisal. If they strike one of our leaders, we take one of theirs. If they take one of our informants, we take one of theirs." Nali gave Tel a slight nod.

The farmer stood, clearing his throat many times and wringing his hands then grasping them behind him as he spoke. "Pedr would'a outlined all the goods and bads. Things like: it could step up and the reprisals get worse. He might'a said that it wasn't quite right for Shandeans to stoop to the level of the Minarians when it comes to violence. And he might have noted that killin's killin' and since we're not in battle, there's something a little more off about it, kinda not like Shandean folk to go all vicious. In the end, after layin' out all the problems with the plan, he'd go ahead and vote for it." Tel turned to Nali with an expression Nali never thought could darken the mild-mannered farmer's face. "I think out of respect for Pedr he deserves to be avenged."

The assembly cheered and clapped as Tel sat, red-faced and sweating. All hands rose in favor of retaliation. Jan grinned at Nali.

"This'll open a few eyes," Nali muttered.

"Aye, Nali, that it surely will," Jan said, his chuckle having a sinister note more like that of Konner of Tasch-el.

Early the next morning, well before the sun got up, Nali, Jan and four other Gnats crept into a palace room on cat's feet. Each knew the repercussions from this act would pale those of the past, but the memory of Pedr's curse still echoed in their ears.

A soft snore broke the silence of rooms once occupied by King Ebon and Queen Sala. The Gnats froze. Nali moved first, tiptoeing to the bedside of his enemy. He gripped his dagger as sweat spread from his hands and face and drenched his shirt. When Jan reached his position, both men slashed down at the same instant, clapping hands over the mouths of the two sleeping figures, twisting their daggers to inflict more damage. Other Gnat hands came to their aid while Nali and Jan continued to muffle the cries and gasps of their victims. As first one, then the other, stopped fighting and gave in to their fate, waiting Gnats hoisted them and carried them from the room while Nali and Jan erased markers of their attack.

A device propped on a chest beside the bloody bed caught Nali's eye. He recoiled to discover a giant medallion. Huge gems the size of a horse's eye held a soft red glow. The thing gave him a sick feeling in his stomach.

"I feel as if he's right here." Nali gagged.

Jan swung his arm, sending the device crashing to the floor. He emitted a squawk of pain when the medallion burned the flesh of his forearm.

"Like as not some magic," Jan gasped. "Destroy it. It makes me feel watched."

Nali hefted the sledgehammer they'd brought for the finale of their plan, bringing it down on the medallion. The gems shattered, spattering like blood to fall glittering and smoking, pitting the floor. The two men stared at one another.

"When we get hold of Laria Keeper, I bet she can tell us," Nali said. "Likely she's got lots to tell and will be more than willing to tell it."

"She carries his child," Jan stated.

"More than enough reason."

"What a proud grandfa Aron'll be." Jan's sarcasm burned like the red gems pitting the stone.

They pushed out into the corridor, Jan taking the lead as the Gnats sped their bloody booty to the Tower of the Sun, that uppermost tower overlooking the city. When Nali and Jan reached the door to the tower, they found a dead Minarian propped just inside the door, a Gnat standing over him with grim expression. The sentry proved the enemy wanted no more blue flags raised over Shande. At the top of the stair, they paused to catch their breath a moment before climbing out onto a narrow ornamental battlement encircling the tower.

Nali drove a spike into the stonework with his hammer, each blow a metallic clank that made him cringe. Another Gnat uncoiled a length of rope with which they tied the dead bodies to the spike.

A warning hissed up the stairwell.

Taking a moment to place the last touches on the demonstration, Nali brought up the rear as the Gnats sped down the stair and scattered.

As Nali slipped out the tower door, he stumbled to a halt. Two Minarians blocked his path. He threw the hammer at them with a swing of his left arm, ducking between them to dash away. He drew his sword as he ran. Minarian boots slapped stone in pursuit. Nali cursed himself for a fool: he'd taken a corridor that led to a dead end. He hid in a doorway, gripping his sword in sweaty palms and trying not to breathe in gasps. More Minarians joined pursuit. In moments, five soldiers encircled the little doorway.

Any way he looked at it he faced his doom, just like Pedr. Was this the way it would end? Nali brought his sword around, determined to take as many with him as he could. Though he wished for the deadly Shiadin cross-bow with which he'd become so proficient, his training with Kefta and Khoti paid off. The Minarians fell back from his desperate blows. But Nali's skills weren't Khoti's. With one Minarian dead and two others staggering from wounds, at last something struck him from behind and he collapsed in a heap on the palace floor.

Dawn sent a brutal chill and a spark of hope, yet fear, throughout the city. The bloody bodies of Governor Loch

Asmodiel and Matriarch Adesia hung from the Tower of the Sun, their shoulders draped in the Shandean flag, a giant banner proclaiming Pedr's curse on Ghyldism.

As Minarian messengers raced from the city for reinforcements, Gnats haunting burned out ruins along the roads cut them down. Little did they know, Nali had destroyed the fastest messenger.

One bit of news swept the city, tempering the Gnat victory. Defiant Minarians triumphantly crossed a name from the posted lists of most-wanted traitors to the cause of Ghyldus. The infamous Nali Drulson-slash-Bertalson, Sefresal rebel, Gnat, derna and King's Counselor had been caught with hands soiled with the dead governor's blood. Inside the palace yet, people noted with pride for a heroic native son.

In hidden storerooms beneath the city, Jan bit his fist while Tel sat mute, rocking on a crate.

"We can't just leave him," Jan muttered, driving his bloody fist into his other palm.

"What can we do? They'll execute him right quick. You can be sure –" Tel began.

"They'll interrogate him first. And what do you suppose Nali knows?"

"Pedr knew the same."

"Not just about the Gnats. Nali's got the king's entire plan tucked inside his head and they know he does!"

"If Pedr held out, Nali will."

"I'm not going to let them get away with it!" Jan paced up to the hidden door leading up into the palace and dungeons. "Right there he is. Only a few paces away, like Pedr. We got to do something!"

"There's too many guards. We can just hope they'll be so hot to have another execution they won't let their men at him."

Jan shook his head. "You don't think they've started? All that shouting? He's big, Tel. The number of times Nali's name shows up on them lists? They'll be more careful with him. They broke Pedr so bad he couldn't think no more to talk. They've had at Nali a day and already it's too quiet when they ask about the king, and how Nali got in the palace and who helped him. They could break open the entire network." Jan sat on a crate, letting his head fall into his hands as dry sobs shook him. "We can't abandon him, Tel. We've come so far. He's our heart."

A rap on the door to the tunnel brought both men to their feet. A Gnat stuck his head in. "Found a fellow lurking around the river entrance. He claims to have a message for Nali. Bit of a scuffle, too. He wants Nali in person. Pretty mean fighter for a messenger," the man muttered, rubbing a swelling jaw.

"What kind of message?" Jan demanded.

The man shrugged. "Says he's only to speak to Nali. Name's Cydwyn Lockman, from down by Iyrafael. His family checks out. Dead."

With a nod from Jan, the guard disappeared to return some time later with his prisoner. Jan's eyes narrowed when they pushed a youth into the room. Cydwyn stiffly regained his balance, then carefully wiped blood from a bruise at the corner of his mouth as he studied Tel and Jan with a cool regard. He resettled his brown and green cloak over his shoulders and reached to check a weapon the Gnats had already removed.

"What do you want, boy?" Jan demanded.

"I'm to see Nali," Cydwyn stated, leaning back against the doorjamb with an air of infinite patience. "Neither of you meet his looks as they was described to me."

"Be a long wait. Captured, day and a half ago –"

"Not killed!" Cydwyn's studied composure faltered.

"Not yet. What's your message?"

Cydwyn studied the two. "Jan the Innkeeper here?"

Jan straightened, his hand reaching for his dagger. Cydwyn stared at him with an unnerving gaze.

"I'm Jan."

"You look nothing like Jali," Cydwyn mused, relaxing his pose a little. "He must favor his mam."

"Jali?" Jan whispered, not daring to hope. "Here?"

"I'm a courier for Khoti of Tasch-el, the King's Champion and Sword of Shande. We're posted now with Lord Habdelion down in Mershy. Jali's a friend of mine –"

"Jali don't know nobody 'round Iyrafael."

Cydwyn gave him a humorless smile, tight-lipped and cold. "The enemy's prisoners come from all over Shande. Likely, you won't know him no more. Jali's a soldier in Han's army too, and

Khoti's attendant –"

"Jali's a soldier? I find that hard to believe."

Cydwyn sat on a crate, leaving a puff of dust in the air where he'd stood, his hand resting on his empty sword scabbard.

"Look, I'm not here about Jali. I knew you were here and thought you'd want to know. I'm sent as part of the network, to coordinate plans between Khoti and Commander Nali. That's my mission. Khoti'll have my hide if I come back only to tell him I sparred with you. For that matter, he might even have Jali's hide, him so gone on his mentor he'd love every minute."

Jan hesitated. "Tell me about Jali."

Cydwyn sighed his impatience, hands punctuating his speech. "He's a red-headed jokester. He's tried to make some of the Akora's shellfish into a stew he claims is fashioned after his mam's chowder, which he claims is famous. You'd never know it from the concoction he comes up with. You'd starve with him as Cook. He says he sat watch on the Harbor, something about a lighthouse –" Cydwyn stopped when Jan wiped at his eyes and turned away.

"Boy never could figure the right side of a pan." Jan wiped his face with both hands. "They claimed him dead. You've made me happy, Cydwyn."

"That's not why I'm here." Cydwyn chewed his lip. "They got Nali? He knows too much."

"We know that," Tel said.

"Gotta get him out of there, or help him die." For a long minute Cydwyn studied Jan with a penetrating gaze that forced the older man to look away. This boy-man had befriended Jali? What would he find in his son? Finally, with a resigned sigh, Cydwyn launched into the news he'd traveled weeks through occupied lands to bear. Jan and Tel stared at a youth whose years didn't justify the calm with which he spoke of things so impassioned.

"Nali's got to know," Tel said when Cydwyn finished.

"Where is he?"

Jan gestured at the concealed passageway. "Lock-up."

Cydwyn stared at the door. "Why not just break him out, or slip him some poison to ease his suffering?"

"It's not that easy," Tel protested.

"He got Khoti out of Sefresal's lock-up. It can't be that different."

"But –" Tel began.

"Look, Kia's special to me, and Rena. I can't tell them their fa's dead and our entire strategy given away 'cause his own folk refused to do anything." Cydwyn's steady gaze judged Jan with such unnerving assurance as if he could see through him. "You got to do something, and soon."

Jan slowly sank onto a stool. He let his head dip in a slow nod, ignoring Tel's sputtered protest. He couldn't lose Nali, the heart of their entire army. He let Cydwyn be his prod, and prayed they didn't act too late.

7: Blood Rage

Another blow fell, numbing. He'd gone somewhere beyond feeling them. Nali flexed his fingers by twisting his wrists to send some little pulse of blood beyond the shackles. He had never done anything quite so stupid as getting caught. Maybe he'd become too cocky, taking that extra second to hang the banner and drape the flag over the imperial couple. He smiled to himself, inside. His lips were too cracked and bloody to respond.

Suddenly a searing pain ripped his forehead, smashed through his skull. It broke through the delirium in which he'd wrapped himself. His interrogator held some device to his face. He writhed, sickened and terrified at the feel of it and the way it seared into him. Something twisted, wrung his gut, wormed its way into him, repelled him, in him.

"Terremar."

Whether his prayer, or just saying the word, he felt stronger as if he might resist ... the device. Something, he couldn't be sure what, perhaps himself, faced a power in the device ... medallion. Ghyldus assaulted him. He couldn't withstand ... Dream-like he saw himself shrieking his pain and fear, yet calmly answering questions, calmly evading the truth though he couldn't lie. Terremar. Nali groaned, gasping from the burning pain in his head. He retched.

"Where is this Dyndevas dog!"

The question loomed so large. But Terremar. Spells wove about him. He couldn't lie. "Dogs?" he managed.

His head cracked against the stone. He smelled his flesh burning beneath the medallion. Terremar ... strength surging upward at him.

"Where are your supporters?"

"Everywhere." Who answered? The words weren't his.

"How did you get into the palace?"

The medallion at his forehead seemed to writhe– Terremar ... "Dalak's way," he sputtered around swollen lips that sprayed blood like the droplets of the shattered medallion smoking on the stonework of Loch Asmodiel's rooms. Why did the name of a dead engineer memorialized in the caverns come to him?

"Where's Dalak?"

"I don't know." The words came from him, but he'd reached beyond. He laughed, hysterical, shrill, his forehead still afire though they had pulled away the medallion.

"Terremar," he mouthed, welcoming back his delirium.

Long after his inquisitors left, grumbling they'd have to execute him before he could die, he hung in his shackles, legs limp beneath him as he both fought off and welcomed the haze of unconsciousness.

The dungeons fell silent but for the shifts of restless prisoners, an occasional moan or sob, a whispered comment. The interrogator returned several times, his visits a blur of red-eyed medallions, the lash and warring gods in Nali's soul. At last, they came to tell him he would die come morning, as if Nali cared. No slurs would he utter as Pedr had. They would cut his tongue out first.

Again, the vision stood before Nali. A mirage-like Cree held out a thick tome with the solutions to all his dilemmas written in the pages. Nali tried to dismiss the vision as more of his delirium, but it haunted him, eyes open or closed, standing before him, insistent, beckoning. At last, he entertained the dream for a while, analyzing it to take his mind from his misery. He found thinking impossible. Yet each time he closed his eyes, Cree stood beside him, telling him he must read from the book to survive, to help Arshal. But he'd die before he could help Arshal. Why wouldn't this vision cease tormenting him?

A scraping sound intruded on the lock-up. Nali opened his eyes a slit. He heard himself moan. He half fancied a door appeared at the end of the long room. Did he view some variation of his odd vision? Would Cree enter the door and hold out a book?

He tried to lift his head but couldn't. The effort made his head throb and fleeting flickers of light pass in front of his eyes. His ears buzzed, but not loud enough to drown out the scuffing sounds of feet on stone. He again tried to lift his head. When a bleary apparition appeared before his eyes he recoiled. His head slapped the stone and fell back to his chest.

"We're here now, Nali. It's over now." Familiar words came as if from a dream. Soon his arms dropped and he sagged, but something held him up. Pressure took him beneath his arms.

"Terremar."

"I wish," the voice returned. Nali rolled his eyes up, seeing the dark doorway into the wall about to swallow him. His arms flopped about, the hands on their ends numb and unresponsive. He must free himself. They took him to execution. He tried to kick his feet free but hands gripped them firmly. He tried to twist his body, but the grip beneath his arms held.

"It's a'right Commander," a voice murmured from somewhere near his feet. "It's friends come to fetch you."

The voice sounded so comforting and familiar Nali sagged limp, letting them at last haul him through the doorway.

Others scurried by him, sobs of relief and groans of pain and voices not his threading among the shadows. Briefly he smelled the oiled-metal and dried-fruit scent of the storerooms before the burn of wine touched his lips. He tried to pull back. What was this place?

"Nali, can you hear me?" They'd captured Jan! "Ah, Nali, they marked you with their evil." Cold, like ice, soothed the burning on his forehead then stung.

"Nali, we got word on your girls," Jan's words fell in his ear. "Kia and Rena, they're with that Khoti fellow."

Nali struggled to open his eyes a slit.

"Khoti?"

He wasn't sure if the words came out. He took a bit more breath, the ache of it in his ribs, his spine. Cree beckoned to him, promising him the wisdom of the gods, the old Visionary a creature not bound by any promise. Nali had to follow.

"What is that stuff? It smells foul," he heard Jan grumble as someone spread salve over his wounds. He roused himself from wherever he journeyed with Cree. Somewhere dark and far. He felt a cot beneath him, the cool mustiness of underground around him.

"Konner's salve," Nali mumbled through clenched teeth, eyes pressed shut, his words barely passing his lips. "I'd know that odor anywhere." He groaned when he shifted, coming alert as welted and torn skin pulled, bruised and broken bones and muscles screaming. "Jan in the Val?"

"It's not the Val, Commander," a stranger said near Nali's ear. "But it's Konner's salve alright, mixed up by Khoti down in Tormor. Handy stuff to keep around."

Nali twisted his head a little to see the youth so gently applying the salve. In a daze, Nali listened as this stranger gave his account, tossing the names of Nali's daughters into his tale as if they were close, not months distant, his cavorting daughters part of an army and Kia with a tally of dead Minarians to her credit. He wanted to sink away forever for his failure, to drift beneath the surface where he could forget it all. As news of Resala, of Detarian and Tormor, of labor camps, assaulted him with more than he could absorb, his head pounded, the hum growing louder in his ears. On the edge of his consciousness, Cydwyn spoke of Shikora's promised support to Euzzeldir.

"Then he's out there," Nali managed, reaching up to discover the softness of a sash wrapped around his head. He felt faint, the heat rushing him to remember the medallion against his skin.

"The king?" Cydwyn asked, not waiting for a reply. "We think so. Prince Euzzeldir wouldn't help before. Something made him go to Shikora. It's only a rumor, but they say the prince came to them in the last days of the last moon."

Nali tried to turn and focus on Cydwyn, his duty to his command and king pulling him up from the dark well he'd sunk into. "He should've been there by the dark moon. Why Euzzeldir? Arshal meant to go to Shikora first."

"You can worry about it later, Nali," Tel said from somewhere beyond Nali's view. "What's important is the message passed on –"

"No," Nali said, his words hoarse gasps as Cydwyn continued to work the salve into his wounds. "Arshal's what's important. We shouldn't have let him go alone. He wasn't ready."

"There can be any number of reasons, Commander," Cydwyn said.

"We'll know soon enough." Jan laid a hand on Nali's shoulder.

Nali winced; the innkeeper quickly withdrew his hand.

"Anything come of their deaths?" he tried to ignore Cydwyn's hands on his wounds.

"Not yet. They were so busy writing your name off the list, and now they're all busy putting it on again, with the addition that you've escaped justice in Sihmad Shal as well. You're a busy fellow, Nali," Jan drawled, unable to hide the fear in his voice. "Not to mention the names of all those others freed with you. And oh, but they're scamperin' about tryin' to figure how we spirited you away right under the guards' noses. We killed off a few to make it look like we come in the front door. Don't you know but they've tightened the guard on the front door? Never even looked for a bolthole out back. If only we'd had the gall to spring Pedr before it was too late. We're just too cautious. We can't play so meek if we want to win, I s'pose." Jan's voice became a frenzied prattle that seemed to want to fill the silence of the storerooms.

Nali wanted to sink away. He felt like retching. The medallion loomed out at him, venomous. He just wanted to sleep forever, could feel it in his limbs, the weight of forgetfulness. "They won. Likely they'll be crossing me off the list again soon enough –"

"Gods, Nali!" Tel gasped.

"No call for that," Jan soothed. "You don't look good, but it's the fever ... and it's that brand festering on your forehead has me worried. If you just want it hard enough, you'll be fine."

"I don't know as I want it."

Jan knelt in front of Nali. "We really need you to be strong, Nali."

"I'm tired." Nali again reached for the cloth on his head. Royal blue, the cloth came from a cloak dyed, perhaps, by the princess herself.

"Think of your girls! They've lived for a dream of being back with you and Bertal. And what of Bert?"

"Khoti's really got 'em?" Nali waited for Jan's nod. Cydwyn's hands crossed a deep tear in his skin. "He was so strong. He never stopped fighting. I just wanted to die."

"That's only 'cause you weren't thinking the right way, Commander," Cydwyn said, moving into Nali's view, his gaze intense in a youthful face. "Khoti says it's all in the mind. Just like fightin'. That's what made survivors in the labor camps. Kia was always telling Rena about things Rena couldn't remember. Kia lived for Rena, and a golden dream of a cottage beside the sea, and laughter, and baking bread. Me, I live for revenge. You gotta have in your mind those things most important. Things you count on to make you strong. That's what makes you survive."

"I don't know if I –"

"You have to! Let me carry your promise to Kia. Her smiles are so special and rare. Let me bring her one from you."

"But –"

"Promise me! Or I'll tell her the lies the guards told are true, her fa didn't care enough –"

"Cyd!" Jan protested.

"Promise me, Commander. Give us all hope. Fight to live!" Cydwyn's gaze bore into him, intense, like Khoti's when the warrior fire stoked in him. Nali just wanted to find the peaceful place he'd been promised somewhere. In a dream?

"I promise," he whispered at last. He heard Cydwyn exhale and rise, the room growing distant, their voices a babble around him, about him, intense, urgent, frightened.

He clenched his eyes shut, trying to see his children romping around his little cottage in the Harbor. The image was too old. Olna always gave him a sad smile in those memories, as if she knew her dream of seeing him become a derna would mark the end of her happiness. Instead, he thought of Arshal. He couldn't have a life with his children as long as Arshal's mission went unfulfilled. But alongside images of Arshal came the figure of Cree holding out an ancient book with letters scrawled across its cover. Flitting through the background lurked a dark-eyed seer with a red gem in his brow, searching for the King's Counselor. As Nali drifted back into his feverish sleep, he called out hope to Arshal and resolved himself to heed Cree's plea as he stroked the long end of the blue cloth the princess had dyed.

The first weeks of summer in Sihmad Shal ran red with blood. While Nali tossed in fever in the bowels of the city, above, his men went on a blood rage in the memory of Pedr and to avenge their founder whose hold on life remained so tenuous.

As each reprisal and subsequent retaliation grew more grisly, more brutal, bloodier, each on the heels of the other, those Shandeans who sought a placid and safe neutrality at last had to pick sides. The Gnats protected their supporters. The neutrals were not so lucky. Rumors raged that the Gnats far outnumbered the Minarians, seemingly proven by the way Minarian messengers rode away from the city to call for aid, but no one ever returned.

As each day of Nali's consuming fever wore on – the Gnat leader not waking to speak or eat, seemingly dead before he could see how great had grown his army – his men grew more ruthless, depleting Minarian ranks and shutting the mouths of informants. No one knew what had happened to the most infamous of Minarian friends, Aron, who had dropped from view.

They couldn't keep up the Blood Rage indefinitely. If enough couriers failed to return some superior along the line would grow suspicious and send reinforcements prepared to put them down. At last, fearing they'd go too far before they could draw the king and Ghyldus together, and not wanting the Minarians to know their strength, not to mention a little frightened by the force of what they'd wrought, Jan and Tel called the Blood Rage to a halt.

The frenzy of those few weeks, ending in the middle of the heat moon, couldn't be forgotten. The range of Gnat supporters and fledgling Gnat units now extended far to the east of Eithira Point to the Otayran border, south as far as Iyrafael and west to some of the tributaries of the Quelica. While the region of the Etaleah Canal continued to be a Minarian stronghold, the number of Shandeans openly sympathetic to the Gnats had grown to near half a million as word of their power spread. The number of Gnat soldiers expanded apace as well. What it told Jan and Tel made them sick. And the Minarians still retained control.

A short time after the Blood Rage faded to only occasional acts of sabotage, as if to prove Jan and Tel's fears, ships dropped anchor in the Harbor to discharge five hundred reinforcements. While five hundred soldiers barely met a month's worth of Gnat recruits, they brought with them the brutal Eidhalt and their terrifying magic to take control of the crumbled government. The enemy traveled in strength to call reinforcements from Saran, Etaleah and Lagdche. When they flogged to death a dozen elders and newborns in the square, promising more brutal attacks on innocents for each reprisal, the silence of fear again closed Shandean throats.

One afternoon a few days after the attacks on innocents began, Jan entered the storeroom alone and sagged onto a stool, dropping his head into his hands in defeat.

"Hard day?" Nali asked from the cot in the corner.

Jan jumped up, whipping around to see Nali's wan face turned to him, eyes alert and piercing in their hollowed sockets. Jan hurried to Nali's side, kneeling to lay a hand on the derna's cheek to find it cool and clammy. Jan dropped his head on his arms and sobbed.

"That unhappy to see me?"

"I failed you, Nali," Jan muttered into folded arms. "I've gone and risked the whole works by letting 'em have their head."

"Letting who have their head?"

"The Gnats. They wanted revenge for you and Pedr. We went too far. We got too big, too fast. Now the word's out. The Minarians sent in extras to put us down."

"It had to come sometime."

"But not so soon! If they send a whole blasted army, we'll have messed up everything!"

"It'll take months for anything to come of it," Nali replied with certainty. "Sure, they can bring in soldiers from all over. But when they do that, they'll just have fewer in those places. Concentrating everything here will make it easier for us to root them out. If you're talking about a whole army, they have to send to Lagdche for that, then gather the men and ship them out. That'd put us at about the cold moon."

"Six moons sooner than we can afford!"

Nali's face took on an expression so familiar Jan let out a yelp. "You're on to something, Nali!"

Nali looked up at him, his cold smile cracking scabbed lips.

"Pull back and regroup, Jan. They don't have to know how big we are. We'll bluff 'em. Make the efforts seem more and more feeble as if the organization is crumbling. Plant lies about a leadership shake-up and make 'em think we're falling apart. The Minarians will forget about us until it's too late."

"We've gotten a bit bigger, Nali," Jan hedged. "Our range grew a bit. It's going to be hard to tell all those new commands that they got to lay low."

"They can train and do the subtle things we used to do. They can still be gathering information, laying traps and building support for later."

"A courier's already left for Lagdche."

"There'll be another. They aren't going to want to anger Ghyldus with news that they can't control a bunch of dimwitted Shandeans. They'll rush to him with any good news."

"It's a lot to count on."

"It's all we got. We have to be ready for whatever happens. But we've got time."

Jan stood, smiling. "It's nice to have you back among the living, Commander." Even though Nali still lay abed, something so strong and compelling about him, some magnetism Jan had never noticed before, made him think he'd leap to his death at Nali's word.

Nali stared at the loose end of the cloth still wrapped around his head, the long strips hanging down almost to his waist.

"How bad am I, Jan?"

"How bad?"

Nali looked up at him with his hawkish gaze. "I don't remember much, enough. Will I leave this bed on my own?"

Jan nodded, a mechanical response. "Nothing's broken but ribs mending. I wouldn't have believed it, the way you looked and the tales we heard of ... how they treated you. How straight you stand might be another matter."

"That medallion. Like some war waged on my forehead. Terremar, I think. Him or Cree. It wasn't me that held my tongue."

Jan peered at him. "Cree's dead, I thought –"

"He means me to read the Lierye; I know it."

"The forbidden book? Are you sure you should?"

86

"All there is to know is in it. I hear him laughing in my head. It's what he meant."

"Laughing? Nali, you're just waked."

Nali smiled and shook out his hands, his legs. He forced himself up to his elbow. "He was a god once. He knew everything and every portent and all answers." Nali sank back onto the cot, paler. "I wonder what he thinks I'll find there. I've studied tracts copied from it, but not the original book itself. Again, I hear him chuckling in me, a sound I've never heard, but I know it's him. He's free now, no longer chained to our world or his promises." Nali took a ragged breath. Suddenly his bright gaze leaped to Jan. "Oh gods, I think I know what this unfettered Visionary would do to me."

Jan stared, waiting. But Nali said no more as he stared up at the rough stone of the ceiling.

"What we got to do is hearten these boys that been praying on you for so long. They went on a Blood Rage for you, Nali. If I'm to curb them at all, they have to know you're against it."

Jan sped into the corridor beyond, already calling for the food to get Nali back on his feet. Nagging at the back of his thoughts was the sane look in Nali's eyes as he claimed a one-time god, unfettered, chuckled inside his head. What did Nali mean when he claimed Cree would do something to him?

8: The Dasirei Swamp

Khoti peered out from among bobbing reeds, his knees and hands sinking into mud. As the scorching sun of the heat moon brought biting flies to his skin in search of the salt his body shed, the vast reaches of the Dasirei swamp hissed in a light wind. The sheer size of the swamp overwhelmed his senses: the moist odors of decay, the living-green scent of slime-slicked waters, felt endless. He couldn't escape the odor. Behind him the dark stretch of swamp put the tangle of Detarian to shame. Trees twisted limbs toward the sky, their roots barely anchored in the tea-colored water. On the ridges of spongy soil where past windfall disappeared into the ooze, a tangle of shrub and plants sent leaves, roots and vines in search of the sun and housed a symphony of birds whose calls deafened.

Where Khoti crouched with the rest of his unit, the tangle gave way to cleared lands. Only rough grass and rushes clung to the tussocks of past roots, and water had turned stale in the depressions where trees had towered, the little pools smelling of rotten eggs and discharging blood-sucking insects in clouds. Just beyond the ring of cleared swamp in the midst of Dasirei lay squares where young laborers tended a grassy water weed cultivated to yield rice.

The swamp formed by the meeting of the Rigannon and Dasirei rivers appeared level. Except for isolated pools, however, all of Dasirei crept southward to Rigannon and beyond, replenishing the roots of plants growing within a network of dikes, ditches and dams. The weed with its starchy seeds grew wild in marshes and shallow lake edges, but here farmers had long bred it into a staple.

Just beyond the cleared area stood a dismal compound housing more than two hundred youths. Khoti glanced at Asteria beside him. The skin of her neck still glared red at him where just last night, in a rite he'd delayed too long, he set his knife on her neck and smeared on her skin the black dye that could bring tears to the eyes of the strongest warrior. The Lady of Sefresal held her stoic silence as she'd become a Tawnkat. She'd let him put his mark on her. He knew of no greater bond.

Suddenly she gripped his arm and pointed. The reeds ahead moved. He heard a few short clicks over the hiss of grass. Kia's head came into view. Khoti hugged the girl to him, hesitant to let her go. How could he keep asking a child so young to take such risks for him? This child of nine honed Asteria's weaponry, waxed bowstrings and groomed arrow flights instead of playing pilfer the pie and weaver's loop.

"Any trouble?" he asked her.

Kia's dark hair clung to her sweaty face where slapped insects and grass seeds collected. "I was lucky to be at Howl," she said, looking up at Khoti with Nali's eyes.

"That bad?" Jali muttered.

"They been treated bad to stop any escape. And the heat and damp has 'em sick a lot."

"But do they think they can do it?" Asteria pressed.

Kia shrugged. "They're not guarded much. It's too dangerous for 'em to go in the swamp. And they're so sick no one thinks of running away. A couple did, but no one knows if they got away. They said they'll try. They didn't want to. I talked 'em into it. I hope I wasn't wrong." Kia's features held the starkness of memories she wouldn't repeat.

Asteria hugged Kia. "They will be better off for trying. They would just keep dying here."

Khoti led his unit stumbling through the swamp to where the rest of his small force waited. Besides his eight-soldier unit, another twenty waited with Chati and Tre in the tangle of undergrowth, prepared to fight all the way to Tormor if necessary.

When reassembled, they slipped back to where the banks of the river seeped into the swamp. After they untied their rafts from twisted trees, the current carried them into the main water course, which swept just beyond hailing distance of the camp. A crude path led from the river bank through the swamp to the camp. There, Minarians kept a guardhouse at the head of the trail to wait for barges that delivered supplies, took away produce, and brought couriers.

As the haunting of nightfall fell over the swamp, the shapes of trees took on ghostly forms while night creatures sent out eerie calls and cast translucent eyes on anything that passed. The soft squish of a foot on a muddy bank silenced the shrill of crickets. Khoti tugged his raft up a span above the water. He calculated his every step, his toes searching the ground before settling into a print.

Other rafts bumped Khoti's. Instead of coming to rest on shore, his warriors tied them loosely to his, all set to flee without a trace. Khoti left Kia and Rena to watch the rafts as the rest of the squad groped along the bank.

Climbing through a web of branches overhanging the water, they discerned the faint light of a lantern ahead. Khoti sent Chati and Tre's units in a wide circle to flank. He took a few more paces before he froze. Close at hand he glimpsed the faint glow of a pipe. In the deep gloom he couldn't tell what snarl of brush lay between him and the sentry to give them away. He tapped Daris, her dusky features melting into the shadows.

With a slowness that dragged the minutes, Daris stalked the sentry. At one point, Khoti could swear the sentry looked right at her. She had become only one of many shadows. She waited until the sentry again turned to scan the dark river, which reflected faint starlight. She tested the ground with each wary step, her pace so slow Khoti measured it in lifebeats.

She stood no more than an arm's length from the sentry when he turned. He peered into the shadows as if sensing something. He stared back toward Khoti. If he turned another span he would look right at her. He pulled the pipe from his mouth and tapped it against his palm. Daris took one more step and slipped the wire over his head and across his throat, pulling it with a snap.

Though no match for the sentry's strength as he fought for a grip on her arms, she held, letting him buck her from her feet, but never shaking her grip. His efforts weakened until he sagged, pulling her down with him. She slipped in the dewy foliage, continuing to grip the wire until Asteria touched her.

Daris stared toward Khoti as she re-coiled the wire and tucked it in her pocket. Khoti nodded, unsure if she saw him in the shadows, but knowing she felt his praise.

They moved on, swift clicks telling them Chati and Tre had reached their positions. Khoti paused at a small stream crossing their path. Pushing a branch into the dark water, he felt it sink into the ooze without finding a firm bottom. Asteria gripped his arm. She gestured at the eastern sky, which glowed as the moon neared the edge of the horizon.

He pulled the branch from the muck then tested the far bank for danger while Jali uncoiled a loop of rope from his pack. As soon as Khoti nodded, the Harbor youth ran and leaped onto the far bank. One foot just missed the water. He tossed an end of the rope across, ready to pull the others to safety if they fell in. Khoti crossed last, facing the dawning moon.

Soon they reached a clearing where a small shed with but one window and door perched just above the river's high-water mark. A rough track disappeared behind it toward the depths of Dasirei. The moon crested the horizon, deepening the shadows and brightening the clearing. They found a bridge over a wider backwater. After crossing, his units fanned out in search of sentries as Khoti dashed up to peek in the window. Seven men slept in the little shed. An eighth honed his sword at a table, his mail and helm lying on the floor.

Khoti touched a spark to dry bracken Asteria piled against the structure. A spiral of smoke rose. Fanning until it flared, he then backed away. If nothing else, this would alert any sentries they'd missed. The fire spread to other dried leaves then licked at the shack. A chair slammed to the floor. The door wrenched open. When the Minarian soldier hurried out to stomp the flame, Jali's arrow whistled true to embed itself in the man's chest. Khoti darted out, sensing death beneath his touch, then eased the door shut and dragged the body into the shadows.

The flames grew, engulfing the shack and feeding on the roof timbers. Shouts arose within as soldiers awoke and scrambled for the door. One darted out, only to be struck by three arrows from different sources. Another stumbled to the door as the structure caved in on itself. Before Jali could shoot, the transom gave way and struck the man in the head. As the last timbers collapsed, he disappeared among the flames, his voice silent among the cries of those still within. Then, silence.

Khoti froze. Instead of the Minarian hut he saw Tasch-el. Von, driven back into the burning barn under a hail of arrows. Von. His dying wails filled Khoti's ears. The burning stable singed his cheeks.

"That is a grisly way to die," Asteria muttered as the rest of the squad gathered around, faces glistening in embers' glow.

"That's why Kia and Rena are with the rafts," Khoti said, riveted by the scene. A knot tightened in his throat, gagging him. Though Tawnkats had used fire before, somehow this felt different.

"Come," Asteria prodded, pulling him around. Her eyes, dark with concern for him, begged him to seek comfort in her. Instead, he shook off her hand as he dispatched his units.

The moon crested the treetops of the other bank and slanted down at them as the fire died. Chati and Tre went for camp while Daris kicked at the little leaders that strove for fuel beyond the shack. Jali and two Tachi left to fetch the rafts. The remaining Tachi stood guard among the ghostly trees. A strange silence fell around him that seemed to quench the buzz of frogs on the other bank of the river. The silence on this side suffocated.

He sat on the bank to watch the moonlight glowing off the few ripples the wind raised on the river. He wished he could just sleep, forget it all. He wanted the sense of home and peace he'd found in Habdelion's camp. He was thinking; he knew he shouldn't.

Before long Chati returned leading shadowy figures who stumbled silently through the dark.

"Any alarm?" Khoti demanded.

Chati shook his head as the slight figures entered the clearing, the moonlight glowing from sweaty faces. Khoti's lieutenant scowled. "They took out the guards. Kia told them they didn't have to. They did it anyway." He stared at Khoti. "They lost a dozen in that foolishness."

"Not a word to Kia," he told Chati as he counted the figures emerging from the shadows, Tre bringing up the rear. He scanned the river, discerning against the glitter the silhouettes of Tachi manning the rafts.

The escapees turned their stunned gazes on him. The knot sank from Khoti's throat into his stomach. Emaciated and listless, likely he'd lose half of them en route to Tormor.

Khoti approached the closest youth as Chati and Tre helped guide the rafts to shore. He tilted the Joffan child's face up to the moonlight. The boy straightened, as if he took strength from something in Khoti's touch. His fingers read the heat of fever in the boy, the swelling in his neck that spoke of poisons in the blood.

"They can't travel far."

"Where? How long?" Asteria asked, already gathering the youngest to her comfort.

Khoti turned away, running a muddy hand through his hair. He gripped a chunk of hair as he gazed across the young faces then groaned his frustration. His arms flopped to his sides. "North bank of Dasirei," he decided as he spoke. "It's dryer, cooler. We'll have to play the time as we see it. We can send the strongest upriver with Chati and Tre."

The youths filed onto the rafts, sitting quietly where told. The shore sped by as Khoti's squad pushed their poles into the muddy bottom. Khoti glanced back at Kia. The girl looked up at him suddenly. He shivered. Whatever had made Kia so slow to emerge from her shell might be nothing compared to what these young Shelans, Joffans and Kalilians had known.

9: The Hainad Road

"Slugs," Baynu muttered as the last of the Minarian boarders disappeared into the dark night on the Rigannon River. He drew his knife in a swift motion as if to stab the Minarian who dared board one of King Wyeff Shikora's craft. "They think they master all of Ea."

"They will learn soon it is false arrogance," the captain assured him in a weary tone. The captain's dark features almost hidden by the deep night of this land, glistened from the heat, or a hint of fear left by the Minarian's boarding. The captain stared into the swirl of water trailing them. The single lamp of their companion barges behind barely touched the shadows of Shandean night. "It is worth the inconvenience."

"Supposedly we are their friends," Baynu grumbled. "If this is how they treat our consuls, why have we not called off our game with them?"

The captain shrugged. "I sail ships, navigate barges. What do I know of court politics? We will move to war soon enough, Champion. It is safer the way things go now. You, Baynu, are a soldier, not consul. You attend your thoughts to your profession and they will watch theirs."

Baynu grumbled as he sat on a covered crate packed with weaponry and stared at the vessel following, which carried similar cargo. The horses crowding the deck stood with heads bowed, exhausted by the rough passage in the cramped hold of the ship left at anchor in Shela. The barge lamps seemed to close the night around Baynu like a damp, woolen cloak. He felt watched, vulnerable, moving like a beacon through a world of dark water and forest.

In Shela, other river travelers had warned them robbers boarded barges and fishing vessels up and down this stretch of river. Not that the Minarians would admit they couldn't completely control their conquest. Baynu whittled at a crate plank, gouging his knife deep into the wood, flipping away a chip that skimmed across the deck to disappear into the dark waters. No wonder the people became robbers. From what he had seen of this occupation, thievery meant survival. He glanced around at the close night then gave another flick of the knife. In their short journey upriver from Shela, Minarians frequently rowed out to inspect their cargo and demand explanations and papers from the captain, even though everyone knew the Kalilian horse herds were diminished. These conquerors avowed no one could plot against them, yet they harassed supposedly friendly traders for the mere sport of it, for the sheer insult.

But King Wyeff Shikora's Champion had come now. Baynu straightened, sending another wood chip skittering into the water. A man such as he could lead these withered Shandeans, become the hero of their lore as he taught them how to throw off their yokes of servitude and follow him to freedom. Perhaps for his service some royal would present him daughter and dowry. He'd return to Wyeff Shikora a lord. How could Shande not honor him? He stood as a father among children. Hadn't he seen how his children had been hurt? When they passed the wharves of Shela, he'd grown ill to see the laborers, bodies scarred, skin hanging on their bones like cerement cloth. Was it a wonder the hungry were thieves? Baynu couldn't wait to serve justice. How they would cheer him!

As the barge nudged northward into Shande, Baynu carefully crafted his fantasy of child-like Shandeans fawning over him, lauding him for strength in this world of despair. More than the wild legends he had heard that doubtless gave hope to their struggle for survival, he came to them a true warrior and savior to honor. The maidens would clamor for the honor of his bed. He would be substance in their petty lives. Baynu! They would chant – their prayer for one sent in the name of the true gods.

Baynu smiled into the night.

Even at this late hour the air remained so warm and damp the tepid river felt cold as they slipped from their raft, their exposed skin clammy. Strong strokes took them close to the brightly lit barges creeping upriver that they had studied these last hours.

Asteria moved out in front of Khoti, swimming in the shallow river toward the first boat. Light from the barge's lanterns lit her face and the sheathed dagger in her teeth. As if realizing she made a visible target, she disappeared beneath the surface, to reappear moments later clinging to the slick sides of the barge. Khoti reached the boat as Asteria crawled over the rail, the horses stirring and pushing, threatening to give them away.

Soft sounds echoed like shouts, telling him the rest of the unit boarded or clung to the sides. A figure rose in front of Asteria, shavings falling from his lap as he stared at her, stunned. She raised her dagger as he moved toward her, lantern light glittering off her wet face and revealing the sunburst birthmark so dark on her temple. It made Khoti's stomach flop. The man stepped back to draw his sword as Asteria ducked around a horse. Scuffles broke out across the craft. Suddenly the man peered at her, his mouth gaping with surprise.

"Shawnsi! Do not fight them!" he called to the men now engaged in skirmishes all over the deck.

"What, and die?" an oarsman cried as he fended off Jali, a red-headed dervish.

Asteria took a step back, eyes narrowing as Baynu dropped his sword to his side. Khoti slipped over the rail, drawing his dagger as he stalked the man.

The man held out his hands. At Asteria's sign, the Shandeans froze, each with one eye on Asteria, the other on an opponent. Folding her arms over her chest Asteria stared at the man with an unruffled challenge that made Khoti want to grin.

"Resistance?" the man asked. Asteria didn't respond. "Come, you are no Minarian. That is written in your face." He took a step closer but Asteria raised her dagger, Khoti coiling for the pounce, his gaze on the warrior's muscular back.

"We claim these goods for Mershy," Asteria proclaimed. "We have no battle with you."

"Sorry," the man said with a smile, shrugging his hands up in apology. "These are for Joffa. We come to help them." He bowed to Asteria. "Baynu, Champion of King Wyeff Shikora." He grinned as if he expected Asteria's stony face to brighten with wonder. "I see this occupation makes the fine ladies of this land soldiers. It is sad, but heartening to see you do not cower –"

He turned as Khoti at last stepped into view, swiftly moving between Baynu and Asteria. Baynu's mouth opened, his glance going from Khoti to the tattoo just above the collar of Asteria's dripping tunic, Rigannon piddling in puddles on the deck as it escaped the fabric. Baynu took a deep breath as his gaze at last came to rest on the battered shackle at Khoti's wrist.

"The legend lives!" Baynu grabbed Khoti's wrist. Before Khoti could protest the Shikoran had raised it for all to see. Baynu's men pressed forward, ignoring the Shandeans they had fought.

Khoti yanked his arm free with so much force Baynu almost flew against the rail. He heard something in the man's tone, triumph? Mockery? It rang insincere.

"You are Khoti," Baynu said, bowing, his crisp dialect giving the name an unfamiliar emphasis. "My honor it is. We hear stories –"

"Exaggerated," Khoti returned finding his voice as his warriors gathered to him.

"No doubt. But legends contain elements of truth. The shackle, the fangs tattooed there," he pointed at Khoti's neck, gestured with his head toward Asteria whose posture told Khoti she, too, doubted this Baynu. "Your light hair. Your eyes are green perhaps? Elements of truth. The legend goes before you. King's Champion, I hear. Commander, as Sword of Shande, I hear. What resurrects long dead titles? What kind of warrior could peaceful Shande make?"

"These horses are for Joffa?" Khoti demanded as he scanned the decks, his face hot.

"Plus weapons, and me," Baynu stated, thumping his thumb into his chest. "King Wyeff Shikora heard your prayers. We are servants to the needy."

"How did you propose to get your cargo to Euzzeldir?" Khoti asked instead of the question foremost in his mind. What role had Arshal played in this boon?

Baynu shrugged. "We expect they await us."

"They aren't waiting." Khoti counted the horses, calculating how many people he had now that Chati and seven Tachi returned to Tormor with the healthier youths from the Dasirei camps. "You say Euzzeldir has no weapons?"

Baynu gestured at tarp-covered crates. "They can be packed on the horses –"

"But do Euzzeldir's people know how to use them?" Khoti muttered to himself.

"Can Han do without you?" Tre called across the deck.

Khoti almost smiled. Tre knew him so well. "He has Chati, Tedwa –"

"The young ones –" a Tachi, Ledak, countered from Khoti's side.

"Daris! How many Joffan?" Khoti demanded.

"Maybe fifty," Daris said, sheathing her dagger and crossing the deck to him. "If you think those sickly things can cross Jashiho you've lost your mind."

Khoti glared at her. "They can ride. It's a better journey than cramped on rafts, or sinking in fens." He turned to Baynu. "We'll take your cargo to Euzzeldir."

Baynu inclined his head slightly as he regarded Khoti with a calculating gaze. "I am to represent my king in what army Shande fields. If I accompany you to Prince Euzzeldir to see the cargo does not turn around and head for Mershy then I will see whether these legends are sound."

"They're sound," Jali said with a growl.

Baynu glanced at Jali, his mouth dropping open as he then scanned the Shandeans on his barge. "Has Shande called her babies to war as well?"

Ledak stiffened. "I am a Tachi warrior!"

"Doubt us at your peril," Khoti warned, one arm shooting out to restrain Ledak.

Baynu took an obliging step back from Khoti's gaze.

"The Shandean tinder is dry indeed. Perhaps we should not delay the great armies of Shande," Baynu conceded.

"Daris, round up the Joffans and fetch Kia. You, Tre and Ledak get your gear to join –"

"The Tachi want to stay with Han," Jali interrupted. "Let me go in Ledak's place. I'm your attendant."

"You're needed upriver."

"Oh, let him come," Daris sniped. "He's so stubborn we'll be here all night arguing. Tachi'd be lost in the desert. It's a fool's mission anyway. Six of us and fifty waifs and you want to cross Jashiho and pass Minarian outposts with two hundred and fifty horses –"

"Three hundred by my count," Khoti said with a wry smile.

Daris sighed. "Do you always look for the slimmest odds?"

"Move, Daris," Khoti ordered. With a shake of wet hair, Daris slipped over the side to swim for the raft a Tachi held steady against the current. In a few moments the raft disappeared into the wide expanse of water where Dasirei met Rigannon.

Khoti turned to Jali, his teeth bared in a warning smile. "Keep your mind on your mission Jali, not on Daris."

As Khoti moved among the horses to inspect the cargo, he noted how Tre slapped the Harbor youth on the back, giving him a rakish grin.

Jali plopped onto a crate to wring out the soft skin shoes he wore.

"He knows your mind better than you do," Tre said. Khoti grinned to himself to hear the tease in Tre's tone.

"He's never said anythin' before," Jali grumbled.

"You're becoming a fine soldier, Jali. Just don't make Khoti regret giving in."

Tre strolled away, whistling his good humor. Khoti paused to watch Baynu crouch beside the red-headed warrior.

"So, what brings a Kalilian youth so far south," Baynu asked with a genial grin.

"Kishman," Jali replied. "Other side the Rigannon." The Shikoran's condescending tone made Khoti's clammy skin tingle and appeared to snuff Jali's usual affability.

Baynu inclined his head. "Kishman. Though your speech places you from the northeast."

"It's all Shande."

"Is it hard to work with such a legend as Khoti?"

"Earned." Jali peered at the Shikoran. "I hope you aren't belittlin' him."

Khoti held up his hand as Asteria tried to draw his attention. He realized that perhaps even Jali read people better than he'd thought.

"You might look at me's just a boy," Jali continued. "Easy mistake to make."

"But you are a boy," Baynu laughed. He held his hands out, appeasing. "You might do the work of a man but time says you are still a boy."

"You can die as easy at any age," Jali stated. "Time's a random marker. In Detarian, at fifteen you're s'posed to marry and have families. In Khoti's mountains, the rites come at seventeen. You claim manhood by custom. I call it by ability."

Baynu chuckled at Jali's confidence as if he didn't notice Jali's scowl. "Pardon, but my young brother, your age, remains at home, still clinging to our mother when the storms sweep through."

Jali had his arm around Baynu's neck, his dagger pressed against the man's throat before the chuckle could die on the lips of King Wyeff Shikora's Champion. Baynu struggled unsuccessfully to shake free of Jali.

Khoti wedged between them, wrenching them apart with his raw anger. "There's enough Minarians to go around!" His warning came out a hiss as Jali panted, glaring at Baynu. "Such a warrior should've learned long ago not to underestimate an opponent, King's Champion or not."

"I was not looking at the boy as an opponent," Baynu said. "He misunderstood my jest –"

"Which was meant to demean him, which makes it a challenge, which establishes opposition," Khoti stated, echoing Eithurdon's lessons. He straightened. "You question my soldier's ability, which implies you doubt my judgment."

Baynu shook his head. "I intended no slur. We work for the same purpose. And we have a long journey to make together. Forgive me a nature lending itself to doubt without proof."

Khoti still stood between the two. He turned on Jali. "Over the side, Jali. When you've cooled off, we'll talk."

Jali groaned, though he sprouted a wry smile. "If a snake kills me, or some other creature drags me under to my death, you'll be owin' me an explanation."

"And I'll give it as soon as I arrive."

Jali sank into the river, hanging on the side until Daris

returned with a raft crammed with the Joffan children.

The Shikorans stared in astonishment as Jali helped the children aboard, the youngsters' ages spanning the scale. When Kia climbed up, dagger at her belt, Jali hefting Rena from behind, the captain brushed by Khoti, unable to look on the tragedy of Shande.

When Ledak and the remaining Tachi waved them off, the barges crept upstream toward firmer banks. Khoti leaned against the rail to stare at the water, scowling to consider the ignorance of Shande's plight heard from the Shikorans. When Khoti described the source of his cold-eyed warriors, Baynu's apology had come through compressed lips as if he swallowed a bitter herb. Khoti sent such children to war for him.

In a normal world he'd be long joined by now, to some young woman perhaps of Lhata or Staph-el. He'd be Von's Second or his fa's officer, have his cottage, perhaps even a child. He'd trek monthly to the Tasch-el mine with Von and then the brothers might hunt a week. He'd tend a patch of garden and share herding duties when the village moved sheep to fresh pasture. By now, Chati and Tre, too, would have cottages beside his, work the mines together, tend the livestock, and seek lifemates. His squad, his survivors, like Jali, just reached the age when Khoti first went into battle with the same self-doubts and desires to prove his worth and gain his vengeance.

The strangeness of it all rose up out of the dark at him, all because Baynu saw his soldiers as children they never could be. The dark water sloughed away from the square bow, the strain of oarsmen's muscle soothing the night, stroking it like the distant chorus of frogs, an undulating lifebeat. His dream of a normal world would never exist. No Tasch-el remained to return to, no livestock, no cottage. If he returned to serve as headman of his village he'd be banished by the lord of his province. And after more than three years a warrior, he couldn't imagine himself presiding over rites and festfires as his father had. In less than a year, Kedtair would rise and decide their fate. Whatever the outcome, the Shande of old was gone. No longer did tribes like the Detarians and Taschians live in ignorance of the world outside their borders. Hard feelings between neighbors and friends would remain. Nightmares would haunt the sleeping. Idleness would challenge warriors like himself. Too much of him would always need a challenge and tests to prove his mettle.

As the Rigannon slipped behind them he tried to wipe the thoughts away. Always he claimed deep thinking had no place in a warrior. But what about a healer, a council member, a headman? None of his titles gave him any certainty of what role he might have a year from now, or whether he truly should hold such titles. He buried his head in his hands, begging to think of something else, anything. His mind conjured a picture of a fiery surface, blazing, a memory from when he was only ten or eleven, and two suns had risen orange from a gray mist in the east to bake the mountains. Kedtair. It had become his prayer.

The next dawn they left behind the barges at the marshes where the Dasirei and Rigannon Rivers joined. They hadn't traveled far before the terrain melted into grasslands that became scrubbier, dryer and hotter as they went. Khoti's nerves frayed as he sought water enough for the horses they herded before them, and worried over the sight they must make against the barren sky. Five days of travel brought them to the Hainad road, their destination still many days distant, Khoti dreading the need to travel on so open a road.

Khoti and Daris crept up to the rim of the shallow valley protecting the road from Jashiho's harsher assaults. Scrub and a few hardy trees hugged the valley bottom where the submerged river ran to meet the swamp and at last the sea, its conniving waters remaining hidden until finding the tidal marshes. As Khoti scanned the road he saw the first of the many wells Daris told him tapped the subterranean river the road's length. Next to the well stood a Minarian outpost.

"I count twenty-five horses," Daris whispered.

"Then assume twenty or more Minarians," Khoti said. "How far before there's another access to the road?"

"Two, maybe three days, with no water." She gave him a wry smile. "You seem disgusted by my desert."

"Likely your desert would look more hospitable without Minarians," Khoti said as they crept back from the ledge. He surveyed the large company they made. More than three hundred horses, most packed with weapons, and almost sixty people crowded a little hollow where Khoti hoped their racket wouldn't carry to Minarian ears.

"We'll have to skip the first well," Khoti announced when he and Daris returned to their camp. "An outpost –"

"How many Minarians?" Baynu demanded.

"Better than twenty."

"Certainly, a legendary warrior such as yourself could take them on with the help of King Wyeff Shikora's Champion," Baynu asserted. "And you tell me your folk are such fine warriors. Certainly, these children can –"

"The risk is unnecessary." The heat rose in Khoti's face making his sunburn sting. "Our cargo's too important. I'm not going to risk children's lives and an army's weapons and mounts for your personal glory."

"Perhaps the legends were exaggerations," Baynu returned, turning his back on Khoti to prove he didn't fear him. "For all you know there will be an outpost at the next well. Then your refusal to hear me will tell. I am a warrior from a land that knows war not one of your infant followers."

Khoti stiffened. "I'm the Sword of Shande, Baynu. Not you."

As Khoti turned away, he caught sight of Asteria's eyebrows hooked up with amusement.

"What's so funny?" he demanded.

Asteria giggled and patted his arm. "You have such a diplomatic way about you, Champion."

He tried to hide a smile behind false indignation. He always failed to fool her. Chuckling, she strolled off to her tasks with a confidant stride unlike the noble in fine raiment she had once been. Khoti frowned to recognize unwelcome thoughts again. She assured him, repeatedly, with an annoying frequency, that their relationship remained one of comrades-in-arms, friends. He reached for the pendant on the chain around his neck, unconscious of the action. He clucked his tongue to summon Fidra only to remember his fine mount remained in Tormor.

Khoti sped their pace, wanting to put the outpost far behind them. He sent Daris ahead in search of a route down into the valley and to scout the next well. Soon they reached barren lands where a storm had swept in sand to choke the scrub. With the next storm, it would likely blow the sand the other way. The horses labored in the loose footing, expending the energy they needed to travel without water.

As evening neared, a full day beyond the outpost and two days since they replenished their water, Daris returned at a gallop. Her face split with a crooked grin that always implied her sarcasm.

"Two hours more," she said. "It's steep, but I made it down and back up."

She handed Khoti a large skin, heavy with the river's cool water. He passed the skin among the children, then to Asteria, Jali and Tre. With several swallows left, Baynu drank deep, laughing when he handed the empty skin to Khoti.

Khoti grinned at Baynu. Asteria's arm shot out to restrain Khoti's hand, which rested close to his sword. Baynu's triumphant smile faded.

Khoti laughed, in this mood a sound that made hair tingle as with a cold draft. He patted Asteria's restraining hand with his other hand. Her fingers released the gold cuff she'd gripped. Khoti leaned over so only Baynu could hear him. "If we're ever in battle, Baynu, you may regret this. When you need help you may find no one there to render it." Khoti goaded his horse, wishing he rode Fidra instead of the sluggish Shikoran mare.

"He has no sense of humor," Baynu said lightly and loud enough for Khoti to hear, though he aimed his comment at Asteria, who pretended not to hear him.

"In a desert such humor isn't amusing, and you should know that, knowing Shikora's lands," Daris said, turning her mount to follow Khoti.

"Water is only two hours away –"

"Anything can happen in two hours. In this land, there's no greater insult than to steal another's water."

When they at last negotiated the steep slope and found the well only a short distance farther, Khoti would allow no one to drink, not even himself, until they pumped enough water to sate the horses, and those he could dole water to only sparingly for fear they would sicken. The night grew old before at last he allowed the children, then adults to fill their water skins and quench their thirst, Khoti again waiting until the last.

"At this rate it'll take us forever to get to Hainad," Khoti muttered to Daris from a sore throat chafed by the arid wind. "If it's a day between wells and half a day watering the horses –"

"Your worries should be with that one." Daris gestured toward Baynu with a toss of her dark hair.

Khoti shrugged. "He's not a bad man, Daris, just accustomed to control. And incredibly arrogant."

"You thought that of Anlon."

"It's not the same. In his land, Baynu earned his arrogance. I could as easily be the same way."

"Well, I'd trust your instincts here more than his and his land is a dry land. At least you recognize danger in an unfamiliar place."

Khoti grinned. "That's the finest compliment you've ever paid, Daris." He tugged her hair. "Even you are coming around."

"Oh, you're impossible." Daris laughed. Her smile quickly faded. "Just watch yourself. He's testing you, and more than likely to get someone killed doing it."

Khoti scanned the encampment. Baynu leaned close to Asteria to relate some confidence, his smile playful. The Shikoran's hand touched her arm to punctuate a statement. Asteria responded with a smile and a short laugh that carried across the camp. Khoti turned away. Daris touched the cuff on his arm. Her smile had gone with not even a scowl in its place.

"Get ready to move out," Khoti ordered. Daris leaped to his bidding, the fresh tattoo on her neck glaring her dedication.

Only a few hours later, Khoti turned to look back behind him from his position as rearguard. He clicked a warning, leaving Baynu dumbfounded when suddenly the Shandean unit spun about and raced back through the haze of dust to where Khoti awaited a Minarian patrol riding hard up the valley.

On cue, Kia and a few of the older Joffans herded the horses before them, goading them to a gallop. Those youngsters tempted to stay their mounts to see what happened Kia quickly herded ahead. At last, with the entire herd moving, Kia galloped away, Rena bouncing behind her.

"There is your outpost," Baynu sneered as the dozen-man patrol approached. "And what did going around get you but more trouble and the lost advantage?"

"Here's the battle I mentioned," Khoti countered. He drew his sword, giving his mount signals only Fidra new. "Dumb Shikoran beasts," Khoti grumbled as he tried to maneuver the horse to the position he wanted.

As the patrol neared, the Shandeans waited for the cue from Khoti that would send them forward. Tre, Khoti, Jali and Asteria released bowstrings as soon as the Minarians came into range.

Baynu laughed, racing ahead into the point of the Minarian charge.

"Fool!" Khoti roared. "We can't shoot now!" The last bowstring fell silent as archers drew their swords. Swiftly, enemy swordsmen surrounded the grinning Shikoran.

Jali and Daris raced to Baynu's aid. The Shikoran faced three Minarians as the rest rode on at the Shandeans. Asteria rested her sword across her lap, balancing it with the heel of her bow. Seeing an opening, she rifled off several arrows, barely acknowledging when one of the swordsmen fell, and another slumped over to turn from the battle. She released three more arrows before the opening closed.

Though it had been a long while since Khoti fought a battle not characterized by stealth and position, as he adjusted to his mount's inability to answer his cues, it came back with a familiarity that coursed through his blood. Tre beside him, the two tore into the fray, weapons rising and falling in tandem.

Though an excellent swordsman, the outnumbered Shikoran tired fast. Jali and Daris attacked with abandon, putting to the test all their training with Khoti. They reached Baynu's side at almost the same instant, their horses locked in among the Minarians as they swung with deadly effect. Daris's blade ripped from her hands, a Minarian's sword coming around to strike her. She lunged with her dagger, slipping under his assault to knock him to the ground among the flying hooves. He still gripped his sword, but Daris fell on him, pinning his arms to the ground just long enough to drive her dagger into his throat. As she spun up, another rider came by, going for Baynu, not seeing her. She scooped up her sword and lunged, letting the rider's momentum impale him on the weapon and throw her to the ground, the hilts smashing into her chest.

As she gasped, on her knees in the dirt, another horseman swept down on her. She tried to scramble out of the way, looking up in the last instant. The horse continued on riderless, Asteria filling the open sky where the enemy had been. Asteria pulled Daris up so quick the girl was on her feet before she realized her danger, Asteria already gone.

Baynu fought so fierce a contest he appeared unaware of the Minarian behind him. As the man swiped at Baynu's back, he met Jali's sword, their horses colliding as Jali fought across the rump of Baynu's mount. With his other hand the Minarian raked Jali with a dagger; the weapon sank into Jali's chest.

Baynu turned as a Minarian slipped from his sword to find Jali ripped open and bloody, a dagger protruding, continuing to hold the Minarian's blade away from Baynu. Baynu stabbed. Jali's opponent slumped backward to tumble from his horse. Jali sagged, clutching himself.

Baynu whipped around to face his next opponent, but none remained. Khoti and Tre, swords sheathed, inspected the fallen, while Daris wandered among the injured Minarians to ensure none could call for aid. Asteria gathered the enemy mounts.

Baynu leaned toward Jali. "Here, boy, let me –" he began.

Jali backed his mount away. "You fool," Jali said around a gasp, arm clamped against the blood rushing down his chest. "You could've got us all killed."

"Look, we are victorious!" Baynu said with a broad gesture at the fallen enemy. "I forgive your insolence. It is only your wound that –"

"In a combined charge everyone's covered by them alongside," Jali interrupted. "You raced off on your own. Daris and me had to ride to your rescue, leaving Asteria unprotected and Daris and me without our flank."

Khoti rode to them, only a small cut beside the shackle on his wrist to mark the battle. From the dent in the cuff, Khoti knew the shackle kept him from loosing his hand. Khoti tore open Jali's shirt to view the deep gash extending across the youth's chest, ending at the dagger.

"Sorry," Jali muttered.

"You should be sorry," Khoti said, grabbing Jali to keep him from toppling from his mount. "I can't lose one of my best because he doesn't know when to duck."

Daris gasped at the sight of Jali, still holding her ribs. "I say kill him now," she snarled, casting a glance like a brace of daggers in Baynu's direction.

"See who's hurt?" Jali asked through clenched teeth. "The ones either side of you."

"Who was supposed to support you besides me?" Baynu challenged.

"Asteria, Daris was end," Khoti stated. "Asteria had to cut out to aid Daris. The line doesn't hold up. But the initial charge sets positions." Khoti spoke calmly, though his tone warned he barely held his anger in check. "I'll need a fire."

Both Tre and Asteria protested at once. Khoti's arm slashed down for silence.

"He won't make it and we need him," Khoti said.

"Not for me, Khoti." Jali collapsed against his mentor.

They rode ahead to find Kia standing watch near the next well, dagger in hand like a Shandean warrior, not a little girl.

As Khoti's long unused sticks fell silent and the fire Asteria had tended slowly died away, Khoti sank into a weary sleep deeper than after any healing he'd ever before performed.

Tre took up a watch over the weary Tawnkat who had returned to his sticks often as he called the spirits to help him mend Jali, somehow some greater intensity, entreaty, in his song than ever before, his medicine as strong as ever but seeming to still not be enough.

Eyeing Baynu, Tre sprouted an uncharacteristic frown as the Shikoran again sat beside Asteria, pumping her with questions about Khoti's magic, his gaze never leaving the Taschian's deathly paled face unless to turn, smiling, on Asteria.

10: Baynu

When Arshal's champion, hundreds of horses and dozens of children, thought lost forever, arrived in New Hainad three weeks later in the worst heat of the early ripening moon, Dynresa had stood beside her father speechless, even as her father introduced her to the Sword of Shande as the king's intended match. No biting retort or dismissive barb could she utter. Though Dynresa had never fully understood Arshal's selfless thinking, she suddenly saw her own reservations about the king's mission as petty and selfish. Stone-faced Hainadan children reunited with families had rallied to the cause of a king they had never met, many of the older youth eager to take up arms in the king's army. Her sweet shal cousin Daris had become a scarred and battle-hardened warrior marked as one of the champion's trusted elite officers. Seeing young Kia, dagger at her side, and Rena tending the weaponry of a duke's daughter, at last Dynresa thought she understood Arshal's outrage at what the Minarians had done. The world was Joffa and Shande, not just Hainad.

The famed Khoti she had heard so much about – haggard with an exhaustion her cousin claimed came from his healing magic – still projected a power that left her breathless, as if some fire burned in him that attracted the devotion of almost all he met like moths to a flame. Daris jumped at his command. Ramel shadowed the champion, seeming to find Khoti even more fascinating than he had the king. Even her normally reticent father immediately gave his trust to this king's man. Everyone except Baynu. She could read the barely restrained disdain between the two men.

Baynu fawned over first Asteria, then Dynresa, offering coy smiles and suggestive banter to the women, instead of the instruction in mounted battle tactics Khoti expected him to provide for the sturdy Hainadans and other Joffans who had trickled in with Euzzeldir's call.

"Baynu, we haven't got time for this," Khoti told him. "We need these people prepared when we meet Habdelion and Sedaik at Shela."

"It is unnatural to teach children and noble women to serve in an army," Baynu insisted. "Children should be playing at their mother's knees and noble women should be dressed in fine gowns, attended by servants. Not pretending to be men-at-arms."

Asteria grasped the gold cuff on Khoti's wrist as he reached for his sword.

"Try me, Baynu," Asteria said. "For a king's champion you appear to have a poor understanding of what makes a soldier, and clearly have a pattern of underestimating everyone but yourself."

Baynu turned to Dynresa, as if expecting her support.

She gave him a cold smile. "And a poor understanding of Joffans."

Baynu held out his hands in appeasement, giving them a disarming grin as if merely teasing, as he turned his attention to the training.

Dynresa had no difficulty seeing through the Shikoran.

The foundation Arshal had built had Euzzeldir's troops looking like an army after only a week, though the grueling training had them asleep before reaching their tents at night.

Dynresa spent long hours with Daris and Asteria, an adept pupil in the stealthy ways Khoti taught. She already knew weapons, taught by a master who had fought in the Great War of the gods. And since the king's departure she'd joined several forays to harass the enemy then dash back to the marshes. She didn't thrill with the heart of the warrior, but like all of Hainad, she would ride among the Joffan troops who would go to war beside the king. They knew the Minarian outpost on the Hainad road awaited only reinforcements to put down the Hainadan insurrection. Thus, when Euzzeldir rode to war for the king, the entire village would ride with him, ancient and infant alike.

Dynresa threw herself into training that left her exhausted and aching, too tired to think of anything but sleep, her dreams filled with drills and Khoti's admonitions about the unity of soldiers acting on a command. She laughed at herself sometimes, wondering what Arshal would think to see her as a warrior going to battle for him, more than curses among her weapons. Yet, she had already killed and bled for him.

Something disturbed her rest a week after Arshal's champion arrived. She rolled, feeling something beside her. Arshal, she thought for a bare instant as her dream of the king ended. A more alert part of her screamed a warning. Her eyes flew open to find a broad grin, a face leaning down to hers. An enraged shriek escaped her to carry throughout the sleepy village.

"Not so loud, Lady," a man whispered. Moist lips pressed against hers.

She tried to pull away but he gripped her wrists in strong hands, huge hands, hardened by years of wielding a sword. She twisted her mouth from his. "You will die!" she promised.

"You will thank me!" Baynu laughed as she continued to squirm beneath him. "I am King's Champion of a noble people! I see you watching me, wanting a man when all around are only children proclaiming themselves warriors. Our peoples have always been close. I could save this land. Look who now claims to save Shande: Jali, a bare boy who cannot even handle your lovely cousin; or this teller of tall tales, Tre the Imager; or the legendary, arrogant Khoti the Sorcerer who hides from his enemy. The way you spend your time with them tells me you seek the strength of a warrior. I have come."

Dynresa tried to scream for help, but a calloused hand covered her mouth as he pulled away the blanket and groped for the skin beneath her tunic. She freed a hand, striking his face with a balled fist.

"Shikoran women dream for a man of my stature, beg the least of warriors to bed them! Your worth is not so great I would beg a woman to please me! If you want a fight –"

The tent flap whipped aside to reveal a silhouette against the starry sky.

Dynresa twisted away. "Kill him!" she shrieked.

Baynu's fist smashed into her face, slamming her into the ground.

The world darkened around her.

Baynu leaped to his feet and reached for the sword beside his clothing. "Dare to strike me!" he bellowed as he tried to make out his foe. "King Wyeff Shikora will refuse all aid, will refuse to honor any nation that threatens his champion! Your war will be with Shikora as well!"

A soft chuckle made Baynu freeze. "When your king hears of this, Baynu, he'll honor your executioners. Maybe Shikora's Champion returns a gelding? You're in Shande, not Shikora. Shandean women go willing to the beds of their choosing."

"Ah, the great Khoti," Baynu sneered. "What are you but a sorcerer playing wetnurse to a gaggle of children? You wonder why you are conquered? A land where men fear their women, and think their wishes worth dying for?" He laughed. "Then, when a true warrior comes among you the legendary Khoti blasphemes him because he fears a true Shikoran warrior will show him for the fake he is. King Wyeff Shikora will not believe such lies of his champion. By the time your words arrive, Shikora will have turned against Shande. This woman tempted me and encouraged me with smiles and flattery. My king understands, as men of Shikora know: she wants this. This is the conquest of a man."

Baynu lunged. Khoti leaped aside. Baynu turned to face the Tawnkat now lit by the faint starlight overhead. They stood off in the dusty space between tents.

"Shande's got no use for Shikora if this is the quality of her aid," Khoti stated.

"That is your assessment. Perhaps your king will disagree."

"Unlikely. When he hears of your assault on the daughter of Euzzeldir, he'll call for your blood. Trust me on this one."

"More likely yours for disrupting his plans."

"I'll take the risk." Khoti snarled. Then he laughed as he surveyed the nude man clinging to his sword, standing so defiant. "Some warrior you appear, Baynu. Where are your battle scars?"

"I am too expert to let any weapon touch me," Baynu returned. He stabbed for Khoti, who parried without pressing.

Baynu took a step back, vulnerable, while Khoti stood firm. People gathered around them, rubbing the sleep from their eyes.

Baynu lunged, the tip of his sword catching the edge of Khoti's shirt but not touching flesh. Khoti arched his back to allow the sword to miss him, then brought his own sword down hard against Baynu's weapon, following through to slide Baynu's weapon away from him.

"I could've had your arm, Baynu. You're too reckless. That's your failing. You do prove to me once again I'm no good judge of character."

"You are frightened of me. If you were a warrior, you would have taken your one and only chance." A few Hainadans chuckled at the spectacle. Others remained sober as if they guessed at the repercussions of this argument.

Dynresa appeared at the door of her tent, her step slightly unsteady, the Shikoran's clothing in her hands.

"Stand back," Khoti told her.

"Kill him," she ordered, throwing the man's clothes into the dirt. "A man who steals water, thief of honor, deserves death."

Suddenly, Khoti stabbed. Baynu fended him off but gave ground, almost falling. Khoti's sword ripped across the man's bare arm when it could have gone for his chest. The Shikoran froze an instant, then grabbed up his clothes and ran, laughter following as the Champion of Shikora raced for a horse and an escape from Joffa.

"You should've killed him and not played with him," Dynresa said, her tone scornful, her words shrill with her rage.

"What good would it do to kill him?" Khoti asked softly, wondering how Baynu could prove such prowess against a dozen Minarians, yet run from one Shandean, a Shandean who still hadn't recovered from visiting the lonely place he'd gone to save Jali.

"What good is it to have him hatching plots and seeding lies about us?" Dynresa demanded. "King Arshal always said you were so merciless."

"What greater harm or insult could happen to such an acclaimed warrior? He's forced to run naked from the very people he disdained."

Dynresa muffled a nervous giggle in the back of her hand.

Khoti peered at her.

"Are you all right?" he asked, studying the bruise on her cheek and the swelling around her eye. "If he's harmed you Arshal will never forgive me."

"I don't need protecting," Dynresa retorted. As Khoti's fingers probed the bruise, she calmed, then stared at him, her mouth opening.

"Looks like you do."

"He caught me unprepared, asleep."

"A warrior's always prepared. You'd better prove yourself better than this before you go to battle. I couldn't forgive myself if I had to face the king –"

"The king. The king. He's probably forgotten about me already."

"I doubt that. If you think so low of him, then maybe it's you that's doing the forgetting."

Dynresa bit her lip. "You were here when I needed help and here I'm attacking you, just as I did him."

"It's that Joffan blood. Daris is impossible."

"What if Baynu's right and Shikora refuses to help now?"

"Then he refuses. What can we do?"

"Arshal counts on all of Ea to support us! We need the Shikoran blockade, the weapons, horses –"

"We'll just have to improvise," Khoti said, satisfied she'd suffered only shock and a black eye. He nodded to the Joffan princess, heading back toward the nondescript tent he shared with Tre and Jali, one in which the king had once slept.

What stayed his hand? Was it weariness with the killing and death, the legacy of bringing the breath back into Jali? He needed a healer's rest, more. It would be at least a year before he'd have that luxury. Perhaps rather than battle-weariness he feared he'd have killed the Shikoran for the wrong reasons. He stared south where Baynu had disappeared and prayed King Wyeff Shikora used more wisdom than his champion. Clearly, Baynu had pitied the Shandean plight. He could see it in the way Baynu watched the Joffan children like a nervous father, how he soothed their fear with play. If Shikora didn't blockade the Sea of Simiriel as planned, a Minarian fleet could ravage these lands when the Shandean armies battled in Sihmad Shal against Ghyldus. He hadn't seen it in Tait. He'd let Anlon go. Now, Baynu. It wouldn't happen again.

He stopped outside his tent, hearing Tre and Jali chuckling over Baynu. Behind him stood the tent Asteria shared with Daris and Nali's girls. Framed by the flap, Asteria looked out at him, her eyes deep shadows with words unwritten. He wanted to hear her assurances, not jest over the exchange. He took a step toward her then stopped. His hands rose then fell before he whirled and entered his tent. The Joffan night advanced on dawn before he fell into a troubled sleep where he once again beat off scavengers while ships filled the Sea of Simiriel, discharging thousands to sweep the land like chaff before the wind.

11: Iyrafael

The thunder shower drifted away to a low rumbling in the distance and the westering sun tinged the clouds and water with mellow gold as the chop abated on the shallow sea. Breathing deep, the King of Shande took in the rich scent of soils feasting on rainfall. The steam of the heat moon cooled behind the storm. Though the winds had died away they still shed gold-tinged drops like creamy butter dripping from the leaves of trees clustering about the tops of the low hills. Stretching out behind him, valleys throbbed green, cleansed as the fresh rain replenished maturing grain and grasslands. He caught no salty scent of the Aziaris Sea crowding into Sihma Harbor, yet the rich earthy aroma beckoned him with the nearness of home.

Arshal let his horse graze on the damp grass at the edge of the clump of trees in which he'd sheltered from the storm. He merely wanted to absorb the sight of the freshwater Sea of Iyrafael glittering below, a place so close to home.

As he inhaled the richness of his home province, the king knew nothing of what went forward elsewhere in the world. Gazing on the peaceful scene, he could only imagine that his officers carried out his plan and soon Shande would be whole again.

More than two months had passed since he'd left Euzzeldir's village. He'd sped through the dry reaches of Jashiho only traveling at night to escape the scorching sun. While Euzzeldir's maps helped, he became lost in Joffa's grasslands when days of rain from black skies obscured the sun and stars. Sometime after he entered Kalilia, a fever forced him to huddle in a damp and dusty hay rick for several days. In Kalilia he crossed regions more populated, forced to shy from his subjects to avert betrayal. Then, compelled to ride around the hundreds of small lakes dotting the Acceber region, he doubled the distance he had to travel. When the weariness of it all settled in, the constant fear of capture and the long lonely days without sight of a friendly face, he found some days he just didn't have the heart in him to move. Then came times like this when he only thought to sit and stare at the vista of his kingdom.

He studied the curve of shoreline to take note of boats pulled up on beaches and a few hurrying out onto the water behind the storm. From here it appeared idyllic, not a land occupied by a brutal enemy. Yet, on closer inspection, he discerned the marks of occupation. Long ago Khoti's scouts reported the thousands of Minarians gathered at the mouth of the Iyrafael River, capable of governing the populous region by sheer numbers and the ability to speed to any area without warning. Now he saw that outposts also clustered beside the sea where many people had lived from Iyrafael's riches. Since Otayr shared this vast body of water, the Minarians were ever vigilant to prevent shawnsi from escaping or Otayrans from entering the region.

An exiled and hunted king knew better than to enter such an area that simply crawled with his enemy. But somewhere north of Iyrafael lived Marol and the thousands of exiles Peshal had led into hiding. Travel near the sea, or crossing the river, would be dangerous enough with so many Minarians. Arshal knew from experience, the stronger the Minarian presence, the more the risk of treachery. His only option: cross the border on this south side of the sea and pass through Otayran lands, risking deportation the entire way or becoming turned around in its lofty western hills and deep forest.

As the sun fell lower and the rumbling thunder faded to leave a washed sky, Arshal at last pulled himself to his feet. No marker told him where the border lay. He might not even know he'd crossed it until he'd traveled far inside Otayr. He could only turn his face east. The golden vision of the sea faded fast. Even though the light still tinged the land with rich hues and the moisture still exhaled from the soil, it had dulled in Arshal's eyes. His heart beat with defeat as he led his horse down the hill, so engrossed in his thoughts he barely noted where his feet fell on the damp grass.

As he plodded down from the wooded hilltop he heard a stir of branches behind him, but ignored it. For months he'd crouched and cowered with every shift of grass or scuffling of wildlife. Each time he found nothing, only his heart pounding in his chest. He turned his thoughts to Dynresa, imagining what she would say about this self-pity of his as he faced vast Shande alone. He smiled a little to himself as he pictured her in that hostile land grown more pleasant in his memories.

The horse pranced at the end of her lead and whickered. Arshal turned. His mouth fell open in panic as a blaze of red light gripped him and seared through his weakened defenses to demand his obedience. With a force that tore the breath from him and made his heart groan with stabbing pain, he leaped for the horse's back and kicked her sides. The few seconds it took to escape the spell gave the three Eidhalt time to break from cover and close on him, their mounts kicking up chunks of sod, the red and orange tassels on their helms streaming behind.

Arshal lay low over the horse's neck, thinking only to race east as he pounded down a muddy trail. A farmer stopped working in a field to peer at the white-haired shawnsi – garbed in Joffan robes – thundering by with three Eidhalt in pursuit.

While Arshal had ridden these many weeks a mare as fine as any, such travel through rough lands on the heels of Euzzeldir's strenuous journey to Shikora took its toll. Perhaps, like Arshal, she simply wearied of travel. Soon her strides shortened and slowed. Her nostrils flared as lather spread outward from beneath the saddle. The better-rested Minarian mounts gained.

Arshal unsheathed his sword. The Minarians had no interest in a battle. One drew even with him, leaning over to try to yank him from the saddle. Arshal pulled the mare up and cut away as they reined in to meet him. The Minarian farthest behind anticipated the move and raced at a tangent to reach him as again the other two caught up. Arshal struck out with his sword, the blade slicing into an out-stretched arm. In the same instant an unyielding grasp pulled him from his saddle. He hit the ground so hard it took his breath. The mare continued on a few paces and then stopped, sides heaving.

Rolling as he struck the soft turf, Arshal lost his sword. The

Minarian mail he wore had jabbed into his skin, pinching his breath. He searched the damp grass, but saw no sign of his weapon. Snarling creatures encircled him, their fangs like daggers, their eyes blazing red as their dog-like bodies thrust lizard heads at him. He recoiled, his dagger unable to halt so many leaping, shrieking creatures. He slashed at one of the leaping dervishes, blinking as it disappeared in a blaze of sparks. A whip snaked out and bit into his hand. The dagger fell as the snapped end struck. He raised his hand in desperation, prepared at last to let his stone do its work. That moment a sharp pain swallowed him as a club crashed into the back of his head. He crumpled, giving in to the blackness, his last image the shrieking creatures, their voices like the wails of a furious wind in ships' rigging.

Low voices and the smoke of damp wood parted the haze, sending the tatters swirling away to reveal unpleasant reality. He slit one eye open, eliciting a painful throb in his skull. He tried to shake away the ringing in his ears and reach a hand up to feel the hard knot on the back of his scalp. He found his hands bound behind him. When he shifted the voices ceased.

Sensing a presence looming over him, he tried to open his eyes wider. A kick caught him in the small of his back, slapping his face into the mud as he opened his mouth in a gasp. He tried to twist away, but found his legs bound to his hands. The movement only cut the bonds deeper into his wrists and ankles.

"Thought you could escape us, demon? So, this is a wretched King of Shande." The words hissed close to his ear.

He tried to open his eyes but they were caked with the same mud that filled his mouth. Taking a deep breath to regain calm, he choked as he inhaled soil. Another kick made his head reel.

"What glows there?" a voice demanded. "Sorcery?"

Through the fury in his head, Arshal knew what the Minarian saw. He tried to roll, to somehow conceal the stone that must have flared in his palm to betray him. Rough hands tugged him and clawed at his closed fist. Something smashed into his face, driving his head against the ground when he again tried to twist away. He struggled against the growing blackness and the small lights that deviled the edge of his vision, but soon the overwhelming darkness came over him again.

Somewhere deep inside, an urgent voice screamed at him. He couldn't respond. He tried to shake away the sound, but it only became more insistent. The voice sounded in one moment like Cree, his brothers and parents. Soon the racket would deafen him. The words grew clearer. He tried to understand the warning. Instead, a throbbing ache drew his concentration. Tremors coursed through him when at last he realized his body warned of some violation. An eye opened, bleary and mud-caked, to reveal the bright light of fire so close he could feel its heat singeing the hairs on his skin. Hands no longer bound, he couldn't find the strength to pull away as he lay on his back in the boot-muddied turf. He could only roll his eyes to see his hand stretched out beside him, a knife prying the opal from his palm.

At last hearing and understanding the noise in his head, he felt the threads of panic pressing his chest like the weight of stone and earth piled deep upon him. He tried to pull his hand away, but a knee clamped on his forearm as an arm flashed by, reaching for a club. The weapon rose, aimed at his temple. He clenched his eyes shut and screamed into himself an entreaty for the strength to save himself.

He heard startled exclamations as the stone flared in his palm. As the club came down toward his face, his eyes snapped open and he twisted his head to see the awesome power of his stone in the tick of a second before the club glanced against his cheek and the light around him again faded.

He felt the familiar fall, taking him deep within where the locked door beckoned like a down comforter on a cool autumn morning. He heard as if down a long and echoing hall Ramel warning him that he must think of himself. The image of a golden dawn glancing off the warm bed and a fresh kindled fire warming the room tempted him from beyond the door, a comfortable place, a place that would ease his burdens. His bloody hand inserted the key in the lock. With a hand on the latch, he struggled with himself, shouting to himself that it was a trick. He forced himself to think of Dynresa, her arms around him full of warmth. In that moment when he only needed the comfort he knew existed beyond the door, he saw her standing on the rim of the valley, the wind shaking auburn hair behind her, her mouth demanding a promise as her eyes taunted him, brown and green and gold in color. The clove scent of her wafted into his face.

As he thought of her, a thousand images crowded him at once. Flickering images of the Shelans, of Khoti, of Ebon's body in the snow, of Peshal foundering in a dream sea, of a dead child in a Joffan tent, of the thousands perished in Sihmad Shal, of a cold grave in snowy Kishman plains and Esthen's body carried from battle. With a bellow that echoed within him but carried no farther, Arshal turned his back on the door.

He shifted with a groan, his hand coming against something grisly soft, damp. He knew instantly: tissue that dared try to separate the gods' gift from the king. He opened his eyes a slit and then retched when he saw what horrors he could project from his desperation. He recalled that brief vision before the club fell, of the stone burning red with a heat that set skin afire. The knife prying his palm had flared and shattered into molten fragments a moment before his eyes went dark.

"He's waking," a voice came from somewhere near his feet.

Arshal's eyes flew open. He tried to sit up but the slight pressure from an unseen hand forced him down. He looked wildly around him, the throbbing of his head swirling daggers of light before his eyes as he tried to define his danger.

"Nasty knock on the head," a man muttered from behind him. "Like to've split his skull."

Arshal tried to speak, but the mud caked over his mouth made his dry tongue and lips unresponsive.

"Gimme some of that water there," the voice behind ordered.

Their voices sounded reassuring, Kalilian. As his vision cleared, he saw his own sword pointed at his chest.

"It's all right," the man behind soothed as if he knew what Arshal looked on. "We gotta protect ourselves. We don't know what happened here."

Arshal choked on the water, spitting out mud and caked blood. He felt a hand on his, inspecting his palm. He tried to wrench away.

"Don't use it!" the man near his feet said around a gasp.

Arshal peered at the man with bleary eyes. From what he could see it wasn't Ramel.

"We're friends," the man's voice soothed as he untied the cords at Arshal's ankles. The man threw a wary glance at another beyond Arshal's vision. "My bet is that's what made this mess."

"So, the old farmer saw rightly," the man behind him mused.

"Well, he brought in that sword."

"Still, exaggeration and rumor's pretty much the rule with him. Talk of some white-robed shawnsi flyin' through the countryside. Sounds more like some sailor's yarn."

"So, what do we do with him? We can't be hauling shawnsi around in broad daylight, especially with that fancy stabber there. And here he's wearing Joffan garb and Minarian mail, man's like to get hung for just seein' him. When someone commences to look for these three dead, Eidhalt by their looks, there'll be trouble for everyone for sure."

"Maybe we should leave him."

"Don't be stupid. That's against our purpose here."

"Maybe just hold him 'til we get approval to let him go."

Arshal shook his head and again tried to sit up. Strangers arguing over his fate was just too much. His ears hummed, his head spinning as he tried to follow the conversation. They didn't try to stop him. He couldn't pull more than his head from the ground, and that little movement made his head throb so hard he thought he'd pass out again.

"You don't gotta be doing that," one admonished. "We ain't gonna hurt you."

They moved away from him. He thought he counted four but couldn't be sure as they stood against the blaze of morning. He knew they discussed him and wanted to know what fate they would leave him to, but already the insistent pull of unconsciousness closed. As his eyes again drifted shut, he saw a man gingerly pulling a dead Minarian toward a thicket, while another peered at him in speculation, his hand stroking a bearded chin.

A door closed below, followed by the creak of someone climbing the ladder to the loft of the small house. Arshal reached for his sword lying on the floor beside him.

"It's Kyne!" the man whispered when the blade came up.

Arshal sat up, rubbing sleep from his eyes, trying to remember which of many little cottages he slept in. Two weeks had passed since Kyne discovered him in the midst of carnage. After the first few days of recuperation in a cramped shack on the shores of Iyrafael they shuttled him from home to home, barn to shed, each move bringing him only slightly closer to his destination, an agonizing pace. The Minarians numbered so many, one couldn't walk hailing distance without coming across some messenger, patrol or outpost. Inspectors of all sorts maintained the lengthy list of curfews and regulations. Yet whatever resistance he'd fallen in with was organized, and growing.

"Tonight's a big move," Kyne whispered. "We'll have you inside Otayr to a friendly old fisher. He'll see you get past Otayran border patrols."

Arshal dropped his head in his hands, weary of the whole game. "I appreciate the risk you've taken for me."

Kyne shrugged. "While I don't know who you are, I'm certain you're no friend of the Minarians. Any enemy of theirs is worthy of aid."

Arshal looked up and smiled. "Do you want to know?"

"Who y'are?" Kyne gave him a sharp glance that reminded the king of Nali's hawkish gaze. "Sure, it's crossed my mind and everyone else's. There's tales of someone like you. A god they say. I don't think a god would have to travel the way you do, nor would he suffer an injury as you did. I don't imagine Eidhalt would trouble the gods. Yet, that gem in your hand's got a sorcery pretty big for any shawnsi I've ever known."

"I'm going to be in Otayr a while," Arshal said. "It won't be easy for me to get a message out. You have a lot of connections." He peered at the man. "Could you arrange a message to Sihmad Shal?"

Kyne sat back on his haunches, chewing his cheek. "It's not a safe thing to be naming any names, you know. So, you tell me to get word to so-and-so, and the messenger starts asking around for the fellow and the next thing you know someone winds up in the lock-up."

"Who are you people?" Arshal asked suddenly, letting just a hint of command enter his tone. He'd used it sparingly with these saviors who helped him. "You're organized resistance, but who directed its formation?"

Kyne peered at Arshal, his mouth opening as if to spill all he knew. "There you go again," Kyne whispered. "Askin' me to relay information that'd get someone in chains."

"Your fellows mention orders from Sihmad Shal a lot. Are you out of there? Is that the base of this, Kyne? Or is it Otayr, or Kishma that's helped you organize? I saw one of your men with a fine sword, not one of the ornamental types some once kept over the mantle."

"Someone wasn't being careful if you heard or saw that." Kyne continued to chew his cheek, at last sighing to himself. "We're local. We're pretty new at this, but the major instructions and planning come out of Sihmad Shal."

"A Harbor man with a limp, one they call Commander?" Kyne's hiss of breath made Arshal grin. "All the way to here." Arshal shook his head. "Send the message to him," Arshal said, gathering his small bundle for the next hop around the sea.

"But what's your message?" Kyne asked, nervous now that he'd said too much.

"That I was at the Sea of Iyrafael and entered Otayr in the first week of the ripening moon."

"But who are you?"

Arshal's face cracked into a broad smile. He clapped a hand on Kyne's shoulder before descending the shaky ladder. "Who do you want me to be?"

Kyne stood mute at the lip of the loft as the king reached bottom and waited by the door. At last, he heard Kyne chuckling to himself. Such a man could be anyone he wanted to. Arshal's host pointed at a wagon in the muddy yard.

"To be ushered from Shande in a dung wagon," Arshal grumbled around a wry smile.

Kyne glanced at him. The man's smile faded as if his heart went out to the exiled traveler. "I don't know what you're up to," Kyne whispered. "But we need all the hope we can get."

"Take what you can," Arshal said as he burrowed in the wagon for the short bumpy ride to the seashore, where he would be forced to swim in the dark to leave Shande, the last leg before returning home. But returning to what?

PART 2. NADIR

12: The Battle for Shela

Sails shimmered as moonlight struck water then glanced up to touch the dingy canvas. The ships nuzzled ahead, testing the water for shoals as they poked among the myriad islands, a bank of clouds in the west threatening to overtake the moon. A light flashed from the deck of the lead ship and in near unison sails slipped down masts and the ghostly fleet turned to mere dark silhouettes on the sea. The clank of heavy chain, then splashes, carried across the water as the ships stood at anchor rather than brave the hazardous passage in the dark.

In the web of blackness on shore, eyes took up the glow from the sea, but all other shapes melted into the twist of fronds and branch as Detarian reached for the open sea with a tangle of arms.

"Ten," Sedaik whispered, his voice a hiss in the night. "This is Anlon's work. If they get through, we are doomed."

"Do not let them through," his father, Perouk, muttered at Sedaik's elbow.

"We will be delayed. We are counted upon."

"It is a command decision," Perouk said.

For many minutes Sedaik examined the expectant faces around him, the long canoes pulled up on the banks of the river near the delta, and the dot of islands all around the anchored ships. At last, he inclined his head, a rueful smile barely revealing teeth.

"Perhaps I am not ready for such decisions. This command was thrust upon me."

"Perhaps," Perouk agreed. "Much is thrust upon us: a need to eat, survive. This is the task chosen for you."

"We will do what we must then."

Perouk stabbed a finger into Sedaik's chest. "You must do it. The King's Sword taught you the knowledge first. You appealed to the headmen. Do not show hesitation. The leader who wavers disheartens his men."

Sedaik groaned. With a few quick signals, he sent his warriors to their craft to paddle out among the islands.

The ships creaked as they bobbed in the baffled waves of Simiriel. A figure dozed in the crow's nest of the lead ship. In others, the watch sat idle as if fearing nothing but a change of weather. The skies remained clear, the first moon of the harvest moon old in the sky. Only a light wind stirred in the rigging.

A man straightened, perhaps hearing some soft sound unnatural to a sleeping ship. In a moment he slumped, an arrow in his eye. Flares of light flashed from many sources at once as tinder met spark to light greased arrows. Throughout the fleet small fires fed on age-worn timbers as startled voices cried alarm and sailors fell from their racks to tumble onto the decks.

The moon back-lit dozens of long canoes that raced to the ships' sides with occupants ready to leap aboard. Arrows whistled through the air, the poisons of Detarian felling many with mere flesh wounds.

While sailors fought the shadowy boarders, some pulling poisoned arrows from the deck to fling back at the furtive Detarians, fires licked at the sails and cries of pain broke the calm night.

Sedaik glanced at Perouk as their craft bumped the side of a Minarian ship. "We are losing," he said, the weight of his decision in his voice.

"It is not over."

"What losses are acceptable?"

"No loss is acceptable. We are committed. No option of surrender exists."

"We lose so many!"

"More important, how many do we take with us!" Perouk shoved Sedaik toward the ship's side. "Be a leader, Sedaik. Be strong. If we must die, do it proudly. Surrender, retreat, those are closed roads."

Sedaik ignored the sting of an arrow grazing his arm. He clambored aboard, trying to wipe away all thoughts but taking as many with him as he could.

The snap of a twig brought Khoti's head around and a hand to his sword, followed by a click of tongue that made him grin in relief. Chati emerged from the dark tangle of the Dasirei Swamp where it had sprawled over to the east side of the Rigannon. Khoti grasped his friend's arm with a strength that made Chati wince.

"You're a hard man to find," Chati grumbled. "Thought an army would leave more of a trail. I've been looking for you for three days."

"We didn't want to leave a trail," Khoti returned. "You must be slipping. I'm gone a little while and my aides get lazy."

Chati peered at Khoti. "You don't look well and sound exhausted. Wounded?"

"Jali, some months back –"

"And you haven't recovered?"

"It was a bit ... different."

"You're thin as a post and you're so pale you glow in the dark."

Khoti chuckled. "Likely the glow of sunburn you're seeing."

"Tedwa went in and tried to make a contact," Chati said. "No luck. They're too beaten."

Khoti scowled as he led Chati to the cheerless camp on the edge of the swamp as a Hainadan woman took Khoti's turn at sentry. Khoti hadn't expected much. He at least hoped a few Shelans would help if they knew an army gathered outside the city. As Chati dug into a bowl of cold rice and drank his wine, between mouthfuls he outlined their forces: Twenty-two hundred regulars, mostly Tachi, and about four hundred apprentices. Sedaik had promised to meet them days ago and hadn't. Khoti sat with his head in his hands, tallying his own complement: two hundred of the northern herdsmen, almost as many from the southern tribes, another two hundred Hainadans and hill folk.

"We should outnumber them –" Khoti began.

"On that count you're wrong," Chati said around fingerfuls of rice he shoved into his mouth. "Reinforcements are coming in all over the place. Shela must have better'n three thousand now."

Khoti let out a low whistle. Where did Ghyldus find all these troops? Had the Pladde rebellion been put down? "I wonder if Anlon –" he began, but didn't finish.

Chati looked up at him from beneath hooked brows then shoved another fingerful of rice in his mouth.

"Cyd's back," Chati glanced up at Khoti warily. "'Parently Nali got strung up in the dungeons. You know the story. They freed him but he's a bit twisted."

"So, Nali – " Khoti prompted.

Chati scooped out the last grains of rice from his bowl. "The Gnats are having a hard time since Nali helped execute the governor and his lady." Chati nodded at Khoti's stunned expression, a fleet smile. "The problem's reinforcements. Guess the Gnats got a bit fractious when the Minarians captured Nali and killed another one of their leaders. They exploded all over the region. We may get to Sihmad Shal and find no Gnats to help us."

"And no word of Arshal?"

"Rumors, old ones. A scout found us a few days ago with a story of some wizard frying outposts full of Minarians with a wave of his wand. Could be just another fanciful tale. But too many versions tell of the same white-haired god as other stories. And one version clearly points to the king because it mentions a sword carved with an eagle and a lion."

"Where'd the tale place him?" Khoti demanded. "If 'frying outposts' he must be in trouble."

Chati shook his head. "Story comes from Acceber. I guess it came to them from the north." Chati gave Khoti a sour look. "Sorry. Maybe you left things in the wrong hands."

"It's not that at all. We know too little! We're supposed to be communicating, but it takes months to learn anything!" Khoti buried his head in his hands. "Three thousand in Shela."

He looked up at Chati with eyes that burned from days of staring into Joffa's glaring sands, and months of dust.

He poked a stick into the soft mud, once again hearing the eerie sounds of the Dasirei swamp surrounding them. This side of the Dasirei shifted from swamp to briny marshes crowded with waving grasses and an occasional stand of twisted scrub. Nearby, the road to Hainad ran along a dike, their only route to Shela.

"We're only guessing on numbers." Chati helped himself to more rice. "Maybe Sedaik will bring enough warriors to tip the odds."

"We can't wait. It's too easy for someone to stumble on us now especially a force as large as Han's is. And we don't have the provisions to wait for Sedaik."

Euzzeldir strolled to them, yawning. The prince stopped, looking from Chati to Khoti to register Chati's tattoo and Taschian features.

"Can we be ready at dawn, Zel?" Khoti asked.

"I'll trust your judgment. You're the commander. You know our forces better than me."

Khoti gave the stick a twist in the mud. "Remember Zel, I'm just a wetnurse to children."

"If you're a wetnurse, then I'd be praying for an army of nannies to storm Shela."

Khoti stabbed his stick deep into the soft ground and stood. "Dawn then. We'll need a few squads from Han to balance our forces. And send someone to find Sedaik."

With a nod, Chati slipped back into the dark. Euzzeldir, too, hurried off to gather his officers. Khoti remained by a cold fire, staring west to where Shela lay at the far-flung delta of the Rigannon River. Something about the upcoming battle had him nervous, more than any other battle in which he'd been engaged. Maybe he still recovered from healing Jali, a feat he should have followed with days of rest. Instead, he'd survived on only a few hours each night for months. When he did sleep, his dreams lay before him a panorama of dead bodies scattered across the vast reaches of Shande. Shandeans sprawled in muddy battlefields as their armored conquerors danced at victory feasts among the carnage. The stench of death seemed to rise up from Dasirei to taunt him. His stomach growled but it had been days since he could stomach more than a mouthful of bread or rice. Less than a year. He tossed the muddy stick far out into the marsh. A warrior couldn't think on anything too deeply, especially on the eve of battle. He just prayed they didn't ride into the slaughter of his nightmares.

A few hours after dawn, hazy sun revealed a semi-circle of soldiers on both sides of the Rigannon, closing on the eerily silent city. They had no choice but victory. Not some skirmish to harass an enemy, they needed Shela to win Arshal's war.

Dawn had revealed that by blunder or treachery, they'd lost the edge of surprise. Along the ditches and dikes outside the city, Minarian archers and pikemen tensed, their cavalry held in reserve beyond the range of Shandean marksmen. The marshy terrain limited the approaches and gave even greater advantage to the defenders. Approach by land forced the attackers to file across the bridges and dikes where archers could target them.

Once a city of some twenty thousand, the exile and death of shawnsi and officers, the children taken away, the leaders, midwives and derna killed, a harsh occupation that left bodies stacked in the streets to be dumped in the Dasirei, had left Shela a ghostly town of a mere five thousand Shelans. Left leaderless and beaten, almost as many Minarian soldiers repressed them. Bolstered by Minarian merchants and sailors and various officials, all told Shela had more Minarians than Shandeans. Without Sedaik – who should have met Habdelion days ago – Khoti's combined forces, including attendants, met only half that number.

As they slogged through swamp and trotted across dikes, Khoti's Army of the South beat against the stench of the decaying bodies of Shela's dead rotting in the swamp, the odd silence broken only by the gulls and crows rising in angry clouds as the troops passed. At last, they halted on Khoti's signal. The standards they bore: the white and gold of Euzzeldir's house, brown and green of Habdelion's, the blue of Shande and the Tawnkat emerald and beige flapped in a salty wind that drove biting flies at them.

An undulating yell echoed across the river from the Tachi as eight hundred of Habdelion's soldiers raced along a dike to cross the wide bridge over the Rigannon to balance Euzzeldir's force. The Joffans returned the cry with a high-pitched hunt call like the flesh-eating bird that patrolled the desert fringes.

Asteria raised her voice with them.

Though a veteran of many a skirmish, Asteria had never faced such a battle. She felt only cold fear knifing through her belly, though she rode beside Tawnkats and the hardy people of the Jashiho.

Arrows fell among them as they raced at the ditches in which the Minarians hid. Horses kicked up in their faces clumps of sod and splattered mud stinking of death. With a yell, the Minarian cavalry leaped from hiding. The Minarian merchants and sailors set aside bows to bring up pikes to impale the Shandeans. Three thousand Minarian horsemen leaped the ditches, their armor flashing as in unison they raised their swords like the hackles on a spitting cat. While most of Habdelion's soldiers had stolen, crafted or been given either light mail or protective leather armor to turn arrows, most Joffans wore nothing between tunic and skin. Only one hundred wore armor stripped from Minarians felled in Hainad or at the outposts in the desert. Asteria cringed inside herself, feeling naked as she raced into the fray. Already their opening gambit appeared doomed as archers pinned Habdelion's reinforcements on the bridge, a cluster of swordsmen and pikemen blocking their escape.

As the Joffans met the Minarian cavalry charge, momentary chaos reigned as horses slammed together. Jostling and shoving preceded an uneven melee. The Minarian cavalry broke through the Joffan line, turning back to encircle them. Asteria ducked a spear thrust, forced to turn and strike over her mount's rump as she struggled to escape the press.

Pinned against Jali on the right, Khoti in front of her, she could only maneuver on her blind side where Daris had been, the girl now battling ahead beside Khoti and Tre. Reins looped over her horse's neck freed both Asteria's hands to counter her imbalance. The din of battle and stench of blood set her mount rearing and prancing out of control. She ducked, a sword falling on her horse's flank. The animal erupted in a terrified frenzy.

Asteria tried to parry the blows a Minarian warrior aimed at her, each attempt coming up against only air as the horse twisted beneath her.

She tried to goad the beast toward a break in the chaos, but the horse's wound lamed it so that it barely stumbled in the direction she indicated. While free to strike with more confidence from her right, a second attacker approached fast on the left.

The horse stumbled to its knees. Asteria jumped free, staggering up to swipe at an approaching Minarian mount, her blade slitting the beast's neck. The Minarian horse fell and rolled, crushing its rider beneath it. Confidence returned now that she stood on ground that, though soft and wet, remained stationary. She rounded on her other attacker, striking him in the side and unseating him. His horse raced on riderless. He struggled to his feet.

She saw her danger in her foe's face, turning too late as a swordsman rode in from behind. Swinging indiscriminately at all in his path he sped in pursuit of Khoti. In the rider's wake, Asteria lay in the mud, her blood pouring into the soil of Shande.

Khoti's mouth opened to shout a warning, too late. A Minarian blade fell on Asteria as if to sever her head. Blood splattered upward. In an instant, she sprawled in the churned mud of Dasirei's graveyard, passing hooves narrowly missing her, battle coating her in mud, sod and blood. He tried to escape the press and reach Asteria.

"Khoti!" Tre bellowed as he fended off a Minarian filling the gap Khoti created. "Kia's coming! Mind to business!"

Khoti hesitated. A wild whoop came from the bridge as Chati's detachment broke free, his Tachi and shawnsi troops streaming behind the fair-headed warrior as he rode to their aid, leaving more than one hundred dead and wounded Shandeans on the bridge. In all the chaos, the Minarians appeared not to notice tiny Kia racing to them on a Minarian horse. When she reached Asteria, Jali and a passing Joffan lifted Asteria's limp body to the horse. The girl fled back to the rear, Asteria's body flopping with the horse's lurching gait, to the provision wagons defended by noncombatants and apprentices armed with pike and bow.

She couldn't have survived such a blow. He went cold; his edge gone. His warrior instincts fled. He fought with mechanical motions. The image of a sword arcing down, Asteria's mouth opening, how she crumpled instantly, replayed in his thoughts. He'd finally lost her. His arms felt leaden as her spirit in him fled.

Chati's men flanked the enemy cavalry, a cluster of Joffans holding around Euzzeldir's standard. Here and there small gaps in the Joffan line opened to spew enemy horsemen that raced among them with abandon. Just beyond the Minarian line, Shela loomed, vast and silent, her people hidden.

A blow from an unhorsed foe eviscerated Khoti's mount. The beast catapulted into the ground with Khoti beneath it. He struggled to his feet, only to have his knee buckle beneath him, already swelling. Dazed, only his tawnkat instincts told him to duck as a blade arced at his head. Another came from behind. He stumbled, confused. He couldn't seem to regain his bearings. The sharp sting of a sword sliced across his unprotected back. He fell to his hands in the mud, struggling to rise as the wet ground stinking of death sucked his balance. A hoof glanced off his hip, sending him to his knees.

He scrambled for footing. His ears hummed as light flickered before his eyes. His stomach knotted at the stench of lives picked away by carrion. Minarians bore down on him. His grip on his sword slicked by mud, he barely fended off a thrust from one side just as he noted the glint of another blade racing toward his head. He pivoted on his twisted knee, preparing to absorb the blow. A horse girt in Shandean trappings filled his vision, almost bowling him over. Cydwyn. As Khoti drove back one attacker, Cydwyn struck down the other. Khoti barely felt Cydwyn's grasp on his arm, but instinctively swung up behind his protégé. The dour youth sped them from the melee to where Chati's men held the Minarian line.

Still dazed, Khoti scanned the rear area for Asteria's body among the fallen lain out like cordwood, a growing wall on the perimeter. Cydwyn reined in where Chati's attendant held Fidra with Chati's spare mount. Khoti landed on shaky legs and limped to the twitching mare that like some mount of the gods had remained sure-footed and intuitive, a beast made for battle, made for Khoti. He fell against Fidra's side. She nuzzled him as he clumsily mounted.

Cydwyn gazed at him, upper lip curling slightly. "Shake it off, Commander." He turned back toward the battle.

"Asteria –" Khoti began. It was more than he could stand. She rode to her death for him!

Cydwyn cut him off with a motion from a bloody hand. "Use it! Like you taught us! They've killed everyone you care about, your whole family. We need a commander, not a mourner. Don't think about it! Know it! They killed them all!"

Cydwyn kicked his horse and raced in search of battle, mud clods flinging up behind him.

Khoti felt so tired, so ready to quit. He didn't want anyone else to die for him. A horse screamed. Instead of the battle, for a bare instant his eyes looked upon a burning stable where Von's figure sank in the flames. Khoti tried to swallow but couldn't. He looked down at his sword hand where the shackle glowed dully. What damped the fire in him? Beside him, Chati's young attendant took in the swings of battle, barely to the rear of danger, hand ready on a dagger awaiting that moment he could gain his vengeance for his captivity among the Minarians.

Khoti took a deep breath and clenched his fists in Fidra's mane. Everyone he cared about. And it wouldn't stop.

He had to regain his wits. He tried to shake the weakness from himself. Concentrating on the burn of the cut snaking across the flesh of his hip and back, he narrowed his gaze on the battle, studying the line for weaknesses. Horses wailed. Warriors shouted for help or cried out their pain, many in the high pitch of youths. It kindled, burned like the wound on his back, like all the scars Minaria had laid upon him.

Everyone he cared about.

His throat opened in a tawnkat's screech of rage, like that of a she-cat's wail for threatened cubs, or of a wounded creature fighting for its life. The raw rage that crept into that bellow sent Fidra leaping forward, her head outstretched as she flew to battle. His throat burned with the moment of mourning he could spare, just enough to make his hand grip his sword until knuckles whitened and his fingers froze to the grips.

Fidra carried him toward a line of sturdy resistance where the Minarians pushed the Shandeans back in prelude to a breach. Khoti sensed someone falling in beside him, riding in Asteria's flanking position. If he looked, he knew he'd find Cydwyn, as dour-faced as his mentor. Another rider paced him on the other side, Daris maybe, or Jali, it didn't matter who. As he roared at the enemy line his troops met to fall in beside and behind him as he became the tip of a spear head, a tawnkat fang with Khoti at the lethal point.

He slammed into the enemy line, his arm rising, falling, rhythmic. Chati and Tre joined the wedge. Euzzeldir and his house were drawn in, flooding Khoti's wake to take on those the King's Champion missed. The Minarians stalled then fell back. The Shandean line swept in from the sides to drive the enemy before them.

Shande only gained a bit of ground before a Minarian captain regrouped his soldiers and they turned to face the charge. But the tenor of the battle had changed. For now, the warrior in Khoti gave his soldiers heart.

When nightfall came and Khoti assessed their position, he found the lines almost unchanged. Habdelion took the narrow ditch and dike the Minarians had held at the outset, but could gain no more. Khoti fared a little better. His units pushed the Minarians back to the first few buildings of Shela, forcing the enemy to make a stand behind overturned wagons. Riddling the marshy fields and ditches that had been the day's battlefield lay the dead and wounded of Shande, attendants standing in for the fallen.

Khoti stared at the buildings of Shela glowing in the starlight, hating the constricting touch of the mail vest he'd pinched from a dead Minarian. After his odd dream of Minarians feasting unscathed among the carnage of unprotected Shandeans, he'd ordered the Minarian bodies stripped of armor and weaponry for all who had none. The grisly task went to the youngest attendants and noncombatants while the Shandean army rested and gathered its dead and wounded. They'd been foolish to ride into battle so carelessly armored. Would mail have turned the weapon aimed at Asteria? His error left a bitter taste.

With weary eyes, that strange light-headedness coming on

him again, he studied the dark shadows of the overturned wagons. So close, yet unreachable. He couldn't use fire against his enemy and risk Shelan lives. Besides, in this damp air likely nothing would catch. Nor could he wait for enemy reinforcements to arrive by sea while his own troops starved. His hands twitched at his side as he considered the options he'd have when battle resumed. A soft step on the churned turf caught his attention. He turned, expecting a scout. Instead, Dynresa's wry smile found him.

"How thoughtless is the man so caught up in battle he hasn't the time to think of a Lady so long his companion," she said.

"That's cruel!" Khoti gasped, his whole body suddenly trembling at the rush of grief.

Dynresa grabbed his shaking arm. "No one told you?" She pulled him toward the rough camp they'd made, calling for Fidra. "She's hurt, not dead. A considerate friend would have inquired."

Khoti stopped, dazed, as Fidra's reins dropped into his hands. For a moment, he couldn't move. He found the will to mount and gallop to the rear area.

Slipping from Fidra's back, he stumbled to his hands and knees before he could catch himself. His legs remained shaky beneath him as he righted himself and limped toward the tents where herb-masters tended wounded with medicine no match for Khoti's. He ignored the pound of hooves behind him, a shout. Then someone wrenched his arm, spinning him around on his twisted leg. He would have fallen if Chati's grip hadn't held him up.

"No, Khoti," Chati said in a voice softer than his expression.

"Out of my way." Khoti tried to pull free.

Chati held firm. "You've no right to help those close to you and ignore others."

Khoti's breath ripped from him. "And who's the sneak who saw to Eithur's healing at Eilime?" Khoti's voice croaked out, hoarse and surly. He felt too weak to even pull free of Chati's grip. As if realizing that, Chati's features softened to concern. Khoti didn't want it.

"That was different. You were a mere soldier, the duke our leader. Now Asteria's the mere soldier. You're the leader. War's no place for a healer. How could you even consider taking such a risk knowing what responsibilities you have? You used medicine on Jali months ago and look how it left you! When do you think you'd rest now, in the midst of a battle we've barely begun?"

"Jali was different." Khoti sagged, letting Chati lead him to a wagon tie where he sat.

"Look, you're exhausted, not thinking right," Chati chided, holding his hand up to faint torchlight to see blood on his fingers. "You'll be worthless if you go thinking with your heart instead of your head." Chati's fingers probed beneath the Minarian mail for the source of blood on Khoti's side. "I know how you feel for her, no matter what you say about friendship among comrades. At least, I surely hope you don't look on me and Tre like that when we sleep."

"I can't just abandon –"

"Don't be stupid," Chati retorted, Khoti wincing as Chati's fingers found and probed the gash on his back. "She knows if you put down the urge to do anything heroic and stupid, you'll never forgive yourself for leaving her to suffer."

"What makes you so knowledgeable about what's going through Asteria's mind?" Khoti glared at him. He felt as if he might pass out. When had he last eaten? Or slept? He couldn't recall. He could smell the Otayran threespice on Chati's breath and it only made him feel like retching.

"And you called Jali on his distractions," Chati teased. "I'm going to get some salve for this. You stay put. I'll check on her. Then you're going back to camp to sleep."

"Look whose giving orders, now?" Khoti muttered. Chati grinned as he dashed away for the tents of the herbmasters.

Khoti tried to work out the ache in his twisted knee, which throbbed as idleness allowed the joint to stiffen. Soon Chati returned with the salve he promised, a poultice, and a wry grin.

"The delicate lady you worry after had a blistering rebuttal to your offer to help." Chati shook out his hand as if he had burned it. "She suggests you do your job and leave her alone." Chati tugged open the medicine pouch hanging from Khoti's belt, rummaging a moment before Khoti yanked it away.

"They don't have any feverweed to spare."

Khoti stared at him.

"You're burning up, fool." Chati took the herbs Khoti drew from the pouch, poured them into a wineskin and made Khoti drink while he applied the comforting salve. "I don't know what kind of poison you took from Jali, but it sure is a wasting thing."

"She's –"

"Fine," Chati said as he worked the salve into Khoti's wound. "Nasty blow to the shoulder. Probably broken. She's out of battle for a good while." Chati looked up at him. "She's got a lot of spies, like Kia, reporting our every move, so you'd better not slip up."

Khoti pulled out the pendant dangling from a chain at his neck, a gift shyly given when she still held him special in her heart. He winced as Chati worked the salve into his wound and adjusted a poultice. He lifted his gaze to notice the wounded awaiting treatment, the dead tossed in wagons and piles like sacks of grist for the mill as the feverweed-laced wine and salve worked on him.

"Where's Sedaik?" Khoti gripped the pendant in a trembling palm. Eight moons. He needed to survive just that long.

For two more days, the Battle of Shela sputtered.

In all the councils Khoti called, none of his officers could arrive at a swift solution. What would happen if they at last routed the Minarians? The enemy could be supplied by sea and evacuate the same way, only to return with reinforcements to retake what the Shandeans paid so dear to gain. The longer the struggle continued, the more likely a ship would arrive or a courier escape to bear a warning to Lagdche. A Shikoran blockade should be here to prevent just such a thing. He saw no fleet and Khoti kicked himself for not stopping Baynu. They needed Sedaik – what could have stopped the determined warrior? Treachery? Khoti doubted even Sedaik's archers could break the siege. So, the Army of the South waited, watching meager supplies dwindle with each passing hour and the ill humors of the Dasirei invade their wounds.

On the third evening since the Battle of Shela began, Khoti stood with Tre at the edge of a marshy estuary where the Rigannon dotted the sea with little islands sporting a few grasses and isolated trees. Just beyond bowshot of the Minarian sailors lining the waterfront, they counted the ships in the harbor, and the many fishing craft pulled up to the docks.

"They're waiting for something," Khoti said. "Reinforcements by sea?"

"No one's tried to sail with a call for help," Tre offered with a shrug.

"By river then? Down from Etaleah or Tormor?"

"Look there." Tre pointed at a dark smudge on the western horizon silhouetted in the westering sun.

"By the gods." Khoti leaned on Tre to take the weight from his purple knee. "They've been awaiting a fleet. We can't retreat only to have them nipping at our flanks all the way to Sihmad Shal. It'll be a slaughter! If I hadn't let my arrogance defeat us, we'd have Shikora –"

"There's no sails. Why would a fleet be at oars? Could it be Shikorans after all, delayed, coming from the west to fool them?" Tre turned to Khoti, his eyes bright with hope.

"We'll know soon enough." Still leaning on Tre, he limped back to camp as the ground sucked at his feet, making him stumble against his aide. He hated his weakness, the way even feverweed couldn't shake the lightheaded feeling he had. He needed sleep that didn't haunt him with the stench of death, and an appetite that didn't make him retch at the sight of food. Catcalls from the Minarians chased them like scavenging gulls as the enemy, too, spotted the smudge on the horizon.

He watched from his camp as the smudges enlarged to shapes, bringing a breath of change in the breeze that cooled Shela. Cydwyn sped into Khoti's camp, his horse prancing so close it almost trampled Khoti who couldn't move away quick enough.

Cydwyn's eyes shone bright and brutal. "Sedaik."

Khoti's hands clenched at his sides with impatience as he called for an all-out assault on his cue, not daring to hope it would make a difference.

The sun sank bloody to the west. Minarian taunts drifted from the city with offers of clemency accompanied by raucous laughter. As night arrived and the smudge of craft disappeared into velvet darkness, Khoti allowed himself a brutal grin. Concealed by night, long canoes manned by dozens of Detarian paddlers sped into the harbor. Before the Minarians knew the danger, arrows from the sea fell among the startled Minarians lounging at the rear of their lines. As the Detarians clambered ashore, Khoti gave his cue to charge the barricades set up around the sweltering city.

Fifteen hundred Detarian archers swept ashore to surround the Minarians. Shortly, assaults fizzled as the Minarians hid in houses from which they sniped at passing Shandeans, or attacked from behind with dagger. But the Shandeans excelled in stealth, played such warfare like performers in theater, their lines well rehearsed, their roles memorized. Soon they drew Minarians from houses unwitting, stole upon snipers with a cunning derived from the forest and the desert, their silent moves like a deadly dance as they moved unseen through dark Shela.

Khoti grinned when at last he found Sedaik in Shela's square as the first streaks of dawn lit the night's carnage. The Detarian leader waited arms akimbo, giving Khoti a weary smile.

"What kept you?" Khoti demanded. "You know how many people we lost?"

"It is a pleasure to see you, too, Khoti," Sedaik returned. He shook his head. "I am surprised, Commander. I expected to find a Shandean flag flying when we arrived."

"We didn't want you to miss any of the fun. We were outnumbered two to one."

Sedaik's smile faded to a blank expression that implied more than it said. "We were detained." He motioned with his head toward the canoes pulled haphazard on the wharf. "We met a fleet. A gift from Anlon." Khoti's mouth opened. "Confirmed by a prisoner. It was no simple feat to undo his work. What we did not burn to the water line, we boarded then burned. No prisoners. A nasty business. I lost five hundred men."

Something disquieting in Sedaik's gaze made Khoti's stomach squirm. It seemed to echo Khoti's own weariness as if some spell drew from their armies' leaders the heart that kept them going.

"Maybe I am not of the ilk to lead an army," Sedaik admitted. "In my first taste of leadership I lose the numbers of four villages in one encounter, one quarter of my force. I do not care for this responsibility. If they had been prepared for us?" Sedaik shook his head and shrugged. "Where were the Shikorans?"

"'Parently I'm not a diplomat."

Sedaik's smile was a thin line. "No one ever claimed you were." He gestured at the low stone building which had long served as the city meeting hall. The Shandean pennant rose into the morning.

"It won't stay long. It draws too much attention to itself without people here to fight for it, or a blockade to secure it."

"The Shelans do not come out to celebrate their liberation?" Sedaik scanned the square, frowning.

"There's few Shelans left to celebrate," Khoti whispered, looking away.

"They are –"

"Mostly dead. We lost a thousand, Sedaik. A thousand dead and too many of them the little warriors freed with you. So, the great Army of the South is a mere thirty-four hundred soldiers. Some army. And with this we hope to liberate Shande?"

"You are so bitter. Something inside you gnaws at your nature."

Khoti snorted. "And why not? Of all the Shelans there's maybe three thousand left, most too weak to save themselves. The Minarians started killing 'em after we struck. You worry about five hundred lives on your conscience, Sedaik. I've thousands."

Khoti turned at Habdelion's derisive snort. The duke leaned on a spear as a cane.

"The decision was war, Khoti," Habdelion said in a battle-hoarse voice. "The consequence: casualties. That is a given you should know. You teach it."

"It's never been my sole responsibility before."

Habdelion's eyebrows lifted with a skeptical sneer, his face haggard from the pain of a gash the length of his thigh. "Every skirmish is but one small element of the same war." Word of Anlon's role in their losses likely gave his words the vicious twist that made Khoti wince. "What, would you go home? Finish what you start! By the gods, you are the Sword of Shande! These people knew what they did when they took up arms."

"And the Shelans? They died 'cause we came to rescue them against their will."

"The consequence of inaction," Sedaik said. "The objectives of this war are for hundreds of thousands. A few hundred cannot

141

halt us." The Detarian studied him as if suddenly seeing him. "Some illness festers in you, Khoti. Hear how it twists your thinking? Perouk can tend you. We bring many herbs of our land."

Khoti barely heard him as he stared up at the pennant until his eyes burned. When he looked away, the image of the pennant flapping against the dawn sky echoed before his eyes. What had stolen his edge, made him doubt again? He felt so hollow and empty, the light-headed feeling rearing up at him from his gut.

He felt a touch on his arm, expecting to find Sedaik or Han. Asteria, pale in the sunlight, peered at him as if measuring his health and mood against rumor. Habdelion and Sedaik had moved off to speak with Euzzeldir and Dynresa, the Joffan princess watching Asteria for any sign she tired.

"Should you be here?" He wanted to fold her into him. His arm went out to support her, fitting easily around her waist.

"I heard about the Shelans. I knew you would blame yourself."

"Resa talks too much. I feel the illness in you yet." He cupped her face in a trembling hand. "I thought you were dead. I couldn't think. I guess I've gotten used to having you beside me all the time. Cyd's a poor substitute."

"I heard how you acted the perfect fool –" she began.

"Is that all people have to do during a battle? Gossip about me?" He shouldn't have betrayed his feelings for her, especially when she had only judgments to proclaim.

"Chati said you –"

"I don't want to talk about it," Khoti stated in measured words. He gazed at her, seeing the illness in her, but also how something in his touch seemed to make her stronger. Impulsively, he stroked her cheek. He'd already revealed his feelings; it made no difference now. "You'd better recover soon. I'm worthless without you to keep me humble."

She poked his chest then shook her finger with exaggerated pain. "It is about time you took to protecting your skin. Is that the stuff making you so sour?" She plucked at the dull glitter of chain mail peeking from beneath his tunic.

"We've got about a hundred prisoners," Chati's voice came from behind him like the clank of weaponry, grating and cold.

"Kill them," Khoti ordered without turning. "I'm as bad as they are."

Asteria pulled from him, concern crossing her face when he staggered to regain his balance. "And what quarter would they give? They set the rules. You cannot waver now."

"I'm sick of fighting! I'm sick of seeing people die and being responsible –"

Dynresa closed the distance in an instant. "A fine time to start thinking that way." She took Asteria's arm. Asteria touched the cuff on his sword arm where it dangled so loose he could have slipped it off.

He wanted to lay his hand on Asteria again, to see how she seemed to draw comfort from his touch. "If Shikora –" Khoti began.

"Oh, back to Baynu again," Dynresa said with a roll of her eyes. She pushed him aside so hard he almost fell and had to bite back a gasp as he twisted his knee. Dynresa guided Asteria away, leaving him standing in the humid square alone.

He looked up at the pennant, each flutter like a life cost to raise it. How long could he continue to harbor two such powerful emotions as compassion and rage, and not lose his mind?

He turned his back when Chati led the Minarians into the square to stand before the gallows where they had executed so many Shandeans. As the traps on the gallows dropped – the thunk as hollow as the empty pit of his stomach – Khoti took note of the Shelans emerging to view the deaths of their oppressors. Khoti tried to avoid their gazes as he witnessed the executions, his back to the victims, eyes closed, their death sounds to haunt his dreams. Suddenly he discovered a Shelan man staring him in the eye with his face but a span distant.

"You're the King's Champion," the man said.

"We couldn't know this would happen to your people," Khoti said in apology.

"And who's at fault?" The man asked, taken aback. "The king came and we didn't listen. We chased him away. Habdelion's men came. Sedaik's men came. And we didn't listen. You came anyway, even after we spurned you. If you hadn't come?" He left the question unanswered. "Now, there are fewer Minarians in Shande. We'd be dead in time anyway." The man peered at him.

"Don't pity fools, Commander."

He turned and disappeared among the growing crowd of Shelans watching the gallows.

Khoti shuddered at the clatter of the traps falling open. He clenched his fists and limped from the square. No matter what assurances they gave, Khoti doubted he could ever shed this sense of guilt. He needed to wipe everything from his mind to be a strong warrior. He stared north to where supply wagons crept over battle-churned ground toward the town, scavenging supplies from among the dead and scattering flocks of crows and gulls seeking the booty of the battlefield. All too soon his troops would head north with nothing, no Shikoran blockade to stop the enemy from sweeping back in, and only three thousand warriors to come to Arshal's call.

He slammed his fist as hard as he could into the swollen thigh above his purple knee and concentrated on the pain. He twisted his torso to feel the burning cut on his lower back. For now, he must be a soldier, not a healer, or the curse of his dual roles would drive him mad before this campaign ended. It was enough to fear for Asteria, his friends and the little warriors attending his soldiers. Now, it seemed, like Arshal, he mourned the enemy whose executions he ordered.

Catching the hint of acrid smoke in the wind, he forced his thoughts to turn to the hateful images he had tried to both forget and remember. He heard again the Minarians' raucous laughter, the screaming horses, Von's silhouette against the flames as they drove him back within, his dying wails shrieking for help, for Khoti, for purest agony. And Khoti had crouched lower in the dark and the image collapsed in the flames, not to rise, silent, and through its silence, deafening, as the Minarians moved down the street, his grandmam's voice rising to join Von's in the silence. Khoti concentrated on the image, on his name shrieked from Von's scorched throat. Khoti's eyes ached, itched. As he limped through the blood-stained streets of Shela, with chain mail peeking from beneath his buckskin and sword clutched in a clenched fist, the expression he wore forced those he encountered to blanch and step aside, unsure whether he had come to terms with his doubts, or at last been mastered by them.

13: A Current in the Air

The Year of Kedtair closed on them. All of Shande, all of Ea raced to meet a designated hour, the players counting on plans laid long ago in the Val by men still ignorant of their opponent.

Arshal struggled against impatience as first it took weeks to gather the Shandean exiles in Marol's care, many even doubting the white-haired wizard in Joffan tunic and braids could be their king. Then he led his many exiles not west to Shande, but northeast to King Farlal, a host grown to twelve thousand traveling through bitter Otayran winter to beg the mercy of Otayr. Even with Marol's influence, weeks more passed before the King of Shande at last faced King Farlal of Otayr. It would be no easy task moving this eastern king.

While Arshal's persuasive voice had grown strong, King Farlal's council ordered their sovereign to stand firm for the country's best interests as his advisors saw them. While sympathetic, Farlal refused to risk the enmity of his council, a group apt to stir rebellion if the sovereign strayed far from their guidance. Already delayed, now he faced a standoff. The Otayrans demanded the Shandeans depart at once. Arshal refused to leave without ships to carry his refugees home and weapons for the exiles now able to help defend their country. The exiles camped outside the Otayran king's gates through the dark days of the cold moon. King Farlal's council insisted Arshal fought a fool's war that would merely extinguish the people of Shande, and the boon Arshal asked cost too dear to throw away on certain loss. The council refused to see the King of Shande in person, convinced he somehow enchanted Farlal. So, the long days of a bitter winter in Otayr passed with Arshal's hordes of

145

refugees besieging Farlal's city, the Shandean sovereign and patient Marol pacing daily to Farlal's audience as the moons took them closer to the Year of Kedtair.

Far south, the Shikoran fleet sat idle as King Wyeff Shikora pondered strange dreams of blood raining from the sky. While outraged by all that his trusted champion told him of the arrogant Shandeans, he couldn't help but wonder if his dreams were not the result of his idle fleet. He hadn't had a peaceful night since he'd ordered his navy to stand down.

As Khoti's Army of the South, joined by a few hundred Shelans, began its long journey north along the Rigannon, no blockade kept the Minarians from retaking Shela. Khoti ordered Shela burned, her refugees whisked into the safety of Detarian, leaving nothing behind worth fighting for.

Meanwhile, the militias in Detarian and Tormor forests diverted the enemy's attentions from Shela by increasing their harassment of outposts, deviling them until the Minarians wasted their arrows on the mere whisper of wind in the trees. Though outpost captains vowed to end resistance, they seldom found those responsible, nor had any sense that such isolated skirmishes marked a larger movement.

Reinforcements arriving in the Jashiho desert found neither rumor of resistance, nor of Hainad, but a beat-up, old, shack and a half-buried glassworks.

The south tensed as Shandean troops and messengers crept north, leaving death in their wake. Minarians accustomed to unquestioning obedience sensed belligerence, though the people they ruled deferred to them with the same fawning pose. They heard distorted tales of the Blood Rage, or rumors that their god sought some upstart rebel god trying to sabotage the occupation. They heard of thousands of education camp internees escaped, of wagons full of Shandean goods dwindling on the roads, carrying leaner cargo, and even a rumor that an army of Shandeans carried rebellion to Shela. Something charnel seemed to hang in the air, a sense of the thin thread of a tenuous occupation unravelling, weaknesses hinting the thread might break to blast apart the web it supported. Desperate outposts sent dispatches to Lagdche, daring to traverse the mountains in deep winter to beg reinforcements.

In the far north, the Lharan Guard had split to cover the broad plains of Kishma. Eithurdon worked east along the Quelica River, Kefta along the Eilime. They traveled with the heavy hearts of those hearing doom in Hothur's warnings. In all the assumptions they'd made long ago in the Val, they never considered the parity of forces. While Shande covered a much larger territory, it had few areas of dense population and the occupation had eroded even those. Minaria had more people. A few hundreds of Shandean farmers might live in a region as large as all of Minaria, while the Minarians crowded the coasts, millions strong and easily assembled. Ghyldus could face Shande's tens of thousands with hundreds of thousands. If Ghyldus came, he would bring all to show his mere ability to command such a force, those warriors filled with the demon's enchantment, constantly refreshed and strengthened by his presence.

As the Lharan Guard moved east across Kishma, each day brought only a few more recruits. When he looked to the stars to mark time's swift passage, Eithurdon often gazed south in vain search of some sign of his daughter. He sensed, as if it were some current in the air, the tension flowing up from the south, the anticipation, the rumor of an exodus of peoples crossing lands in a rage. He knew she would be in the thick of it.

In the northwest, Shiadins patrolling the border with Minaria discovered the Minarian troops retreating, unit by unit. Messengers rushed to King Keyen to warn that the time came at last. Minaria gathered her armies.

In the mountains of the northwest life seemed almost to have returned to a pre-occupation normalcy. The Val remained untroubled. In Eilime and Sefresal, couriers came and went, the ruse of occupation apparently unchallenged. Yet the Shandeans watching the Ymmenay River and the Staph-el and Lhata roads had a sense of foreboding that only grew as more and more messengers rushed west on the Staph-el road, keeping to themselves the reasons for their urgency. Orders streamed into the mines at a greater pace than ever before. But a sense of some trouble about to close made Tawnkats and Guardsmen alike watch the shadows with apprehension for any glint of a Minarian's medallion.

In Arenh, border skirmishes faded to memory as Minaria abandoned that quarter as well. King Azren fretted to recall the timetable Arshal gave him. Minaria moved too soon.

In the northeast, the Gnats had grown so inactive the occupation declared the rebellion over. Yet a sense of some subdued tension remained, a pause as something coiled to strike, something glimpsed in the eyes of farmers or artisans when the tribute wagons arrived to collect.

Like the great arm of a catapult winched back, all of Ea tensed. The eve of the Year of Kedtair arrived, no sudden marker stating the next moon would be a new year. Even those who remained blind to what passed in Shande felt its approach, an ominous pressure, some dark stain that spread. Shandean hopes fought against fears as the people watched each day for the symbol that told them what they awaited, while the enemy among them grew only more afraid.

For those who knew, they knew it came too soon.

14: Precarious Positions

Jeret held his face with his hands, the circular scars on his cheeks puckering into deep furrows. It seemed so long since that day Tsevon of Tasch-el had convinced him, against his father's wishes, to raise the Pladde against the Hogde. Now the handful of Pladde gathered in his tiny shack mourned more of their comrades lost in raids on the Minarians.

"We have no choice but to somehow save ourselves before it is too late," he said.

"You cannot quit!" Teshet declared. "This is when we are needed most!"

Jeret slammed his fist on the table. "We lost hundreds of men, Teshet! I understand your loyalty to Princess Resala, but you cannot let that blind you. Your people are being annihilated!"

"They sail soon. If we let them, all those who died, died for nothing. Our plans are working. We cannot let them go yet."

Jeret sighed. "Teshet, you do not understand. What are we supposed to do? We cannot gather enough men to raid a food shipment. How can we think of stopping the demon from sending his armies to Shande?"

"There has to be a way. We must find more soldiers. There are thousands of Pladde –"

"Too scared to help," the door guard mumbled.

"Uncle, how can we just give up? Resala can devise a plan."

"She has enough troubles keeping that demon in check." Jeret sighed. "If you continue with her as you have, you are bound to be caught and executed. Our only hope is to disband and find refuge in Shiad or Arenh. If we wait much longer, they will walk right in on us. It is safer if we just escape."

"And you the one who was so hot for battle when Tsevon came," Teshet retorted, her face wet. "Are you going to take Resala with you? She risks death daily for this rebellion."

"What will stop his army if he chooses to send it? Nothing that we have."

"We know their movements but they do not know ours," a man offered. "And we have Verdred."

Jeret stared at the man.

"What have we got to lose?" the door guard urged.

"Our lives, for one," Jeret replied. "We cannot count on Verdred. I am not sure as I trust him."

"It was you that said a life of servitude was no life at all," Teshet said. "They will just come down on us harder."

"The issue is still that we have no men to do anything."

"Then find them! The Shandeans started with a handful. Now they have armies." Teshet's face had gone crimson.

Jeret stared into calloused hands. "What does Resala expect?"

"Something to make them hesitate to leave Lagdche undefended just now, or a set back." Teshet pursed her lips. "He listens too well and wants to go too soon. Then the traitor Anlon urged him on. But the Shandean soldiers will not be at Sihmad Shal if Ghyldus departs now. We need to delay the fleet a few moons is all."

"With fifty men, we are supposed to delay thousands?"

"How many Tawnkats were with Tsevon?" the door guard queried.

"What did it get them? What they destroyed of Lagdche has been rebuilt, and with our labor. Their foray came to nothing."

"Did it?" the door guard challenged. "Since then, the Pladde arose and found tribal pride again, long enough to give Shande time to gather armies. Hogde fear us now. They think long before beating a Pladde servant in fear the next morning will find them floating in the reservoir. All this because a handful of Tawnkats came here. We are five times that number. If Amhese could kill Mol Azezial and if Halieri could destroy Lagdche, then certainly we can do something to slow an army."

"When are they scheduled to sail?" Jeret mumbled.

"Two weeks," Teshet said. "We cannot have them leaving

before the greening moon."

"Four moons! How can we hold back an army for so long?"

"It takes time to reorganize after any delay," Teshet said.

Jeret scanned those gathered. "I suppose we cannot fail if we do not try –"

"We cannot succeed if we do not try," Teshet stated.

She jumped up and slipped out to race back to Ghyldus's halls before someone missed her. Jeret wished he could still feel her determination. So many of his people had died for Resala's dream.

Teshet gave the sentry a pert smile. She tossed her head, dark hair bounding over her shoulder. Beyond him stood a warehouse crammed with the food stuffs and supplies vital to Ghyldus's fleet.

"My mistress sent a bag to be stowed but packed a dress the Great One wishes to see her in. I am sent to fetch it," Teshet said with a bright smile.

The sentry raised an eyebrow, placing a suggestive hand on Teshet's thigh. "It is a large warehouse, missy. To find one bag, it could take hours." His face became a leering grin.

Teshet's lips curled to a coy smile, her eyebrows raised with subtle invitation. "Would I look fine in that fancy get up?"

The sentry's eyes widened. "A delight!" he cooed, turning to grasp his lamp and rush her into the warehouse.

Teshet freed the club hidden beneath her cloak and brought it around to smash into his skull. He crumpled with a soft groan. She grabbed up his lamp and closed the door behind her. She searched the warehouse, at last finding a barrel of lamp oil. After wrenching off the lid, she pushed the barrel over with a bang that echoed through the building. The oil spread to coat other crates and the wooden floor, sheathing the timbers, now trailing by bolts of sailcloth, now trickling by crates of dried meat, now soaking a bale of osfothye. Another barrel tipped to brush against the wooden walls and send grasping fingers around barrels of liquor, crates of tack, bales of fodder, sacks of grain and bundles of bows and arrows.

At last, Teshet backed to the door with her lamp, leaving oily footsteps in reverse and nearly tripping over the still-groggy sentry just rousing from the blow. She pursed her lips, staring at him a moment before yanking open the door. With one backward glance at the sentry, she lobbed the lamp at the nearest puddle of oil and dashed away.

Jeret lifted one rail after the other, using the shuffling of the horses to hide the scuffing sounds and block him from view. One of his men snuck up behind a guard to slit the man's throat. As flames erupted near the waterfront, Jeret and his men spooked hundreds of horses destined for the holds and decks of the ships, sending them fleeing into the broad and fenceless countryside where it would take weeks to again gather them.

The horses scattered, spurred by rancid smoke carried on the briny wind. A ship, still on the ways for repair flared as the fire spread along the waterfront. A clamor of voices rose; bells clanged alarm, too late to halt a fire that would forge weapons into grotesque shapes like a mad potter disdaining his wheel.

Such easy success made Jeret wonder a moment if he invented excuses to quit. But horses could be corralled again. Lost food stuffs could be replaced. Weaponry and fittings might take longer, but they would come. When the ships were again ready to sail in a moon's time, there would be a heavier guard on the warehouses and corrals, and a tighter rein on the Pladde.

Jeret glanced at one of his men, signaling for the others to hurry into hiding. "You," he muttered. "Get to the mountains. We must stop shipments from Lharan."

The man grabbed a laggard horse, mounting bareback and guiding the animal with a strip of rope from around his waist, then tore off into the night. Jeret stared at the hungry fire. Hundreds had gathered already, forming bucket brigades that stood dwarfed by the flames. After a few minutes, Jeret turned away. Ghyldus would still reach Shande too soon.

Resala stared out the window at the glow of fire and the scurrying silhouettes striving to put it out, her breath small gasps of eagerness as she cheered on the hungry flames. Though sealed against the cold winds of winter coming off the sea, chinks in her window allowed the sour odor of burning meat and tar to seep in. Her throat constricted as the smell clung to the sweating glass. A roof gave way in a cascade of sparks, like the dormered roofs of Sihmad Shal collapsing at the hands of her enemy, their memory a haze over the region for weeks. This fire hungered over only a thin stretch along the waterfront, nothing like the blaze that burned thousands out of the Harbor and Sihmad Shal.

Resala turned when the door opened. Teshet slipped in, checking the hall behind her for the guard who had gone to fight the fire now threatening to spread to the market district as the wind dribbled sparks onto neighboring roofs.

"Think it will help?" Teshet whispered in a smoke-choked voice.

Resala nodded, turning back to the window.

"May I clean up a bit? I smell like oil and I stained my shoes."

"You did it?" Resala turned to stare at Teshet. "There must have been sentries. Why did you take such risks for me?"

"It was done. And not just for you."

"You shouldn't have," Resala admonished, hugging Teshet.

"As well me as any other. I had an excuse to go there. We have grown few." Teshet washed her hands and face in the cold water on the dressing table, shivering as it hit her skin. "It will not delay long." Teshet bent to examine her shoes, trembling. "It is the best we can do. It falls in your hands now. They will regather all they need in perhaps a moon."

Resala nodded, stroking her cold arms as she paced away from the window. "It helped."

She looked over her shoulder out the window. The firelight tinged the waves in the harbor orange, a fiery color that had dominated the last few weeks in Sihmad Shal.

"The Year of Kedtair is coming," Resala whispered. "Can you feel the difference, Teshet? Never before have I felt this way. It's as if all of Ea waits for something." She pressed her face against the pane so she could look northeast. She shivered.

It closed. The last moon lay only a few weeks away. Then, three moons into the Year of Kedtair, some time around Long Day, Arshal would face Ghyldus and defeat him. Her ordeal of nearly two years would end.

"Soon, Teshet," Resala muttered as she continued to press against the glass, the stench of smoke strong. "Then you will be free of my depressing company."

"I will join you," Teshet said as she dried face and hands.

"You can't."

"I will. I think of you as a friend more than a mistress. I cannot let a friend go into such danger alone. What have I to lose? I have only Jeret, and him with his own children to think of. It is a long journey of idleness. One in which, with Ghyldus aboard, you may need someone to talk to, a friend among enemies."

Resala gave her a comforted smile. "If he can be convinced to go. I'm still not certain he intends to. He won't say."

"He will go. You will convince him. And at the pre-arranged time, your brother will meet him and defeat him," Teshet stated, chin thrust out with desperate determination.

"Maybe," Resala said softly. "It's my prayer."

A few days later, Resala stood at her post behind Ghyldus's throne, wooden as each comer brought his report. She stiffened as Ghyldus scowled. His mood felt like a physical blow.

"Loch Asmodiel assassinated," he muttered as a courier knelt beside the ship's captain, awaiting Ghyldus' judgment. "Why was I not told this before!" he demanded.

"The winds, Mighty One, they fought us all the way," the courier said in a whimper. The man shriveled before the Great God of Ea, begging mercy from his angry god. "They destroyed the governor's medallion and the few Eidhalt with the powers to use such magic were far south pursuing rebel gods and demons."

"What do you know of Eidhalt magic?" the god demanded. "You know your tale too well." Ghyldus made a sign to Verdred. Ghyldus's Malice laid his hands on the shoulders of his victims. Their eyes went wide. They knew they'd been consigned to carrion. Resala felt no pity.

Ghyldus peered up at her with one murderous eye. "I will tolerate no more of this," he rasped in a voice that pierced her armor. "My education camps deserted, my messengers and couriers killed, open rebellion –"

She tried to hide her fear behind a shrug. "I dare you to put him down," she said with less conviction than usual. He appeared stronger than ever, seeming to emanate power, his mere glance enough to wilt the greatest warrior. She had found the strength in herself to thwart him before, to guile him to do things he thought he chose. But now ...

"You have doubts." His smile made her heart falter. "You think perhaps your esteemed brother is after all nothing against God. Perhaps I should rule from the center of Ea, take up my residence in that city Loch Asmodiel could not control. You could again wander your home halls. That would please you, perhaps? It would certainly hearten your people to see their princess standing again behind the throne, in her proper position of deference to the God of Ea." He laughed as her eyes widened at a humiliation she had never considered.

She gripped the back of the chair. "He'll be waiting for you, ready to cut you down," she whispered, seeking the strength she had called on through her misery.

"Hah!" He laughed with genuine humor. "You forget I am God! What power can this false hope of yours possibly possess?" Ghyldus seemed to fill the lofty hall. A shadow like deepest night among the tangled roots of trees closed around them, his web drawn tight so that only the two stood there, all others gasping in the suffocating darkness, unseen. Ghyldus filled her vision, a towering presence. His scowl raised writhing hairs on the back of her neck. Trying to avoid his eyes, she sought Verdred in the deep shadows, finding nothing but ultimate night. The floor shook as he glared at her. "I can make the ground open at my very feet to swallow you. What can this king of yours do?"

She drew herself as straight as she could and stared him in the eye.

"He can call Terremar to strike you down." Merely uttering the name heartened her and threw Ghyldus into a rage.

"That false tale still dwells in you?" he bellowed, slapping her. The blow threw her against the stone wall, almost knocking her unconscious. "I told you never to utter that name in my presence. Until now you were wise. You made a very foolish mistake." He bent over her where she cringed against the wall.

She stroked the hard lump on her cheek, a bone likely broken, and it had been an idle slap. She spat blood onto the stone at his feet, drawing herself up.

"It's you that's erred," she slurred, the strength returning to her heart from somewhere, seeming outside of her. In the corner of her vision, she saw the shadow wall of the spell tatter and Verdred rush forward to his master's aid.

"What has your false god done for you?" Ghyldus's words hissed like adders. "Has he protected your land from the fury of the real God of Ea? You serve only one God. Me."

"You're but a puppet of Fyraer. You're nothing but what he made you, no thoughts of your own, no strength, merely one of many tools –" She faltered, awed by the transformation of rage in Ghyldus's face. He struck the wall with his fist, splintering the hard stone into powder but leaving no mark on his hand.

"I could have smashed you!" he declared, his words slithering up her spine. "I chose not to. Your brother will be like this rock!" Dust fell from his hand as he turned to stride from the hall. He paused, glancing at Verdred. She couldn't collect herself in time to stop it, felt too deeply stunned. She sensed Ghyldus drawing from the vacant mind all that he expected to learn, long kept hidden by her will: messages of dead warriors littering Shande, of trouble throughout occupied lands, of a king last seen near Iyrafael. Deeper than that was only the charge to protect. With a sign, Ghyldus propelled Verdred against the wall to await his master's orders.

Ghyldus stared after his champion, his words meant for Resala. "I did not want to hurt you." It almost sounded like sorrow. "You have pleased me. I know you have defied me and likely terminated my offspring to thwart me. Do not forget I can still keep you in chains. You have lived with privilege. You are created by me, made by me, alive only by my grace, my servant. You had best learn that and act accordingly or I may tire of you." He turned and looked at her, as close to an expression of tenderness as had ever crossed his face. "I doubt I will find as fine to replace you. I did not wish to harm you."

He strode away, leaving Resala frightened and confused, her head throbbing as she spat out more blood. This demon god liked her. A hysterical laugh escaped at the birth of the incredible concept. She hated him more than ever, if possible. Through the fuzziness of her aching head, she realized that now she held a truly precarious position. She gambled wrong. He had publicly addressed her intractability. He must feel some new confidence from somewhere. If so, she no longer could control him. If no longer in control, she would not only fail, but die.

She looked to the abomination lurking in the corner. Verdred peered at her. She shivered with a thrill of apprehension. She must remain strong to keep Ghyldus from gleaning news from Malice. Oddly, it seemed the bare glitter of eyes from the shadows made that same appeal.

15: Sage

Sprouting an uncharacteristic, broad smile, the man the Gnats called Commander, but more often now addressed as Sage, flung aside his weathered cloak to reveal a sword at his side and derna robes wrinkled and bright. He drew a rumpled blue cape from his pack, and, as Jan followed suit, clasped it at his throat.

The two men looked at each other, grinning as they clasped arms. "We stick out like the only geese in a duck pond, Jan," Nali laughed as a pale, cold moon sun rose toward noon over the Harbor.

"No, we're real soldiers, Harbor Gnats again. And it's about time," Jan crowed.

In step, they paced the timbers salvaged from the original boardwalk, hands resting on sword hilts.

As they passed a bunkhouse, Shandean workers filed out to fall in behind them, most of them Gnats already displaying swords long hidden or nocking arrows in bows fetched from hiding. Others grabbed loose boards and tools as they rallied behind the two Gnat leaders whose faces symbolized resistance. Now and then, they heard the rap of a tool falling to the ground as a man recognized the outlawed Jan and Nali in forbidden Shandean cloaks, their faces set for battle. A few startled faces peered out of the grimy windows of a mean building next to the first of a long line of warehouses. Moments later, the door swung open and several dozen Pladde padded out, pulled up boards and silently fell in step with the Gnats.

As the two leaders passed the first warehouse, Gnats torched the empty building. The grim-faced processional continued on as fire once again fed upon Sihma Harbor. A belated alarm clanged in the strangely silent village, echoing from silent cliffs out onto a silent sea.

Sailors stumbled from inns. The Minarian lighthouse keeper signaled to ships beyond the breakwater, begging assistance. Before any vessel could drop her tenders and send support, a hasty exodus of foreigners crowded the docks to escape the rebellion.

And a rebellion on a large scale it must have appeared to those few Minarians on the waterfront. A throng of men and women marched behind two stone-eyed symbols of resistance. The Minarians drew their swords with none of their usual bravado.

Shande met Minaria halfway along the silent boardwalk in front of a space that had once held Jan's inn, a plethora of bright-hued merchant stalls and the crackling excitement of a living city, and not far from the toppled statue of Maura. It stood silent now but for wind and wave and the shuffle of their feet. Instead of the heady scents of a chaotic market, came the faint odor of charred timber, brine, and now, again, the smoke of fire.

Nali stopped with one hand on his sword hilt.

"It's over," Nali called to the Minarians gathering to rush them. "Your ravening ends now. Surrender, or die for a witless cause."

A Minarian captain wagged his finger at Nali. "You are mistaken. I see you are a fugitive. You will find our dungeons less than accommodating." The captain took a step forward, his confidence not reflected in his eyes.

With a deft move that stunned even Jan, Nali drew his blade and pressed it against the captain's throat before the man could lift his foot a second time.

"I've had the pleasure of your dungeons, sir."

The captain made to grab for the weapon. Nali's arm jerked. The captain sank to his knees, clutching his throat, blood overflowing his hand.

Nali paced toward the startled soldiers as fires among the warehouses sucked at the air with a hungry sound. First one, then the entire cluster of Minarians turned and ran for the stables in search of horses for the race to Sihmad Shal for help.

Three pounded south from the group, making for Etaleah and reinforcements. Nali and Jan didn't worry. Gnats held all the roads.

They drove more than one hundred Minarians before them. On Jan's signal, Gnats busted open caches of arms hidden beneath the boardwalk, tossing them to dock workers and Pladde hungering for revenge. A contingent of Gnats settled in to hold the Harbor, keep troops from landing and scour the narrow alleys as the rest of the throng rushed over the bridge and up to the plains above.

By the time Nali and Jan crested the eastern bluff of the Rigannon, Minarian dead already scattered the fields, Shiadin crossbow darts protruding from their armor. Gnats rummaged the bodies, their crossbows slung at their backs.

Nali had no time to contemplate success. Too many details crowded the top of his mental checklist. No Minarian escaped the swarming Gnats Nali had at last called up. Kyne himself delivered the message that the king had crossed into Otayr south of Iyrafael. The man went crimson to learn he'd unwittingly sheltered his own king. It was the cue Nali had awaited. He called up the Whittea Gnats who trickled north, a gathering that took months to accomplish. Nali named Kyne a captain and sent him back to ready the Iyrafael Gnats for the final cue. On Nali's mark they would cleanse the Iyrafael region of the enemy. Then they would meet near the confluence of the Iyrafael River and the Etaleah Canal to await the Army of the South, a force Cydwyn expected to reach ten thousand strong. The combined army would likely be just enough to stop that massive gathering of Minarians at Etaleah from reaching Sihmad Shal before Arshal.

Now, Whittea Gnats snaked through the dry prairie, discernible only by the parting trails in the grass. Two thousand figures stalked a city now guarded by more than four thousand well-armed Minarians who had arrived ignorant of the Blood Rage. Nali hoped Maura heard his prayers and sank the courier ship carrying the grisly tale. Though, unlike most Shandeans, he doubted few of the fanciful stories he heard. He sensed treason sent these extra soldiers so sudden and unexpected.

Behind him, he heard the racket of the five hundred Gnats

left in the Harbor. They pillaged Minarian stores, burned anything the enemy had built, and with a cheer, re-reraised the statue of Maura and began to cleanse her of the Minarian defilement. Smoke rose, a warning to those in Sihmad Shal.

Nali and Jan accepted the two mounts offered by their attendants, girding themselves in the uncomfortable and blood-stained mail, still warm, pilfered from the dead bodies of messengers. They raced south to the entrance of Peshal's Tunnel, leaving behind the wave of Gnats rolling across the prairie.

When they stalked into the cavern the two leaders wore smiles grim with victory. They had no time to gloat. Tel waited with the Gnats' best warriors, all stiff and nervous in stolen garb or gear found in the city's storerooms. The crowd shifted and muttered among themselves, their faces flushed.

Nali scanned them as he passed, barely acknowledging the pats of praise on his shoulders. Eight thousand waited in the city above to heed his cue. Hundreds ranged the countryside to waylay messengers and dismantle outposts. These few hundred counted most.

Nali stopped on the first step up from the cavern into the corridor leading to the storerooms beyond. Turning to scan the crowd, he occasionally found some face that glistened with a sheen of fear. He gave a brief nod. Then he mounted the stairs and strode down the long passage to the doorway into his storeroom command post. The men filed behind him, feeding on his power to ease their fear as they followed his wordless commands. Grips tightened on weapons. Eyes glittered in the torchlight. Sihmad Shal held its breath.

Nali opened the door into the hidden tunnels. Padding a well-known path, the Gnats' muffled their passage, rags quieting footfalls and clinking gear. He pressed his ear to the door. Beyond, Minarian captains heard petitioners, apparently oblivious to or unconcerned by the smoke rising from the Harbor. Nali opened the door, a gaping darkness revealed in the back wall of the reception hall, concealed by the curtained dais. He crept behind the curtain, followed by a dozen men. Hefting his small crossbow in one hand, he set a bolt and checked the position of his sword. Tension hummed in his ears.

He gave Jan a grim grin when the older man's head peeked around the doorway. Jan surveyed the hall before leading another cluster of Gnats to an unguarded door up into the officers' living quarters.

When Jan cleared the alcove, another cluster followed Tel up the same stairway to bleed into other sections of the palace. Others remained inside the passageway, awaiting Nali's cue.

Nali took a deep breath then stepped into the open.

For a frozen instant everything paused. Then petitioners' eyes widened as guards' hands darted for weapons. Gnats disguised as petitioners whipped out daggers. Nali aimed his dart at the Minarian on the throne. The man came out of his decadent sprawl just as the dart took him in the forehead. With one hand, Nali wedged the crossbow against his knee, popped in another dart and cocked the weapon as his other hand drew his sword. In the meantime, Gnats dashed from behind the curtain to shoot guards, while those disguised as petitioners held prisoners at bay with daggers or sealed off the room. Three petitioners sympathetic to Minaria were led away, dumbfounded, to the Minarian's own lockup.

Nali gave a curt nod, sending the rest of the squads fanning out to scour the palace. He yanked the dead Minarian from the throne, letting him slide to the bottom of the dais before blood could stain the fine satin cushions.

"Spare the prisoners?" a Gnat called.

Nali shrugged his indifference, then nodded, his heart beating the sheer thrill of his revenge. He didn't want the feeling to stop. He gripped his sword and crossbow with the eagerness vengeance brought him.

Then he recognized a young woman led to meet him. More like a girl. The fire in him died. Eyes down-cast, belly swollen with Loch Asmodiel's treachery, Laria Keeper's knees bent in courtesy. She remained silent for his sentence.

"She came to us," her Gnat escort offered. "Says she'll give you Aron."

"You'd turn on your own fa?" Nali queried.

"He sold me!" Laria declared with such venom that Nali felt the pain of it stab through him. Reddened eyes, wounded with a hurt and humiliation he knew he'd never understand, but likely would find in his own daughter, made her pale face a beautiful tragedy. An image of Resala tossing her hair over her shoulder came to him. Before he could stop himself, he had sunk to a step, head in hand. He nodded then and waved them away as the pleasure of his vengeance lost its sweetness.

In an hour, Gnats had secured the palace, the Shandean prisoners in the dungeons replaced by Minarians and traitors. While a secretive search continued for Aron, Gnats returned to the hall to await Nali's cue, their anxiety making them grin foolishly. At last, Nali nodded, sending a man scurrying up the stairwell to once again raise the Shandean pennant over the palace. Another peered out a side door of the hall, dropping his arm when he saw the pennant unfurl above.

The three Gnat leaders and their men burst through the wide doors of the reception hall and raced into the courtyards. Gnats throughout the city attacked at the pennant's cue. From far distant, came a wild shriek as Gnats outside the walls took the outposts before the gates.

A few Minarians tried to burst into homes to seek cover. But residents quickly reported them. A few old men and women had no qualms about clubbing some Minarian holed up in an alley or seeking refuge in waste piles.

Before sunset this blustery day three weeks into the cold moon, the Gnats accounted for every Minarian in the city and Harbor. Forty known traitors idled in the dungeons beside another one hundred Minarians who surrendered. Seventy Gnats fell.

While Jan and Tel supervised the establishment of defenses on the walls, and other Gnats busted arms out of hiding and broke food from the Minarian coffers, Nali paced the long stair up to the Window of the Sun.

It had been a victory. Easy to gain, in retrospect, but accomplished by less than ten thousand regulars. He hadn't even called up those west of the Harbor. It only proved the occupation should never have occurred. And Laria's wounded expression kept reappearing in his thoughts, pushing out more important details. When he tried to turn his mind away, it was with a toss of Resala's long hair before his eyes, or a giggle from Kia in his ears, or Olna's sad smile as she trudged into the unknown bearing a child destined to die at the hands of Minaria. He pictured the broad belly hanging on Laria like a burden to be shed at the end of a wearying journey, something not quite part of her. His hand reached out, stroking the smooth stone sill. Shande should have been able to resist. Victory twisted his face into a sour scowl.

He peered down at the Harbor, hearing Bertal's shrill voice at the base of the stairwell as the boy spoke to one of Nali's aides. The Minarian ships had fled. It would take months for the enemy to call up an army, provision ships and sail all the way to Sihmad Shal. By then, certainly, Arshal would arrive. The timing would be just right: Kedtair would rise as the Minarian fleet accompanying Ghyldus arrived at Sihmad Shal, while all the armies of Shande stood ready to defeat him. At that same hour as Kedtair left the horizon, the Pladde would break open their rebellion, Arenh and Shiad attack, Shikora blockade the straits into the Sea of Simiriel, and Otayr hold the Minarians from retreating out of the Harbor. First, Ghyldus must decide to sail with his fleet, and come to Sihma Harbor. The thought made Nali go chill. They counted on so much.

As the sun sank into a bank of clouds looming in the west, sending shafts of orange light out to gild the city's walls, Nali found no euphoria in standing openly in this tower again, wearing his derna robes, commanding. Sage, they called him, a courtesy title reserved for Visionaries. They hung on his words, followed him without question, and revered his name. If they knew his doubts, they might have thrown down their arms and gone home. The cloud bank overtook the sun, only streaky shafts reaching out to give a creamy glow to the haze hanging over the sea, before winking out to leave a gray dusk.

Below him, an old man clung to the rail as he climbed up to a battlement. The silhouetted man carried tools to repair the destruction the Minarians had wrought. Bent to a task so menial, yet important, he reminded Nali of his fa, Drul, running at one end of a litter. All over the city, people cleansed and mended, clanged and rattled and shouted. Once again, Sihmad Shal girded for war.

The one comfort to which Nali clung as he pondered the variables in his plan came from the strange words he memorized from the Lierye. Cree had foreseen this event, even foreseen Nali, though the Visionary never relayed that information to anyone but an ancient book, and appeared to have forgotten much of what he'd written as the centuries passed. Only historians and scribes perused the Lierye's pages, a tome that mostly recounted weather, the fortune of crops, commerce, officials visiting, or treaties signed, and the census. It listed the prophecies read at the birth of the royals and detailed the actions of sovereigns or justice meted out.

Hidden in its pages, Nali also found the osfothye dreams of kings and Visionaries, all duly noted by Cree or others of his guild. Snippets of Cree's foreknowledge before he lost it held import in ways historians had never imagined. The power such Visionaries once possessed stunned him. Cree, a counselor in Ebon's time, had been so much more in the young days of Shande than statistician and advisor. He had the power to command kings to his will. As Idenai, he knew the minds of the gods, and thus the minds of the enemy in the Great War. There Nali found the key Cree left for him, the weakness.

If Nali could use the ancient knowledge correctly, he could foul Ghyldus's imagery about which he'd heard so much. He memorized words Cree had penned for him in an ancient tongue that Nali didn't know if he could pronounce, or even interpret truly. Though long dead, Cree gave Nali an inheritance of knowledge like none the gods had ever before imparted. This small glimmer of hope made Nali's decisions easier. It couldn't erase the doubt entirely. He may appear undaunted, his mere words oddly compelling men to honor and obey him, but he never felt completely sure he didn't merely lead them to their dooms.

Nali stood long in the tower as he watched the stars pop out after the last light faded. The moon as it approached the western horizon glowed out sudden and bright with the sun's departure, highlighting the wisps of smoke still rising from the burned warehouses and again turning to a creamy haze of mist on the sea. It glimmered on the Harbor water, sending a sparkle of light upward as it had that night when Arshal called the fog. Nali whirled and stared east toward Otayr, in silent plea for Arshal to hurry home.

At last, he descended into the darkness of the cheerless and stripped palace to hear the cases of the traitors imprisoned in that dank dungeon where Cree had come to Nali's feverish mind.

He also must again face Laria, whose woeful eyes bled so freely from her hurt.

Nali could see that she had no bile left in her to hold in contempt her mewling father. His bleating excuses mixed with guilt-ridden charges against Nali's arrogance, or the king's absence, each word falling from his mouth like sour milk, spittle dribbling from his red face in its effort to vindicate sins committed by coercion. Laria cringed with Aron's every word. Nali had to wonder which fate was worse, hers to have been sold so high to witness a fall so low, or her nine siblings, who may, or may not have survived her fa's attempts to help them.

Having dispensed with all the other petitioners, Nali at last stood from the blue satin cushion two steps down from the throne. He faced Aron Keeper, his onetime friend and comrade, the man who had sold Pedr, and by extension tortured Nali. He felt physically ill.

"Your sentence is death," Nali whispered, striding past Aron's red and stricken face to the door opening onto the courtyard. He wondered, as he gasped in the freshness of night, if Shande could ever be sound again.

16: Unmasked

"Afraid you might be proven a fake?" Resala challenged, gathering her robe to cover herself. She pulled from his gentle grasp, lip curling with distaste. Two high blotches of color in her cheeks gave her face more life than he'd seen in months, yet emphasized the deathly paleness of her skin. She brushed her fingers through her hair, letting the long locks splatter his face before tossing them aside as she spun from his bed.

He shook his head, smiling. How she challenged him! "Testing, testing, always."

He tried to catch her gaze, but seldom could. She always found some unimportant mote of space to stare into with unflappable concentration. He wondered if he would ever pierce her armor for good, strike her heart the killing blow and at last mold her to his needs. But then, he might miss the challenge.

"I think you fear you'll be proven nothing but a pawn in your master's game." She looked him up and down with a critical eye. "Nothing but a tool. You are no god, not even a man. Just the machine of a power larger than you, like Verdred or the Hogde are to you."

"Tisk, tisk," he laughed with a leer. "Why would you want to speed the demise of your fool brother? Likely, my men have already taken –"

"They haven't. And he'll destroy you."

"Tomorrow I will order a fleet of nine thousand to Shande. That will prove –"

"It will prove nothing," she asserted. "You are inflated, living high on your laurels. What are your nine thousand? Shela's taken now. There are rebellions in Sihmad Shal. Obviously,

Habdelion's forces were too strong for your fleet. What did Anlon's warning mean? That you sent too few. They're not enough."

"Habdelion's cur suggested your brother thinks he will be strong enough to face me when the star is overhead. Would you urge me go forth now, in the last moon, when I will arrive early? That would foul your plans."

"Are you afraid that under Kedtair Arshal can defeat you?"

"Maybe I can make the star never rise," he threatened.

A shrill laugh escaped. "You're just afraid."

"Still, the matter lies, I would arrive too early."

"By the time you gather your men, and sail –"

"If I choose to."

Resala paced to the door of his chamber, pulling her robe tight about her and clasping her arms across her waist. Did she know how strong she was?

"Then you will forever be fighting this war. When all of your reinforcements are gone, when the children are sent, the old men and women, when you've run out of soldiers to fight for you, finally you'll have to face the King of Shande. Then we'll see who is stronger. Yours is but a show."

"Look for me in your dreams, dear one," he laughed as she opened the door.

She spun and left, but she couldn't escape him. He filled her dreams with his mocking smile long hours after she had fallen into bed, nightmares that held the evil threads of his spells, dreams where her acquiescence would bring Esthen and Peshal smiling from violent graves, dreams that ripped bodies to shreds with each day she resisted, that twisted everyone she had ever known into a bloody pulp, that begged her for mercy. She was strong. But he was God.

He stood at attention, his master having arrived to hear the case of yet another petitioner. He stared at the small window in the hall as a first moon storm blew up, banging the sash, flickering candles, and sending a cascade of papers to the floor. As rain lashed in through the window, a haggard ship's captain told of the suffering of his men as, with short provisions, the ship had retreated from Sihmad Shal because of rebellion. He cited flaming arrows scorching decks, catching on the sails, and good men dead. Under spare canvas, they had made Saran for repair, forced to sail all the way home with insufficient supplies, and short of crew.

His master's face grew livid as the man recounted his story. A finger pointed at him.

"Two hundred and fifty ships, to depart immediately. Catapults, horses, one thousand warriors per ship. This will end! I am tired of it!" his master declared.

The princess's face broke into a smug and mocking smile. "So, you hear my counsel?"

"We will arrive before expected, and not where expected, Lady." He gave her an evil chuckle, reaching up to tweak a pale cheek. "And you will join me, to see the last of your family erased with my contempt. On my ship no more will handmaidens deliver poisons to foil me. I will see you plump with offspring, repayment for the trouble you brought me."

He could not understand why he felt anger at his master's declaration. The mere tone used with the princess made his heart pound in his chest, the blood rise to pulse against his cheek guards, his hands clench at his sides. He couldn't fathom why his breath exhaled as a hot hiss through bared teeth.

"And," his master continued, "I have no doubt you will relay this information to your Pladde contacts. Do not give me those innocent eyes! I know your games! Your servants will not leave the palace. When we make landfall at Canwyn Point, there will be no infant army to slow us. We will sweep victorious through the land. This upstart king of yours in whom you hold such unfounded stock, will be left no support to feed his goals. When I am through, the people will call for his death to stop their own suffering."

"Canwyn Point?" the princess queried, as if she hadn't heard what followed.

"Would that be a tidbit of news to pass to your Pladde friends?" he laughed. "We will strike where they least expect it and this ridiculous rebellion will be crushed. If we leave within a fortnight, we will land long before your star rises. The seas and navigation of no concern. You are a fool, dear lady. You played your role too well. Yes, you will draw me to Shande as you promised your brother. It will not be to his benefit. I will not allow a gaggle of Shandean farmers to defy me. This rebellion will end if I have to decimate the land, if none of your beloved shals remain. The land can be repopulated with the faithful, the deserving –"

"How could you?"

Laughing, still staring at her, his hand waved in the air. "Verdred!" he ordered. "A fleet of ten thousand to Shela. March five thousand to Sefresal. Yes, I recall Anlon's warning. I know that is the heart of resistance. Do you think my couriers are blind to the games played in those mountains? I played them into my hand, will crush the fools who dare to toy with the God of Ea. Ready my fleet to sail within a fortnight, to Canwyn. Assign extra guards on the princess and her handmaidens. None of her servants may leave the palace nor anyone her servants contact."

With a swift glance, unseen, at Resala, Verdred departed to issue his silent orders. Somewhere inside of him he sensed he shouldn't. As he gestured to his underlings, signing the God of Ea's edicts, he remembered he had a purpose: to protect the princess, the mountdoe-like creature so pale he imagined milk when he tried to place the lustre of her skin. What would her interests be?

Once out of his master's sight, he stood long, trying to remember that small thought he sensed inside of him, but couldn't quite place. He sensed his actions should be different than what his master ordered. But what?

The princess's servant ambled down the hall on some small errand. He grabbed her arm and yanked her into an alcove, ignoring the whimper that escaped the girl as she tried to squirm from his grasp, deadly hands clenching her arm like the talons of a hawk around a field mouse, leaving dark bruises.

He shoved his face into hers. "Ships to sail. He knows her connections. Landing at Canwyn Point," he rasped at the wide eyes gazing up at him.

"They were going to strike the warehouses –" she stammered. Why did she admit so incriminating a truth?

"Stop them! He'll think she ordered it!" What did his mouth

say? Some other demon manipulated his words. How could his mouth defy his master's wishes? He remembered Teshet, and a small shack somewhere beyond the edge of the city where he had given her a token. But why? Were these people against his master? Why would he defy his doting master?

"Just don't do anything. Just stay with her." The words came from his mouth, a mouth he knew was mute. Yet the words came. What did he say? "You won't be allowed to leave the palace. Cancel all plans. He knows she plots against him. I will send word to the shack beyond the city."

Treason. The word echoed through the almost empty recesses of his mind. Weren't traitors killed? To whom was she a traitor? If he abetted her, didn't that make him a traitor too? Must he kill himself to save his master's honor? The word honor sounded strange in his thoughts, a word not in the collection of concepts his master had drilled into him. How could he speak when he knew he couldn't, think thoughts not in him to imagine?

The mouth he knew contained no voice continued to speak at the frightened girl. His deadly fingers, which could have moved so swift to her throat and ended this confusion, loosened on her arm. Then he released her and shoved her into the hallway, prepared to give the rest of his instructions in sign, not understanding what possessed him to speak to the inconsequential Pladde servant. And moments later he could not remember doing it.

Teshet stood trembling before her mistress, her eyes wide with fear. "It is too soon, true?"

Resala paced, furious, her face twisted with her concentration. But no answers came. She paused at one end of a path worn before the window, her hand slamming down on the wash stand so hard a small vase holding the first pre-spring blossoms overturned. Her hands balled into fists as she stared at the spreading pool of water trickling away from the vase. She grabbed the offending vase and hurled it at the window where it smashed into fragments against the sill. Her eyes bore the caged cast that most frightened Teshet, brought the princess closest to harming herself. Like a pent animal, her chest heaving with frustration, her eyes red with her fury, she again took up her frantic pacing, ignoring the crunch of the broken vase beneath her slippered feet.

"Lady –" Teshet prodded.

"It'll be a slaughter. All this for nothing! Peshal died for this! Your people! For nothing! He'll destroy us and go on undaunted." She shook her head, continuing to pace, faster and faster as if it would focus her thoughts and reveal an answer.

"You cannot give up hope!"

"It's over, Teshet!" Resala shrieked. She spun at one end of her pacing. "He'll come too soon!"

"A message went out –"

"Do you know how far it is? By the time our armies reorganize, and take to the road for someplace they've never seen, never planned for, ships will have arrived –"

"You do not know this, Lady." Teshet feared her mistress's tenuous hold on sanity.

"He knows everything!" Resala shrieked. "I thought I had him duped. He saw through me all along, knows everything in my head."

"I do not believe that."

"He knew about the remedy you brought. He knew! He knew I passed information and plotted his ruin. How did he know if not through my own conceit thinking I hid it from him?"

Teshet shook her head, lips pursed. "It was a servant caught unawares by his gaze. You must believe that! You have a power over him! You cannot give up! Perhaps you can convince him to sail on to Sihmad Shal after all. Perhaps you can slow the departure. You must try. You cannot give up without a fight."

Resala sank to the edge of her bed. "I've been fighting so long, Teshet. I've no will left inside me."

"It is there. You are just determined to ignore it."

"He's grown too strong!"

"You are letting him steal the initiative. Take it from him! As you did before. Foul his plans! All you need is a few weeks' delay. Slow him!"

"But it'll still place us in the wrong port."

"It may be enough time for Shande to adjust plans." Teshet's tone prickled with thorns, a harshness she had never before used with this woman she so respected. "Do you think your brother gives in to despair?"

"Who knows where Arshal is," Resala muttered.

"Exactly. The demon does not even know. Your king evades Eidhalt, has rallied armies and sovereigns to his aid. You must be as strong as he is."

Resala hung her head. "I feel like a wasted entity, like Peshal and Esthen who died too soon. All martyrs for a lost cause. We must delay them. Perhaps another raid –"

"No," Teshet said. "Verdred says any action by the Pladde will be blamed on you. I fear for your life, Lady. It must be with guile if you are to slow him."

Resala looked up from her hands. "Verdred? Why would he, how could he?"

"How should I know?" Teshet stammered, her palms growing slick. "You must not think of it, ever, especially around Ghyldus. I should not have spoken."

"Explain this to me! Have you trusted some spy –"

"No," Teshet turned from the wounded expression on Resala's face. "You have enough concerns. Just concentrate on belaying Ghyldus. Everything else is out of your hands. Pray if you must. The only help we count on now is within you."

Teshet sped from the room, the door slamming behind her to cut the princess off from her only comfort in this dismal land.

Resala sagged, thwarted by her only friend and deceived or kept ignorant by the only person she could trust.

She appealed to the cold, gray beams above her for some answer she had yet to find. She could pray the winds would fight them, or the sea. Her eyes narrowed. The sea. The route Peshal chose. An image of the dark amethyst depths of her own eyes seemed to somehow swirl before her like a rush of waves. She turned to the mirror atop her wash stand. Her face appeared stark and pale, like the ivory froth cresting the dark amethyst waves in the Harbor, rising up in wine-colored swells to break on the lavender coral in the shallows. Her hair coiled about her shoulders like dried seagrass on the shore. She must think of the sea, the back of the beast that would carry her home, bear her to her disgrace. She must pray it swallowed them all.

She stared into her own eyes, mesmerized by the sense she had of falling inside of herself. Is that how Latra felt when she gazed at her? Is that what locked Verdred's mind from Ghyldus? Is that what stole Anlon's voice? Had they fallen within themselves when they saw something mirrored in her eyes? Or had they fallen within her?

Staring into herself, she saw a power she never admitted. Something fought her for control. She sensed Ghyldus's enchantment strong in her. His will prevailed when she despaired. She mouthed a plea. The name 'Terremar' reflected from the face in the mirror. Calm entered her limbs, eased her panting breaths and slowed her pounding heart. With each lifebeat she sensed the blood surging through her veins with less fury, felt the heat drawn from her face.

Pacing to the mirror, she leaned on the water-splattered top of the stand to press her face close to her image. Again, she breathed her appeal as she stared into her own eyes, seeking solace from all the fears nagging her. She prayed to herself, to Terremar, to the waves and winds that would carry her to Shande on swift wings if she couldn't convince them to honor her plea. She found an answer, or the sense of some such, locked beyond her knowledge, but within her eyes. She called on things, elements, not part of her. But she sensed they were hers to beg. The answer existed within her like a great treasure she would one day reach.

Hours passed before a knock on her door brought her gaze from the mirror. When she entered Ghyldus's adjoining chambers, a different woman answered the summons.

17: Home

The ship dropped anchor up the northeast coast of the bay, within sight of the soft glow of the lighthouse. The thick fog of a greening moon-warm night meeting winter-cold sea concealed the vessel and the shadow of its companions further east from all but gulls stirring from sleep to investigate the wake for bounty.

A boat dropped with a slight splash, followed by a lone figure wrapped against the damp fog. With a soft hail from the ship, and a bare wave from the figure, the oarlocks creaked as oars plowed into the light swell with experienced precision.

Soon the natural current and the tug of shore-bound waves eased the rower's labor. With the experience of one familiar with these waters, the rower guided his craft around the reefs and breakwaters, gliding into the fog-veiled harbor unnoted by lighthouse or guards as dawn tinged the fog ice-white.

The shadow of the Rigannon River bridge loomed out of the mist as the rower labored against the strong current greeting the calm of the Harbor delta. The water swirled around piles charred by fire as the river, swollen with rain, fought to throw him back to sea. He knew this river. Soon he rowed in a rhythm, cutting across currents with experience as he found the calm water to speed him to his destination with the least effort. He passed the ghostly shape of enemy ships without raising an alarm and now rowed into the unoccupied stretch of countryside. Once again, he tempted danger and escaped.

The fog thinned as he left the cool sea behind. Dawn passed and a watery sun burned away the mist at sea's edge, promising a warm day to come. He pulled at the oars, the effort barely raising a sweat as his chest drew even breaths. At last, he found the marker he sought, not far beyond a small stream cascading down the scarp. On the right, a twisted old tree clung to the top of the bank.

Stopping short of it, he pulled his boat ashore on the east bank among the jumbled boulders strewn by the river's force. At last, he reached the spot he sought. Without a pause, he stepped through the entrance of Peshal's Tunnel.

A spear pressed against his chest, scraping armor but halting him in the entryway. Before he could react, the guard spun him into the tunnel, propelling him against the wall. An instant later the guard had fallen to his knees, grasping at the hand bearing the signet ring.

"Forgive me, King." The guard's voice quivered with something other than fear.

"Is he here?" King Arshal asked with quiet authority.

The guard pointed his spear down the long torch-lit tunnel then raised his horn. Arshal shook his head, pressing a finger to his lips with a small smile that made the guard's hands shake.

Arshal noted the wear on the tunnel floor, the new niches carved in tunnel walls where empty pallets lay in low rooms. The empty rooms gave Arshal an eerie sense of space and solitude as his footsteps echoed before him. He counted on thousands. The silence became ever more oppressive until finally he entered the cavern beneath the market square. After so many long months, he stood again beneath his city. He noted long benches propped against the wall and a floor worn by the daily passage of hundreds. Minarian ships stood at anchor in the Harbor. Had they decimated Nali's forces? Had recruitment fallen off here, the Gnats around the Sea of Iyrafael an exception?

He took the steps up from the damp cavern to the dry tunnel beyond. At last, the corridor took a long turn and he saw a square of light ahead, the door into the storerooms propped open.

He slowed as he neared. A figure bent over a massive book, scribbling notes on crumpled parchment. Hunched over, back to him, Arshal had a fleeting thought of Cree, or even Ramel.

Nali's hawkish green eyes turned to him. Arshal noted the blue and white sash across the derna's brow, braided from long strips of cloth that hung down his back as part of a single plait of hair. Arshal sensed something dangerous and unpleasant caged beneath the band and felt glad Nali kept it hidden. Scars marred the contour of Nali's neatly trimmed beard, and the face had a pinched look, dark circles ringing his eyes. But the glitter of delight and humor in his gaze hinted of his old friend.

"You're late," Nali stated as he rose to his feet.

Arshal grasped Nali in a hug that forced the air from the derna's lungs. "Not too late I hope." Arshal stepped back to study Nali. "You haven't gone and won the war on me, have you?"

The two stared at each other. Arshal noted how Nali stooped a bit and wore chain mail beneath his robes. Nali circled Arshal, clicking his tongue against the roof of his mouth.

"Why, Arshal, you actually look like a king." Nali gestured at the glint of stellan breastplates peeking from beneath a thick, royal blue mantle.

Arshal flung back his cloak and turned for Nali to view the garments crafted by Shandean refugees waiting idle outside Farlal's halls. Nali plucked at a white linen blouse, embroidered in blue, and the light blue quilted tunic that protected him from the press of armor. A skirt of chain mail reached halfway to his knees – a gift from Farlal – and again stockings, not mountbuckskin, hugged his legs. But his high boots were tough hide and laced just beneath the knee, a dagger sheathed at the calf. Nali reached up and touched one of Arshal's braids bound with black leather wound with gold.

"Sporting a new fashion I see." Nali chuckled as he yanked on a braid.

"Is that a way to treat your long-awaited king?" Arshal grinned as he settled on a crate. He thumbed a page of the book Nali had left open. "The Lierye?" he asked with a raised brow.

"Much to be learned," Nali said, closing the book and moving it beyond Arshal's reach. "From all quarters. Kyne gave me the last news of you, moons ago, and that on the heels of all sorts of rumors. You've a bit of a tale to tell!"

"So, where are your soldiers, Nali? Gnats took me in out by Iyrafael, but here I see only empty mats. What tales do you have to tell?" Arshal grabbed Nali's wrist and held it up to view a shackle scar in the lamp light.

Nali yanked his arm away, rubbing his wrist, his expression a closed door. "I got cocky and paid for it. As for the Gnats? Come and see for yourself!" Nali's face smiled bright again, as if a shade had opened.

The derna motioned for Arshal to follow him to the open door into the passages above. Arshal paused at a door on a landing, closed, but with muffled voices and calls coming from beyond.

"Lockup," Nali offered. "It's a much nicer place, now." That veiled look briefly flitted across Nali's face again, before the twinkle came back into his eyes.

When they exited behind the curtain in the reception hall, Nali pressed a finger to his lips and guided his king up the stairs, then down the hall to the open door up to the Tower of the Sun. Not a soul had they seen. So, the palace rested in Shandean hands, yet Minarian ships anchored in the Harbor.

Arshal stared out at the city lying below him, opening up before him like a flower to the sun, unfolding in all its brightness and a flurry of activity. No gods' gardens grew on the battlements, nor in the courtyards and window boxes, but everywhere royal blue-clad soldiers ranged the walls, archers staring out onto the plains, wagons moving to and from forges, carpenters hammering and masons bricking. Unlike the eve of war three years ago, the scene appeared organized. They moved about their business with ease in their roles, like Lharan Guardsmen.

"Gods," Arshal muttered, shaking his head. "But –" he pointed at the Minarian ships in the Harbor.

Nali laughed. "Just another prank. We took them off the ways, or confiscated them when they came to port. It's to foul Ghyldus when he arrives, and gives us an edge when enemy ships come into port. It's confused more than a few. Our fleet grows."

"I always said you had the head for command, Nali."

Nali shrugged and turned away. "Learned the hard way. We've lost a lot of good folk. It took a while but you've got yourself a real army now. I don't know how Khoti or Eithur fare, but there's about twelve thousand Gnats here on the walls, thousands more around Iyrafael and down by Etaleah, and west along the Quelica, awaiting your call or Eithur's. We've another ten thousand Home Guard, a militia as fine as any. This is the army we should have had, Arshal."

"We had fifty thousand during the invasion," Arshal said, his smile faltering.

"Fifty thousand what? Oh, sure, if you want to count fire brigades, cooks and attendants we can come up with a higher score. The soldiers we fielded then, King, were all cooks and firemen. We've got the real thing now: fine warriors, armed and trained with attendants to serve them. No one's got to use a club or bare knuckle because he's got nothing else. No one's without at least leather armor. All know the bow, as well as the sword, and we got ourselves Shiadin crossbows and five hundred marksmen to shoot them. These aren't soft clay just shaped by the potter. They've been through the kiln and are ready to serve. We've remolded Shande, Arshal. We're now a nation of warriors. Our women sport swords at their hips, not children. Our elders weave bandages, not tales by the fire. The youths play Kill the Minarian, not Pilfer the Pie. They wear their daggers proud, little soldiers, like Khoti's made. My boy's down there somewhere." He waved an arm at the scene below. "Attending a soldier. My girls – " Nali didn't finish, but peered up at Arshal. "Are you ready, Arshal?" he whispered. "Did you figure it out? The things I didn't know enough to tell you?"

Arshal straightened, dragging his gaze from the Gnats on the walls. "We won't know until the time comes, will we?" He tried to place just what felt so strange about the encounter, about both of them.

"So, you've learned to use your voice." Nali nodded. "Very good."

Arshal chuckled. "You're sounding like Ramel, a cantankerous and bothersome Visionary I butt heads with in Hainad. He had strange methods of teaching."

"Ah. He taught you about the stone, and for you to have made it this far, I'd say you learned to stay away from that room Cree always sent you to."

"How did you know about all that?" Arshal demanded.

"A lot of things are in the Lierye. Cree's a patient teacher on paper. The problem is he remembered things wrong when he trained you. Perhaps even this Ramel guided you wrong, not meaning to. Some things aren't in the Lierye." He shrugged. "Some things are just in me. You can defeat Ghyldus if you learned what you must to face him. You need all the elements –"

"Ramel said that."

"Did this Ramel tell you how to manipulate those elements?" Arshal shook his head. "And I can't just tell you, either. Partly, because it's speculation. Partly, because you have to seek it in yourself, though you likely can figure it from hints." He gave an exaggerated sigh. "Well, King, in the short time we have, I'm afraid you're going to have to suffer through more lessons."

Arshal groaned before he let out a chuckle. "My fisher-counselor will teach the ways of the gods?"

"Don't mock me."

Arshal felt the sting of a power he never before heard from Nali, but somehow sensed he'd awaited. Something from a vision.

"I didn't mean to offend."

Nali waved the apology away. "I know. I haven't been a fisher since the day we met." Nali rested against the sill, staring at Arshal as if measuring him against the role he must fill. After a moment, Nali sighed and leaned forward to rest his hands on his knees. In broken snatches at first, then in a scholarly and succinct manner, Nali chronicled all that had occurred since they parted, and what news he'd gathered.

In contrast, Arshal's account of himself spilled out like flood waters bursting banks, a search for assurances he'd made the right choices. When both finished their tales, silence remained between them more awkward now than their first meeting. The door banged open, Bertal running up the stairs to stumble to a halt on seeing Arshal. Nali's hand dropped to the boy's shoulder, an instinctive move Bertal didn't shrug off.

"Jan sent me for you, Fa. He's seen a ship of Otayr to the northeast."

Nali patted the shoulder. "Your duties finished?" The boy nodded. "Laria needs help –"

"Watch that demon's whelp again?" Bertal demanded in a tone likely heard among the soldiers.

"You've been very lucky, boy," Nali said softly his words carrying an odd mix of power and menace. "Don't be judging people whose suffering you'll never understand. The lady didn't want the child, nor the child want the fa. What's made's made, and not for you to judge."

The boy squeezed from the room to run to his father's bidding.

"I'm certain you haven't given yourself credit for anything near what you've accomplished," Arshal said to break the awkward moment. "From thirty Gnats to tens of thousands!"

Nali shrugged. "I'm certain we took the longest and hardest roads just to end up right back where we started, facing battle."

"It had to be this way. I see that now," Arshal admitted. "We were like children who didn't know the first thing about how to be who we're meant to be. I had to nearly die to decide I wanted to live, to learn to use common sense, to learn to survive, to hate." He cocked an eyebrow at Nali who courted a secret smile. "Was that in the Lierye? It wasn't in our visions."

Nali's eyes became small points filled with keen interest, the scholar researching a metamorphosis. Arshal had a crawling sense of nakedness as if the derna evaluated each bit of the king's tale and decided how it had transformed him.

"You've changed, too, Nali," Arshal said, surly.

Nali sat back with a smile. "I make you nervous?" he asked. "Some habits are hard to set aside, even among friends. Yes, Arshal, we're still friends. Soon the strange in us will feel familiar." Arshal straightened at the telling remark. "Some things aren't in the Lierye," he admitted with a pleased chuckle.

"You're so different. Maybe you should study yourself –"

Nali laughed again, holding his side though his laughter was soft. "I already know what's muddled my mind. I'm just looking for similarities. I know you've grown by this ordeal, Arshal. I just still feel we could have saved a lot of heartache, somehow. I suppose it all paid off. It took every shred of power in your voice to talk Farlal out of his fleet."

"Speaking of which, those poor people have been crammed for weeks on the smallest ships Farlal could find. Children to grace the city again –"

"On the eve of war? Can any of these folk fight?"

Arshal laughed. "You and Khoti, no thoughts but your armies. Three years gives us a lot of youths capable of attending and a few old enough to learn a thing or two. They're a long way behind us. Instead, they can be a big boon in support."

"You should've left them there until the end. More mouths to feed on few enough supplies."

"We're well enough supplied," Arshal grinned. "Otayr was more than happy to see us leave. It cost less than us consuming all the regions' supplies before they reached the city. I'm thankful Shande's kings never kept such councils. The king is powerless without his gaggle of entrenched advisors, each with a region for which he wrangles favors. And if the king resists, the counselor encourages revolt. It's such a game."

"Nothing like ordering your liege lords to cough up an army or else." Nali chuckled. He laid a hand on Arshal's shoulder. "I spent the night poring over Cree's horrendous scribblings. I need an hour of sleep, perhaps two, and I'm late to meet Jan and Tel. Let's bring your ships in."

With a distracted wave, Nali left, the braid bobbing on his back in a carefree last image as he took the stairs down, two at a time. Arshal stared out the window at his altered home. Several burroughs were merely charred ruins, lean-tos and shanties the only shelter, garish and crude, the light and color stolen.

He studied the open ocean, seeking the glimpse of sails that would herald the Minarian fleet. He reached into his tunic and pulled from his pocket the one treasure besides his sword, ring and crown that survived Simiriel and years of travel to be returned to its promised destination. He laid the Minarian arrowhead on the sill, staring without seeing the broken stub of wood that still held traces of his father's blood, returned home as promised.

A servant came and left to carry out his orders, leaving him feeling as if he stood at the helm again, the best sailors manning his ship. He leaned on the sill and peered at each distant breaker that momentarily appeared like a phantom sail on the horizon as his fingers worked the splintered and broken arrow shaft. Soon he'd ride into battle for his vengeance, Marol bearing the new standard his people had crafted based on the devices on his sword: an eagle clinging to the back of a lion trampling the flames, the name 'Dyn Eadon' beneath it. Power of Ea, Farlal had named him.

As the greening moon of the Year of Kedtair stretched into the blossom moon, the rising of Kedtair but a moon away, Arshal slipped into the role of sovereign returned. Quickly, he officially named Nali his advisor, and affirmed the tripartite Gnat leadership.

Unlike his father, his quarters and hall remained austere, the treasures of Shande remaining hidden until true victory. Only the small circlet crown and the glimmering raiment his people had made for him denoted his rank. His sword remained at his side, always, as did the armor he wore, occasionally even in his sleep. When he needed to ease his tension, he sought challenge, anything he could do to constantly test his reflexes, agility and skill. He sparred with Nali, who imparted what wisdom he cared to share between parries and thrusts as the two worked hours each day beneath the spring sun as if their practice could speed Shande to freedom. It was between those parries they spoke, too, of the personal things. Arshal talked of his fascination with Dynresa, his fears and failures. Nali described how he fed on the pain that still haunted him, a pain that brought him shouting from his sleep at dream demons bearing medallions, how something about Laria drew him, or of his fears for what his daughters had become and his failure to save Olna. Finally, they realized the friendship they feared lost hadn't been found until now.

One balmy evening in the middle of the blossom moon, Arshal and Nali sat in the reception hall as the last petitioner departed, sunset scattering the light from the two windows beside the dais. The warm glow took the cold from the austere hall. Nali sat in a high-backed chair that now stood beside the throne, an indication to all of how important the king found his Gnat commander.

About to go to their meal, they paused as the courtyard rang out with the clatter of horse hooves. A familiar trio stalked into the hall, a herald dogging them and demanding their business. Hard journey marked their clothing, dust clinging to the crevices in their faces and sweat-dampened, wind-whipped hair. Arshal and Nali leaped up to greet old friends.

Konner stared about him, his slashing grin sizing up the austere hall. "Such a waste of space," he said when Ahrwesz and Aibak prodded him to speak.

"You can't tell me a desire to sightsee brought you here!" Arshal said with a laugh.

Konner's grin faded. "Not much could bring me from home but plenty of news, bad. We tried to find Eithur, but gave up. He's travelin' to be unfound and this is too urgent. We heard Kefta was down along the Eilime River. Teckhan went that way, alone. We lost Gelter at an outpost near Saran, but found a farmer we hope delivers our message to Eithur before too late."

Arshal signed for an aide to bring the men chairs, drink and food. He sat on the steps of the dais, leaning forward and staring at the trio. "You take the long way getting to such an urgent message. So, what brings you?"

Aibak took a long drink from his ale then wiped his forearm across his mouth, leaving a streak of dark dirt. "Well, I am here as King Keyen's representative. I meant to join Eithur. But as Konner said, we found no trace of him, only rumor. What that means, we cannot say. It is difficult to conceal an army."

"And we didn't mean to come this far," Ahrwesz muttered. "Thought we'd be home safe in Sefresal by now, watching our own backs for what's to come. If we'd known, we certainly would've sent someone else. We didn't dare trust this to folk not prepared to die to deliver it –"

"And that message?" Nali demanded. "You're mighty slow getting to it."

"Just catching our wind," Konner said with his characteristic grin. "Tale's never so good as when you have to wait for it." He held an empty mug out for the servant to refill. "It was late in the first moon. A Pladde rider came over the Staph-el bridge, blew right by real Minarians, not dressed-up Tawnkats. He kept right on going, stuck full of arrows. Poor fellow died that night to tell us Ghyldus aimed to sail in the middle of the first moon with two hundred and fifty ships crammed to the crowsnest with warriors. He sent a smaller fleet to Shela, and five thousand troops march on Sefresal. Man said Ghyldus had his fill when he found out about Loch Asmodiel." Konner paused to grin at Nali and take half his ale in one gulp.

"It's good news, Konner," Arshal said, his breath quickening. Resala had done it! "Remember, we wanted this –"

"Begging your pardon, Arshal, King," Konner corrected

himself. "But we didn't want him sending armies on Shela and Sefresal! We hope Shikora and Arenh have the straits blockaded, but they might not have the stomach for that much fight. And Sefresal's got barely five hundred to fend off five thousand. Segan's trying to work something out with Shiad and the Pladde to make 'em pay for marching on Sefresal, but we can't make no guarantees. The Tawnkats pretty much used up their store o' tricks. The Minarians are wise to us. And the Pladde resistance numbers less than the Tawnkats was when we started. And I hadn't finished about Ghyldus yet."

Konner took the rest of his ale and held out the mug again. "Ghyldus says 'sure, I'll come to Shande and face that cocksure king,' thinking in his words, mind you. He doesn't have to go just where the king wants him to. He wants to make landfall at Canwyn Point, not Sihma Harbor. Then he can cut across the country and strike without warning, wiping up all those outer defenses. And even if you did notice the change in plans, he figures he'll have more advantage in open field battle with his spears than fighting you dug in on home turf. Canwyn's no one's stomping ground. You don't know its advantages, and neither does he. His intention is he'll be there, and you won't, and with so many soldiers, he's got the numbers to just roll right over us."

Arshal leaned back against the steps, watching Nali from the corner of his eye. "It's what we worried about all along."

Ahrwesz nodded. "He's probably counting on drawing away support by hitting Shela and Sefresal. That way if things don't go his way, he'll still have a foothold, always having us running somewhere or another to stop him while he's building up in the places we're not."

"And," Aibak asked, "Did Shande plan to face so large an army? How many can he hold on two hundred and fifty ships? Five hundred? A thousand? Can Shande call such a muster?"

Arshal stroked his chin. "So, he throws a puzzle at us," Arshal said after a long silence in which Konner put down his fourth ale. "We had to draw his strength, so they're too weak to support another minion of Fyraer. And we need to destroy Ghyldus himself. If he sailed with his army, then we can still hope for success. We need only keep his warriors at bay so I can do my task. Likely, after Ghyldus's demise the majority will surrender –

185

"

"We're hoping on a lot of things again," Nali warned. "For one that you can even reach Ghyldus through all those soldiers. He seems the type of omnipotent creator who will sprawl in comfort in his sedan during the bloodshed and come forward only when it's time to gloat."

"He's to prove a point, won't step out until there's no threat to him," Konner agreed, swallowing the echo of his ale.

"In the meantime, they'll outnumber us –" Arshal began.

"If we're there to face them." Nali stood, his spine snapping. "I can call the Gnats ready by dawn, a call to arms for the outlands takes longer and our supply lines will be far behind. But we can march on light rations."

"And if Canwyn's a ruse?" Arshal posed, massaging his temples with one hand. "What if he leads us from the city then sweeps in when we're gone?"

"Then he does, and we lose," Nali declared. "The militia will be here. We'll still have Peshal's Tunnel and thousands of troops." Nali took the newly filled mug of ale from Konner's hand and emptied it down his throat. "We can field maybe thirty-five thousand –" he began.

"Against over a hundred thousand?" Arshal asked with a smile.

Nali shrugged. "We're counting on Khoti, Eithur and Kefta, wherever they are."

"First moon," Arshal mused. "If they sailed on time, how long would it take? Before Kedtair rises? How long can we hold?"

"It's no good speculating," Konner said with an ale-bleary grin. "If we can't stop 'em, well, we die trying."

"But can we beat them to Canwyn?" Arshal asked.

Nali held Konner's mug out to the servant. "It's Ghyldus's move. At least we have Aibak and Tawnkats with us." He took a sip of the ale, wiping foam from his beard as he handed it to Konner. "With an uprising all around and armies swarming the plains, you can't make it home."

"We resigned ourselves to that." Konner grinned. "I was hoping I'd find Khoti again, see how the boy does."

Nali glanced at Arshal who nodded. "And a messenger to Khoti, if we can find him."

Konner stood and bowed deeply. "Ahrwesz and me would be honored to take on the task after a night's rest and a fresh horse." Konner stumbled forward, Ahrwesz catching him before he fell.

"It was a long ride for a big thirst," Ahrwesz volunteered.

As the three stumbled after the herald, Arshal sprawled in the spacious seat of the throne, one leg dangling over the chair's arm. "They take all this with such good nature when I feel as if the world's falling away under my feet, happy it's ending, and terrified."

"Think of your new standard, Dyn Eadon," Nali said with a cynical smile, the name uttered with the same teasing twist as the title 'Sage' held when Arshal spoke it. "The armies of Shande are that lion trampling the flames, you giving them direction, holding them firm in your talons as you guide them to an end. It's not their task to think on the consequences. Though, you can be sure, Konner's role as one of your talons has something to do with how fast he puts down an ale. Just remember, the lion's feet can't lift far from the ground. The eagle has wings to rise above it all and see things from a different perspective. You're responsible if the brawn's led astray, the soldier's only duties are survival and following your lead."

Arshal grinned. "You've found more meaning in my devices than I ever did. I merely found them intriguing, somehow appropriate."

"They were yours long before the smith made them," Nali said, watching Arshal from the corner of his eye. "You're King. Your role's to lead your people, and when the time comes, deal with the ruler of the enemy. And Ghyldus's role's no different. You just have to soar higher and see more than he."

Nali departed with a rustle of robes. Arshal sat in the darkness of dusk, waving away the servant arriving with a lamp. He no longer entertained thoughts of his certain death, unless to view it as some ultimate test he had to pass, an extra challenge to make the contest interesting. He'd made a promise he would try to keep because his honor required it of him. If Dynresa rode with the Army of the South, as he imagined she might, he wouldn't want her to come so far only to witness his final failure.

Shattering his reflection of Dynresa came an image of the

stone's power, that scene he had glimpsed beside the Sea of Iyrafael when Minarians had dared try to remove his stone. He gazed down at the opal glowing in its own soft light. He wasn't certain he could do all that Nali told him he had to, but he doubted he could ever be more ready, his mind jammed with the advice of seers and long dead kings.

He studied the colors glowing in the palm of his hand. Always the stone had lain in his palm predominately blue. Since that battle near Hainad, flecks of orange and milky white marred the stone's perfection, giving it an illusion of greater depth. He gazed at it. The stone flared a deep red, Ghyldus's color. He closed his fist, quenching the color in his palm, extinguishing it with a thought. He didn't like the way it marred the beauty of his stone. But he wouldn't forget how to call it forth.

He stared into the deepening darkness, his thoughts crowding in faster than he could sort them out. At last, he slammed his fist against the arm of his throne. He had to remember Khoti's admonition: a warrior could not afford to think too much. A healer couldn't think of anything but compassion any more than a warrior could think of anything but his sword. When a just and compassionate leader aimed to take his country into war, both roles needed coddling, each always trying to suppress the other warring within, a constant conflict of doubts and guilts, sniping at one another, a war he knew Khoti waged as well, alone and victorious. He grasped a distant scent of cloves in the air from some mulled wine served somewhere. Survival, he decided, must take his concentration above all else when doubt threatened to suffocate him and dig holes in the confidence he projected. Survival: so he could lead his country back from the abyss of war, to health.

At last, he padded up dark stairs to his rooms. Late into the night he honed his sword and packed his few needs, his mind going over that one goal when the vicious fears scrapped and babbled for his attention, like demon hounds leaping for the jugular.

18: The Army of the South

When Khoti's Army of the South rode north from Shela, but three thousand strong, Khoti split his forces to either bank of the Rigannon. While it might make communication difficult, it would ease their provisioning, improve the range of recruitment, help ensure no Minarian outposts remained behind and allow squads to range through the countryside in search of enemy scouts and stragglers. Often, Khoti and Euzzeldir on the east bank lost sight of Habdelion and Sedaik on the west as the river stretched into broad tangles of swamp or wide expanses of water where other tributaries joined.

When at last they left the Dasirei behind and entered firmer lands where horses grazed on grassy hillsides above brush-filled valleys, a trickle at first, then a steady stream of scouts and messengers found them. Finally, when the army reached the confluence of the Acceber, Eilime and Rigannon rivers, from the cover of wood and vale, by units or singly, clusters of soldiers joined them. Gnats, they claimed. Gnats: weeks south on a fast horse from Sihmad Shal.

Khoti prodded his army north for months. Sometimes days passed before they could bring the entire entourage into one camp, their path so narrow troops moved only a few abreast or in single file, vulnerable, their feet and the hooves of cavalry horses delving a trench in the soils of Shande that soon became a quagmire. Soldiers often went on days-long forays in search of game or Minarian coffers to rob, and supply wagons lurched through undergrowth along marshy riverbanks swollen with winter rains. At first Khoti worried about remaining unseen, rather than making speed. Yet he also needed local squads to find them and needed to destroy the many Minarian outposts along the Rigannon's banks and tributaries.

As the weeks stretched into months to reach the broad banks where the Iyrafael River joined the Rigannon, their ranks quadrupled to twelve thousand on a road that took Khoti's scouts only three weeks of easy riding. Khoti no longer tried to conceal the passage of so many, especially not since they'd developed some shadow of Ghyldus, pacing their every move. At last, he conceded the two commands must converge. They had wanted to come on the Minarian fortification at Etaleah by surprise, but the enemy's shadow assured them otherwise.

Late one night, the creak of oarlocks, the swish of paddles and the thunk of waves rippling against a craft's bow rang out like shrieks in the dark, still night. As Khoti waited on shore for the vessel, he glanced skyward again. A familiar shape swirled across the stars with a glimpse of red eyes then shot away north. If only he could have such messengers. Some Eidhalt imager clearly had cast the hideous illusion to trail them, a cat-like creature with giant red eyes, long canine teeth and leathery, featherless wings. It glided effortlessly above them, its guttural howls and yaps like childhood nightmares come to life. Whether the creature relayed information, or meant only to frighten them, as fast as archers shot one from the sky with a cascade of sparks, another appeared. Somewhere Eidhalt watched them beyond the skill of scouts to find them.

The craft bumped the shore. Euzzeldir rushed to greet Habdelion and Sedaik as they disembarked. The closer they came to Etaleah, the more dangerous it grew to hold these midnight meetings. Khoti scanned the sky again. Could a few Eidhalt with Ghyldus's powers of illusion threaten an army?

The darkness yielded up the sounds of stumbles and missteps and the grumbles of soldiers unsatisfied with cold and cheerless fare as they huddled in their bedrolls away from insects, or camped near their horses in the hopes the larger target would draw the biting parasites away. They hadn't lit a fire since the howling-yappers, as Jali dubbed them, appeared more than two weeks past.

Khoti leaned against a wagon tie, hiding a yawn behind his hand as his officers gathered, their greetings low and weary, but never so tired as Khoti. It had been almost a year now since he'd healed Jali. He realized now that what killed Tsevon had been the lingering effects of bringing Khoti home from a place the spirits had kept him. Khoti knew better than to attempt a healing on a warrior's road, yet it hadn't kept him from saving Jali. And he'd yet to find a healer's rest. The army spent each daylight hour on the march, the officers spending most of the night overseeing their troops and supply lines, settling disputes or hearing and dispensing scouts and messengers. Clearly, Khoti decided, the role the gods saw for him could only be as Arshal's sword or the spirits would have granted him the stamina to put Jali's poisons behind him.

Now, far from the ears of his troops, Khoti oversaw the last of the many meetings as a split command, the night too dark to make out features, though his voice relayed his fatigue.

"Cyd's back," he said as Habdelion and Sedaik settled around the wagon, all of them lost in shadow. The ghostly glint of starlight from the river reflected from the cuff on his wrist as he swatted insects. Chati and Tre stirred, impatient, their feet squeaking in damp grass that gave off the earthy scent of perpetually soggy soil. They knew the news.

Khoti sighed. "We thought they had nine thousand at Etaleah. It's more like fifteen."

"So, outnumbered again," Habdelion muttered.

"I could have told you that," Ramel said from Euzzeldir's elbow.

"You knew they had reinforcements?" Khoti returned with a hint of humor.

"Of course not," Ramel retorted. "But it is only obvious. If Shela had reinforcements, if Gnats are openly running Sihmad Shal, with the king's threat broadcast far and wide, any idiot should have expected to find more troops here."

"Well, Ramel," Khoti drawled. "We're mere Seconds in the scheme. It's your folk that came first and made the mess we're expected to mop up. Care to take a stab at strategy?"

His musical chuckle soothed the night. "Too tedious. I have already seen one such war. I am here only to witness the outcome. It is my people that left Fyraer strong enough to rebuild. I do not think you would want my advice."

"Then if I may?" Khoti prodded. "Cyd found no trace of Iyrafael Gnats. We've got to make a go of it on our own again. We can't count on reinforcements arriving fresh from sinking an enemy fleet."

Sedaik's teeth glowed out in a sliver of a cold smile.

"I think maybe we've got the advantage of surprise, yet," Khoti went on. "If the howler-yapper was more than just an irritant, I think they'd have come for us by now. Maybe the Iyrafael Gnats drew their attention. For whatever reason they've missed us. We haven't got much longer before they'll notice. So, we can't just wait for Iyrafael. Maybe the Gnats planned to show up on Kedtairday –"

"Which could be any day now," Ramel said. "Can you feel the ground tensing beneath you? The wind falls from the east, a hot wind, unusual from that direction. And see how the horses grow skittish, the air heavier? Kedtair will be soon. Perhaps in days, no more than weeks. I would guess just over a week."

"Attack tomorrow," Habdelion said. "Who knows how long it will take to clear the canal and get to Sihmad Shal. We do not want to be too late to see the destruction of Ghyldus."

Khoti grinned. "It's not something I want to miss. It's just we have uneven odds again. Now we've got Gnats that, though trained, haven't got the gear or experience the rest of us have." He nodded at Kyne, captain of the nine thousand Gnats who had ridden in, squad by squad, from southern Kalilia. The entire southern half of the province had emptied of young and old alike. "And while, as a whole, we're better armed, have more cavalry and initiative, it's a risk."

Kyne cleared his throat. "I only got about four thousand that aren't outfitted to a passable degree. I'm sure we can ransack the dead at Etaleah for a bit more."

Khoti chuckled at the one-time Iyrafael fisher's confidence. After Nali bestowed upon Kyne a captain's rank, Kyne took it upon himself to move south and organize the reaches of southern Kalilia, inspired by the soft-spoken king whose dedication filled Kyne's heart.

"We're about an hour's ride south of the canal," Tre offered. "Cavalry can ride ahead. Infantry would follow a few hours behind. But almost their entire force is on this side of the river."

Habdelion and Sedaik sighed as they rose, reflecting their dismay that their weary troops would have no rest this night. They would leave the hundred or so Minarian soldiers on the western bank of the Rigannon untroubled. Khoti needed the combined army to face so large a garrison as dominated the eastern bank.

With night aging, Habdelion and Sedaik once again rowed across the Rigannon, the howler-yapper winging overhead with its mournful sound like the pleas of the dying.

As the moonless night aged, ropes guided wagons and troops across a broad expanse at the confluence of the Iyrafael and Rigannon to land on the north bank of the Iyrafael, which soon became a mire as troops already on the eastern shore crossed the shallower Iyrafael to join them. Khoti could allow them only a brief rest before the combined cavalry formed up, eight thousand strong.

They rode out an hour before dawn, the troops uncertain whether they guided their mounts into fens or bogs as they peered into the dim pre-dawn. Khoti took the lead, Asteria his standard-bearer. The flag of Shande, among the pennants of many houses, unfurled to greet streaks of gray in the east. As they departed, the infantry assembled to follow and teamsters packed for the difficult trek. Though the bulk of the army rode in columns of four behind Khoti and his captains, they raised no racket but the snorts of horses and the creak of gear.

At sunrise the howler-yapper disappeared.

When the sun still clung to the horizon, as if hesitant to dawn this day, the cavalry fanned out in a semi-circle around a sprawling stronghold at the southern end of the Etaleah Canal. The Minarians could only retreat into the river and Khoti's scouts had already severed that path. Clothes dripping river water as they shivered in the damp of dawn, his scouts watched as a handful of attendants guided ferries and barges beyond reach of the besieged.

When the sun at last broke free, Khoti winded Habdelion's horn and the cavalry charged as one against the stronghold's walls. Arrows filled the crisp morning as Minarians answered his challenging blast with their own call, confident.

Sedaik's expert archers flung flaming arrows over the walls

into the Minarian stronghold. Soon Minarian archers ringed the wooden walls, holding Sedaik's marksmen at bay.

"By the gods! Come out and fight!" Khoti hissed as the gates remained closed. He peered at the stronghold from his position atop a high levee built with soils dug from the canal. Something in the picture, something he should notice, didn't fit. He stared at the cleared fields encircling the fort, the river with no barge marking its surface, the walls looming better than thrice a man's height. The answer eluded him.

He glanced at the knot of officers around him awaiting his order. He pointed at Chati. "Take a squad and round up their horses. We can use the spare mounts."

The Minarians' passive posture infuriated him as Chati and his unit dodged arrows to drop the bars of the corral and herd the horses stabled outside the walls back to the waiting army.

"Anything else?" Chati grinned as he inspected a tear in his cloak where an arrow had struck and bounced off the leather armor he wore. Two of his squad fell victim to the barrage of arrows. A dozen horses quivered from light flesh wounds.

Khoti studied the corral where two Gnats lay in the dirt, Minarian archers taking shots at their lifeless bodies, jeering as they did so. He scowled, the bright morning making his eyes sting and water. He missed something. A haze hovering over the river on the horizon promised a hot day, probably one of many to come in a summer of Kedtair. The enemy jeered at Habdelion's colors now. All knew of Anlon.

He simmered at the sight of enemy arrows sticking from the two dead Gnats. "At least they're wasting their shots on the dead. Ah, there." He pointed as a Minarian captain shouted for his archers to conserve their arrows. Silence returned to the walls of the stronghold.

"How long will it take to starve out fifteen thousand?" Tre asked with a grin.

"Longer than we've got," Khoti returned. "Before that they'll come busting out, looking for blood." He rubbed an insect bite on his unshaved chin. What was he missing? Fifteen thousand. "How many horses was that?" he called to Chati.

Chati surveyed the nervous beasts. "About two hundred."

"They must have more somewhere around here," he muttered,

glancing at Cydwyn. "They can't have many within the walls."

"There's a herd a half hour's ride north," Cydwyn said. "It's a large grassy area, a few herders, no fences. No way these fellows can reach them."

"But we can," Khoti said. "Take what you need, Chati. Cyd can guide you. Hurry. We may need those mounts." He scratched his chin again, trying to pinpoint the thing his instincts read. He ordered Jali to make a circuit of their position, unable to say what he sought, but certain if it existed, Jali would find it.

"They couldn't have more than a hundred horses in there," he muttered. "So, if they come out, they'll make an infantry charge. But horses would make their food stores last longer." While his captains waited for some plan to emerge from his musing, he scanned the ring of horsemen. "Sedaik, the maximum range of bowshot?" Sedaik pointed at a few bushes here and there serving as landmarks for a perimeter of fire from the stronghold's walls. "How many bowmen with at least minimum protection can we field?"

"Guessing, about five thousand if you are not counting archers delayed with the infantry." Sedaik's forehead creased as he tried to guess Khoti's strategy.

"No, mounted only," Khoti said. "Though, if they arrive in time, we can divvy up the captured stock." Khoti stared down at the faint perimeter Sedaik outlined. "The east wind should serve. Have men gather tinder and wood. I want a ring of fires all the way around the stronghold. Make them good and smoky. And keep them stoked in case they try to escape come nightfall."

Soon fires blazed some hundred paces from one another. A slow procession of horsemen gathered to wait just out of range in relay ranks, their arrows dipped in lamp oil. When a few Minarian arrows fell among them, fire tenders adjusted until the fires marked the exact perimeter of the enemy's range.

With an undulating shriek, Khoti raced from the hilltop to the nearest fire and dipped his arrow into the flames. Cueing Fidra with his knees, he reached the point of a loop, fired his arrow to crest the wall and raced back as the rest of his cavalry followed suit.

A barrage of Minarian arrows scattered among them, targets

foiled by billows of smoke as fire tenders threw on greens. A few horses went down. Several riders fell. Most of the fallen scrambled to safety among the pelt of hooves as archers continued their mad race, churning the ground like bread kneaded to a pliant dough. The beat of their passage, the whinnies and shouts, the suck of flame and hum of bowstring, formed a discordant symphony that thrilled Khoti's blood.

When each had shot a dozen arrows, they pulled back on Khoti's call. He nudged a prancing Fidra to the crest of the bank so he could see above the smoke. Fewer heads stared over the walls. Others looked over shoulders to the fort's interior. Smoke coiled up from several sites, but not nearly enough.

"Again!" Khoti cried and leaped forward, the Shandeans flinging arrows by the thousands. Khoti paused in his pattern to study the scene. A few arrows had fallen short, smoldering in the grass outside the walls. Some stuck in the wooden walls where archers rimming the stronghold doused them with water. Several dozen men lay still in the space between the fire perimeter and the walls, the dying horses scattered among them scrambling to rise with pitiful flails, or lying on sides, flanks twitching with each close passage of riders. Many soldiers ignored flesh wounds, or examined mounts lamed by arrows protruding from their rippling skin. More coils of smoke rose from within the walls.

"Now," Khoti said between deep breaths constricted by the smoke. The blood of the challenge, sour and wicked, coursed through him. "Get those fires smoking. Gather oil from everyone who's got even a spoonful in his pack."

Soon thick smoke billowed upward as more and more greens smothered the fires sending up a cloud and stench that threatened to turn day into night.

Hugging deep grass yet untrampled and the cover of dead soldiers and their mounts, a cluster of Tachi crawled toward the stronghold, each cradling flasks of oil and grease. Every pace or so, the Tachi lay flat in the grass, affecting the pose of the dead, before again crawling on. A gust of wind threatened to carry the smoke away. They froze for long minutes until again the smoke lowered like a pennant losing the breeze. At last, the Tachi reached the walls and splattered their grease and oil on the gates and walls, then dashed back to safety, dodging arrows as they ran. A few fell among those on the field. Several Tachi stumbled and limped on. Smoky and red-eyed, their battle grins stark and evil in their faces, the Tachi cued the fire tenders.

Firemen at each blaze cast brands into the undergrowth where the Tachi had trickled oil. Though damp with dew and trampled by horses, the tops of last year's underbrush and grass remained dry and brittle before the flames.

"Be ready if any break for it!" Khoti called as his eight thousand horsemen gathered just outside the perimeter.

Soon fire crept on the stronghold, fanned by the warming east wind. He cupped his hands to peer through the haze, but he couldn't even see the stronghold for the thick smoke.

When the fire's leading edge raced away, and the perimeter fires again burned clean, Khoti discerned the frenzied figures on the walls dumping buckets of water on trailers of flame sputtering at the base of the structure. The Tachi had thrown the majority of the oil at the barred wooden gates, which flared and spit as the flames reached them. Smoke rolled upward from within the fort's walls, a flight of sparks scattering skyward as some roof caved in on itself, sending out clouds of dust and ash like puff seeds hovering over a field.

"If you build a wooden castle, better have a good fire marshal," Asteria said.

"That's why I prefer stone castles." Khoti turned to find her, sweat- and smoke-streaked. He wanted to reach out and wipe her face with the orange Detarian scarf holding the sweat from his eyes. His hand started to reach for a strand of loose hair, but stopped when her gaze went to the offending limb. He jerked his hand back and then swatted the air to send a flurry of ash feathers floating away, her gaze following the motes of ash swirling in front of them.

Khoti scowled. While fire weakened the walls, they didn't fall. Though the gates burned, the army couldn't draw near.

"They outnumber us. Why won't those demons come out!" Khoti demanded as he slammed his fist into his thigh.

"They don't have to!" Cydwyn gasped as he crested the levee, soldiers parting to let him through. He supported Chati before him. The Tawnkat lay folded over Cydwyn's restraining arm.

Khoti went chill at the blood running down Chati's left arm, sheathing the horse's side to drip into the grass, and Cydwyn's blood-streaked face. Only three of fifteen warriors returned.

"They might've had fifteen thousand in there yesterday, but not today," Cydwyn gasped. "Howler-yapper or Anlon, but they got thousands about an hour north, making for Sihmad Shal. They must've left just before we got here." When Ramel lifted Chati from Cydwyn's mount, Cydwyn sagged forward to lean over his horse's bloody neck in search of breath. The Taschian flopped to the ground. A trickle of blood ran from a gash on Chati's scalp.

"I knew it!" Khoti's gaze locked on Chati's pale face. His palms itched, burned. "That's what I missed: too few horses, confidence. They expected their comrades to hear their call." He clenched his fists to quench the fire in his palms, taking deep breaths. "When Jali gets back, he'll tell us there's a trail north. How could we be so stupid!"

"What did I tell you?" Ramel said, not looking up from Chati's wounds. "They are finally doing something about these pesky Gnats. The ones in the stockade figure their friends will see the smoke, or they do not care as long as the main host got off. They probably intend to join Ghyldus's troops, a flank movement we were not expecting."

Khoti slipped from Fidra to look over Ramel's shoulder as the Visionary examined Chati's scalp.

"The infantry will be here inside an hour. They can set a watch on the stronghold." Khoti looked around at his officers. "Order them to mount up. We can't let them reach Sihmad Shal!"

As his officers sped away to call up the troops, Khoti pulled apart the edges of a deep gash on Chati's muscular upper arm, glimpsing bone.

Chati's eyes fluttered open. "Don't even think it."

"I'm not a fool." His palms twitched. "It's not even a wound worthy of note," Khoti hid behind a weak smile when Chati demonstrated that he couldn't make a fist, the blood continuing to flow from the wound. "You never were very strong." Khoti turned his attention to the cut on Chati's head, a large lump forming beneath it. He plucked a piece of bark from Chati's bloody hair. "Some excuse, Chati. To go complaining of a little cut to get out of battle. Don't even think of deserting me, Lieutenant." He looked around to find Cydwyn on unsteady feet. The young scout leaned against his horse as he wrapped a light wound on his forearm.

"We stumbled right into them." Cydwyn said as he caught his breath. "Fools! We should'a known better –"

"Yes." He peered at Cydwyn a moment before lifting the young man's sword arm, ignoring the scout's wince, to find the seep of blood where a stab penetrated leather armor. "Stay here and tend Chati. Bind his arm tight and apply salve to his head wound, and to yourself. Maybe Ramel can find some herblore to help when we return." He squeezed Cydwyn's shoulder. "Next time fight like you've been trained. No one should get under your sword like that." He tried not to think, tried not to let it in, but he knew. Chati would bleed to death before any of them could do a thing.

Khoti whirled to leave, only to stumble into Asteria. She looked on him with sympathetic eyes, soft and dark and comforting. Her glance went to Chati. Moving to brush by her, he halted at the bare touch of her fingers on his arm above the battered cuff. His skin tingled. He hated that she did this to him, that in the midst of battle he wanted to hold her, that she might pity his pain.

"He will survive," Asteria said as if by saying it, it would happen.

With a nod, Khoti pushed by her and took to Fidra's back as the first ranks of infantry reached them. Snarling like a cornered wolver, he rode prancing Fidra at the head of the column. Soon the southern cavalry loped in pursuit of its enemy.

To lose even one more of his dwindling mountain people, another brother, drove Khoti like a storm into the dry uplands hugging the canal. Ramel's voice carried over the pound of hooves and jangle of gear, the seer preaching caution at him, warning him not to let fear for a friend make him a reckless fool.

Khoti knew his own prowess better than Ramel. He needed the rage like he needed food and drink, comfort and friendship. Too often he let his rage run off without him when the burdens of command made him think too deeply. In Shela, he almost let compassion and fear for Asteria drive the warrior away. He savored the hatred now, like fresh game on the fire after a long day of scouting.

Forcing the long litany of death and suffering into his thoughts, he felt his inner warrior stir, his grim scowl making those near him shiver. He glanced over his shoulder at Ramel. The seer fell silent, his godly eyes widening at what he must have seen in Khoti's gaze.

"Go with it, Khoti," Asteria called, her mouth open to welcome the wind and dust and whip of mane as she lay low over her mount's neck. She clutched in her left hand the staff bearing the Shandean banner that snapped in their passage, Khoti's own sandy beige and emerald colors gracing a streamer beneath it.

He nodded as a scout drew even to tell him the sprawling line of the Minarian forces followed the bottom of a long valley ahead. Khoti swung one arm out to the right and then veered left.

Half the cavalry streamed behind Euzzeldir and Habdelion to the east rim of the valley. Habdelion's hunter green and brown bobbing from a staff among the heads of hundreds of Tachi in woodland brown, shawnsi with faces set grim above their green cloaks. Behind Euzzeldir, a gold and white banner, once carried to battle by Dynfearn the Lost, jangled as the bells on its purple tassels rang shrill with the pace. His white-garbed Joffans appeared like winter in Habdelion's austere forest.

Racing to the west rim behind Khoti, Sedaik sat a tall figure with the orange standard of Unified Detarian fluttering from a staff in his father's hands. Detarian archers wore bright orange sashes at their waists and had wrapped their heads in orange scarves like the one Khoti tied across his brow, orange gracing the braids of many a head. The motley gathering of thousands of Gnats rode to the blue and white standard in Asteria's hands, Tre and Khoti in her father's buff and pewter. For a fleeting moment, as Khoti gained his first glimpse of the black, orange and red of Minaria marching below, he found war colorful, vibrant, alive. He suppressed the thought as he lay over Fidra's neck.

Both wings of the army raced just below the outer rim of the valley, their figures leaving no silhouette against the sky, though their passage might echo before them above the Minarian racket.

When the two groups had outpaced the army below and encircled them, they came to an abrupt stop on Khoti's cue, turned toward the valley and waited just below the rim. Khoti pounded over the top, alone but for the colors clinging behind him in Asteria's hands.

Tre, Jali and Daris broke to join them. When Khoti and Asteria were halfway down the hillside, the Minarians brought archers around to face them. Khoti opened his mouth in a shriek of the tawnkat. Euzzeldir and Habdelion's wing swept down from the east while Khoti's companies leaped over the rim behind their leader, their warrior cries raising skyward as one tremendous shout.

From a hilltop to the northeast, a man not quite twice Khoti's age cupped his hands to view the scene, a paternal pride and fear both swelling and deflating him. He watched a Tawnkat and Guardsman, but also a commander of armies, and champion of his king. When Fidra leaped forward, Khoti's weathered Lharan cloak flared out to cover Fidra's chestnut flanks, her gray tail streaming behind her to whip Asteria's mount in the face, the streamers of Khoti's followers hanging suspended in the stiff east wind. Fair Taschian locks, unshorn in months of travel, blew back from his face, breaking free from their Joffan braids. And even at this distance they could see the hint of menace the champion could project. The king had chosen wisely.

When an unearthly screech carried above the wind to him, one to make the blood pulse, high and eerie like an eagle's distant scree, or the shriek of a tawnkat, support rushed to the Sword of Shande, rallying to his cries as his weapon flashed in the high sun of mid-afternoon.

"That's a bushel of Minarians the king wasn't counting on, eh Konner," Ahrwesz muttered.

Konner sprouted his slashing grin. "Just where I 'spected to find him, right in the middle. Should we join the fun?"

"Oh sure, die before we deliver an important message and have the king so mad he'll kill us again, then spit on our rites for good measure." Ahrwesz cupped his hands to scan the hillcrests to the south. "He must have support lines for so many. Wagons, spare mounts, at least an infantry. His whole force can't be in cavalry."

About to turn his horse's head south again, Konner's grin faded when he threw another glance at the battle in the valley. Khoti fought like the Taschian spirit unleashed, the west wind his father had been, falling from the mountains, piercing, cold. Though Khoti still fought with a fury beneath his standard, too many fallen already dotted the battlefield. The warriors in white had a few wounded scrambling from the fray, horseless, evading the pikes of Minarian infantrymen rendered nearly useless against the swift charges. The brown and green, those in orange, they too battled on with few losses, the wounded fighting from their knees. But royal blue littered the field, as did many with no colors to mark their allegiance.

Konner glanced at Ahrwesz.

"The two of us won't make a difference," Ahrwesz said, nudging his horse to gallop south.

Cydwyn stared at the fort as he chewed a piece of jerky as flavorless as a hank of rope, more an exercise for tooth and jaw than for taste or stomach. He glanced at Chati, whose face appeared death-like beneath the stained rag wrapped around his head. Cydwyn wished he had Khoti's touch. He should have known better than to leave the stronghold unwatched while his men stole the barges. A whole army escaped his attention! How could he have missed the trail north? And now thousands of infantry sat on their hands when they could be tipping the odds in Shande's favor in a battle Cydwyn had no doubt would be ugly. Only an hour from their haven, hale with months of ease, the Minarian mounts had the light hearts of beasts fresh from pasture. Such an army would face those who had ridden hard for five months on the heels of devastating battle, and had already fought half the day without a night's rest. The Army of the South had overrun dozens of outposts, battled wounds and fever and damp. And those who fought at Shela lived with that nightmare, even Khoti tossing in his sleep, awakening with a shout on his lips, bathed in sweat.

Cydwyn studied his one-time home. The familiar countryside

no longer resembled the memory he'd relished. His house had once stood within the walls of the Minarian fortress. Did his stone cottage still stand, with its hearth stained by his family's blood? Or had even that been changed and mutilated like its former occupants?

Cydwyn examined the low ridge hugging the canal waters. A retractable pier once jutted into the canal where barge crews tied on to visit the small town while waiting for the water to rise and fall within the locks. The high levee on which he now sat came from the dredgings of the canal, and served as the haven the townspeople sought when on rare occasion turbulent waters overflowed the dams and crept over the lip of the canal.

He glanced again at Chati, finding him staring up at him with feverish eyes. "Sleep," Cydwyn said, turning back to study the water.

"Where's Khoti?" Chati mumbled, gripping Cydwyn's wrist with a hand grown so strong around the hilts of a sword that despite the Tawnkat's weakness Cydwyn couldn't pull away.

"Gone to fight that army we seen."

"Gotta take the stronghold," Chati rasped, his gaze taking on focus.

"I know. But how? We're ordered to stay put –"

"Meant to be broken." Chati tried to sit up but flopped down, turning to stare at his arm swathed in stained bandages stretched beside him. "I'm gonna go fighting, not lying a-bed."

"You're not going anywhere, Chati." Cydwyn yanked his arm free. "When Khoti comes back –"

"He can do no more than herbmasters. There's ways to stop bleeding –"

Cydwyn shook his head. "The muscle's –"

"And whose to fix it? It's all Ramel can do. I may not be a healer like Khoti, but it's in my line and I've learned a few things watching."

Cydwyn turned from Chati's intense gaze and stared at the ring of fires around the stronghold, the entire perimeter rimmed by idle soldiers.

"Cyd, I'll die before they come back. They need the infantry. We got to get that stronghold."

Cydwyn stared into his hands, his jaw keeping pace with his

heart as his teeth clenched and released in unconscious agreement with the lifebeat in him. He would never forgive himself for the lives lost because of his sloppy scouting.

"You got an idea?"

"Do it like the Tawnkats, not the Army of the South." Chati's voice grew distant. "This is your country. You got to know things you didn't think were important."

Cydwyn peered down at the lip of the canal's banks and nodded. Images etched in his memory like a second reality beside the occupied world he lived in reared up.

He leaned close to Chati as he relayed anything he thought important and in return absorbed the experience Chati had gained watching Tawnkats create fear and weakness in their enemy. But Chati held his advice for a boon, a promise, Cydwyn felt loathe to honor.

Later, as night fell over the stronghold, Cydwyn studied the dagger in his hand. His thoughts replayed the way Chati's entire body trembled, how he'd made no sound but to take a horrendous breath Cydwyn thought would suck all the air from the world and leave them all gasping, bursting Chati's lungs. No bloody rags remained to remind him how the wound had bled and Chati writhed as a Hainadan midwife sewed what she could inside the wound, as if trussing a bird for the pot or mending a shirt, small stitches that dragged seconds into eternity. Now beneath a clean bandage and a poultice of egg and salve, seeped an ugly burn, a thing Cydwyn couldn't believe he'd inflicted on his friend.

As an officer in Khoti's corps of scouts, a title he'd held for only a few months, Cydwyn already tired of ordering others into danger, inflicting pain, making decisions. He dug his dagger into the soft mud. He shouldn't have such duties. At sixteen he hoped to lead thousands. With all the experienced officers gone with Khoti, and Chati too sick to think clearly, he held rank over many far older and wiser. He didn't want this! But he was one of the survivors.

He glanced at Chati, wondering what poisons he'd sealed in with the blood. Chati remained pale, a sheen of sweat still lingering in the glow of the fire. Dark settled around them. Cydwyn winced when he at last pulled himself to his feet, tugging on the leather armor that had foiled a sword's blow, leaving only a nagging wound in the flesh of his side. He stuffed rags beneath the shirt before lacing the protective coat, the cut on his arm swelling against the bandage. He only wanted to crawl into his bedroll and sleep.

Cydwyn beckoned into the shadows, knowing she watched him, though he saw nothing. Kia, dagger at her slender hip, stalked to Cydwyn's side.

"Watch him," Cydwyn whispered into her ear. He looked down into her unnerving gaze, laying a hand on her shoulder, giving her a sort of smile, as much as his face ever expressed. Perhaps because that slight turn of one corner of his mouth came so rare and special – only a few knew where the vestiges of his humor lurked – for some other reason he hadn't found, he was one of the few for whom Kia smiled. He had to force himself to remember she was a child. They thought so much alike, calculating warriors, their silence conveying their thoughts. If this child-woman could take on tasks well beyond her years, certainly he could accept the responsibilities thrust upon him, the price he must pay for begging to fight beside Khoti. He gave a last glance at Chati and nodded at Kia. With the distant sound of Khoti's army trumpeting retreat as night fell, Cydwyn headed into the darkness, making for piers and gates known to the Lockmen of Etaleah, the infantry silently streaming behind him. He only prayed his memory held true, that time hadn't eroded this image as it had all the others, leaving golden tatters trailing from a rent and bloodied canvas where trees toppled and buildings broke and gardens lay choked with weeds.

A quarter moon glowed in a bank of clouds just above the rim of the east valley. Below, watch fires flickered around the Minarian camp, pickets holding themselves well out of the light. Soon the moon would rise high enough to light the valley.

Khoti nodded at Kyne and held up two fingers. Though so exhausted he stumbled, rubbing his eyes to clear them, Khoti couldn't sleep. Somehow, he had to salvage this army he'd built. He couldn't see Kyne's two squads moving through the deep shadow to cross the muddy stream at the bottom of the valley, then creep up the eastern slope toward enemy watch fires. A figure disturbed the light, then another. No sound came but the soft snores of Khoti's troops scattered about him, a few groaning as the aches of wound and weariness troubled their sleep. Khoti nodded at Sedaik. Detarian's best marksmen crept into the darkness on the feet of fog.

He peered into the dark, unable to discern figures as the light fog rose from the stream.

"Simple as spittin'," Kyne said at Khoti's elbow. Khoti startled, clutching at his dagger. Kyne sagged into the trampled grass beside Khoti and dropped his head into his hands.

A cry from the opposite camp brought Sedaik's marksmen sprinting across the stream, already rushing for their bedrolls as Sedaik roused a second shift of archers.

"Give them half an hour," Khoti told Kyne. "Send three squads. They'll have increased the watch."

"No one's to get much rest," Kyne said, gazing up at the moon. "I've a couple squads pilfering gear. But we'll still have more, desperate, without armor, dead before they hit the field. We're going to be short."

Khoti sighed but made no answer. He could do nothing.

When he heard the tally for a lousy night's sleep, one hundred enemy dead, Khoti shook his head. Not enough. "Maybe it'll suck at their stamina," he said around a yawn. Euzzeldir and Habdelion joined him, fresh with rest and chewing the hard biscuits of a cold camp.

"You stood the whole night, didn't you?" Euzzeldir demanded when Khoti tried to shake himself alert. "Don't try to be the hero today, Khoti. Stay to the rear, save yourself for the greater battles ahead. You've got officers who can call your orders."

Habdelion nodded. "The king will want his sword to be sharp when he calls for it."

"You're sounding more and more like Eithur, both of you," Khoti growled. "They're rousing over there. Call your ranks up." He barked his orders in a voice growing hoarse. The faint dusk of morning grew about them. Euzzeldir and Habdelion stared after him, stunned by something in his tone. He refused to look back.

Khoti shook out his arms, stamping his feet and twisting his neck as he waited for an attendant to bring Fidra to him. Asteria offered him a ladle of water. He gave her a tender smile, brushing his hand against her cheek, seeing her as if she again sat beside the fire in his cave, her face flushed with winter, not smudged with grime. For an instant, she seemed to wear that quizzical expression she'd worn when he had presented her with his dagger. As suddenly, he realized what he had done and knew that the look she wore was startled and concerned.

With a snarl he yanked the ladle from her hand and splashed water in his face. He couldn't afford to have his mind delude him this way. He sought the rage he needed to survive. Almost unscathed, more than once he'd turned a deadly blow by his sheer anger. But anger alone couldn't keep him sharp. Even dragging up the ghost images of Von, or Chati's deathly face brought only a knot that choked his breath, not the smoldering hatred he so desired.

The enemy took the advantage early, striking before dawn while Khoti's men still staggered from bedrolls. With the wind still from the east, the enemy set fires in the trampled undergrowth to frighten the Shandean horses and obscure their approach. But when the Minarians raced in behind the fire, prepared to strike a final blow, no Shandeans remained. Stuttering to a halt, they turned to find Khoti's cavalry thundering up the blackened hillside behind them. The melee that followed felt like a continuation of the day before.

As the day grew old, neither side took advantage. Khoti began to wonder if he'd fallen into some nightmare of endless war that kept him in the field forever, a special kind of punishment, an eternal suffering as blood saturated the battered turf in perpetuity.

Darkness brought thunderstorms and a call for retreat. Soldiers flopped into the mud beside bedrolls, falling asleep while they chewed their repast as rain pelted them and lightning crackled overhead, the ground trembling with its thirst for ever more blood to sate it. Again, a weary exodus of Shandean soldiers filed onto the field in search of armor and weaponry. Again, archers crept into the Minarian camp to bedevil an enemy grown wise to such attacks.

Khoti strode among his troops, his step light as he passed a third night without sleep. His body moved by his will alone, his thoughts and perceptions a keen edge. He couldn't rest now and lose this odd euphoria absolute exhaustion brought. Images flitted before his eyes, odd thoughts crept into his mind, but he'd never in his life felt so intensely alert, so awake. Everything he looked at appeared new and bright, never before seen by any but he, each with some special significance he only just discovered. He swelled within himself with an indescribable pride and love for those who fought for him. His eyes went moist as he moved among his troops, hugging some sentry to him or squeezing some archer's shoulder. No enemy had routed his soldiers from any field. None of his soldiers snuck away home in fear of the odds. He'd built the finest and most loyal warriors Shande could field! How could he contain this pride he felt in them? He barely noticed the glances and double-takes following him as he passed the night humming an old harvest hunting tune as he checked the perimeter.

Morning brought no change in their endless battle as storms gave way to gray overcast, as dull and cheerless as those below it. Many began to mutter that battle would only end when all the soldiers fell from exhaustion, not enemy blows.

Khoti struggled to regain that strange euphoria he'd discovered the night before. But his eyes strayed, glazed. Images flit before them with annoying frequency. He fought on instinct, his arms numb and shoulders tingling, as he gasped out the strength to lift his arm just one more time, to parry just one more blow.

A sword caught him beneath his arm. He heard Kefta berating him for letting the weapon sneak by his defenses, and his own chastisement to Cydwyn. The enemy blow drove the mesh of his Minarian armor into his ribs with a force that stole his wind. Losing balance, he waited for the killing blow to fall on him as he struggled to raise his sword to his defense one more time. Instead, he sagged forward. He heard the blast of horns in the dimness closing on him, wondering what new delusion his mind conjured. Battle still raged around him, weaponry clanking and men screaming, and Fidra's blasts of breath in his ears.

He couldn't open his eyes, and moments later, at last his endless battle ceased.

Asteria's sword flew from her hand, lost in the churned mud. She brought up the staff bearing Shande's standard to fend off her foes. She saw Khoti sag to one side in his saddle. Fidra stumbled, trying to keep her feet in churned turf as Khoti's weight and skewed balance drove the mare to her knees, her master tumbling to the churned and bloody ground.

Asteria's heart went into her throat. Just beyond, Jali yanked a bloody Daris from her saddle, pulling the dazed woman up behind him while parrying an attack and turning his mount's head from the worst of the fighting.

What had happened? The end of her staff snapped and flew into her face. The Minarians seemed to rally to something: the horns she heard a moment before? Though defenseless with a stump of staff, she couldn't leave Khoti. Dismounting, she ducked beneath a blow to grab the sword from Khoti's open hand.

She found no comer. Her foe retreated. She first looked to Khoti. No one challenged him where he lay pale and motionless, Fidra standing over him with head hung and haunches twitching with exhaustion as first one hind leg, then another, rose to favor inflamed tendons. Asteria scanned the field, seeing nothing but mud-coated warriors. Not a single face turned her way. Then she looked up to the crest of the western hills. Her mouth fell open as the Shandean infantry streamed down into the valley, dark silhouettes to a gray sky. A horrible shriek of challenge ripped from their throats as they came fresh from victory to find the slaughter of their cavalry, the dead and down littering the field.

The enemy hemmed in and the weary Shandean cavalry maintaining pressure, the battle soon turned. As worn and wounded as Khoti's troops, the Minarians fell back from the envigored onslaught, many at last breaking and running.

Asteria startled to find Chati, like a specter, circling the battle as wagons rumbled to the rim. In a hoarse voice, he directed support troops to fetch bows and pick off Minarians fleeing the battle to keep them from pillaging the countryside.

Chati paused, wincing and reaching for his arm when his horse came to an abrupt halt beside Asteria. She bent to retrieve the standards struck from her staff, pulling them from the churned mud with reverence. Chati sheathed his sword and dismounted to unsteady feet and nudged Fidra aside to reach her still master. Flagging down two old Hainadans, he ordered Khoti borne from the field. Fidra trotted behind without a lead, like a dog following a shepherd to pasture. Chati mounted again with a groan, pulling Asteria up behind him before she could protest.

"I am able to fight, Chati."

"You're lousy afoot, Lady. You know that," Chati returned. "We've got things under control."

Asteria stared out upon the field to see the infantry's swift success.

"You wore them down for us. Now it's our turn to clean up." Chati turned to look at her over his shoulder as he loped toward the wagons, cradling his wounded arm in his lap. "Besides, I don't think you're quite as hale as you think you are." He glanced at the stub of staff left in one hand and the pennants tucked into her belt. She felt the blood flowing from her head down the side of her face, more seeping from a wound on her leg. "Eithur will never forgive us, bringing back a battle-scarred warrior for an heir."

Suddenly, feeling the weariness she'd tried to ignore, Asteria had to cling to Chati's waist to keep her seat as his horse labored up the slope, one hand unconsciously stroking the mudded emerald and beige pennant at her belt. She sensed the tension in Chati's muscles. But her thoughts were far away, on Khoti's pale face pressed into the mud, on the warmth she felt clinging to Chati's middle, the feel of a mountain life in the midst of death.

PART 3. KEDTAIR

19: Maura's Breath

While Pladde messengers raced to reach rebels in the Lharan Mountains to deliver news of the Minarian fleet's imminent departure for Shande, the city of Lagdche frantically tried to assemble the fleet Ghyldus ordered.

The God of Ea fumed in his stony halls to learn his fleet could not sail because this necessary item or that could not be found. The first moon of the Year of Kedtair sped toward the greening moon, Evenday passing, and still his main fleet waited on the ways. The ten ships destined for Shela would be delayed even longer, and the troops set to march on Sefresal could not even guess at a departure date.

His generals swore the Pladde uprising a mere annoyance, already fading into memory. But the irritation proved to be a mere symptom of a more serious disease. Ships' captains fumed as they sought such minor fittings as hooks, rope and line, clips, hook-eyes, pulleys and chain, to no avail. A hoard of shipwrights assigned to outfit the fleet scavenged for equipment and building materials. Vessels left dry dock without fittings or enough sailcloth to take the full wind. Armor and weaponry amounted to less than ordered and often flawed. Farriers clamored for shoes, but no metal could be found.

The nation's stores had fallen to a dangerous low, the

storeskeepers too terrified to report shortcomings to leadership known for fatal judgments. And now the caretakers of Ghyldus's realm understood why their god sailed so suddenly on Shande. All had enjoyed the prosperity the God of Ea brought, the bounty of a rich land filling the coffers of a poor land, the regained honor of a warrior people, and a promised future as rulers of Ea appearing no longer a dream.

The sea of riches had evaporated to a puddle.

Warehouses once crammed so full of Shande's cargo that the walls bowed outward now stood half empty. Workers discovered the odor of rotting meat in barrels that should have been cured. Sweet wines gave off a sour smell, their contents a cloudy vinegar. The aroma from so-called bales of osfothye hinted of seaweed and straw. Stems and seeds riddled seasonings, still-damp leaves dusted with mold. Cloth goods unraveled at the touch; fine metals weighed too light for their kind. Barrels of apples and bags of tubers leaked dark liquid while insects fed on coarse grains. Spools came rife with splinters, lantern chimneys cracked and thin, candles soft and short-wicked, rice damp, green and full of worms, cheeses runny and green. Moth-eaten blankets, moldy leather goods, harnesses unsewn at the seams, buckets and bedding, utensils and tools, machinery and weaponry, all soured by a bitter Shande.

Ghyldus sent his soldiers to citizens' homes to seek the goods to meet the army's needs. Even as the populace watched laden wagons creaking away from the door, so firmly had Ghyldus's enchantment taken root, they imagined it an owed service to a country and lord who needed help, warriors conscripted to help him wrest his due from the heathens of an arrogant and sinning land. If any wondered if they could justify the conquest of Shande, if they calculated the expense in lives of Ghyldus's proposed conquests, they kept it to themselves. The believers rose too strong, too numerous, too ready to reveal their neighbors' lack of faith.

Finally, when the last day of a windy first moon dawned, a flotilla so large it staggered the senses drifted beyond sight of Minaria's barren seaside hills, its sails filled with a benevolent wind and masts colored with the banners of war. As numerous as the waves, they seemed, or stars against the sky, or pebbles in a brook bed, as the seascape fluttered and boiled with ivory sails and bobbed and creaked, carrying the din of thousands.

Faces lined rails. Captains had crammed the holds so full with the needs of war that hundreds would sleep head-to-toe, elbow-to-elbow beneath canopies on the deck. Horses staggered on decks and in holds, the mounts of Minaria's finest cavalry companies cared for by masters who relinquished sleeping space to their tack, sharing their beasts' bedding, the hold filled with tuns of water and bales of hay. Oarsmen locked oars above the waves like wings, ready to take flight if the wind died. Crates of capons emitted flustered cackles from where they dangled from rails. A hubbub of grumbles filtered up from the open traps, where troops fought the stores for space, knowing all too soon dwindling supplies would make them wish for the cramped quarters again. A steady stream of soldiers climbed the ladders from below, seeking the fresh wind, and the light to work their weapons in idleness. The creak of hammocks holding lazing troops kept cadence with the swish of water flying from bows as the ships turned all sail to the wind.

As the ships sped from home, leaving a scant few behind readying for the departures to Shela and Sefresal, stark remained the image in the memories of those few left behind of their god standing, arms-upraised as if calling the wind, in the bow of the flagship. Indeed, as the armada littered the horizon with sails, with troops gathering in the fields beyond the city for their march on Sefresal, with ships standing ready to sail on Shela, with reinforcements to Shande having emptied the city well in advance and with only a handful of old men, women and children left behind, all of Ea seemed at Ghyldus's command.

Distant shores sped by.

Leaving behind, at last, the brown hills of Minaria, the snow-capped mountains of Shiad rose, peaks tinged blue by the dawn behind and gilded by sunset as the days of the greening moon passed, a time of rough weather forgetting its season. No storm hindered them. No rain troubled them. A wind from the southwest filled sails as stars shone clear at night to guide them.

Resala headed home at last, after two years as Ghyldus's prisoner. They would come too soon, Arshal unprepared. Unless a message sent by Verdred arrived. She thought of the black-garbed figure, a dark statue at his master's elbow. What treachery could that be?

Resala paced the narrow confines of yet another cage, loyal Teshet at her side. The speed of their journey, the seeming success despite their long delay, had Ghyldus in high spirits. Again, he wove his enchantments about her, through a feigned, or not so feigned, sweetness. Certainly, he aimed to catch her off guard. What was his game? Courteous, less demanding, he smiled his evil smile with black eyes glittering in the sun's glint off the waves. So strong!

Soon she would step on the soils of Shande again to witness the fruition of Arshal's plans ... or the failure of them. She drove the darker thoughts away, would not consider any afterward if defeated. She couldn't let soft-spoken spells enter her mind to bring her despair. She had found something in herself, glimpsed in a mirror, something never before contemplated, a strength that belonged to her line. She didn't know how to use it, if a usable commodity. But she knew it existed and fed from that knowledge.

When the fleet rounded the northern tip of Shiad, marked by a lighthouse standing beacon in the distance, it seemed on cue the wind shifted west to fall in behind them, billowing out sails with the fullness of its power. In only four weeks at sea the ships stood off the Ymmenay River's broad delta, a journey known to take weeks longer. Could Ghyldus force winds outside his lands to honor him as well? The gusts exhaled hot and moist, chasing the swells before it. Yet, only the first of the blossom moon, the coolness of night in the north should have been in the air. Ahead lay the shores of Shande. At this pace, they would reach Canwyn Point before moon's end, before messengers could reach Arshal and speed him there, before the rising of Kedtair.

But as Resala stood on the deck, watching the northernmost peak of the Shandean Lharans rise out of the dawn, the wind died like a door closing. She turned to gaze upon a storm brewing on the western horizon. At first no one appeared concerned. A few commented how a little rain would replenish their water supplies.

Resala glanced at Teshet who gripped the rails with a fear of sailing that the long journey had yet to abate. The ships, hundreds of them scattered across the sea like shells on a dark beach, slowed to a halt as sails fell limp in search of a breeze.

"So close, but the wind dies as we near the border," Resala muttered in Teshet's ear.

"You think it is a-purpose?" Teshet asked, eyes widening.

Resala shrugged. As the sailors trimmed sails, their gazes turned to the fast-darkening sky boiling toward them. The tumble of thunder became a steady drum roll. Men unlocked oars from their perches and set them at rest just above the piling waves, prepared to close their oar ports if they seas grew too heavy or in readiness for a call to row to keep the bow pointed into the waves.

Darkness raced at them, black and white rolling in the squall line. The trimmed sails lowered when someone spied the green glow of hail-filled clouds behind the squall line. The crew swiftly lashed down anything that might shift. Fidgeting horses squealed when lightning overhead tingled spines, blinded eyes and sucked air from the lungs a mere instant before a prolonged, rending crackle shattered the air, to roll on for long minutes with resounding booms and grumbles as if the bowels of Ea itself protested hunger. Rain came sudden and then hail that collapsed canopies with its weight and terrorized the livestock lurching against their bonds, piling white pebbles on decks and bounding over rails.

Resala clasped her hands together, huddling against Teshet beneath a sagging canopy as rain splattered her and spray flew at them, hailstones unsettling their footing. She watched the beckoning peak marking Shande dissolve into gray streaks of rain. This violent storm felt too much like a threat after prolonged calm.

Moments later the sea erupted with a plume of spray.

"Maura!" Resala breathed as a giant beast crashed against a ship fading from view in the steady rain. Rising so slow from the surface, the beast moved like a huge, slate-gray wave concocted by the equally gray sea and sky. She heard only the wind and a distant crack, a mast toppling as the creature slipped beneath the waves. Resala clenched her eyes shut. The legend lived. She opened her eyes to see the beast again emerge from the crest of a wave.

Moving across the water, faster than any vessel, head above the waves, the beast's eyes blazed in the gloom. It leaped, crashing upon the decks of a ship, spilling men into the sea and smashing masts and rigging.

Resala gripped the rail, ignoring rain and hail to watch the beast return again and again to strike the ship, moving on to another while the omnipotent barked orders at signalmen. A barbed spear snaked from the bow of a ship, striking the flank of the beast as it arched its dark back to dive beneath a vessel. A furious flip of its massive tail proved the weapon's aim. The creature bellowed, a deep and anguished cry, as it broke from the water and then veered away.

Any urge to cheer died on the sailors' lips when a larger creature sped in from the open ocean, a fury that made Resala tremble to look upon it. It circled a cluster of ships maneuvering to pull men from the water, beyond the reach of spears. Faster and faster, it circled as if the wind of a cyclone. The sea swirled in its wake, at last spiraling inward. Lightning crackled above them, the strength of the gods scattering sparks across the waves. Spinning waters sucked the vessels into a whirlpool fanned by the beast's fury.

As it fled the watery cyclone it had made, a spear raced from a ship to strike the beast. The mariner who threw the weapon fell silently into the sea, clutching his chest as his weapon struck. The beast rose from the sea, a giant wave, smashing the ships near it as blood splattered from the sky in giant steaming droplets from the rent in its side. An icy gust fell from the back of the passing storm, laying ships on their sides as the beast's form raced away, a dark shadow just beneath the water leaving behind a smoking plume in its wake.

The creature sped for the flagship. Sped for her. Resala looked upon eyes glowing in a head set barely above the waves, maw gaping as if it could swallow the ship. Resala's mouth fell open in a silent gasp to see Ghyldus had gone pale. Then he reddened with his fury, the gem on his brow blazing. His hand stretched out, an accusing finger pointing at the smaller beast that lurked in the distance.

"Your oath!" Ghyldus bellowed at the large beast all knew must be Maura. Rage made his voice crackle the air like passing thunder, an echoing, resonant timber that made the decks rumble. A glow gathered in his palm. Then, a red bolt like a glowing dart, guided by his intent, propelled by his anger, swept from his fingers toward the smaller creature at the rim of the destruction. That beast dived to save itself as the fiery blast of Ghyldus's anger, like the dart from a crossbow, skipped across the ocean's surface until it fizzled in the crest of a wave. Maura rose, too late, from the water to thwart another attack, a wordless wail coming from her gaping mouth. The beast reared up as if to strike the ship, but its gaze fell on Resala, its deep eyes – reservoirs of the sea – seemed to implore her for that instant before it veered away.

Resala locked her gaze on Ghyldus as the fire in his hand grew to a glow. He flung it toward the distant creature, to miss.

Ghyldus let his murderous anger fall on Resala. "I warned you." Snakes coiled about his words. "You defy your master!" He then screamed at the beast. "You could return if you wanted, but no longer."

Another wail broke from Maura's mouth, one only Ghyldus seemed to understand. Resala trembled, knowing she witnessed a god at last intervening for Ea, breaking all oaths with One. But why? The glow grew in Ghyldus's hand. He pushed Resala aside so that she stumbled to the deck and almost over the side. The second creature arched and dived in the distance. Ghyldus brought back his arm and splayed his fingers to scorch Maura's back as the dart flew true. A hiss of sparks scattered skyward.

"You cannot threaten me with Aziaris!" Ghyldus bellowed as Resala pulled her face, wet with spray, up from the waves. "It is a lie. He is gone! Destroyed! I rule here!"

Maura veered away, a shadow beneath the water as she rejoined her companion and sped away.

Resala stared at the turbulent water, ignoring Ghyldus's rantings, unable to stop trembling. A god at whose existence she had scoffed had emerged from legend to smash Ghyldus's fleet. Old nursery tales spoke of Maura the loner who spurned the gods as lovers, finding them too predictable. She no longer swam alone.

Clearly, Ghyldus feared the name that brought another nursery tale to life: Aziaris, whose name graced the sea beneath them. Tales claimed when Maura returned to Ea after the Great War, not to become a mere Visionary and weaken over time, but to safeguard her sea as a god, she spurned the gardener Aziaris who remained with One. Though master of soil and the rains to feed his fields, he could not adapt to the watery realm Maura ruled. In desperation – an example, storytellers attested, of how love could dim the wits of even the gods – Aziaris leaped from the high cliff on Eithira Point to punctuate his vow to come to Maura's call if ever she beckoned, whatever her need. Legend said spikes of rock tore him, a great lightning and thunder accompanying the passage of the body he had assumed. The spirit, tales claimed, remained in this sea.

Resala stared after the retreating beasts, her breaths coming in small puffs. Threatening clouds hovered over the mountains as if ready to return if the fleet dared continue. The wind swung around to the east with a swiftness that confused the waves and revealed a carpet of weeds that choked and calmed the sea's surface ahead. Had Maura called Aziaris, and, after eons, he came? Did two such powerful gods willingly spurn their vow to One for private goals that paralleled her own? Speculating made her look too deep. She embraced the hope.

While devastating, the attack barely dented Ghyldus's fleet. Of his armada, thirty ships had been smashed and sunk by the smaller beast's fury, another fourteen vessels suffered such damage the captains abandoned them, dividing what cargo, crew and troops could be salvaged among the other craft. Rescuers only plucked some hundred men from the water. The remainder went down with the dozens of vessels sucked into Maura's watery cyclone. Not a keg or board or even a flask rose to the surface to prove the ships ever existed. The blast of wind behind the storm laid ten ships on their sides. In all, Ghyldus lost some thirty-five thousand in the carnage, a gaspingly huge number of warriors, yet only a single tine on Ghyldus's fork. If only Arshal could lead such a pair to war! And here nursery tales destroyed more warriors than any army Shande could muster, only a seventh of Ghyldus's fleet. More than two hundred thousand warriors remained. Ghyldus vowed now to utterly destroy all that stood in his way. He would accept no surrender, no quarter, he vowed to his dark Malice, Verdred, raising his voice for

Resala's benefit. He would destroy Shande in one fell blow.

The benevolent wind gone, the east wind calmed and fidgeted, forcing them into a languorous zig-zag across Aziaris's weed-choked surface. At times oarsmen rowed, but the weeds sent tendrils around oars and rudders to weigh them and make the ships unwieldy to steer. The carpet of green and gold weeds bloomed with deep purple flowers, becoming a thick mat that sent up a perfume that made food and drink taste like their scent in the throat, thick and sweet and bitter. Eyes watered and throats choked as the odor hung about them, no matter the wind. This strange growth on Aziaris's crystal surface and the charnel odor of the amethyst blooms only made Resala feel stronger as each day brought her closer to home.

The blossom moon crawled by as the fleet limped toward Saran. In two weeks, it made a distance they had covered before in three days. As each day opened wide before them, Resala rejoiced that some landmark still remained on the horizon, having barely crept nearer in the long night's travel.

But as the hills of Saran rose, Resala noted that despite their losses and delay, a menacing grin fouled Ghyldus's face, a blemish on the day. When his glittering gaze touched her, his laugh held an evil sound that made her skin go chill.

When they reached a point just east of Saran, Ghyldus's ship closed on the stony shoreline. With morbid curiosity, Resala watched as soldiers led Verdred's horse to the rail and lowered it from a sling into the sea. Verdred then leaped into the icy waters to cling to a rope around the beast's neck as it swam for the rocky shore. After only a hundred paces the horse found bottom and – shaking its sides with a splatter of water – raced through the surf to revel in its freedom from the swaying decks of the ship, Verdred on its back. Resala turned to find the God of Ea chuckling with smug satisfaction.

"Scouting out the enemy, my dear princess."

"We are far from Canwyn Point."

"Canwyn?" he laughed, shrill and caustic. "Did I say Canwyn? It must have been an error on my part." He laughed at the implied illogic of the statement. "I know you thought you could out-wit me. A mere shawnsi deceive God! Let your brother race to Canwyn Point. If he gets your message."

Her mouth opened. Her resolve had ridden into the surf of Shande. She had no retort.

"I know you sent one!" he shouted, raising a fist but not letting it fall. "Nothing escapes me! I am God of Ea! Let your play king fortify Canwyn. Let him stare out to sea, lay his plans, gather his troops. You thought you manipulated me. Instead, I led you, willing, into my trap. Let him sit, flank wide open on the advice of his spy he sent to serve me!" He laughed so loud soldiers turned to stare. "You serve me! A slave sold by her brother to his arch-enemy. A fool! Like no other pollen you have drawn him to me to destroy!"

Her limbs went cold, a swell lifting the deck to meet her sinking heart. Her years living this dream wouldn't, at last, let her completely despair. She thought briefly of Malice cresting a hilltop, fouling the pure soils of Kishma. Whether that thing hidden within her, yet unexplored, or the thought of Verdred, or Maura's support that leant her strength, somewhere inside she found her resolve. She had her mission and would think no further. She took a deep breath, sensing, but ignoring Teshet's fearful face peering at her from the shadow of crates.

"To destroy?" she murmured. Her voice, still her own, gave her strength. "So, you send Verdred ashore. That will destroy the King of Shande?"

"He is merely a pawn in the game," Ghyldus said with a dismissing gesture. "He reports what he sees, my eyes until I leave this ship."

Resala stared up at him as if untroubled by the spell in his glare. His gaze lost its sharpness as he fell into hers. All expression fled his features for an instant. He shook his head as if to rid himself of drowsiness.

"My brother will annihilate you," Resala stated in such a flat tone that he blanched. She turned and swept by him, never more certain of her convictions, never more uncertain.

"He knows," Teshet cried into her hands later when the two sat on a tiny bunk in Teshet's cramped cabin near the bow of the vessel. Here, the vessel's pitch only added to Teshet's lengthy sea-sickness. Face pale beneath a fall of dark chestnut hair, blue-black circles hugged her dark eyes. "We will be executed."

Resala shrugged. "Maybe. He will not hurt us yet. He will use me to bait my brother into a foolish move."

Teshet stared at Resala with open mouth. "You would let him do this?"

Resala smiled, untroubled. "What can I do to stop him? He talks as if he knows everything I have thought, planned or done. Maybe he only guesses and has a success on the first try. If so all-knowing, how come Pladde raids succeeded, and Tawnkats remain untroubled in the Lharans? If he knows everything it does no good to stop him. But if he guessed, and doesn't know all there is to know –" she shrugged again, leaving the question there. "The mistake was trusting that abomination. His purposes are his master's. We were led into a trap –"

"Maybe not." Teshet studied Resala from the corner of her eye, a calculating gaze. From the pocket of her skirt, she drew a small cloth pouch sewn from a royal blue cloth. She dropped it into Resala's hand. Though only three fingers wide and a long finger long, the pouch weighed heavy for its size.

"What's this?" Resala untied the white drawstring and emptied the contents into her palm. A sapphire glittered there, dulled only by the fingerprints of much handling. Her head jerked up, her eyes narrowing on Teshet. "How did you come by this?"

Teshet pointed at the chain around Resala's neck.

"Verdred!" Resala hissed the name as if it summed up every pestilence that might invade a world. "What treachery is this? You didn't tell him anything else, did you? He gave you some token stolen from the body of a dead shawnsi –"

"Think what you like," Teshet retorted, surly with seasickness. "I cannot say anything but that he said you would recognize it, and that you must not despair, instead draw strength –"

"How can Verdred say anything!" Resala almost shrieked. Zopher must be dead if his bridegift to her, waiting only for his selection of its setting, came from the hand of Ghyldus's Malice.

"I cannot tell you –" Teshet began.

"It's more treachery, Teshet! He keeps leading us into traps. Ghyldus sent this to destroy my hope, my resistance to his spells. Verdred slew Zopher at the reservoir that day. And these trinkets are part of Ghyldus's arsenal."

Teshet pursed her lips but said nothing.

"Teshet, what have you told him!" Resala wailed. She had visions of the Val invaded by Ghyldus's troops and Tawnkats hacked to death in Lharan mines, Arshal falling beneath Ghyldus's fiery darts as Kedtair sank into memory.

"It is not a trick," Teshet whispered. "I believe there is something still alive in Verdred that hates Ghyldus more than it hates what Ghyldus has done to him. Soon enough, Princess, you will understand why I must keep secrets. The risk is too great to tell you. Remember, even your own mind has been open to him."

"But Verdred, Teshet. Of all Ghyldus's servants, none is more dangerous, none more under his control!"

Teshet inclined her head. "Maybe. But maybe that is to our benefit."

She would say nothing more, clenching her jaw and nibbling her lip as Resala rubbed the prints and dust from the gem before placing it once again within its little pouch and tying it inside the belt at her waist. She would let the sapphire give her strength, as a reminder of all Ghyldus had taken from her.

He crouched behind a boulder molded by some furious ancient sea, though the rock now sat high on the hills at the edge of the vast ocean. The women disappeared down the road, the cackling of chickens they carried in crates on their backs drowned by the east wind.

Why had he hidden? What threat were a gaggle of old women to Ghyldus's Malice? He clenched his black-gloved hands into fists, terrified and frustrated by his confusion. He had been three weeks on this foreign shore. Or was it foreign? The ground itself seemed to beckon as if it were the bosom of a mother he could not remember. He stood upon the land of his enemy. His master awaited his word to destroy it.

He had much to relay with the square of mirror tucked in his pocket. All over this land he found rumor of something about to happen. He couldn't understand just what he sensed, as if the land held its breath. Besides old women and a few old men, he saw no one. He considered racing west to Saran to warn the outposts. How could he explain a sense of foreboding, he who couldn't speak? Yet words erupted from him to the princess's handmaiden. He had heard them fall from his mouth, not the words his master would have bid him speak if he could speak. From where had the gem come? What memory that he couldn't grasp compelled him to leave it for this princess who churned his confused mind into a complex knot each time he saw her, drove him to do things his mind said he couldn't do?

His role was not to think. He served as his master's eyes on this foreign soil that disrupted the god's visionary powers, the evil here so deep. He would tell his master where enemy troops gathered, the traces of their passage, now old as spring passed into summer and fresh growth overtook the worn trail. He would select the fleet's landing site using the mirror to relay the information back to the shadowy armada lurking off the coast.

He felt the warmth of pride at the honor entrusted to him. As he thought that, once again the war in his thoughts surfaced. The indecisiveness in him was the flaw that fed all the others. Something irresolute claimed he acted wrongly, broke some vow, defied some loyalty. This voice in him made him seek cover when a Minarian patrol passed several days back. He'd hidden from his own servants, who might have spewed volumes of information at just his glance. And the old Shandeans he had passed? With a twist of his fingers against their throats, a wrist-flick from the hand holding his knife, they might have spilled more information than even they themselves knew. What stopped him?

He knew many ways to kill, fast and slow, painful and painless. He had extracted confessions from sinners before their sacrifice, forced mothers to betray children, and children to betray fathers. He took pride in his work. His master had taught him well, this god who could turn a person inside out with a bare glance. Ghyldus's Malice could take pride in the way he extracted confessions to justify executions to the populace. He had such a rewarding role to play, to so please his god, to reinforce his word, to bring men to his command by the mere laurels attending a dreaded name. No one dared face him in battle. No mere King's Champion as the meddlesome Verdaen, Verdred was God's Champion. What higher calling could there be?

Then why did treasonous thoughts enter the untroubled vacuum of his existence? Why did he so often do things alien to his role, contrary to his lord's wishes? When important news reached him about events in Shande, why did he wait until the princess stood beside his master before reporting? Why did he gaze on her, not his master? Why would he use a mirror to relay his messages, the magical medallion that could have opened his mind to his god left behind on the ship as if by accident? He sensed the secret inside him must be dangerous, and fatal.

He turned his face to the sun and pulled out the square of mirror he had carried ashore with him. As he gazed into it, the sun lit those features always in shadow. Much of his helm sheltered the rest, an armor he wore even in sleep, for reasons he didn't know. Something about the eyes he glimpsed in the glass unsettled him. Gray, they hinted of some other tribe, not Hogde. In this mood they appeared soft, nothing like the gaze that disciplined his men. Normally the angle he tilted his head hid them, though he did not know why he had such a mannerism, unless a vestige of deference learned in the service of his master. A hint of dark brows showed above the eye holes in his helm, but not so dark as the Hogde. He tilted the helm up a little to reveal where the padding rubbed away the skin, leaving a scar of callouses that ran across the ridge of his brow. Above that ridge three parallel white marks tweaked some chord of memory. He had an image of a giant tawny cat, bleeding and gaunt, leaping at him. He remembered emotions inconsistent with his role. Then, too, he had served this strange princess who so befuddled him. If he shifted the helm from his temple, he knew he'd find a demon's mark, a shame he barely understood. And at the base of his neck was that mark of fangs, usually concealed by a cowl of metal rings. Thinking of that mark gave him an instant's memory of flashing emerald, of warmth and camaraderie, before it, too, faded. He had no comrades, nor need for their companionship.

He resettled the helm on his head and turned his back on the sun. Gazing out over the sparkle of sea, he could just make out the fleet's shadow on the horizon, a few specks like distant birds or some fishing vessel or a cluster of merchant ships seeking the swiftest currents off shore, not like an armada of hundreds of ships. He grinned, a thin-lipped smile. He would see his master victorious. His mission would assure it.

The old women had shrunk to small dots of color against the green hillsides. He considered racing to catch them, like a black hawk swooping down, talons outstretched to wrest from them with his most pleasing arts anything that their minds would spill. Aged matrons would succumb quickly. Not much sport, they would delay him no more than moments, giving him the most information, tripping over themselves to beg his mercy, tell him their darkest secrets. He drew a knife from a sheath in his boot, examining its sharp edge with his thumb, staring after the women. Cresting a hill, they disappeared from sight. With a last glance, mouth twisted by a wild-dog sneer, he replaced the weapon and mounted his horse. They would have to wait. This part of his mission came first. Later he would have time to find some hapless old midwife or cobbler and learn all there was to tell, of things true and fancied, anything he wanted to hear. He could make them confess to be the King of Shande if he so wished. These false admissions never failed to bring up his raw and lethal anger. Many Kings of Shande passed through Lagdche's dungeons.

Once again, his mind lurched ahead with some tangential thought, some inkling of something hidden deep beneath a black-cloaked façade, something that chafed like wool in summer. He imagined a fair-haired man with soft gray eyes and a laughing smile, like a comforting embrace. He wore a circlet encasing a sapphire at his brow, and in his palm a hint of blue from a gem embedded there. The vision seemed a memory of hope. He shook his head. Some fancy from his youth. Yet he remembered no youth. Perhaps his master made him whole and these images came from the bits of minds his master had stolen, a comforting thought. He must be a perfect creation if God made him.

With this thought confidence returned. He rode to the crest of a high peak overlooking the ocean. It would take a long time to empty so large a fleet, and it might yet be several days before the ships could slip into the bay he had found. If enemy scouts lurked nearby as he suspected, his lord would have to disembark under cover of darkness until his armies assembled.

With the square of mirror, he flashed his message across the bright sea from this great height above the pound of surf below. While his hands mechanically delivered his message to the distant ships, his eyes strayed southeast, and he thought that what he did with this mirror might be wrong, not part of his true mission at all, not consistent with some promise or vow he had made. For some reason the feel of this land beneath his feet, the sense of something in the air, made the doubts he had learned to subdue more virulent than ever. A spark lit at sea and the comfort returned. Praise came in glittering code, the greetings of his Maker.

20: Kedtair Eve

The old man standing before the Duke of Lharan still fought for breath following an urgent ride and the roughing the scouts gave him when he crashed through their pickets in the deep of a cool Long Day eve.

"I tell you, that's what I saw," the man insisted.

"That can't be right," Ytri mumbled, squatting in deep grass and peering up at the man silhouetted against a scatter of stars.

"Describe again what he wore and did," Hothur said, the man hesitating a moment at Hothur's Minarian accent.

"All done up in black, from gloves to boots, with helm covering most of his face," the man replied. "He had a mirror aimed to sea, sending some signal. I described it to a fellow who used to tend the lighthouse up that way and he said it was no reg'lar maritime sign. I made out a few ships way out, and saw a glitter come back. Then he made camp like he planned a stay, even to making sure he had a good blind to hide in."

Eithurdon stroked his chin. Ytri glanced at him and then looked away. "Why were you there?" Eithurdon asked. "There are no villages, no roads. What brought you that way?"

"Militia, Lord," the man said. "When we heard the enemy was making for Canwyn, we started watching the shoreline. We have three elderwives walk an old path along the ridge to the lighthouse every day. They saw this man hiding in the bushes. They thought certain he'd kill them he had such an evil feel about him. They hurried to warn us and I went to check it out." He shrugged. "Since I'm the only one as still has a fast horse, I got to come deliver the message."

Ytri looked from Hothur to the old man. "We just heard

yesterday that the fleet was making for Canwyn. Maybe the Minarian merely assures them of a clear passage."

Receiving Konner's message so late, relayed through a rancher who spent weeks finding their trail in such a vast country, they now had a week's back-tracking just to reach Canwyn Point. Now this messenger told them they must travel much farther and would still be late. They had long since given up hope of reaching Sihmad Shal on Arshal's schedule.

The old man shrugged. "You're the folks who know about warfare and all that. I'm just passing the tale. The man looked as if he planned to stick it out a while. We heard rumor of him before, up and down the coast from just east of Saran. He raided a few farms. There's a dead man, neck snapped clean that 'parently stumbled on him in a chicken coop –"

"Verdred," Hothur straightened to turn glittering eyes on the duke.

"What would that mean?" Eithurdon asked.

"Verdred would not be far from his master, and not for long. Where along this coast could they discharge cargo?" Hothur demanded of the old man.

"He was at Lanis Point, which has a good view all up and down the shoreline, one of the highest bluffs," the old man said. "Most of the coast east up to Canwyn is a mess of huge boulders, not a place you'd want to come ashore, too deep to anchor, and too steep to scale the bluffs if you did reach shore."

"So, he must be making for Canwyn and a good beach –" Eithurdon began.

"I wasn't quite finished, Lord," the man interrupted. "At the base of Lanis Point, to the west, there's a sheltered bay. A peninsula juts west and being so high and stuck out so far, the waves are pretty much broke up and the sands have filled in. You can anchor in the lee of the point and have a long sloping beach and a calmed harbor. There's a stream emptying from the Kric into the bay. It cuts a defile in the bluffs, a regular funnel up to the top."

"Send for Kefta!" Ytri barked his order at a scout lounging nearby. "Lanis Point's the marker! He's tricked us again."

Eithurdon nodded. "We must assume that. If he has not landed yet –"

"He may have," Ytri broke in. "They intercepted the message ten days ago. He could be gathered and ready to sweep through the country already."

"How fast did you ride to get here?" Eithurdon demanded of the man.

"Faster than your folk can move, Lord, I'll bet."

"We'll see," Ytri said his face suddenly lit with a luminescent silvery glow.

They turned to stare east at the strange light of the moon on the horizon. It stood out so bright it obliterated the stars in the sky and revealed Eithurdon's soldiers in a white glare like prolonged lightning overhead on a dark night.

"Tomorrow," Eithurdon whispered. "Tomorrow it rises. If he has not landed his fleet yet, then, at least, he will not have calm seas, or the cover of darkness."

"And neither will we," Hothur grumbled. "And you will ride with your five thousand to face his two hundred and fifty thousand. What good will we do, Duke? And where is your king, and your Army of the South? Where is the King's Champion?"

Eithurdon scowled at the reference to Khoti, his fists clenching at his sides. He looked south where his daughter likely rode in Khoti's company, a blatant affront to her father's honor, his daughter playing soldier in an army but most likely seen as a camp follower, no matter what her role. Eithurdon wished he could go just one day without having Khoti thrown into his face. He only awaited the day he could regain his honor.

"We can do only what we can do. And we will need messengers to those commands as well." Eithurdon dismissed his officers to call muster. They would use the eve of Kedtair to light their path.

When Khoti opened his eyes to find Habdelion rousing him, he looked upon a twist of bodies scattered across a battlefield like autumn leaves on a forest floor, Gnats rummaging among them for gear. His mud-stained and bloody standards fluttered in the cool damp from a staff pressed into the ground at the edge of a stream cloudy and stinking of death. Birds of war already gathered for raucous feast, beaten back by Hainadan midwives eyeing up the beasts for cookpots. He gasped at the pinch of fractured ribs. His exhaustion still wrapped tight about him. As Habdelion detailed the points of battle he'd missed, he felt numb to the center of his being.

Three thousand lost. It paled the devastation of Shela. Yet Habdelion grinned, like a skull's bleached features, as he tallied a Minarian defeat so total only a few hundred prisoners remained of fifteen thousand troops. In silence, Khoti absorbed news of how young Cydwyn slipped through a secret door from the riverside of the stronghold while feinting at the gates, the victory at the stronghold averting the cavalry's annihilation.

Habdelion went on then, with a litany of dead and wounded: Daris would likely lose an arm, Kyne's leg slashed, Chati fevered, Dynresa with a broken arrow embedded deep in her thigh, Asteria fighting fever in her wounds. The deepest of the wounds Habdelion related last, in a voice soft and hoarse with mourning. Tedwa gave his blood to soils far from home, the cairn his people set over his ashes high on a bank facing distant Mershy.

Khoti looked up from his contemplation of the cuff on his wrist to realize he heard hoofbeats drumming the rain-softened sod. Habdelion had left, Khoti didn't recall when. As the wind stilled with dusk, the deep gray of rain clouds lurking near the horizon until they mustered their strength, he heard a challenge. Rising out of the storm came a breath of home that pulled at a corner of his mouth. Konner and Ahrwesz screeched out a Tawnkat battlecry as they raced to greet him.

Khoti let the numbness settle in his limbs as Konner detailed their adventures and his meeting with the king. Yet, at their message, Khoti didn't leap to call his troops to march on to Canwyn. He couldn't ask those who'd fought the spirit right out of them to move on so soon, and still the Iyrafael Gnats had not come.

With an oddly soft expression, Konner tugged a bundle from his gear. Soon, a paternal grin spread and the Second's cheeks glowed ruddy beneath watery eyes. "Arshal thought of you," he said. "He wanted you to know and didn't know how to say how he trusts you."

Trust, it echoed like that wintry day in the Val when he roused the king from his deathwalk to have the sovereign proclaim his trust in that waking moment. As dusk darkened the afternoon, Konner touched Khoti's arm, a healer's touch, a touch of pride and home and fealty brushing the skin he had bled for.

"He named you King's Champion and Sword of Shande," Konner went on. "Well, the last, Nali says, was a servant of Dynfearn, certainly there must be something in the royal clutter. So, here's a king and his counselor rummaging the darkest recesses of the palace storerooms, setting to raise a dust like a gaggle of grandmams sweeping out winter, to send, well, this."

Konner held up a stellan-plated helm, thick quilting adhering to the adanan shell.

"You won't find many blades as will dent this!" Konner rapped the metal with his knuckles. Blue and white tassels fell from the crest so long they would reach down Khoti's back. Khoti thought certain he'd look the fool in such a get up, but felt the warmth returning to his middle, a feeling he hadn't known in so long. The king hadn't ceased his search with the helm. He'd included stellan-plated breastplates polished to a high shine and embossed with the coat of arms, a snowy white padded undertunic to go under thigh-length mesh, an overtunic of light blue and a cloak of royal blue.

"If I don't just fall over in all that gear, I'll die of heat stroke," Khoti managed around the knot in his throat.

Konner's face took on a stubborn bent. "Don't you be disobeying your king's wishes that you wear it. We got ourselves a real sovereign like the old tales. I wouldn't be nay-saying him, if I was you. He looks able to drop you on your ear if you smart off."

Khoti plopped the helm on his head for their inspection, managing a laugh to imagine how comical it must appear, with its crest and plume and noseguard. Just seeing Konner and Ahrwesz, hearing the lilting speech of men who had lived the better part of full lives never knowing anyone but their own mountain folk, he felt a tiny glow of hope creep back into him. Then Konner had spied his nephew Chati lying like death under Cydwyn's care.

Despite the urgency of the king's need of his southern command, Khoti let his army rest while scouts and attendants gathered barges. Four days later, he nudged his army onto the crowded barges for the journey north, joined by two thousand Whittea Gnats who heard of the muster to Canwyn too late to meet Arshal.

The short rest barely rebuilt the soldiers' stamina, and it would take much longer to mend the seriously wounded. Khoti wanted nothing more than a deep sleep in a soft bed, for a month, at least, to regain a year's worth of sleepless nights. Images of the quiet fires in Habdelion's forest taunted him, the soft nights when he surrounded himself with the laughter of friends.

During their first day on the river a few hundreds more trickled in from the little hamlets along the canal as the army, no longer the Army of the South, but instead of Three Provinces, drifted by. While they still had room to spare for a comfortable journey that would allow them to rest and recuperate, and travel faster now that the wagons wouldn't slow them, come the next noon Cydwyn raced along the bank with an excited cry. Minutes later the marching columns, prancing horses, and clattering wagons of the Iyrafael Gnats appeared, more than doubling the size of Khoti's command. It brought a small lump into his throat. Such awesome responsibility all these lives! Thirteen thousand infantry led a cavalry of seven thousand, far fewer than Kyne hoped. Battle for the region around the Sea of Iyrafael had been stiff with Gnat losses heavy. The soldiers augmenting Khoti's ranks were battle-hardened survivors.

But now the barges were so cramped and uncomfortable, sitting low in the water, the battle-weary army had to sleep in shifts. And they had many days of travel ahead yet.

As a second night on the canal advanced, Khoti huddled in a corner of his barge command post, a crowded place sour with unwashed warriors. Canal water rippled against the bow as the creak of wagons shifting and the stomp of horses rose into the silent night. Silhouettes of oarsmen stood against a starry sky as they dug poles into the canal's bottom in cadence, propelling them toward the next lock.

The other rafts, barges and boats loomed dark against the canal's starry surface before and behind them. He shifted, his legs tingling. He had only bare inches between tack and gear and weaponry piled upon the barge's deck.

He could only wish for the day they would race across the open grasslands of Kishma in search of Canwyn Point, long prairie grass concealing their passage. The horses would not want for feed and the soldiers could flop in the grass at night. He intended to use the barges as long as they could after leaving the canal, the speediest way to by-pass the marshes at Quelica's mouth and bring the infantry and support wagons to firm ground. He planned to send the worst of the wounded on to Sihmad Shal. He could allow nothing to slow them. After poling up the Quelica beyond the marshy lower reaches, fifteen thousand cavalry would take to land and speed to meet Arshal, the infantry continuing up a tributary of the Quelica to place them only a few days behind the cavalry. Arshal would likely be engaged by then. Khoti couldn't help it. He was just one man and his troops bled too freely.

Khoti dropped his head in his hands. He needed more sleep. Dangerous thoughts suffocated him again, threatening his grip on reality, himself.

A brush against his bare arm made him turn to find Asteria peering at him in the darkness. He scrunched down closer into himself, moving away from her. He gazed into his scarred and calloused hands. Too much depended on this campaign and too many of his comrades were dead. Tedwa's silent chuckle came to him, the woody smell of the man as he'd leaned close to the fire so the flames would dance in his eyes as he related some tale in that musical dialect of Tormor.

In the raft behind, Ahrwesz held high a lamp so Konner could tend a soldier. All the powders healers carried, all the herbs the Detarians brought, none could help Daris. Jali hovered over her just beyond the light of Konner's lamp. Other soldiers succumbed to lesser injuries on the damp and dirty battlefield. And each day Khoti fought the desire to mend this wild creature tamed to one handler. He owed Daris for her loyalty. But when the wounded continued on to Sihmad Shal, no healers, not even Jali, would be aboard the barge to defend her decision to keep the useless limb. He knew Chati would die trying to follow alone if Khoti tried to force his lieutenant to travel on to Sihmad Shal with Daris. Chati fought his fever so valiantly, Khoti had to relent. That he dwelt on the injuries of his friends, not those of all his warriors, made Khoti scowl his ill humor.

Something made him look up at the shore. He felt no wind, yet the dark shapes of trees moved against the sky, and ripples sprouted from the shoreline. He glanced back at the following raft, a sudden wave pressing it against his. Ramel leaped aboard a moment before the raft slipped away again, the waves rolled back within the canal's narrow walls.

The seer pressed through fidgeting horses to meet Khoti, who stood to study the banks and the shape of the waves sloshing in the canal like water in a pan. Asteria's fingers gripped his arm, but he pretended not to notice as horses emitted nervous snorts and squeals, their legs braced against the rise and fall of water threatening to splash over the banks and splattering over the barge's wales.

"Tomorrow," Ramel stated when he reached Khoti's elbow.

"You're certain?"

"The ground shakes. On the open sea it is worse. The star makes tides surge, builds storms with devastating winds and seas. It comes. I have witnessed its arrival well over two hundred times." He pointed at a glow on the eastern horizon.

"The star's rising now?" Khoti asked, searching for the dim memory he had of his last Kedtairday nine years ago, as a child, when its mystery loomed even more incomprehensible.

"No, the moon, lit by Kedtair. Tonight, there will be no night."

As if to punctuate Ramel's statement, the sky brightened like a room to a lamp as the moon crested the horizon. Soon it would breach the high levee blocking his view. A muted white glow grew around them, the shadows sharp and as dark as the deepest mountain caves. Ripples no longer spread from the shores, but the waves had yet to abate within the canal's confines, each tipped white in the odd light. A scatter of high and rainless clouds scudded silver against the sky, blazing out a blinding white moments before a crest of moon flashed over the horizon. So bright it made the eyes water to peer at her, the scars on the full face of the night sentinel hid. The moon almost appeared to give off rays like the sun. With an effort, Khoti dragged his gaze away, the light against the dark sky seeming so much brighter than the day sun.

"And this is only the eve," Khoti muttered to Ramel. "I remember now: heat, avalanches, the snowpack melted, sheep and goats' milk went dry and the lambs and kids had to be weaned early. The mountains shook, landslides closed passes, the wildlife desperate and crazed."

"Kedtair's effects are like that everywhere," Ramel admitted. "Think of Jashiho's heat with a wetness like impending rain in the air, and a wind driving the sands in to choke the grasslands so herders must drive their stock to Kalilia to find range. By summer's end, this canal will flow a pace or two shallower, its source waters evaporated, to suddenly rise when some storm dumps the ocean on the land. Think of the oceans! Waves as high as ship's masts and stars hidden in light!" Ramel shook his head, but his face held a stark eagerness, as if instead of hundreds of times, he contemplated Kedtair for the first time. "You might find when we take to the Quelica that a great flood will rush down."

"But Kedtair dries up springs –" Khoti began.

"First the snowcaps will melt, rushing to streams that feed rivers that feed the Eilime and Quelica. And the storms. We will have to watch ourselves or be driven back hours along our course if we lose bottom and the current picks up."

Khoti clenched his eyes shut against the bright imprint of the moon still ghosting his vision. "All men to oars," Khoti ordered Tre without looking at the officer he knew awaited his decision. "Every man. We have to make speed. We're a long way from Canwyn."

Tre nodded, hurrying to follow Khoti's orders. Khoti returned his gaze to the moon, feeling a profound foreboding, as if a live thing breathed in his face, not the touch of a star's reflection. His skin crawled, hair prickling across his scalp as he watched the moon's slow passage across the sky. More than the arrival of Kedtair, this harbinger impressed him. For reasons he couldn't fathom, Khoti felt he must study this event, this eve of Long Day and eve of Kedtair and dawning of Kedtair's first day, as if the event would never occur again. Perhaps, if Arshal failed, it never would.

Around him came the soft calls of oarsmen to man the poles. Gasps of surprise filtered to his ears as the pace of the barges picked up, the waves filing out from the crafts' sides with urgency. He felt a lurch in the pattern as someone chanted a cadence and the poles dug into the bottom, pushed, came up as one, then dug in again. The shores sped by, nervous chatter heightening the tension as soldiers and support troops realized the import of the day to come.

Khoti leaned back against his saddle pad and the bundle of ancient armor beneath. Asteria crept closer to him, her gaze, too, locked on the orb chasing the starlight before it.

"It will be a new world tomorrow," Asteria whispered.

Khoti turned to her, the full moon super-imposed over her face until his eyes adjusted.

"What comes tomorrow," she shook her head. "I feel so minor, as if I have no right to even think about what might come of it."

"It's bigger than us." He wanted to put his arm around her, certain she would reject it. He wanted to ignore her.

She nudged him hard and giggled. "But you are one of the major players." Her giggle died, sounding hollow and shrill on this strange evening.

His hands clenched and unclenched beside him. "So much depends on this star's rising, on timing, on interpretations of omens and dreams. I'm a healer and a warrior. Which role am I meant to play?"

He studied her face so bright and pale, her dark hair a deep shadow from which she peered. He touched her arm, a light brush, charged. Her skin puckered with the chill beneath his touch. Her other hand rubbed the spot as she turned to look at him, his gaze seeming to steal her breath. He again stared up at the sky.

"And here," Khoti continued, softer, "My greatest fear isn't Ghyldus, or his two hundred and fifty thousand. It's facing Eithur when we meet again on the battlefield."

He smiled at her a moment only, before looking back to the sky. He reached an arm around her in search of a comfort for which he couldn't ask. He sensed her watching him with that quizzical expression, but soon forgot everything but the enormity of the eve of Kedtair unfolding before him.

"Too soon," Nali grumbled at Arshal's elbow, scowling.

The king turned from the moonrise. "Our birthstar rises come morning," Arshal said lightly. "Who will light the festfires for Long Day?"

"Festfires? Long Day's no festival no more. It marks the anniversary of the call to arms, and Ebon's abdication, and the start of another war. Like I said, one giant circle we've made."

"But we didn't have Kedtair, or the stone, or armies."

"At least we were there when they made landfall."

"We'll be there," Arshal insisted.

Nali wasn't so sure. They marched out of Sihmad Shal more than a week late, not the next morning as Nali promised. Then, delays kept them in the hills and forests around Mania Point. Now, an army near forty thousand strong, they grew daily as more and more recruits found them. Yet they could field only seven thousand cavalry and with so much infantry and so many to support, they crawled west, their supply line strained. They had been on this march a month already. A lone rider could have done the journey with comfort in under two weeks if not saddled with the logistics of such a trek. And they rushed the muster, troops and beasts pushed mercilessly. A little over halfway to Canwyn, time fled before them. As Konner had said, no one lives near Canwyn. They carried and cured what they could; behind them the soft lowing of cattle greeted the rising moon, attendants such as Bertal herding pitiful stock that wouldn't serve so large an army long. At each camp, teams of butchers labored through the night to cure what should have been on hand were they not an occupied land, were they a land steeped in the logistics of war.

As Nali studied the glare of the moon, he wondered if Ghyldus had already come ashore, now marching at them, better prepared than these troops that had trained to defend a city of full larders. Would the godhead meet them far from Canwyn, the king's strength scattered under four commands? What if Canwyn Point was a ruse?

As if sensing the turn of Nali's thoughts, Arshal gripped his counselor's shoulder with such strength Nali winced.

"Sage, don't go soft on me now."

Nali stared up at his king. The moon silvered Arshal's hair, his gray eyes like stars in a shadowy face. The stone glowed softly, a blue-white glow in the palm of the king's hand. He projected such confidence it took Nali's breath from him.

"Arshal, how do you feel this moment," Nali whispered, gripping Arshal's forearm.

"We must drive harder tomorrow," Arshal stated, staring out into the night as if he saw a map he would follow. "We won't reach Canwyn for three weeks at this pace."

"How do you feel!" Nali insisted.

To Nali's surprise, Arshal laughed. "Ask me when Kedtair rises in the morning. This moment?" Arshal turned from the moonrise. "I wish I stood on a desert, watching that moonrise while contemplating my abilities beneath the reproving tongue of a Joffan princess." He laughed again, a soft chuckle to himself as he examined a private thought. Arshal clapped his hand on Nali's shoulder. "Instead, a Sage who's wiser than he'll admit joins me this romantic moonlit night, a bloodthirsty army in the background. It steals from the ambiance."

Nali emitted a snort. "And now, how do you really feel?"

Arshal remained silent a long time as he watched the moonlight sparkle up from the dew, like millions of stars set in the tall grass. "I've never been so terrified, excited, and happy, all at once, in my life. I'm ecstatic that at last this will end and we'll realize everything for which we've strived. It'll be a final test. For some strange reason I've come to yearn to prove myself against myself, to test my skills. And what could be the ultimate test but this?" His words trailed away into a whisper as he gazed at the moon.

Nali stared up at him, nodding with imperceptible acknowledgement. Nali had learned much from the Lierye. The derna couldn't read the future, but he knew what should happen at dawn if they did what needed to be done. Were they ready for it? He shook himself, realizing Arshal still spoke.

"But then, I'm terrified. At the pace we've been traveling we'll reach Canwyn only a week before Kedtair sets. That may not be enough time. I'm terrified I might fail. I tense up with horror when I think all of Shande makes sacrifices for a vain challenge by me that can never be accomplished. What if they lose hope on the field? What if I fail? What will then become of us? Or is it vain as well for me to even think the country needs me to function? And all the things you told me, all the things you're teaching that should've been taught long ago –"

Nali gripped Arshal's arm and spun his king to face him. Arshal's eyes didn't have that haunted cast, the bereft look he'd once had when his fear threatened to carry him away.

"I'll overcome it." Arshal pulled his friend to him in a reassuring grasp. "You'll have the wisdom to support me. Khoti will lend me his strength. And together we'll destroy Ghyldus."

"There's more to it," Nali said, his tone more and more like that of Visionaries, cryptic and sour.

Arshal laughed. "Odd the way you found such wisdom in a book written by the long dead. What changes will we find in Khoti? Gods. It's been two years. I can just imagine his doubts. He has such a gentle passion and pity about him –"

"Are we thinking of the same warrior?"

Arshal chuckled, turning his back on the moon. "I'll count on you to say the right things at the right time, and to remind me of things I already know. I'll count on Khoti to keep me alive to the end. As long as we have the night lit for us, I guess we'd better press on. We don't want to keep the enemy waiting."

"Nor the gods that made this evening possible," Nali said, his tone acid as he signalled Jan to relay the order.

"It may be the gods' fault," Arshal admitted as they fell into step. "But at least they didn't just abandon us to their mistakes. They've tried to guide us –"

"We think. Who knows what the dreams really mean –"

"There's the stone, your powers." The corners of Arshal's mouth lifted with that playful cast from his past. "You can't tell me you don't have them. I feel the command in your tone, the gods in your thinking. And look at Khoti, with Terremar's touch, but a fire and drive in him more like Fyraer –"

Arshal stammered to a stop as if he'd stumbled on something he should know. Nali peered up at him, eager. But the wisp of an idea eluded the king, as if stolen away.

"It's all of Ea coming together, Nali," he mumbled. "And I don't want to nay-say one bit of it." Arshal turned his glance over his shoulder at the moon.

Geleg, dressed in a Minarian cloak, stood on the high stone walls of Sefresal, staring out over the silvery plain to the east as the moon rose. A hand fell on his shoulder and he turned to find the pale light thrown back from Steadon's gaunt face, his shawnsi features gathering shadows.

Geleg nodded. Tomorrow he would be a Guardsman again, curse the courier. He would never again carry on the ruse of being Minarian, never have to don the dismal black, but again honor his duke in the buff and pewter. Not that he thought his ruse had been successful. Recent weeks convinced him the courier performed his own game of lies, feint and fakery. Geleg heard the same from his counterpart in Eilime. Certainly, the courier knew by now of revolts in the southern Lharans. Certainly, doubts had surfaced when men didn't respond to summons or letters from home, or transfers never showed. Sefresal stood at the heart of a vast network of sabotage, of goods that fell apart or food stuffs processed to spoil. What game did the courier play as troops marched on them from the west? If the courier dared come again, he would never leave.

Geleg unpinned the clasp at his throat that held the black, orange and red cloak. He flipped back the hood to reveal his burn-scarred features and dropped the uncomfortable, fingerless mesh gloves from his hands to fall on the stone at his feet like sacks of sand.

"Remember, at least a dozen Minarians are here to challenge you," Steadon whispered.

"Remember yourself," Geleg retorted as if addressing a peer. "You're standing bold here with your shawnsi face, Steadon. Tell me you can run inside and hide after so long waiting for this eve." He turned to find Steadon's smile.

"So, we move a night early," Steadon said, chuckling at Geleg's battle grin. They both knew it didn't matter. Nothing went by the rules anymore. Nothing would be the same: the duke and his daughter at odds, most of the original Guard dead or maimed, Khoti banished, his people dead and scattered, villages lost and burned. Steadon wasn't Eithurdon and would not let rules stop him.

"Well, if we are to cleanse the city by morning," Steadon muttered with a sigh, ignoring Geleg's broad smile.

Geleg grasped Steadon's arm a moment, pulling a flask from his pocket. "First, we must toast what will come," he said with his rakish grin. "Gods above, I wish I could be there to see it!" Geleg's eyes grew moist as he stared into the bright night. "To see Arshal riding into battle with that stone of his, Khoti beside him, and Nali."

Steadon shuddered. "To Kedtairday, and the end of this war with no others to come," Steadon mumbled, accepting the flask pressed into his hands.

Geleg glanced at the shawnsi, hearing empty words, as meaningless as cordial greetings. His smile faded. He had the image of a vengeful Eithurdon, thousands of his reflections beside him in an unending war beneath a ghostly moon.

The moon stood a marker to all of Ea, a lantern, a beacon.

Far south and east of the walls of Sefresal, a cluster of ships dropped anchor in the harbor off silent Shela. As the captain of the small fleet looked skyward at the moon tingeing the mists trailing from the Dasirei swamp, he ordered his men ashore. When the morning came, the furious winds of Kedtair would likely rip across shallow Simiriel.

"Do we abandon?" the first mate whispered in his captain's ear. "If we go ashore, we could lose the ships if they swing off the wind."

"To lose the ships is a better alternative," the captain returned. "Ships can be built; a country must evolve."

The mate stared at the captain, who shook his head and gave the man a shove to hurry to boats that would take them ashore before the morning came. The captain stared up at the moon briefly, then at the ghostly shore. Shela didn't have to be empty this moment. If it hadn't been for that warrior he'd transported upriver so many moons ago, a man with a childish anger. Better to see the port empty than to look on the emaciated forms of the Shelans that had labored here, died here.

As the sailors stowed sails, lashed down everything on the

decks, and unloaded supplies to last them the month of Kedtair in Shela, far away in a high room facing east, King Wyeff Shikora let out an audible sigh. The dreams had not returned since his fleet sailed. When the truth of what truly occurred in Joffa came out, they led his champion away in chains. King Wyeff Shikora's lips drooped down. Baynu's foolishness, his arrogant pride, cost the lives of thousands.

Far to the west, at the narrow Strait of Tebez, a shadowy line of craft bobbed in the swell where Simiriel met the colder waters of the western Sea of Tebez. High bluffs stared down at the dark water, their inky shadows hiding the ships below. Lashed together, the ships' sides splintered and cracked as the swells threw them together. On the north side of the strait, the large, bulky vessels of Arenh loomed dark in the stark shadows. The lights of a village on shore twinkled on the water, seeming detached and no more consequential than sparks against a starry sky. But high in the rocks above the village, a swarm of archers from the ships peered out to the Sea of Tebez.

At about the midpoint of the strait, the ships became smaller, squatter, flatter, their drafts designed for the shallower bays of Simiriel, not the deep ocean off Arenh's western shore. Shikoran flags flew from their masts, and on the southern shore, Shikoran archers awaited confrontation. Aboard the vessels, sailors made their last preparations they hoped might spare their vessels from the worst of the buffeting when Kedtair finally rose.

"Night ceases tonight," a Shikoran sailor said as he peered up at the sky, unable to find the guiding star paled to nothing by the moon.

"It will be day each night from now on," an Arenhian sailor agreed as they hefted their seabags and crossed the rails of adjoining ships, prepared to find shelter on the shore.

"When the star sets, it will be night forever if Shande is lost," the Shikoran shouted.

"Then we had best not let them lose Shande," the Arenhian returned as he leaped to the deck of another ship, the flitting figures of hundreds of others following the same path to shore. The loss of so many ships would be slight if it kept Minaria from ruling Ea.

Farther north, in the seaside city of Ar-Tebez, King Azren of

Arenh rose from his vigil in his courtyard when the moon finally crested the rooftops of his house. He turned his face up to the white light and raised his glass.

"Destiny is what you made it," he toasted. He mulled over the fault of the gods on this ominous evening, gods who created this war as they created Kedtair and the evil they left to trouble Ea. Gods who had left mere mortal servants to finish their tasks. Azren drained his wine and raised another, the one he'd set out for the white-haired king who had come so singly to Azren's hall, hidden in his cloak, no entourage, no pretense, only his voice of command. Azren made his toast in silence. It was no good for him to chastise the gods. They knew their errors and had eternity to contemplate their mistakes. It was not Azren's role to judge, but it would be Arshal's.

Far to the east King Farlal contemplated his weakness before his council in defense of the Shandean king who held such an odd power over him, comforted that his last gesture would be an apology and surprise. To the west, half a dozen Otayran ships dropped anchor beyond the lighthouse in Sihma Harbor. The sailors stared up at the silhouette of the city of Sihmad Shal looming above. The moon stood directly behind the city, a glow bounding from the walls. At its uppermost elevation, the Window of the Sun blazed, its prismed windows sparkling blinding light like sun glint on seas. Shades of silver and blue scattered with white and deep lavender as the moon peeked through the bright eye of the tower. Like a beacon, the Tower of the Sun drew people to gaze on her, find hope like a yellow square of window calling a traveler home at night. Despite their intent to surprise the King of Shande with Farlal's greetings, the pilot boat rowed to meet them, hails greeting them as if expected. Farlal had made no such promise.

21: The Rising of Kedtair

Dawn rose like no other could or would again.

Never had such a dawn meant so much to so many. All of Ea paused, expecting life to somehow change this moment. Never had its oddity, the light and color accompanying it, the set of the dew, or the shape of the clouds attracted so many to view it.

Dawn. The sky glowed all the way to the west, a purpling that faded to lavender and at last to an almost powdery blue, but clearer and sharper than that. The color of the gloaming clung about it, that sheen like thick glass shedding reflected moonlight. When the sun rose, it blazed out sudden and bright, not yolk-yellow as a summer dawn was wont to wake. Moments later a hot wind exhaled from the east, drying the dew in its blast. Trailing the true sun by the distance of a thumb held against the sky, a small white star blazed fiercely, its rays paling the sun's. While on the horizon, the sun could fit within the circle of thumb and forefinger held against the sky, Kedtair followed like a tiny dangling pebble. Kedtair burned so fierce it almost seemed to draw the sun's light away, leaving the sun strangely shadowed in its presence.

Heat overtook the dawn, drawing the dew in steaming wisps from the ground. Then, from ponds, lakes and rivers, a steady stream of moisture rose, coiling puffs of cloud racing upward. When the wind blew the tendrils of mist against some hill or across some larger water, storms would erupt to rain their strength in moments then rise again in steam. In the warm waters of the south, the sea rained into the sky to soon whirl into sucking storms that sent their fury out from trailing spirals across vast reaches of ocean. The tempests would crash into land with winds that toppled trees like blades of grass before the shears, and send tides like city walls surging inland.

Once the two suns rose free of the horizon's muting haze, they became impossible to look upon, and only a white blaze could be discerned from that patch of sky they guarded.

The tide rushed in, lifting ships in harbors and flooding the mouths of rivers. The wind whipped seas into a froth. The ground trembled in places, mortar cracking and walls crumbling, shaking Ea from its mesmerization with the dawn.

As Kedtair rose, trailing the sun in a stately march that took it south of the sun's path and at a faster pace, a cue went out across the land. Throughout Shande shals threw down their tools and gathered in those places where Minarian outposts remained. The conquerors didn't expect this sudden fury with which Shande revolted. Shandeans broke weapons from hidden caches as children emerged from cellars across the countryside, pale faces blinking at the light. Caches of metals emerged. Mobs busted open coffers or tore down Minarian structures stone by stone, pelting any Minarian they found with their labor.

In Sihma Harbor, Otayrans struggled ashore against the surf, preparing to defend foreign soil if Ghyldus sent any ships so far. In Sefresal snowmelt rushed streams and shifted rocks as Tawnkats attacked the Minarians guarding the river. Segan looked down from the redoubt, watching as the bridge over the Ymmenay River at Staph-el crumbled once again. Mines closed. Once again Tawnkats took to the hunt as an army marched on the Lharans.

In Detarian and Tormor, trees creaked in a wilting steam as heat rose from curling leaves. Tachi retook Habdelion's ancient seat, his daughter Habda standing by with a smug smile as the last of the Minarian defilements were swept away.

The rough Sea of Simiriel smashed ships into one another like twigs against shore as the southbound Minarian fleet plowed through heavy seas and fended off attacks from the bluffs above the straits. One ship's crew already tried to quench wind-whipped fires kindled by a flaming arrow.

And in the secluded bay sheltered by Lanis Point, a few ships at a time discharged their cargo as waves crashed among them, threatening to pull all beneath the surface. A few vessels foundered on the rocks after their cargoes were mostly ashore, the rest rescued as giant breakers carried the supplies landward.

Ghyldus's frenzy drove them as they disembarked beneath the dark stare of Verdred on the bluff above. It might take days to assemble.

Ghyldus's Malice had served his master well. The old women who might have warned of their arrival lay in a twisted heap in a ravine a few paces away, their necks snapped by a dispassionate Verdred. They had told him little he did not already know. That their landing had already been reported escaped him.

Soon, as Ghyldus planned, they would flank their enemy. In the distance a dozen ships fought the rough seas en route to the city of Sihmad Shal. Ghyldus would accept no quarter, no prisoners, no surrender, would allow no traitors in his secured land. Ghyldus's Malice smiled at such a thing, the glow of Ghyldus's praise flowing up at him. All the doubts of before had fled. He had brought his master ashore at the place that would best serve vengeance and victory. He served his master well.

The troops wading ashore would prove Ghyldus's might. The god never need soil himself with the evil of Shande. He would watch his troops destroy the King of Shande and take the pleasure of watching Shande's soils feed on her people. The god already spun a web to trap the upstart king. Perhaps Ghyldus's Champion would have the honor of slaying him.

The rising of Kedtair passed swiftly.

The star sank in the near southwest many hours before Long Day ended in the west. When welcome dark came with a coolness like a sigh over the land, the moon rose blazing, like a watchful eye, again turning night into day. A few hours later, Kedtair rose again. Its light fell on Ea pale, muting the day with an eerie dimness like those rare times when the moon mostly eclipsed the sun. Like the brightened moon, Kedtair created sharp shadows, its half-light bright enough to sew by, but not as golden. It appeared as if hundreds of torches lit a square with a luminescent, opalescent, lunar glow.

The light faded briefly at moonset, while Kedtair hung to the south for several hours after the sun rose. Kedtair would follow its faster path for half its journey overhead, each day setting more westerly than the last until at its zenith it would follow the same path the sun had taken on Long Day, leaving no shadow at the midpoint of its course. Then, slowly, Kedtair would swing northwest until it stayed there, hidden, as it had every nine years since the Great War sent the gods back to One. In that month night, true night, might only come for a few brief minutes when the three lights in the sky joined at the back of the horizons. The moon would lose her phases: the new moon fainter than full, yet lit by Kedtair; the quarters lasting an hour as Kedtair shone from some other angle, brightening dark edges like a face partly in shadow.

Before Kedtair set for the last time, Shande had much to do.

At the rising of Kedtair, Nali paused. He pulled his mount away from the path the others followed. Dismounting to watch the sun breaking the horizon, he leaned on his sword. The vibrations of Kedtair's power surged through his weapon, trembled in his hand. He stared at the white star, remembering each lesson, each morsel of knowledge Cree had passed from beyond his pyre. The derna studied the blaze. Then he closed his eyes to recall its light, calling deep within himself to do what Arshal must discover on his own, perhaps prodded by Nali, but not led. It was the secret of Kedtair, the spark that would bring together all that he'd learned, all the powers both latent and discovered that lay within him.

His emotions churned, the knowledge shuffling within his mind like tiles in a game. An order emerged in the wisdom learned and lived, organizing the volumes he had gathered, codifying it into an understanding more profound than even the Visionaries had known, more accessible than the scholars' library, more calculated than merely leafing through pages. He felt as if at last he found a book in a word that provided the answer to any question ever sought, all within him. Kedtair.

His breaths came in rapid gasps. His face flushed as he stood paralyzed, closed lids contemplating the ghost of the star. He cast his thoughts within, finding answers, divining a mystical sense of himself, of what he was capable, a startling knowledge that made his heart pound in his ears. Could he do what his mind insisted? He had struggled to decipher the Lierye, now his mind filled with those meanings. Like a flood gate opening, understanding crushed him, his head pounding, aching, his lungs catching fire. He expected this. How would he help Arshal deal with the gifts he'd earned for his trials if only he found the key to open them?

Panic struck him, his breath sucking in with a throat-tearing gasp. What if Arshal hadn't learned the lessons, explored the thoughts he must to find admission to Kedtair? Nali didn't know what the king needed to undergo to be accepted, to be unleashed by Kedtair. It was an unleashing, Nali decided, an awakening.

They had thought something more tangible would come from this rising, not this inner knowledge, not this extension of power through contemplation of the star, through acceptance of all the elements, that finally they must grow to Kedtair to unlock themselves.

At last Nali opened his eyes. He discovered he'd fallen to his knees, gripping the sword hilt, white-knuckled, as he leaned on the weapon to avert falling. His face dripped tears and sweat, his hair limp and damp, stuck to his brow. As he glanced about himself, placing himself in this new world, he first thought to test himself to see if his mind could really do what it claimed.

He scanned the columns of troops passing by him. Few even noticed him crouched in the deep grass.

"Awake, King, come find me," Nali thought to himself. He made a fist and pulled it to his chest as if to draw Arshal to him. He closed his eyes. They flew open when a hand fell on his shoulder.

Arshal stepped back from Nali's gaze. The king appeared haggard, as if tormented, now twisted by fear for his counselor who still knelt, clutching his sword for balance.

"I thought I heard you calling," Arshal said as he studied Nali as if he'd never seen him before. He stared into Nali's eyes as if drawn into an abyss, yet repelled. "Are you well?"

"I called," Nali gasped, wrenching his hands from the sword and sitting back on his haunches, wiping his palms on his knees. He tapped his temple. "Kedtair's promise is quite a promise." He staggered to his feet. He ignored Arshal's questions, the king's supporting hand, waving them away like so many flies circling his head. As they approached their mounts, he regained his strength and the alien feel in his limbs seemed to fade though he clung to the sensation of discovery that had so enveloped him.

Mounted, Nali studied the King. "You don't look well," he stated, delving, digging, sifting as he studied Arshal's drawn face.

"I'm not sure what's wrong with me," Arshal said. "Anticipation maybe. I feel I must do something. I don't know what. I feel torn, wounded. It's hard to explain. Maybe nerves. I had a poor night. I can't seem to think clearly, or concentrate, as if there's someone badgering me with inane questions that have no answer, but are taking up my time."

Nali studied him silently for many minutes as they caught up with the head of the column. He looked away only when Arshal began to squirm under the inspection.

"Concentration is key."

"There you go getting cryptic on me again."

"You have to find it yourself," Nali returned. "I can lead you in the right direction but you have to make the discovery, Dyn Eadon. I can't do everything for you. Use your reason! Everything you need is inside of you. All you need's the right trigger to put it in order –"

"What makes you so sure," Arshal cut in with an irritable wave of his hand. "Is this more of the undecipherable scribblings you think you may understand out of the Lierye, but you're not quite sure –" Arshal faltered at Nali's perilous expression.

"No. I found the answers," Nali whispered.

Arshal started to speak, but Nali's hand flew up. Arshal stared in awe, gasping, unable to speak. Nali gave him a small, smug smile before he lowered his hand.

"This is interesting." Nali mused. "But what power if in the wrong hands! No wonder gods dole their gifts so sparingly, with tests and trials and suffering. I must explore this."

"How did you –" Arshal began.

"It's from Kedtair, Arshal. And, gods! What I've found! I can't imagine what you'll discover."

Nali nudged his mount and disappeared into the columns of troops marching for Canwyn Point, leaving Arshal to mull the derna's words.

In the bay off Lanis Point, Resala tossed in an uneasy sleep.

She ignored the presence beside her who wormed through her thoughts. Something happened. She could feel the swell of the ocean beneath her, the insistent pound of waves and creak of wood as the ship protested. She didn't recognize the thoughts passing through her, but sensed she was meant to learn, to achieve, something. Something that would give her enough strength to rid herself of the presence beside her. It related to Kedtair. She must think on Kedtair.

She remembered the day she stood before her mirror and saw a truth she couldn't name. As then, her mind now brought strange images before her, as if she must recognize these thoughts before she could reach a wholeness that would give her strength. With a sense of awe, she realized she needed something of Maura, and something of Ghyldus.

She tossed again, hearing through the vestiges of sleep a chilling chuckle. She sat up and stared into the darkness toward the dark place she knew. When her gaze found him, his laughter died, though he certainly couldn't see her in the dark cabin.

She knew he crawled inside her mind.

"You are granted some little power by your star," he said with what sounded like sorrow. "Thus, I must destroy you. First, there is a role I have for you to play."

"Bait," she stated. Her voice shredded the darkness like a shard of glass.

"You will bring him, reckless, to me."

"No," Resala stated. "I will bring you, reckless, to him."

He leaned away. "What are you? From where do you draw this power to defy me? It cannot merely be the much-diluted blood of my siblings."

She stared at him, undaunted.

"Perhaps I have, indeed, harbored this long time a very dangerous entity. What fortune you cannot see that. This will be one of the easiest conquests of my long battle to be shed of One's rabble. Already this day I draw tight the noose. Last eve I cast my spell, triumphant, used the anchors my faithful Eidhalt set long ago, years ago. My skill deserves so much more than your derision. Go."

She rose, her body stiff as she pulled the robe about her and left the cabin to face the rising of Kedtair. The ship groaned in its anchorage.

When the dim light of the passageway fell on her face his gaze narrowed on her. He saw it, she knew he saw it, the features of a woman torn by confusion.

"Even in sea sickness you are a marvel to behold," he said, drawing his conclusions. "You need not rush. We have plenty of time. Kedtair will set with your king unawakened."

She continued along the passageway, as if she had not heard him.

As the vessel groaned beneath him, Ghyldus pressed his hands to the gem at his brow, turning inward to appeal to his mentor. If his spell, set so long ago, failed, if this king knew himself, perhaps at last Fyraer might need to show himself through his emissary.

As Ghyldus hovered over himself, a burning presence brought searing pain from the ruby at his brow, the only pain the god had known but that inflicted upon him by One. His limbs grew hot. His body trembled with unsated desires. Sweat rushed to bead up on skin tingling with fury.

Within himself, the weaker Ghyldus sighed. He might be the maker of illusion, but Fyraer had the power to make the King of Shande believe what he saw. Fyraer was Ghyldus's stamina, his resistance against any enemy weapon. And Ghyldus could not command Fyraer's power, a power greater than anyone but One or Terremar could face. With eager heart, Ghyldus welcomed Fyraer into himself.

Above on the swaying deck, oblivious to what horrors she might find in the visage of her keeper, Resala studied the horizon.

The sun had yet to rise high enough for her to see it above the cliff crest. She waited patiently, ignoring the queasiness the bobbing ship brought. She'd gain no comfort from Teshet, who would be ill until put ashore.

What had Ghyldus said? Kedtair gave her power. What did he see that she couldn't? Something about Kedtair ran through her strange dreams. She felt as certain of it as of her meeting with Maura. Often since Maura had attacked the fleet, Resala dreamt of the god. Maura filled her dreams with comforting words, guiding her, giving her the strength to face her enemy, her words seeming to penetrate the hull of the ship and come to her ears alone.

Resala had soured at the idea she must live some destiny penned in an old book. In her dreams, Maura assured her she and others rewrote their fates many times. They exceeded the expectations held for them. Maura showed her paths as originally drawn: Khoti, a healer of great passion, his brother Von a warrior beside their brutal leader, Tsevon. Though the gods gifted Khoti for a role in Shande's future, that he encountered the king, or saved his life, or became a warrior of renown were flukes of the fate. Would he have accomplished all he did if the gods directed it? She had rejected the dreams as the feverish meanderings of her despair. Now, she wondered.

On the rolling deck trying to ignore the nausea rising in her throat, Resala contemplated what transpired in the world, events relayed in dreams. She couldn't doubt, the details felt too real, whether of Khoti and Asteria or Arshal or Nali or any of the armies searching for Ghyldus. Aziaris and Maura gathered the news of wind and wave and fed each morsel to the trapped spirit in Resala. She knew it, accepted it as she accepted the strangeness of sea creatures assaulting Ghyldus's fleet, or deep seas choked with amethyst blooms.

A glow fell on the side of her face. She turned into the hot wind to see the blaze of sun finally crest the bluffs above. She needed to see this rising of Kedtair, though hours old. She had prayed for this day, thought on it with such a sense of finality. She gasped when Kedtair crept into view, too bright to perceive. She clenched her eyes shut, nearly blinded by the view.

"Think on it ..."

The words had come from Maura, many times, filtering through her dreams, weaving like seagrass through her thoughts. She felt the words in her again, but now they were not in Maura's voice, but of all things, Nali's.

Think on it. On what should she think? Did Nali stand on the bluffs above? How could he come to her mind? Why would he even appeal to her thus? She stood in absolute silence her confusion gripping her so tightly she forgot to breathe. Her body forced a quick gasp when it demanded air. Behind clenched eyelids she saw the memory of the sun beside Kedtair. She turned her attention to the ghost of Kedtair. She tried to picture how it had appeared in the sky while still low in the mists, when she might discern its shape and see through the blinding image.

Suddenly, she felt a jolt, a shock that made her twitch as if lightning ran through the ground to find her standing in a puddle. Her hair tingled across her scalp, her skin prickling into bird flesh. She gasped her thoughts to herself, incredulous as she stood frozen, hands gripping the rail. Knees locked, her body bobbed with the sway of the ocean's fury. Maura. Her mind demanded she recall her own eyes reflected in a mirror, a hatred she'd cherished, a deep power like the depth, the mystery of Maura breaking the water.

She almost cried aloud when the truth came to her, when it all revealed itself, all the truths Maura represented, all she had spoken, all the mystery, vigor and power she breathed into Resala. As if her body suddenly shed the tension of a lifetime, or a rope securing a heavy weight fell from her shoulder, she straightened, freed, her breath deep and complete. She needed more, all the elements, the rage, the hate, the deep revulsion the black visage of Ghyldus's Malice brought out of her. She had an image of him watching her from the shadows, his evil purpose surrounding him, his black-gloved fingers dripping the blood of his victims. It stabbed through her, sudden, blinding. Power like none she'd ever imagined infused her, a knowledge deep and instant and as hot as the sun and Kedtair burning her skin. At last, she knew what she could do, her strength. One with herself she felt at peace for what seemed like the first time. In that moment of awakening, hours after Kedtair had risen over Sihmad Shal, Resala felt something touch her thoughts as some other on Ea absorbed the world of knowledge, testing the meanings of his own awakening.

Nali. She mouthed his name. She sensed surprise. Delight. She needed to learn and explore so much without discovery. They needed Arshal. It couldn't be without him.

A heavy hand dropped on Resala's shoulder. Her eyes flew

open to discover an enraged Ghyldus looming over her. The light, comforting touch that had found her, faded. She looked on a sea where the swells built higher before Aziaris's dark storms.

She imagined as she looked upon hatred, that Nali jerked away, repulsed by the touch of this alien creature who kept her. She sensed in the distant friend the unspilled tears of grief.

The days of Kedtair advanced, a furnace banked by treacherous storms that left stifling humidity. Shandean soldiers walked beside their mounts, pushing on twenty hours each day in the odd, darkless world to meet a timetable long expired. To spare their horses, cavalry alternated riding and walking. Others forced their legs to carry them, blisters growing atop each other. It seemed all of Ea moved in some army or other, seeking each other like filings to a magnet.

It took four days for Ghyldus's troops to gather on the high bluffs overlooking the ocean at Lanis Point. Minarian horses fed at leisure on tough, windswept grasses. The bulk of Ghyldus's army spread across the plain like crabs chasing the tide. Soldiers assembled catapults, pulled by teams of men and horses. Cavalry fit their thin spear-like lances to boots slung from saddles, secured knives and daggers at calves and belts, and slung bows, battleaxes or broadswords at backs. Fingers tested blades sharpened to a wafer edge in months of travel and secured well-oiled straps, grips and bonds. Once again, the well-rested would face the harried.

Unchallenged, Ghyldus's troops marched along the rim of bluffs, planning to turn south, then swing north to approach Canwyn Point from the southwest and thus trap the Shandean army with its back to the sea.

Eithurdon had other plans.

At last, the Duke of Lharan had found the armies of Minaria. His Guard set camp in the Kric, a cluster of craggy hills that opened south and east onto an expanse of boggy marsh. To the west and north, sheer bluffs of ancient stone left few footholds, the only access to the hilltops by a narrow path along the Kric's southeast base, flanked by bogs. The Minarians marched for a slim gap between the Kric and the drop from lofty bluffs to the sea. Ytri's scouts figured the Minarians intended to pass though the gap and then march on to Canwyn. It might take weeks for such a force to venture around the Kric.

Eithurdon and the five thousand troops he gathered in his journey across the plains peered from an aerie in a cleft above to look upon more than two hundred thousand experienced warriors trampling Shande with confidence and contempt. Enemy scouts barely scanned the lands before them in their rush for Canwyn.

Eithurdon's scouts sped away in search of the armies of Kefta, Arshal and Khoti, but Eithurdon held little hope Shande could muster the warriors needed to stop such a host. Eithurdon's scouts had returned many times with the rumor of Arshal's host and Khoti's Army of Three Provinces. Weeks ago, his scouts positioned them so far from Canwyn they might as well be in Shela yet. Only Eithurdon stood between Lanis and Canwyn to stop the demon.

Within the craggy niches of the Kric the Lharan host could maneuver a favorable position. They couldn't let Ghyldus flank the bulk of their forces rushing for Canwyn, nor draw the enemy out onto Canwyn Point to be besieged. Ghyldus had to be stopped here, where the land gave Shande a tiny advantage.

With his horses, wagons and gear hidden from view on the other side of broken hills, Eithurdon and his Guardsmen watched the Minarians approach for two days, the sheer size of the enemy army and the height of the Lharans' perch in the Kric giving them a panorama that twisted their guts with despair.

At last, at the zenith of Kedtair, the second week of the heat moon beginning hot and sultry, Eithurdon had to act. His scouts hadn't returned with news of barges littering the Quelica, the southern command split in two as Khoti pounded north for Canwyn with fifteen thousand cavalry, far from the duke's need. And scouts hadn't returned to report that the king had only just reached Canwyn Point, his scouts searching for news. Alone, forty times outnumbered and weary of months in the saddle, Eithurdon at last turned to Ytri with a fatal smile.

"Send word to the king, and prepare to attack," Eithurdon croaked in a hoarse whisper.

Ytri swallowed, his expression unwavering. He bobbed his

head. When Kedtair stood directly overhead, the mid-point of its month-long journey, the Lharan Guard silently mounted. Eyes straight ahead, not even banter broke the quiet among the ranks. With a nod from Eithurdon the men of Lharan, of Kishma, surged forward.

22: The Kric

For almost two days Eithurdon's command harried and sniped at its enemy and held its scrap of rock. Reckless and encouraged by the weak resistance, an enemy thirsting for blood to sate their god threw itself at Shande. The warriors of Lharan, fierce and skilled, faced company after company of reserve while the main body moved onward like the tide, a force mere blood couldn't sate. Eithurdon's gambit slowed them. Guardsmen slew the horses towing the light catapults and shot the mounts from beneath the Eidhalt. Wagons carrying the massive army's supplies burned, dark smudges against the sky.

His honor already tattered, in desperation to stop the enemy host from rolling on through the Kric barely touched by the duke's feint, Eithurdon built on the ruse that the king held the Kric. The ruse violated all the codes of warfare Eithurdon thought sacred. The duke hid his buff and pewter standard, raising only the blue and white and winding Dyndevas calls on his horn to direct his troops against the enemy. Ghyldus sent scouts to confirm what nuisance he faced. His scouts didn't return. The multitudes of Minaria marched no farther.

A night lit by Kedtair meant there were no respites for the weary warriors. He knew as another dawn approached that he could throw not one more sortie at Ghyldus, nor call one more charge. Their arrows had dwindled and many had fallen or suffered grievous wounds, yet all knew that they were all that stood between Ghyldus and the end of Shande.

A rumble from the east drew their attention, but as it did, dawn revealed Ghyldus' impatience. Throbbing drums overwhelmed lifebeats. The beat quickened. Rattles hissed with venom, punctuating the drums' cadence. Banners flapped on standards. Red and orange and black they challenged, gold fringe whipping in a hot wind as bearers shook the standards to the rhythm of drums and rattles. Now and then a blast of horns rose above the din to cue companies to a path marked in some marshal's head. The entire army was about to descend upon the Kric and overwhelm Eithurdon's Guard.

As the red drums' beat quickened, marchers pacing themselves to its cadence, a sudden blast of trumpets drew the weary defenders to again look east where a cloud of dust rose against the morning, an unmistakeable rumble building. The trumpets, louder now, joined in song by the horns of many houses and clarion calls rising skyward.

The King of Shande had finally arrived.

Cavalry seven thousand strong rose out of the dawn, silhouettes behind the king's standard as they pounded into the gap between the Kric and the sea. Behind them, rank upon rank of infantry, more than thirty thousand, marched in song. Spears and pikes held up to Kedtair glittered like icicles in the pale sun of a cold moon thaw.

Whoops echoed from the Kric as the Minarian troops scrambled to assemble. The Gnats had marched day and night after Eithurdon's messenger found them at Canwyn Point, but the grim faces peering west reflected no weariness, more like a simmering anger waiting to boil.

Drums rolled and rumbled like some giant's belly, followed by a low call on a horn. Shande surged ahead to the distant cheers from the Kric. Flutes trilled to counter the harsh monotone beat and adder-like rattles of Minaria. The field sparkled, a mass of movement, like colored glitter scattered by a capricious hand as horses neighed, leather creaked, wheels groaned and trappings jangled. With a horn blast, Minaria halted its march, a silence overwhelming the music of Shande. As one, Minarian spears and swords clashed against shields in cacophonous warning, a challenge, like a wolver's teeth gnashing before the lunge.

Shande's horns bellowed a retort. An undulating yell rolled over the plain and marsh and crashed into the crags of the Kric as forces lurched ahead and drums once again sounded the attack cadence.

A cluster of standards swam in the flaming dawn of twin suns as the King of Shande rode forward, dressed in the clothing woven by his people, awash in their hope. Beside him rode the king's Sage, upon whose gaze few could long look, the scarf at his brow concealing a sense of veiled danger that leant severity to his bearded features.

Marol, dressed in the florid colors of Otayr, bore the blue and white standard of Shande, with the King of Shande's personal pennant of eagle and lion fluttering beneath it, and the smaller crimson and gold pennant of King Farlal. Beside Marol, Aibak of Shiad rode grim-faced and weather-stained, his huntsman's gear drab but for the long purple scarf hiding his braids. The silver and black pennant he carried had a place of honor beside the king, symbol of Shiad's long and unbroken friendship with Shande.

Jan and Tel sat their mounts in stony silence, viewing the field with grim grins, blue cloaks clasped at their throats despite the heat. No other marker named them leaders of the mass of blue-cloaked soldiers behind them.

As squad leaders and company captains darted among their men, exchanging orders in preparation to meet the oncoming threat, the knot around the king halted on a slope at the base of the Kric.

Nali held the king in reserve. Likely Ghyldus hoped the king would rush into the fray with youthful bravado to be hacked apart long before reaching his target.

Arshal raised a silver horn and blew a call to thrill the blood. Jan and Tel pointed their spears ahead. As the cavalry galloped toward the front lines behind blue and white banners long stored in the smoky eaves of dining halls, the remnants of Eithurdon's northern command raced to their mounts and sped at a tangent to join the battle. The two forces surged together with a shout, the melee fierce, each side fueled by desires so close, so within reach, so long awaited.

In the Kric, bloody men sank back against the hot stone. Among them, high in an aerie in the Kric, Ytri cradled Eithurdon who had finally collapsed, knowing he had done what he must, as the first ranks swam out of the dawn. The duke's blood sheathed the rocks. Ytri couldn't imagine that any blood yet remained in his duke to be shed. After the first assault in his gambit to stall the enemy, the duke had hobbled back to his perch, ignoring the broken spear protruding from his side. And from here he had called his orders through the long night when his men used the ghost of Kedtair in the moon to sabotage their enemy's camp with the skill of Tawnkats. Throughout the next day Eithurdon weakened, his gaze ever drifting east in search of the king.

Ytri stifled a groan when he bent to lift his duke. Eithurdon made no sound, only gave Ytri a clear and paternal gaze. Of the one hundred original Guardsmen, perhaps a dozen remained. With each man's death, Eithurdon grieved, as a father losing a son.

"Do not bother, Ytri," Eithurdon whispered through dry lips. "It is my time. We did what we came to do. It falls to you to lead what remains of us."

Ytri stumbled and leaned against a rock wall, the blood of the dead rising in a stench from the hills. More than half their force lay dead or dying in the crevices of the Kric, the pools of the swamp and the fields beyond. At least five hundred men suffered grievous wounds, unable to fight and uncertain to live. Not a man among them went unscathed. The Guard rallied to the duke, died for him, in the best tradition of their long history. But they had held.

"Be a little less stubborn and you might live long enough to hear the king praise your effort," Ytri grumbled as he stumbled down the path, the duke in his arms. He couldn't tell over the din of battle beyond the Kric whether he could hope to move the wounded back or even find a moment's rest.

Eithurdon smiled up at Ytri, a feverish glint in his eyes. The duke's dark hair, now speckled with flecks of grey, had plastered against a brow grimy and smudged with blood. Ytri paused again, leaning against a jut of stone as he caught his breath, weakened by exhaustion and many light wounds. He laid the duke against an outcrop of rock. Filling his hands with water from a small spring, one of many bubbling out of the Kric's crevices, he splashed his face before taking a sip. Then he tore a rent sleeve from his tunic and wet it to wash Eithurdon's sweaty face.

"It is wasted effort, Ytri. If you are determined to take my bones home to Lharan, come for me when we are victorious."

Ytri growled at Eithurdon, his lip curling in a snarl. He grunted with the effort of again lifting the duke, pushed himself away from the rock and stumbled on down the path. "You've survived worse."

"But he is not here."

Ytri glanced down at his duke, startled by the caustic tone. "You'll never forgive him?"

"Never. All I have is my honor. If I live to see him, I will kill him. I loved him as a son, Ytri. Who could not be proud of the leader he has become? That the man who stole my child from me to make of her a camp follower was my trusted, my savior ... like heat on a burn."

Ytri looked away. The duke wouldn't even name him. It had become an obsession, one that would send five thousand against hundreds of thousands. Ytri stumbled down to the spongy turf at the foot of the Kric where the Guard's wagons gathered up the wounded and maneuvered to reach the relative safety of Arshal's supply lines. One bore the duke away from his command.

Ytri turned from the departing wagons to find a chiseled face beside him. Ytri startled, his hand reaching for his knife in the instant before registering recognition.

"I make a rather convincing Minarian," Hothur said with a tight-lipped smile that held no humor. "With your leave, Captain, I will advise King Arshal as I am able." Hothur waited for Ytri's nod. "You should have gone with the duke," Hothur admonished. He plucked at the remaining bloody sleeve of Ytri's tunic. "The Guard earned a rest. In all my years as a soldier I never saw such grit. It has been my honor to fight beside you. But others have come. Let them earn some glory now."

Ytri gave Hothur a sour smile. "We're trying to hold back the sea with a sponge. Everyone counts." He winced when Hothur's hand came down on his back. The din of battle in the gap echoed up into the rocks. The cadence of retreat, regroup, charge, rallying calls beaten and blasted and rattled as soldiers maneuvered in the narrow gap between the sea and the Kric. He paused when they reached the knot of Guard horses whose masters had fallen. Ytri stared across the expanse of marsh.

"Verdaen will come." Hothur gave Ytri an impatient tug.

"He better not come before the duke," Ytri said with forced levity as he swung up onto his mount, gaze still turned southeast as they spurred their mounts to battle.

All that day the lines see-sawed with no gain or loss but of the blood that soaked the soil. The blaze of the two suns in the sky left a dark crimson crust in dry and churned turf. Heat drew steam from the ocean and marsh to coil around them, the humidity making even their weapons damp and sticky as they gasped for a fresh breath. From the marshes came hordes of biting flies. Gulls circled overhead by the thousands, their cries plaintive as they waited for a lull. As each regrouping left an opening on the field, the gray flocks descended, only to scatter in anger when the lines once again met. Soon other birds from the plains and perhaps even farther gathered, scavengers settling in the high crags of the Kric or spiraling on black wings overhead.

The gap between the Kric and the cliffs overlooking the sea saved the Shandean army from destruction. Ghyldus could not commit his entire army in the narrow space and held most in reserve. The western face of the Kric couldn't be scaled, and the range stretched too far to go around with any kind of efficiency. They could reach Arshal through the gap or not at all, yet Arshal could not reach Ghyldus through the multitudes of the Minarian army, as he must. If the enemy had passed through the gap to the open plains around Canwyn Point as planned, they would have overrun Shande.

While Shande struggled for survival, no small measure of spirit drove their enemy. Ghyldus wove spells to feed his soldiers' frenzy. They threw themselves recklessly into the fray, dying as if they had lost the instinct to live. This crazed enemy battered Shande, each regroup call on the Minarian horns eliciting a collective cringe from the Shandeans, the sign the enemy sent a fresh command onto the field. No replacements so bolstered the Shandeans. Their grand schemes in the Val only proved they had no experience in tactics.

When Kedtair set and the sun neared the horizon, Nali nodded at Jan, who raced for the Kric. At least two hours of true darkness would reign before moonrise, all three denizens of the heavens hiding behind the horizon.

After reaching the saucer-shaped cirque Ytri directed him to, its edges bowing out toward the Minarian army, Jan winded his horn. The echoing call rang out: the Minarian order to retreat and regroup, heard as if from the Minarian lines.

The Shandean line thrust forward, throwing the Minarians back in turmoil, and at last evicting them from the gap. Moments later the last light of sunset faded, plunging the field into a night like pitch following days of blazing light. Both sides groped in the darkness, huddling behind watch fires for a sense of dimension. Night fell so total stars went unnoted in the sky, their faint glow not enough to light the gap. When the moon at last rose, the armies let out a collective sigh, the light giving context to the night, defining shadows, and lending life to the movements heard in the dark.

For several hours the Shandeans rested while the Minarians rotated their reserves. But Shande now held the narrow entry to the gap, and once again archers scampered over the rocks of the Kric, able to shoot at the enemy below. When the moon stood overhead, daylight-bright on the field but for the depth of shadows, the Minarians horns called attack. Only will kept the Shandeans from being driven back. And that will wavered.

Arshal stood on a ledge high up in the Kric overlooking the narrow gap, Nali silent and brooding beside him. Battle waged below in a wash of silvery light, each command's movements marked by squares of colored flag, muted gray.

"I wait for him and he won't show," Arshal muttered, gazing out over the milling masses of Minaria defiling Shande.

"'Cause he can destroy you without lifting a hand," Nali stated without looking at his king. "He figures his troops will reach you first."

"His fanatics are his strength," Hothur agreed. "Even if you faced him, and his devotees wavered to witness his weakness, there are enough who will fight to the death whether Ghyldus leads them or not. They are the ones who would kill for the sport. They are the type whose honor will not let them quit, or those who have come to believe what Ghyldus tells them about Shande though they may not support the demon. It is the fanaticism of his devotees that makes him strong. He will not let them see him truly challenged."

"You're both a vat of good news," Arshal grumbled. "So, what's the point, if there's no point? He'll destroy us before we can ever face him! What were all our plans if not for this?"

"What have I told you?" Nali demanded, his eyes boring holes so deep into his king. "You have to figure it out for yourself. When that'll be, gods know, but it better be soon or you'll have wasted our time and our lives. Kedtair's waning. You've got to figure it out."

"Then what move do I make now? Can't you just tell me that? You're supposed to be a counselor. So, counsel!" The stone flared in his hand.

A smile pulled at the corner of Nali's mouth, but his eyes remained stony and hard. He glanced at the stone glowing a faint orange in Arshal's hand.

"You gotta go to him," Nali said. "He isn't going to face you unless he has to. Our fear of him makes him strong. He feeds off his ambition. We need Khoti –"

"Eithurdon's scouts found him too far to reach us without wings. If we wait for him and he doesn't show –"

"He'll show," Nali said. "You know he wouldn't break his word. If he has to crawl –"

"So, he crawls and is too late."

"The point is," Nali said, his tone like a cold wind in the Lharans. "You need Khoti. We'll never bust through to Ghyldus wedged in this gap like this. Eithur's plan worked as well as it could. Now we need Khoti to push them beyond the gap and out into the open. Then when we spread out, we can ride for Ghyldus."

Hothur nodded. "You gamble on Khoti having enough troops to tip the odds."

"I count on Khoti's slicing a hole through their lines."

Arshal stared at his counselor. "So, then we're supposed to hold until Khoti shows, if Khoti shows?"

Nali's eyebrow rose in unspoken speculation, a small smile tugging at his face.

The hard eyes took all the gaiety from Nali's rare smiles. The expression felt mocking. Arshal didn't see in him the man he'd known. This counselor fit more truly the Sage men named him. Arshal couldn't forget the way Nali had silenced him with a gesture. He could only wonder what Nali had become when – He himself should know what it meant!

The battle waged on. Arshal watched, making an occasional suggestion as to his army's deployment. Still, the king remained more a figurehead than a leader. Hothur and Nali had the experience to detail plans and Khoti and Eithurdon had the cunning minds for strategy. Runners came to Nali from Ytri, Jan or Tel as he used his vantage to shore up weak spots in the line or anticipate movements. Arshal peered at the field below, twisting his hands in idleness.

The gap line wavered as day broke, the men too exhausted to move. Stoic infantry held as the Minarians rolled through the Shandean cavalry. A wedge of line buckled as morning wore on, Ytri's men driven back in a swirl of screaming horses and flashing weapons as Minarian lancers rode forward, spears down, pushing Shande before them. When the line ruptured, something snapped elsewhere. As if the Minarians swept aside a clutter of dust, the entire Shandean line gave way. It looked like a rout as the infantry struggled to hold pikes in the face of Ghyldus's dwindling cavalry. The body of Minarian infantry surged up behind screaming Minarian horses. Medallions flashed out on their chests as Kedtair rose in the east, firing the red gems with the fanaticism of their bearers. Blinded by the red glare, Shandeans fell back from the eerie glow on their enemy's chests and shielded their eyes.

Arshal gasped at the sight. He shook off an aide's attempt to speed him to the rear lines in case they lost the gap, thus leaving Arshal's perch in enemy territory.

"This is sorcery!" Arshal pointed at the medallions.

Nali nodded, face grave. "The ruby's Ghyldus's stone, like the sapphire's yours." Nali leaned close so Arshal could hear his mumbled words over the din. "Cree chose the opal in your hand wisely because it holds all the colors." Nali peered at Arshal as if expecting Arshal to understand some hint.

The king gave him an impatient glare. Again, the derna spouted gibberish at him.

"As your stone flares blue when you're filled with a regal

passion," Nali went on with a scowl, "His flares red. He uses his ruby to infuse the medallions with his ambition and drive them into a frenzy."

"Then it's merely a message to his men –" Arshal began.

"The streaks of light you see are more than Kedtair reflecting from them," Nali warned. "They're an illusion to frighten us. Our warriors have to concentrate on other things to overcome it. The illusion they believe real, is more powerful than the sword they face."

"I met his illusions and they're real. I have the scars to prove it."

Nali shook his head. "His greatest weapon is that illusion. He'd defeat us with fear. Our minds believe what he shows us. It drives us to flee from imagined threats. The imagination of your enemy is a powerful ally."

For a moment Arshal wondered how Nali could know so much about the mind of their enemy. The doubt crept on him, alien. How could he doubt Nali? He remembered Cree speaking of the prophecy of Kedtair. Those born under the star could attain great evil or good. He felt the evil presence of the medallion's shape branded on Nali's forehead, hidden beneath the scarf. Had it somehow turned Nali's good heart?

Nali chuckled suddenly, true mirth in his glance. The king had the chilling feeling that Nali had read his thoughts and as he thought it, realized he held unfounded and ridiculous fears. He saw Kedtair in Nali, not evil.

"Then how do we defend ourselves?"

"Remember that if you believe it, it exists. If you don't believe it, it doesn't."

"Then I can wish Ghyldus away."

Nali's glance stabbed up at him, knife-like. "It's not a joke. When you face him, you'd best be prepared to defend yourself. You'd best remember what I've told you. And you'd best pray his weapons will be directed only at you and not our armies. Only the stoutest of heart and the true skeptics will survive such an assault."

Nali's prophecy played out below them as the Minarians punched holes through the Shandean line, which crumbled. The Minarian weapons took on an eerie red glow thrown by the medallions. The Shandean faces registered their fear as the crimson glow fired their enemy's arms as if the blades themselves hungered for Shandean blood.

A horn blast rose above the din, of different pitch from the many they had learned.

"Look!" Hothur grasped Arshal's arm and pointed southeast.

"It's not Khoti," Nali said as he cupped his hands around his eyes. "And if it were, there wouldn't be nearly enough."

From the gap below, Ytri let out a whoop, chased by a wild yell from the Guardsmen.

"Kefta!" Hothur crowed. "We feared them trapped, or already overcome if they approached from the west."

Fifteen hundred horsemen broke from an equal number of infantry as Kefta's detachment of the Lharan Guard pounded toward them, delayed by the long circuit around the Kric and marsh. Kefta's troops amounted to little in the parity of forces, but they arrived unscathed, fresh from a night's camp. If Kefta arrived, perhaps Khoti and his rumored tens of thousands of seasoned warriors might be close behind. They needed that hope to survive.

Somehow the Shandean army found its feet and held the gap, Kefta's arrival infusing weary troops with new vigor as they moved to the fore to take the brunt of assault.

When moonlit evening arrived, the enemy retreated, an odd reprieve when it would take little to overrun Shande. Ytri's scouts found no secret weapons creeping forward, no attempt to flank or slip past watch fires. But when true darkness arrived a few hours before morning while the Shandean army slumbered, cries of terror erupted across the length of the gap and echoed up against the cliffs of the Kric. Sentries discerned fleeting shapes before their eyes. Their shouts brought their comrades from their sleep to scream in horror. Shadows of the dead shimmered up from the blood-encrusted ground, wailing out to their comrades to give up the battle. Arms reached out, smoke-white, like steam from the marshes, eyes blazing red in their faces.

Rousing, Arshal gasped as ghostly Peshal, Esthen and Zopher reached out to him. Nali gripped Arshal's arm and forced the king to look at him.

"I see nothing," Nali stated. "Your mind conjures your fears."

When Arshal turned back, the smoky dead had departed. But around him and below in the gap soldiers leaped up, throwing their hands to their faces and crying out as the visage of a relative or friend loomed before them.

"It's an illusion!" Arshal shouted into the night, the command in his tone carrying across the plain, compelling, insistent. Those nearby turned to look up at him. He stood, hands upraised, the opal blazing blue in his palm. "It's the Enchanter's illusion. Don't believe it and it will disappear." A few skeptics turned to him, then back at the apparitions. Some registered surprise, discovering the visions gone. Others still cringed in terror. "Turn to me!" Arshal insisted. "Look to me. Believe in me and they won't harm you. Believe no strange sights!"

The glow flared from his hand, appealing across the vast battlefield where soldiers huddled about the embers of watch fires. He had their attention. Some moved closer, their gazes riveted on the blue glow in his palm.

"Believe in me!" he demanded.

Nali turned at the strong tone of command in the king's voice. Warriors lurched to their feet and cried out their fealty.

Arshal sat down beside his advisor and dropped his weary head in his hands.

"Listen to yourself," Nali demanded.

Arshal started at the power in Nali's voice. "Is this another veiled hint? I don't care for the way you play your powers on me, Sage."

Nali turned away from the king. "You're no dim-wit, no idiot. Why do you resist? Here, for a moment, I thought you'd awakened. But you performed your own illusion for them. All the things we spoke of in the past, nothing."

Arshal stared into the faint glow in his palm. He didn't, couldn't understand. Everything Nali said fell on his ears as odd as the language of the calling stones. He should wonder at it, should think on the oddity, question it. But too much demanded what little energy he had.

No more apparitions rose from the bloody soils as the dark hours passed. When Kedtair rose before the sun, the Minarian army awaited, rested, volleys of arrows taunting the weary

Shandeans as the first streaks of light brushed the sky. Boiling heat again rolled at them as another day of shifting lines and grueling battle passed. Warriors fell now to heat and exhaustion, wounded by Kedtair. The ocean sent occasional squalls at them to bring brief respites, but left behind mud and humidity so pressing soldiers gasped for air. At one point the ground itself lurched under foot. Calls rang out to regroup as soldiers shook with their fear, still stumbling from the feel of the ground pitching like a ship beneath them, fissures opening before them as they dodged rocks chucked from the Kric.

The pause didn't last. Night would not come this day. As the hours drew on, each call to regroup brought fewer Shandeans staggering back. Arshal gave what hope he could. He stood upon the ledge and called out his support, hand held palm out so the most distant troops could see the faint light of the opal glowing blue in his palm. To this marker, the Shandean army moved with the fatalism of martyrs: all saw the orange pennant bearing the black shivered arrow the Minarian commands rallied around. The flag promised no quarter, no mercy for the captured, the surrendered, the wounded or even the dead. Shande's warriors had no choice but fight to die. Their certain death drove them into battle with a vengeance.

"I can't stand this, Nali," Arshal mumbled when the moon and Kedtair stood overhead, several hours yet before dawn. "I have to do something. I can't just keep sending them to die for me. At least I can fight alongside them!"

Nali merely looked at him, a glare from red-ringed eyes. The derna's patience waned, like Kedtair overhead. With each setting, the star moved north. Eventually it would remain there, along with the king's hopes of destroying Ghyldus.

"You'd better hope Khoti comes soon, or you get your wits about you, King. Your time runs out."

If he hadn't known better, Arshal could swear Cree spoke to him. The same barely restrained impatience and self-assurance filled Nali's words, while Arshal felt only a growing sense of inadequacy. He failed the very people who sacrificed the most for him. When he looked at Nali, he had to force himself not to stare at his sash-covered forehead.

An hour before dawn only the fainter glow of the moon

remained in the sky, the Shandeans gaining an hour's rest. Again, shapes sprouted from the shadows. Wolvers, jaws dripping blood, eyes flaming red, slunk among the sleeping Shandeans, raising their throats to the moon with the mournful wail of their kind, more unearthly, more chill than any wolver had ever called. Too weary, many soldiers slept on unaware. Of those who woke, many looked up to find the king again standing watch over them. One man near the foot of the cliff Arshal stood upon leapt up and ran as a wolver neared him. It lunged at his throat, ripping. The man fell to the ground with a sickening thud.

Arshal turned an accusing gaze on Nali.

"If you believe it, it's real," Nali said in that cryptic tone that so infuriated the king. "The man believed."

As the camp grew chaotic and confusion and fear brought soldiers awake, the sun again rose and the horns, drums and rattles of Minaria again challenged the whip of the wind rising from the sea.

Arshal felt certain the last day of battle had arrived. Reinforcements would do little good with half of Arshal's troops slain by exhaustion. His weary warriors stumbled over themselves, while Ghyldus merely rotated fresh soldiers onto the field to rush the narrow gap. Arshal felt no nearer to discovering the secret at which Nali hinted. Ghyldus counted on that, Nali assured him, and likely knew Arshal remained – 'unawakened' Nali called it – or the demon would come forward to challenge. Ghyldus needn't show himself, especially if Arshal awakened too late to drive through and face the demon. Arshal's stone alone couldn't bust through the enemy lines. He didn't dare risk it all riding to the field unready.

Desperate, Arshal said a silent prayer, his eyes skyward in appeal. They just couldn't hold any longer. He sensed Nali watching him, the Sage's hands gripping forearms in a prayer that Arshal at last figured it out. But the king appealed to Terremar.

"Fool!" Nali cried silently into himself, so loud, with such intensity, that the king turned and stared at him. Arshal knew Nali hadn't spoken aloud. Yet he'd heard the derna's voice in his mind. Arshal thought he sensed some other dismay within him as well, not his own thoughts, but something from outside of him slipping into his mind. Arshal sank to his knees. His hands gripped his hair as if it might prod something he'd overlooked. He groped through everything Nali had said, all his hints. It just wouldn't come to him. What did he miss? Empty words came back at him, without concept, meaning. He begged of the sky, barely feeling Nali tugging on his arm to pull him from his knees. He stared at the glitter of ocean through bleary eyes, begging for help with the appeal of one who, helpless, holds the world's fate in his hands.

And drops it.

When the day grew old, defeat imminent, an intense blackness built over the ocean to the northwest. Surf pounding the beaches below carried up to the battle. Lightning flickered far out to sea and soon a low rumbling overcame the din of battle as the wind picked up in damp gusts, increasing in intensity until a steady wind lifted up dust and sand and even fragments of stone and threw it in their eyes. The king turned toward the fury, blasted by the gritty wind. He felt as if he held his breath to watch the approaching tempest, his cloak snapping out behind him and wind plastering his clothes to his body.

The storm crawled toward them, several hours passing before the first lashing rain whipped them. Thunder rolled constant, at times indistinguishable from the surf. The sky opened up with such a deluge neither army could move. Shandeans collapsed where they stood, the rain pooling on the parched earth as clouds hid the star and sun behind a thick mass of slate gray pierced by lightning. Soon, water stood a span deep, turning into a pasty mud in moments. It took shouts and prods for the army's commanders to urge soldiers to their feet and into some semblance of an orderly defensive position, words torn by wind that boxed ears and sent men stumbling to knees.

Fierce winds spiraled in. While the Shandeans had the partial shelter of the Kric, the Minarians bore the full brunt, wagons tipping, rains driven sideways into them, cloaks and command tents rent. Furious seas roared against the cliffs with a force that shook the ground and foundered the vessels at anchor. Lightning and thunder crackled off the peaks of the Kric, forcing soldiers to duck as each fork prickled scalps and sent the rain more intensely.

The Shandean army huddled around fires that wouldn't light. Most sat in miserable groups. They pulled cloaks over their faces and struggled to rest, unable to move unless they crawled. The ground, churned by days of battle, became an ooze.

The storm raged through a night turned so dark they could see nothing but lightning ripping the sky. Late in the night the fiercest winds howled in the rocks above, threatening to pull Arshal from his perch. Then came an eerie silence and the sky opened to reveal the pink streaks of dawn above them. Mud and water splashed with the steps of soldiers slogging to their posts. The wind abated to a soft breeze, the cooks stoking fires near their overturned wagons as the rain diminished to a drizzle. The respite lasted only an hour, the armies still assembling, when again the wind picked up and rain returned. This time soldiers found the patches of ground above the mire. They scavenged for soggy bread, cheese, and jerky, eaten with muddy fingers, then settled down to weather out the back side of a storm determined to creep over them at a snail's pace.

"I've never seen anything like this," Arshal yelled in Nali's ear as they huddled in the Kric. Somewhere above the dense roll of clouds dawn again brightened the sky. And Kedtair waned. While sheltered from the rain by the angle of the rock they huddled beside, the wind howled so loud around them it threatened to deafen them, on occasion sending a cascade of rock at them as it whittled chunks of stone from the ancient ridge. "It'll probably flood the Quelica –"

"And delay Khoti," Nali finished the thought for him. "Khoti must have left the Quelica a long time ago. Scouts found him at the canal weeks ago –"

"Then why isn't he here yet!"

"He lost half his force! How long did it take us to get here? He'll be here!"

The storm that had stalled over them for almost two days finally drifted away. Only a week remained of Kedtair, the Minarian army showing no signs of budging. If it hadn't been for the storm they would have routed the Shandeans days ago.

The clouds dissipated into shreds with the last rays of Kedtair sinking to the north, clearing during one of those rare times when true night settled above them. The storm tatters glittered silver in the last of Kedtair's white rays. Then came absolute darkness. A light haze of clouds hid the stars. Everything dripped, ran or trickled. The wind died, leaving only silence in the Kric, and the distant hush of surf. Soldiers shed and wrung sodden cloaks. The muddy army tensed, awaiting some devilry of Ghyldus to trouble their night. Despite the wind and rain, most regained some measure of strength, so weary they slept through the worst storm the region had ever witnessed.

And out of the dark hordes of poison toads hopped from the marshes, and snakes slithered from their homes, biting insects swarming at them.

"What's real, what illusion?" Arshal demanded.

Nali threw an unforgiving glance at him. "Figure it out."

Arshal's face betrayed his hurt. He nodded then. "A stupid question. Insects I believe. Not the toads and the snakes." He looked down on the muddy plain below. It stopped seething. He sighed, ready to once again assure his troops, to let the shielded glow from his palm give substance to the night. When would Ghyldus tire of these games? As he wondered, he realized that it was exactly that: a game. Ghyldus baited him by displaying his power. Arshal could create no illusions to torment the Minarian army. But Ghyldus, far back behind distant lines, could direct his illusions right into this camp, his mastery such he could manipulate mists to take the shape of those for whom soldiers grieved. He controlled their fears, and Arshal could barely control their hopes.

As the night grew old, Nali sighed and stood. He stared at the faint edges of what should have been a new moon. Kedtair would rise again soon, followed by the sun. The heat would strike the muddy ground and turn it into a sticky, steamy mess.

"Today, Arshal," Nali said at last. "Whether you're ready or not, we have to make our move. If we don't, Kedtair will set."

"Do you think I'll figure it out?"

"Gods, I hope so." Nali sighed, sounding less harsh and forbidding than he had. "You've got to wipe your mind clean and think on what's important. You'll find the answer. We're doing no good waiting. By evening, we'll have weary troops again."

"What are you suggesting?"

"Make our rush at dawn, while we're fresh. We'll use the darkness to maneuver close. Then we can try to drive through. They've taken a beating, but the Guard's still our best. Let them lead. Ytri and Kefta have fought Khoti's style, reckless. It's what we need to open the way."

Arshal nodded. Soon startled aides roused commanders and they their troops. The silent sloshing noises drifted up to the king as the troops moved forward, concealing other sounds that might have given them warning of what the morning would bring.

Nali stared into the darkness to the east, waiting for something, yet uncertain what. Impatient, he decided, for Arshal to figure out the secret of Kedtair. He wanted to bellow out the answer! Even then, he wondered if Arshal could discern the truth. Obvious hints eluded the king. The awakening had to be voluntary, learned, a reaching out. It was part of the test, part of earning the secret of Kedtair, the secret of himself.

A furtive sound carried to Nali through the twists and crevices of the Kric. He peered into the darkness. Against the mists hovering over the marshes two darker shadows moved, riding in from the south along the foot of the Kric where he'd posted no sentries.

Nali tossed a stone at an aide. He signed, pointing into the darkness toward the figures who remained some distance from the camp at the base of the Kric overlooking the gap.

Nali's heart pounded in his ears. When the two riders reached a point where they had a clear view up to where Nali stood, they stopped. He knew they looked up at him, as if they could see him standing against the dark rock face. A light flared out below. Neither figure attempted to flee, but dismounted, the torch revealing them. Light-colored mud spattered their clothing. A darker grime clung to patches of skin. He saw nothing recognizable, no color or feature revealed beneath their hoods.

It seemed to take hours for them to climb the slope. Nali barely acknowledged Arshal rousing to come to his side, except to motion him to remain out of sight. Nali studied the movements of the arrivals. An air of confidence clung to them, a certainty, reserve. They reeked of danger.

At last, two bedraggled men stood before him, the king hidden in shadows beyond the torchlight. Nali could now see the dark, mud-spattered green of their cloaks, and boots and breeches mud-caked and stiff. Beneath their cloaks, their tunics hinted that the soiling ran deep. A sentry pushed the first forward. His hood flopped back to display an unruly tangle of long chestnut hair spattered with clumps of dried algae. His face sported a grimy knot of youthful beard.

"Cydwyn!" A memory dimmed and surrounded by pain lurched up at him. It took a moment's struggle to maintain the reserve he expected from himself, his hopes racing on ahead. The man gave him a curt nod, holding his silence as the sentry's sword pressed against the young man's back. At Nali's sign, the sentry sheathed his sword. The derna peered at the other figure. He nodded at his aide, holding up a finger. The man dashed away.

"You've grown, Jali. He'll never recognize you." Nali knew the look in both men's eyes, a look frightening to see in his friend's son. Jali stood at stiff attention under Nali's scrutiny, his freckles lost beneath a scrub of beard darker and browner than his hair. He'd wound his long red hair in Joffan warrior braids, like the king's. Nali motioned for a torch, noting a mark at the base of both men's necks.

"Ah, Jali, you're not a Gnat like your fa before you," Nali whispered. "And what it must take to earn Khoti's mark."

Jali smiled broadly, gesturing with his head to defer to Cydwyn who ranked Jali in Khoti's loose network.

Cydwyn accepted a cup of wine with a grimy hand. "It's good to see you, Commander, in better health," Cydwyn said when he'd taken a deep drink and passed the cup to Jali. "We're scouting ahead. We came through the marsh –"

"Through the marsh?" Arshal echoed from the dark.

"Along the foot of the Kric, but that gets lost in the marsh," Cydwyn explained, adding a hasty "Lord," when he must have caught a glimpse of the king's finer raiment, or perhaps heard some accent too familiar for Nali to note. "We left Khoti 'bout three days ago. We can move faster than him, and with the storm, they might've stayed put."

"You didn't," Nali stated.

Jali gave Nali a grim smile, his glance touching Cydwyn. "Not likely," he said with a wry twist of his mouth.

Cydwyn gave Jali what might have been a smile. "The infantry's 'bout two days behind the cavalry, if the storm didn't wash them out. We're here to check your positions, see if there's even a battle to be fought yet. You don't look too secure here so we'll have to be heading back to call him in after all."

"Will he have enough?" Arshal demanded from the shadows beyond the torchlight.

Jali grinned at his feet. Cydwyn nodded. Both turned as someone ran up the trail behind them. Their hands went to weapons. Jan stumbled into the torchlight, his mouth falling open to see Jali drawing a dagger.

"Jali," the name came out in a whisper.

The red-headed warrior peered at his father. "So, here's the famous Gnat leader I hear tales of!" Jali laughed.

Jan grasped Jali to him. "I didn't believe Cyd when he said I wouldn't recognize you."

Jali pulled away with dignity, and took a step back from his father. He finished his wine with a quick motion.

Jan poked at the Tawnkat tattoo. "You're this fellow Khoti's man now? He better be right by you." Jan's voice had gone husky.

Jali shrugged, no longer smiling. "We're Tawnkats, earned." Jali didn't elaborate. "We gotta be goin' or Khoti'll be worryin' after us," Jali added without looking at his father. "There'll be time later for reunions." He glanced at Nali pointedly.

Nali went chill. His daughters were near.

"Sage," Cydwyn asked softly. "Is the Duke of Lharan in this camp?" Arshal's hiss of breath replied. "The Lady Asteria would meet him again."

"He's dying," Nali stated

Cydwyn's head bobbed. "Then maybe he'll meet her."

"He won't," Nali cautioned.

Cydwyn shrugged. "She'll accept that."

He passed his cup to the aide and pulled his hood back up over his face, wiping away the insects that had gathered on him.

"Look for us," Cydwyn said with a nod. He gripped Nali's

forearm in a familiar greeting. "Glad you kept your promise, Commander."

The pair melted into the night. Soon hoofbeats splashed through the camp at a light trot. Then, they galloped east on the north edge of the marsh.

Nali laid a hand on Jan's shoulder. "They return, changed. Will Kia and Rena wear Tawnkat tattoos? If they do, I won't care. I'm not the same either." Nali brushed by Arshal without a word to return to his perch and stare out over the dark camp.

The king glanced over his shoulder. The sky paled, but it remained too dark to define more than an occasional silhouette. Streaks of gray highlighted the clear sky above a bank of clouds clinging to the eastern horizon. Darkness would end soon. Arshal and his company waited at the base of the Kric, their horses slipping in muddy ruts. Soldiers' movements rang out loud, but a northwest wind carried their racket out into the harmless reach of marsh.

In only minutes, Arshal would raise his horn. He touched the sword at his side. He would ride to battle again. Cavalry under Kefta and Ytri's command milled about ahead of him, silent, resigned, ready to beat their way through to the death.

Calls rose behind him, angry rebukes of sentries, then the thud and splash of horse hooves in the churned turf. A horseman raced at them. Had Jali and Cydwyn met trouble? Arshal stared into the fading dark, his hand gripping the hilt of his sword. A silhouette rose from the faint eastern glow then lurched to a halt in front of them.

"Ernik, King," the man stated in the soft dialect of Arenh. His fist struck his chest in salute. "I am King Azren's hope, his witness. I fought for Shande many times now as a warrior in the Army of Three Provinces and witnessed victory earned by the blood of thousands. I gave my own blood to Shande, more than promised. I begrudge not a drop. I will fight to the death for such men as Shande bred. I will fight for you, Lord."

Arshal's mouth fell open at the passion in Ernik's words as Nali moved to the king's side.

"Are you alone?" Arshal demanded.

Ernik laughed, his eyes glittering in the growing light. "No, Lord! Indeed!"

Day grew around them with each moment, light enough now to discern features against backgrounds, the world a ghostly gray without color when all wore the ashen cast of the dead.

"Arshal you must call them," Nali pressed. "It's dawn!"

Arshal brought the horn to his lips. He took a breath, but a distant call came from the east to echo against the Kric. The horn's voice rang deep like a buglebuck's trumpet echoing through a mountain forest. It thrilled his blood with some primal call that spoke of a land untamed. Another call entwined the first, trill and clear like bird song echoing above a secluded lake. A yell rose toward crescendo, high-pitched whoops that made his heart flutter as other horns now rose to greet the continuing songs of the first two. He recognized the tune of Jashiho in a high piercing note like the ring of crystal, and then a deep bass note Arshal knew to be Detarian.

"Khoti!" Arshal shouted, his throat tight with his hope and relief. He poised to goad his horse to battle.

Ernik grasped his arm. "Hold, Lord King. Stand your men aside and fall in behind. The charge will not slow for greetings."

Arshal jabbed his aide, ordering the man to trumpet Ernik's orders. The man hesitated, pointing at the Minarian line, which grew clear as dawn arrived, ready to rush them if the Shandeans retreated as ordered. Arshal raised his sword to strike the aide. The man's eyes went wide as his trumpet blared the king's orders.

A moment of chaos reigned as commanders and captains turned confused gazes to the king, beside whom Ernik planted the aqua and gold pennant of Arenh. As they hurried to pull back, the startled Minarians staged a hesitant rush. They saw their error too late.

It was the kind of day that follows a week of rain. Crisp, the air crystalline. The sun lifted above the clouds. In that instant of dawn, a blaze of light erupted from the trappings of fifteen thousand horses thundering at the gap. Mud flew up from hooves. Standards whipped in their wake as many-hued cloaks billowed behind them. They pounded through the supply line that rushed to right wagons and pull them out of the way.

Arshal could only stare agape when he saw them, full of a weary joy. The multi-colored flags of the Army of Three Provinces floated in a cluster around the knot of warriors riding in the forefront. Orange sashes of Detarian, faded by the elements, bespattered white tunics of the desert, rent hunter green and brown of Tormor, the grimed royal blue of the Gnats, all appeared bright in the sparkling morning. Before them all rode Khoti. The sun flashed from his stellan helm, the blue and white tassels blowing back from it like a horse tail as Fidra took the bit in her teeth and extended her stride beyond the reach of the other beasts. Her neck stretched out with the eagerness of a foal in a new world, not a veteran of many campaigns. Stellan-covered breastplates blazed out to the morning as the wind lifted the royal blue cloak high over Fidra's rump, the garments bright, clean beside the weatherworn clothing of his comrades.

Arshal instantly recognized Khoti's officers clustered in his wake, their faces stony, their eyes blazing and eager as they followed Khoti into certain death. Cydwyn, Jali, Chati and Tre rode in a tight knot behind Arshal's Champion. At Khoti's heels, Asteria bore the standard of Shande and the emerald and sand household pennant of Tsevon's line. Arshal discerned Habdelion beside his pennant, and Euzzeldir by his, the flag of Detarian chasing a grim-faced youth who mirrored Khoti's actions to the most minute gesture. Then he spied Konner and Ahrwesz as they brought up the rear of the leading cluster, their swords already drawn, their mountbuckskin garb plain in this flourish of color.

As they entered the gap, their horns echoed through the Kric with a deafening peal that sent horses prancing and men's hands to their ears. Khoti winded the song of Habdelion, the great buglebuck trumpet, before lobbing the horn to Habdelion's standard-bearer and leaning low over Fidra's neck. The shrill screech of the tawnkat wailed from near a dozen throats, followed by the wailing yell of the many tribes of southern Shande that had carried over the plain.

As they made for the gap, Habdelion and Euzzeldir slowed, their warriors bunching up behind them in readiness for their orders. As Asteria passed, she made a small sign. Kefta, Ytri and the rest of the Lharan Guard leaped to her command to fall in behind, the Guard once again rallying to Verdaen, their Lieutenant, their brother.

They drove the stunned Minarians from the gap, racing to break free of the confining wall of the Kric. Euzzeldir led one wing to the right toward the cliffs fronting the sea and the widening curve of shoreline. Habdelion took the other to the left to fan out on the west side of the Kric. The scatter of commands fell in behind.

Arshal searched the passing soldiers for a sign of her. In the blur of cavalry racing into the fray, he noted few wore Joffan garb. A pang cramped his stomach. Far too few Joffans. How many souls of Shande had already died for him, wasted in this foolish war against a power so much greater than him? And now, on closer view, he realized that in this bright vision riding out of the morning he'd missed how clothes hung loose on gaunt frames, stained bloody or rent by past wounds. Some still wore the grimy bandages of past battles. Like no other command, the Army of Three Provinces had fought the brunt of Shande's battles. The Lharan Guard may have been a past hallmark of Shandean prowess, but Khoti's command had collectively shed the most blood. And the king counted upon Khoti's command to save Shande in the battle for the gap.

Arshal found Nali searching the passing cavalry for familiar faces as well.

"Come, Lord King, this is what you awaited," Ernik said. Arshal studied the Arenhian in the light of day for the first time. Rail thin, weatherworn and blood-stained, mud and grime clung to every crevice of the man's coppery face. His dark eyes had that dangerous hunted cast of a man who knows death intimately, like too many of those who passed his review in Khoti's wake. Ernik grinned. "The time is here, King. Prove King Azren's trust!"

Ernik grabbed the standard he'd planted in the soil and dropped the stake into his empty lancet boot. He drew his sword and goaded his mount to the bottom of the slope and looked up at Arshal, expectant, his dark Arenhian eyes glittering.

Marol raised the king's standard and the smaller standard of Otayr as Aibak followed suit, both men moving to Ernik's side.

Khoti and his troops had already pushed the enemy back as

the bulk of his cavalry still passed below. Once beyond the confines of the gap they spread out in a semi-circular line like ripples racing from a stone's drop in a pool. Minarian reserves rushed to grab up armor and weapons as Khoti's men roared at them like the surf in the wake of the tempest.

Jan galloped to the king.

"Quick!" Arshal cried. "Fall in behind. Don't let them regain the advantage!"

Jan spun away to his troops. The Gnats tensed, ready with a renewed vigor. None would forget the visage of the shining warrior rising from the mud of dawn to drive their enemy before him like the best legends come to life.

Arshal motioned for his soldiers to fall in behind him, at last winding his horn for the charge, and thundered after Ernik who cut among the companies of the southern army, racing like a man possessed to chase Khoti's wake.

Like the demon warrior they'd proclaimed him, Khoti slammed into the Minarian army. His rage crested. He chastised himself for the long delay and for what Cydwyn and Jali saw and learned in their brief passage through Arshal's camp, more than even Nali could have guessed. Khoti knew Eithurdon lay dying, that more than half of Eithurdon's northern command had met their deaths and bore the brunt of the battle. His two best scouts reported the way blood trickled from the Kric into the marsh from the bodies of dead Guardsmen yet to be carried away. They reported the legions of scavengers circling the battlefield. They sensed the dismay in the camps, not the least the fear in the king's eyes, Jali knowing his sovereign even as he hid in the shadows.

Khoti glimpsed the circle of birds overhead. How many Guardsmen lay untended, consumed by scavengers instead of being received by the spirits?

His arm rose and fell in cadence with Chati and Tre. Despite the weakness of Chati's left arm, the Tawnkat refused to give up his position at Khoti's side, worked himself harder so that one-handed he wielded his sword with as much force as with two. The injured limb his mark of defiance that he couldn't be driven to Sihmad Shal. Khoti's two Taschian officers, his adopted brothers, moved like mirror images beside him, with Asteria, Jali and Cydwyn at his flank. He missed Daris's caustic wit prodding them on, calling for blood, demanding no quarter like the enemy's flag fluttering orange on the battlefield. She'd almost had the strength to defy him as Chati had. But not quite.

Khoti glanced back to see if Arshal's pennants followed. He made out Ernik's torn colors flying ahead of the other standards. Khoti grinned to himself. Ernik stood among Khoti's best, as determined as any Shandean to see victory. In the same glance, Khoti saw the purple scarf and austere flag marking Aibak, and the bright slash of the Otayran colors. All of Ea rode to battle, rode to the king's call. Except Baynu.

Cydwyn's assessment terrified him. He couldn't doubt the young officer with instincts often more uncanny than his mentor's. The king was terrified, Cydwyn said. And Kedtair waned.

Asteria gasped. He didn't dare look, but glanced anyway. Blood ran from her arm. She fought on. Cydwyn and Jali closed ranks beside her. She bore many scars; she was a Tawnkat. He couldn't afford to think of her any other way. He pushed away a weapon, his tender ribs straining against his mail. They might be fresh to this battle, but, like him, his troops couldn't be called hale or rested. They must reach Ghyldus before they wearied. He knew from the positions of the enemy's command – so identical in every battle – exactly where Ghyldus's command tent stood, without even looking ahead of the next soldier he faced.

With his knees, he stood in his saddle to look back at his followers. Once again, he formed the point of a massive wedge. The flags of Arshal's entourage neared. He discerned Nali's blue and white scarf, and Ramel speeding to join the king's company. Khoti expected that. Ramel intended to witness the great moment of the age, he'd said. That would be with Arshal.

Arshal's company now battled right behind Asteria, flanked by the Lharan Guard. How that must have stunned Ytri and Kefta to receive a signed battle command from Asteria. How it must have surprised them that they leaped to respond, without a thought, to Eithurdon's daughter, a Tawnkat, an officer of the Sword of Shande.

Khoti glanced at Asteria. Rising Kedtair blinded him in the same second he glimpsed the swath of blood sheathing her arm. A great heat welled up within him as the rays of the star filled his vision. He had to force his gaze away. He turned back to strike the enemy before him, ghost images of Kedtair and Asteria's bloody arm remaining before his eyes. It seemed to imply some message, this melding of light and blood. A host of visions, memories, surged through him. How odd this thing he felt. Images, unbidden, flooded him as he fought, his blows still deadly though his mouth had fallen open in amazement as ideas fluttered within him, intertwining with the ghosting of Kedtair. Before him appeared Dynresa's capricious smile, her head tossing to send her braids flying. As if viewing from a distance, he saw himself, reckless, taking on the Staph-el mine alone or racing ahead as the point of a wedge. Nali stood before him in a dark dungeon, jailer, servant, prisoner. A brief image of sticks clacking before a fire dissolved into the flash of a sword striking the gold cuff on his wrist. The flood of impressions, concepts stunned him, his mind like an exhalation of memory.

The star blazed off his stellan-plated helm, blinding his enemy as he struck. He felt like new growth behind a fire. His sword gleamed through a sheath of red, moving in his grasp almost of its own. He battled on instinct, his blows sure and deadly. New strength fell on his enemy, the weariness of months, years, of fighting Shande's war dropped from him. Everything stood out clear as spring water in a glass goblet. He gasped at the sense of strength he felt, the power surging in him needing to be expended. Truly the spirits had taken him like no healing or battle he'd ever known. His fists clenched around the hilt of his sword as his palms throbbed as if he had sliced them on a sharp knife, the lifebeat of his blood filling some wound. He freed a hand and glanced at his palm. His breath sucked in a gasp he couldn't expel. Chati and Tre moved in to protect him in this moment of sheer awe on viewing his own hand. Not fear, too much of another thing poured into him to feel that. He found understanding. The two warring passions in him, the healer and warrior, met, melded, became one.

Kedtair faded from his gaze.

On his palm, the old scars of healings stood out red, as if

blood again filled the cuts. Blood beaded up in the gashes. He feared losing his grip on his sword, but the blood didn't smear. He felt no pain, only the strange throb that followed the slash of a knife.

The battle passed around him, as if he himself had become invisible. He lifted his gaze from his palm with effort, finding Ramel staring at him, stunned. Ramel's gaze shot to Nali, dragging Khoti's with it.

Nali grinned across the backs of enemy horses, a calming expression that silenced the din of battle and soothed his fear and confusion. As if Nali spoke in his ears, Khoti heard his friend's assurances as if again hearing the soft words of hope uttered when he lay dying in Sefresal's dungeons. He recognized Nali's wonderment at how Khoti awakened, at its manifestation. As suddenly, Khoti knew, felt, the power now his. He saw himself as his enemy saw him: grin like a death knell; the dark scrub of beard and long, fair locks gathered at his neck giving him a fierce look; features lean and hard, gaunt; his body all muscle and sinew; the emerald gaze of an apparition so frightening the enemy fell back before him.

"Verdaen!" a wail rose before him.

He swung two-handed, the blow severing a pike and swinging on into the man's face and driving him into another. The shout rose around them, a cry of fear as the warrior thought dead resurrected on the field. An illusion of the Shandean king, some screamed. Shande's warrior rode them down, intense, burning, like the star glittering from his armor as Fidra pranced over the dead like a creature eternal of the gods, untouchable, immortal.

Resistance parted as the enemy struggled to escape his deadly path. He trotted ahead to a small rise, stopping to gaze on the distant canopy of Ghyldus's command. Beside him, Asteria sagged a little, her face pale and pained. The deep wound on her arm bled profusely. He reached out to support her when she appeared about to fall, his heart going out to her. She gasped, staring down at the hand gripping her arm over the bloody wound. Afraid he'd hurt her he drew back. She regained her balance, still staring at him in amazement. His touch had stanched the flowing blood. In its place a mark remained in the shape of Khoti's grasp. Her pain gone.

"Gods," he muttered, knowing at last Kedtair's secret, the power the word had for him.

The dilemma of his life remained. He didn't feel the pain. What would it take from him? It seemed nothing, yet he doubted. For the first time the conflict of his roles merged. With the same hand he dealt life and death. What role was the king's?

23: A Bitter Cup

Despite the arrival of the Army of Three Provinces, the advance faltered, sputtering to a halt as some sixty thousand Shandeans faced three times their number. Even if Khoti's infantry arrived this moment, they would only be another sixteen thousand. Though enough to stop a rout the odds still favored the enemy. With so many troops weak, wounded and weary, the day threatened to go against them. Even Detarian stunning powders didn't give them the edge they needed. The advance halted then reversed. Khoti turned aside to assist the king's company, now hemmed in by the multitude of Ghyldus's forces. Indiscriminate of striking their own, enemy arrows fell among the battling soldiers, taking Shandean and Minarian alike. The Minarians had men to spare.

Now that the Minarians had recovered from their surprise and knew Khoti as a mortal warrior, his enemies came for him, determined to see him dead.

At last, the Shandeans retreated until they backed up against the steep face of the Kric again. The Shandeans didn't panic. The dead and dying, mostly Minarian, scattered the field. But Arshal's troops could withstand little more without real rest.

Euzzeldir's command had spread out to the north, protecting the gap, bolstered by thousands of Iyrafael Gnats. Habdelion held the face of the Kric with Kyne. Sedaik's best archers swarmed the Kric above Habdelion, their long bows and poison arrows aimed on the enemy's foremost ranks while Jan's crossbowmen aimed bolts at the leaders of the Minarian commands. The bulk of Arshal's troops waited in the center of the gap, rotating back to the supply lines to refill water skins and haversacks during breaks in the battle. The smell of curing meat wafted at them with the scent of damp cattle and dung as cooks tended fires now that they no longer stood to defend themselves.

Horns blared from the Minarian lines as commands rushed to regroup. An uneasy lull reigned as the two suns beat down on them. Kedtair already neared the horizon as the sun reached the mid-point of the sky. Kedtair's path shortened; little time remained. Despite the full brunt of the heat beating upon them, instead of falling to their knees, the Shandeans stood patient and ready, inspired by Khoti who, if nothing else, proved a powerful symbol to rally to.

A cluster of commanders and runners huddled around the king's standards as they eyed enemy movements. Arshal watched his champion approach, Fidra dancing like a foal beneath him. Khoti wiped the sweat running from beneath his helm and adjusted the orange scarf that bound the hair off his brow. Strands of tawny hair escaped Joffan braids and plastered his neck. His scraggly dark beard seemed to add darkness to hollow cheeks and the shadows beneath his eyes. Yet in his eyes the emerald glow of a cat regarding its prey gave no hint of weariness.

He grinned at Arshal. The king couldn't stop staring at how Khoti had changed. The Taschian's smile faded as Arshal pumped him for news of the south and Dynresa. The doubt Arshal felt hearing about Baynu and Shikora's failure to defend Shela seemed to make his champion uneasy.

Khoti dismounted, Fidra sighing and her head dropping as if Khoti alone charged her spirit. She shook her head, sending splatters of lather from her neck falling into the light layer of dust already settling over the muddy plain. Khoti ran the tips of his fingers down each leg then gave her a distracted pat on the neck. What care the man must bestow, Arshal thought, when other beasts would have succumbed long ago.

"We'll retire you soon," Khoti said when Fidra nuzzled her head into his chest.

Dropping her reins Khoti walked about, stiff-legged. Arshal didn't know how to react when he learned they had ridden through the storm, the force of the wind shredding the soldiers' clothing, horses staggering or lost. They rode three hours, resting for one, through the entire duration of the tempest. Not better rested than Arshal's troops, the Army of Three Provinces couldn't even claim to be less battle-weary.

Khoti ambled to Nali's stirrup and peered up at the seer.

"Did you know?" Khoti asked, holding his palms out for Nali's inspection. Arshal glimpsed a thatch of bloody streaks.

Nali shrugged, then nodded. "Not that part," he admitted, pointing at the bloody grooves in Khoti's palm. "And not you."

"Will it harm me? I healed Asteria's wound with just a touch! I felt nothing! I just willed her to be well. No weakness, weariness, not the spirits, nothing. There was only this sudden heat, or maybe chill. Will it affect my ability to fight? Will I heal my enemy as I strike him?"

Khoti had found what Arshal could not. And they hadn't even known Kedtair called him.

"You don't feel the spirits in you because you're part of their world now," Nali said so softly Arshal had to strain to hear him. "It's hard to absorb it all. I had the Lierye to warn me."

Khoti's eyes widened to that cat-like stare in which his pupils enlarged for the pounce, then narrowed again.

"What of the king?" Khoti demanded.

"He'll figure it out."

"Can you tell him? The star wanes," Ramel demanded, startling the Tawnkat who hadn't seen the Visionary's approach.

"Ramel is it? You know I can't," Nali returned as the Visionary inclined his head. "You knew that when you tortured him in Hainad," Nali gave the Visionary his ghost of a smile. "He has to find it on his own or it won't be his. He won't understand. I've hinted. He's not listening."

The three turned to gaze at Arshal. He shivered at the speculation he saw in them. They waited for him to do something. He just didn't know what.

Khoti peered at the cliffs above. Konner's figure stood out against the stone as the Tawnkat surveyed the enemy's position. Khoti scanned the length of his command then returned his gaze to Konner. Konner gave a signal. Fidra's head came up as Khoti mounted, his arm swinging up. Arshal turned to look for Konner again. The man had gone.

"It's our turn, king," Khoti stated. He grabbed Arshal's horn from Marol and gave it a mighty blast.

Leaping forward on cue, Shande again took the offensive while the enemy fumbled to regroup. Arshal's troops responded slowly. The commanders of the Army of Three Provinces knew Khoti's penchant for sudden decisions without benefit of counsel. Captains had watched the Kric, expecting such a move at the enemy's most chaotic moment.

His champion raced like a ship into the sea of Minarians, bearings set on Ghyldus's canopy. His men streamed behind him into the breach before Arshal realized the way opened for him.

Before he could follow, Hothur pressed a cup into his hand. The man turned and rode away before Arshal could mutter his thanks. The king emptied the burning wine and tossed the cup to the ground.

He spurred his horse. Nali was beside him, racing for the opening Khoti made. All along the buckled stretch of the Minarian line, Shandeans held the way open for him. Some turned to cheer as they dispatched Minarian soldiers with ease. Khoti raced far ahead as if nothing could stop him from meeting Ghyldus. Arshal followed. On the edge of his consciousness, he heard Nali screaming for him to stop. The distance between them yawned. He urged his mount faster, ignoring Nali's calls. At last, after all this time, he raced to reach Ghyldus and end the bloodshed! The elation made him light-headed. He felt the twist of excitement in his stomach. Nothing could stop them!

A command brought him up short. Nali's voice shattered his awareness. It ordered him to stop. He couldn't resist. Reining in, he stared over his shoulder. He had come far across the plain. Nali appeared distant, though his voice loomed close at hand. Nali galloped after him, the field open now save for a scattering of Minarian bodies. His troops, far distant, battled toward Ghyldus's canopy. Khoti neared the canopy where Ghyldus laughed at the king's laggard progress. As he stared, Arshal discerned the demon reaching up to tweak the cheek of the woman standing submissive behind him. Resala! He lurched forward against Nali's command, his heart laboring in his chest as he sought to defy an order stronger than him. Nali loomed before him now. He tried to wrench free of the Sage's raptor gaze and race to his sister's defense. The pain in her expression pierced him over the great distance, assailed him with guilt. He'd sent her on this treacherous mission. Khoti had nearly gained the canopy. Arshal couldn't expect his champion to wait there until Nali finished cautioning him.

"Don't move!" Nali commanded as Arshal tried to wrench away. Nali's word alone held him fixed, without a will of his own.

The king struggled, only to frighten his mount into rearing up and side-stepping as Nali's eyes bore into him. Arshal turned to retort then froze at the combination of terror and anger in Nali's expression. The king's mouth opened but he could make no noise as the horse pranced beneath him. Nali grabbed for him, but the horse reared beyond the Sage's grasp. Arshal stared about him, seeing only the open field and Khoti battling in the distance. What madness took Nali that he kept the king from his destiny? Had Ghyldus set some spell in the brand on his counselor's forehead?

"Arshal! It's an illusion! You're not seeing what you think you see!" Nali's voice held the power of the surf rushing in with the tide.

Arshal looked around him. Nali's voice was the surf. On Arshal's right, not a span from his mount's hooves, the ground fell in a long, steep slope to a ledge undercut by a drop hundreds of paces into waves rushing over boulders. Hooves sunk into the rain-softened turf and slipped toward the slope where the animal would never regain balance.

"Can I believe what I see now?" Arshal asked in a small voice, gripping the reins so tight his fingers cramped.

"If you see a cliff, believe it." Face pale, Nali leaned forward and swept the reins from Arshal's hands. He towed the horse away from the ledge. As it lurched to follow, its back leg slipped from beneath it, almost sending Arshal tumbling down the slope. Nali's mount backed away, Nali gripping the reins of the king's mount. Arshal clung to his horse's neck. Soon his mount lunged ahead, regaining its balance to stand with sides quivering. Arshal stared at Nali, mouth hanging open in shock.

Raucous laughter echoed in Arshal's head. Sinister and mocking. It seemed to find every recess of his mind. He slammed hands against his ears to muffle it.

"Can't you hear that! He mocks me!"

Nali shook his head. "He can't deceive me with illusion. I won't fall prey because I refuse to believe it."

The noise faded from Arshal's ears. He realized now that instead of following Khoti's path into the battle, he had ridden straight across the gap, behind their lines, to reach the edge of the ocean. The bodies he saw, the canopy, the image of Ghyldus and Resala, of Khoti and the cheering Shandeans, all had been an illusion. Khoti had punched a hole in the enemy line, but he hadn't gone far and the battle appeared stiff. The bodies in Khoti's wake wore both Minarian and Shandean colors. No one cheered. He found only the grimaces of wounded and weary.

His hands shook as he took the reins back. "How do I know what's real, what illusion? What if he deceives me into killing myself or striking down my own troops, or attacking you?"

"It's possible." Nali studied him. "You aren't the confident king who entered Peshal's Tunnel just a few months ago. Illusions weaken the foundations you built in your journeys. He's winning by the very means I feared."

"Can't you help me, Nali? Help me or I'll fail us all! I see it in Khoti. We thought him awesome before! Now he's truly the Verdaen the Minarians feared!"

Nali appeared barely able to conceal some rage. "You aren't thinking. Fight the illusions! Believe it, it exists! Refuse to believe, it doesn't. All that is is you. Be one with yourself! That's the reality that controls illusion." Nali glared at him as if he'd been forced to reveal a secret.

Arshal shook his head. "This must be another illusion. I can't understand a word you say. What infant's babble are you spewing at me?"

Nali sat back in his saddle. "That's it! Some Sage I am. I never thought of it! Illusion! Since the beginning! You can't figure it out because Ghyldus makes you believe you can't! Believe in yourself, Arshal. You must figure it out! Refuse to believe his illusions!"

"But if he's in my mind, how can I escape him!" Arshal demanded. Nali's words sounded like those of a lunatic. But then, wouldn't an illusionist ensure his supremacy in his victim's mind by discrediting sound advice? The words made sense. But the concepts translated into babble. He recalled everything Nali had told him. Just nonsensical words. He couldn't imagine what Nali asked him to do.

"Maybe he isn't in your mind," Nali said, thinking aloud. "Maybe he convinces you he's there. Then your imagination conjures up the things he would try and you believe it. For all we know, you're the one with the power of illusion who brought the snakes and toads and wolvers and ghosts because you believed it could happen."

Arshal dismissed it all with a wave of his hand.

"Remember the eyes in the medallion? Your enemy's imagination is your best ally."

"But the eyes are real!" He just couldn't see what his counselor tried to show him. "So now what? Khoti broke through for me and I'm not there. And if I did ride forward, I wouldn't be sure whether I attacked the enemy or a comrade."

"Gods!" Nali shrieked at him. "You're defeating yourself. If you believe he can command your mind he will!"

Arshal fell into Nali's gaze. The Sage's expression softened, but it lost none of its clarity, or depth, or menace. "I think you could master illusion if you chose to, Nali."

Nali laughed. It sounded so odd on the edge of a battlefield, from a man who so seldom let anything amuse him. "I already have, Dyn Eadon," he said. "Every time I don't see what you see, every time I call you back from your visions, I've mastered illusion. I master it because it has no effect on me. Only reality has an impact."

Arshal tried to evaluate the changes in his counselor since Kedtairday. Perhaps the Visionaries of old felt like Nali did now. Visionaries like Cree and Ramel had forgotten so much. Here, Nali's wisdom reached beyond those who had once stood beside One. Even irascible Ramel appeared to defer to the one-time fisher with only three years in his robes.

"So, counselor, what's your advice?"

Nali remained silent a moment. The day wore toward sunset, though Kedtair would rise again before dusk, making its appearance twice this day as its circuit shortened toward the north. Only three days remained before Kedtair set for the last time. Between Kedtair and the moon there would be no night tonight.

"You have to follow Khoti," Nali stated. "There's no time. Pray you overcome the illusion that you can't do it! Resala awaits and she grows impatient."

At mention of Resala, Arshal straightened. Her appearance in the illusion meant to encourage him to race toward his sister.

"I need help. I know he baits me. If I see her with him, I'm afraid I'll fly into one of Khoti's rages. Just remind me of things I should and shouldn't be doing. Stay with me and don't let these illusions take me."

Nali grimaced but nodded.

Arshal turned and with Nali beside him as guide hurried toward the cluster of standards where Arshal's aides awaited. Khoti stood out far out on the field, the sun blazing from his helm. Though dented and splattered with blood, it still sent a reflection into the sky, star-like. Something about the image made Arshal hesitate, made his heart race, something about the blazing reflection. Then he lost it. He glanced at Nali, sensing somehow that he had come very close to unlocking the secret the derna held. Nali paid no attention to him. The counselor's mouth pressed into a tight line that made him forbidding.

Arshal dug inside himself, seeking some thought he could cling to, some element only his, that couldn't be corrupted. Dynresa. Her image had saved him from death in the hills above Iyrafael. Nali told him to believe in himself, but his nature instead urged him to think of her, to concentrate on the promise he made that he would live to rebuild his bruised country. Dynresa would be the reality he sought, the incorruptible part of himself that would protect him from illusion. From Khoti's hints, he knew she had ridden into battle for him, shed blood for him. Perhaps her mind had changed. Perhaps her contempt had only grown more virulent. Maybe the closeness they discovered lived only in his imagination. All Hainad rode with Euzzeldir. She may not even have thought of him. Her image shined with that golden light, that soft clarity the passage of time gave memory. He saw clove-scented, chestnut-streaked auburn hair and the coarse white linen of a Joffan tunic blowing in the hot wind of the desert, the heat like afternoon on a sleeping cat. The briefest image of her crouching in his tent, stained dark with her king's blood, face ugly with fear, intruded. He cloaked that memory with the shining vision he had created.

Arshal matched his pace to Nali's beside him. Giddy and dizzy, he felt certain the heat and weariness consumed him. His stomach constricted in a knot that made him gasp. He supposed he must suffer the beginnings of heat exhaustion, or the effects of days of tension and poor rations. A wave of nausea came over him.

As they came to a halt where the flags of many lands remained posted in the field, gazes followed him, his wild ride witnessed by many. He didn't even glance when Hothur's hand held out another cup of wine. He felt the heat in him now. He took a sip, afraid to drink too deeply lest his stomach cramp again. Nausea scattered sparks before his eyes.

He heard the calls, the orders, demands and greetings that marked Khoti's approach, but he could only imagine that Ghyldus had won.

Khoti took in the dazed expression in the king's eyes, face glossed by a sheen of sweat. Something he could see ... He turned to speak to Nali, but his gaze fell on Hothur, who handed the king a cup of wine. Dark eyes regarded Khoti with a second's unveiled hostility.

Khoti slapped the cup from Arshal's hand, too late. The king sagged, clutching his stomach. Hothur drew his sword when he saw that others had marked him. In the confusion, aides and Nali struggled to keep the king from falling from his saddle as they rushed him from danger.

Khoti blocked Hothur's escape. It wasn't Hothur. Something had bothered Khoti when he'd first seen the man in Arshal's entourage. The man wore a helm, his features similar. But he'd never even acknowledged Khoti. Now, he could see that while the man might wear Hothur's clothing, might have Hothur's features, his dark eyes did not match the soft hazel of Hothur's. They didn't hold Pladde bloodlines among their secrets.

As the man made to escape, Khoti threw a pinch of Detarian powder into his eyes. The Minarian gave a violent sneeze then stopped, as if unable to remember what he fled. Khoti smiled as he disarmed the assassin.

As he led his prisoner to the rear lines, he spied Ytri relaying orders to Mitte, his hands moving to punctuate his directions. A click like rapping stone brought Ytri's head around. Ytri nodded, darting away before he'd finished issuing his orders.

A short time later, Khoti swept into the tent holding the king, the champion's presence filling the space as spare light glittered from his armor. His attention went to Arshal who lay on a pallet, deathly pale.

Khoti shoved his prisoner forward. The man fell to his knees as the Taschian ripped the helm away to reveal Ghyldus's mark branded on the Minarian's forehead. The man who impersonated Hothur had in his gaze the fanatic expression all feared.

Khoti knelt at his king's side. Arshal's eyes remained shut, his breathing shallow. Taking the king's hand in his, Khoti studied his sovereign.

"Poison," Khoti told Nali, who regarded the prisoner with loathing. Khoti tugged his helm from his head, brushing unkempt hair from his face and readjusting the orange scarf. "If he went to the trouble of sneaking into camp to kill the king, why didn't he just get him with a knife? Why bother with poison?" Khoti glanced at an aide who scampered in, sending him to fetch warm water.

Nali's words seethed command as he demanded answers from the prisoner, who spat in the dusty floor of the healers' tent. Nali's tone changed. His hand rising. Appearing stricken, the man's mouth opened, though his hands tried to hold it shut. A shadow filled the doorway. Asteria held the tent flap as Ytri ducked through struggling to help carry Hothur's burly body with a knife protruding from his back.

A soft moan came from the other side of the tent as Ytri lay Hothur down, the man's unseeing eyes studying the ceiling.

Asteria stared at her father, the man who had gasped at the sight of Hothur's body. The Duke of Lharan regarded his daughter with relief and reserve, both love and hate.

Hurrying to the duke, Khoti crouched, reaching for the poisoned wound in the man's side. Eithurdon grasped Khoti's wrist in an iron grip despite his fevered wounds. Hatred twisted the duke's face. The expression struck Khoti like a physical blow as Asteria knelt beside her father.

"You made my daughter into a camp follower! Of noble house fallen –" He stopped, focusing on her Tawnkat tattoo and the outline of a battle scar on her forehead. His hand whipped out and struck her. She fell back on her haunches. "And you even wear the mark of your shame."

Asteria stood, betraying no emotion. She stared at her father a long moment then touched the red mark on her chin where he'd struck her. In the stiff but upright gait of the mourner, she turned and left. As she did so, Eithurdon's feverish gaze went from the palm-shaped smear of blood over the congealed gash on her arm, to the marks in Khoti's palms.

The healer's aide returned with the demanded water. On a sign from Khoti, who remained at Eithurdon's side, Ytri took a pungent powder from the pouch at Khoti's belt and dissolved it in the water, then forced the unconscious king to drink.

"What have we made of the impetuous boy who ran into my hall in his nightshirt," Eithurdon whispered. "Tsevon begged me to leave you be. I ignored his warnings, prophecy. I made you and can blame only myself –"

"I'm the gods' creation. You give yourself too much credit." Khoti reached for Eithurdon again, but the duke held him at bay. "You refuse life!" Khoti leaned close, his very presence a threat. "You're no better than a coward to give up your command! I'm the Sword of Shande. You refuse my orders and break faith with your country and people to disdain life. And I let your rebuke hurt me. It was misplaced pain."

Khoti returned to the king's side with his back to the duke. He paused only a moment to shake off weariness before he brushed his fingers against Arshal's brow, outlining an old scar. The tingle of a breath passed through him, gone before he could define it.

"You're called to your people King –" He paused, discerning something tucked within the king's thoughts, hidden from all others. "Remember your promise," he whispered. Arshal stirred. Khoti set the heel of his hand against the king's brow. He felt the color drain from his face for the briefest of moments.

"Lazy King," he called. "You've a battle to wage."

Arshal's eyes opened as if commanded. "You're forever coming to my rescue," Arshal rasped. "But your touch has changed –"

Khoti put a finger to his lips and gave Arshal a distracted smile. Arshal twisted away, retching as the powder took effect, cleansing him of the poison. Khoti went to the tent flap, whipping it open so that light from outside blazed in at them.

"The poison was meant to weaken, not kill," Nali said. "Then he would fall prey to Ghyldus's spells."

"He almost died."

"He wasn't supposed to. If he'd known the secret of Kedtair he would have resisted the poison. The spy meant to use the time to identify our strengths and weaknesses."

Khoti nodded then gestured at the Minarian. "Kill him," he ordered, taking another step for the door. He paused and glanced back at Eithurdon's feverish face. "Your time's short, Duke of Lharan. You were to me like my fa. I pity you your pain and forgive you your foolishness." The flap dropped behind him, darkening the tent.

A dim echo of battle chased through the Kric as Khoti stopped outside the healer's tent, scanning the encampment for Fidra. He scowled. How would he see his king through the end with such thoughts as he found within him? How could the duke he loved as a father refuse the life Khoti could give with just a touch? And it galled him that the enemy stood in this camp and Khoti didn't recognize him.

He found Asteria some distance away sitting astride her mount as she held Fidra's reins. Her features clenched and stony, she stared toward the distant battle with the impatience of a warrior. He touched her hand, which jerked as if she'd received a shock. She gazed down at him.

"How can your touch be so comforting yet so fatal?" She rubbed the spot on her skin where he'd touched her. "It is something you project, then, that heals or comforts, or hurts."

Khoti shrugged. "It's no easier." He leaned into Fidra's sticky side where a crust of sweat and dirt gave off a pungent and comforting odor. He ran his hand along Fidra's neck, resting his chin on the damp and sour saddle pad. "Do I treat the wounded with this special gift?" he asked. "Or just play protector to my king? Either way someone dies or suffers who needn't –"

He turned to find haggard Ytri ducking from the tent. Khoti went to him, laying a companionable arm around his shoulder. Ytri straightened, giving Khoti a wary glance, the man's weariness falling away. Khoti felt the briefest flicker run through him.

"Can't you help Eithur?" Ytri begged as a pale king exited the tent behind him.

"The spirits won't minister the resentful, those who refuse their gifts."

"Can't you try and let them decide if he's worthy?"

Khoti laughed, a bitter sound as he mounted Fidra. "Come, King," he said. "Your champion waits to serve you." Khoti reached down and pulled Ytri up behind him to speed the captain to his command.

Arshal mounted, still shaky, from the poison and the powder that made him retch so violently. A king who moments ago staggered near death rode again to war.

"Eithur –" Arshal began.

"Is dead," Khoti said, goading Fidra to again carry him to battle, Asteria, her expression a mask, close beside him.

24: The Enchanter's Web

Again, the horns rang out. A pale king rode in his champion's tracks, the Visionary Ramel on one side, the Sage Nali on the other to keep him from straying.

He faced into the blazing red of the sun setting in a smoky haze. The indistinct horizons gave an eerie feel to the day as the smoke of fires and silhouettes of scavengers hung over the field. As the sun sank, Arshal felt the white heat of Kedtair rising behind him. His thoughts faltered. He sensed an answer so close, but again it eluded him, as if the key to a lock were snatched from his hand.

He could not be so foolish again. The lives it cost! Ghyldus's illusion might be excused, but he should have known Hothur from his assassin. How could he forget the ways of a man he huddled beside throughout the storm? Hothur left camp bearing water skins, returning minutes later without the promised water. Why had no one caught the deception? Why hadn't he noticed the change in the man's voice, the set of his eyes, the unfamiliar mannerisms?

Arrows fell among them. One bounced off the light breast plates shielding Arshal's chest. Another stuck in the small wooden shield he held before him. Still others clattered around him. An arrow struck him in his thigh just above the knee. He grimaced. Though not serious, it throbbed with the promise of pain, each jolt of his horse's gait twisting the arrow tip in his flesh. Arshal raised his hand. A blaze of light erupted. Arrows in the air burst into flame or burned in quivers. A shower of ashes fell among the battlers like snowflakes as arrowheads plunked harmless to the ground with no shaft or flight to guide them. The volleys of arrows ceased.

Perspiration worked from beneath the king's arms, down his back and neck and spread across his chest. Damp hands gripped his sword until his wrist ached. Had he erred again? Khoti turned his cat's gaze on him. Ramel and Nali stared. He knew they hoped he'd found the secret of Kedtair. Another failure.

Enemy commands converged on them now. Ramel, Nali and Khoti labored under the blows of many as they struggled to breach the lines. Khoti's faithful Tawnkat followers crowded up on the sides, Kefta, Konner, Ytri and Ahrwesz just behind on either flank. He heard Aibak and Ernik calling the challenge of their kings nearby and Marol cursing from behind as he fended off attackers with his standard. The entire Shandean army pummeled the line in the shape of a broad chevron, but the battle remained uneven, with many ranks to fight through before they reached their target. But they moved ahead, at last.

Nali's hand bled from a wound Arshal couldn't see. Khoti slowed. The two might possess some spirit greater than Arshal's, but not immortality. Arshal knew he wouldn't survive if they fell. Yet they threw themselves up as shields around their king. Wearied by his use of the stone, the nausea still in him and the arrow wound in his leg, his mind wandered. He felt so ineffectual here in the center of his warriors, no foe coming even close enough for him to draw his blade.

Arshal raised his hand. Nali opened his mouth, perhaps to issue a command, but before Nali could speak, the king's palm disappeared in a white blaze. Enemy swords shattered for ranks ahead of them. Lurching through, the Shandean forces beat down men who now turned to run. The king fell forward over his mount's neck seeking breath after the expense of a power he didn't know he could wield.

He felt Nali's grip on his arm. "You shouldn't be doing that. You're so weak now."

Arshal brushed the comment aside with a wave of his hand, feeling faint. A sudden breath passed through him like the surge of cold air falling from the snowpack in the Val. He caught the scent of pines on mountainsides and the aroma of cedar burning in the cook fires, before the sensation faded. He found Khoti beside him. His champion had already plucked the arrow from the king's thigh and laid his hand upon the wound to stop the bleeding. At the same time, the fingertips of Khoti's other hand touched the palm sheltering Arshal's stone. The king felt new strength.

How did Khoti know what to do? Did Kedtair bring answers? Then he noted how his champion's eyes had dulled and face paled. The Taschian nodded and an instant later the color returned to his cheeks and the life flared again in his eyes.

"I was wrong," Khoti muttered to Nali as he moved to battle forward to his position again. "There's an effect."

"I saw. Is it a weakening, or merely a tiring?"

"Either way, he can't face him without me. But I don't know how long I can give him all my strength and still be of any use. He'll need a warrior at his side –"

"Ramel," Nali stated, nodding at the seer.

Khoti shook his head. "Too distracted by the epic historical event taking place to bother ensuring it occurs."

Khoti spurred ahead, leaving Arshal freshened but feeling no better knowing he stole so much from the lives around him. Chati and Tre moved apace across the field, Khoti reaching them as Ghyldus's canopy became a real target on the plain ahead. But they tired. Along the line, troops fell back to be replaced by infantry. It wouldn't last and again they would fall short. He imagined a demon beneath his canopy laughing at their efforts, knowing they would merely break upon his army like waves on a beach head.

As the white light grew higher in the sky, minds wandered. Arshal could see Khoti's weariness as blood trickled from the many little nicks and cuts on his champion's unprotected limbs. Khoti paused only a second to take a long draw from the skin hanging from his belt, its neck slashed. Water leaked from the hole to splash him, steaming from his armor. He stopped the top in the same smooth motion that opened it. Then Arshal heard it, a distant horn.

Khoti looked up at the sky in disbelief. "It's only about midnight."

Arshal heard the horn again, clear, a low cheer following. An impulsive whoop emitted from Khoti's throat. Chati and Tre surged ahead. Khoti fell back to the king's side.

"King," he hissed in Arshal's ear. "Infantry's arrived, with them your promise. This is the last help to hope for. Trust yourself, King, not others. Ignore the promise you made and look elsewhere for your strength. If you don't, we're dead."

When Arshal turned to respond, Khoti had gone, only the hiss of his voice ringing in ears, and the faint scent of cedar tickling his imagination.

Resala heard Teshet pouring a cup of water for her. The light passing through the orange fabric of the canopy roof failed to brighten the girl's cheeks. Though ashore for weeks, the pallor remained. What frightened her so? Resala almost laughed. Yes, what could frighten Teshet: to stand beside a demon and witness the destruction of lives, to see her mistress transformed from trembling weakness to something ... else.

As Ghyldus had been transformed. Something more dangerous, evil, lurked in him now. She no longer twisted him as she once had, needed more stealth to manipulate him. His presence radiated heat like the giant bonfires lit against the nip of harvest season, but without warmth, only the flame making her skin tingle like the moment before fire singes away the hairs.

He'd left her alone since her awakening. Maybe he sensed how dangerous she had become though she tried to conceal it. But more likely the other presence in him, not the spirit of Fyraer, but Fyraer himself – cloaked in Ghyldus's form – had no need for her. Had Ghyldus had his own awakening, calling Fyraer into him? Resala had no doubt he could do it. She no longer questioned anything strange. She had witnessed the oceans whipped and tangled by Aziaris's wind and gardens, boiling with Maura's fury, pounding with the combined anger of gods defying their oaths to One.

Across the battlefield Resala caught the distant flash of silver, rumor of Khoti. Her heart went to him. Like her, his awakening came unexpected. She sensed him grappling with the power coursing through his veins. They came for her, but so many warriors stood in their way.

"You're afraid," Resala said. "Why else the games?" She didn't bother to mask her loathing for him. That ruse ended with her awakening, with his arrival on this field, with the uncaring demon in him.

Ghyldus looked up at her. She returned his gaze unaffected by his presence, unafraid.

"I play no games." Even his words resonated with a deeper power.

"I think you're weak and frightened. You hide behind your mentor," Resala blurted. "You're nothing. A toy. A tool. Not strong enough to take to the field for fear the mask you wear will shred and reveal the nothing beneath it."

His hand shot out and twisted her arm with such force she shrieked and jerked away. The bone snapped. His touch felt as if it turned her skin to ash. He locked his grip on her arm, ignoring her gasps of pain.

"I will hear no more from you! You will stand mute and witness. Before they die, I will turn all these witless fools to me, and lock them out of the afterworld of your false gods. Their destruction will be complete. When I give leave, you will repeat the tale to the people who remain. None will survive this battle to relay the story! No one who can raise a hand to me will survive. You will see what it is to taunt God!"

He studied her, no hint of any emotion in his eyes but the determination lurking in their blackness, an unknowable menace that might peer from a dark cave or deep well. Ghyldus at least displayed remorse, perhaps even pity, when he hurt her.

Fyraer not Ghyldus, the certainty shrieked at her. She couldn't form words, only the noise of her exasperation as his spell locked her throat. Could Arshal even hope to face Fyraer?

Through the tears the pain elicited, she saw the black blur of Verdred step forward. Something about him disturbed her. She'd noticed it since her awakening but she couldn't define it. A familiar feeling about him seemed to terrify Teshet to the point of hysteria. This abomination had left the necklace and gemstone for her. So much hate filled him, yet she sensed he came to her rescue, his intent protective, not malicious.

Ghyldus released her arm. Verdred stopped. Resala sagged against Teshet who held her as Resala cradled her arm.

Ghyldus pointed at Verdred. "They ride again. Have the

catapults readied." As Verdred bowed to his Lord, Resala caught the bare flicker of his glance touching her before he spun away to his duties.

Something in that glance, not in the expression, drove the pain from her mind. As always, Verdred projected his dedication to his master. But the eyes themselves –

A chair pressed against the back of her legs. Teshet eased her to a seat. Resala tried to swallow away the faintness overtaking her as sparks danced in her vision. Calm, she needed that to work with the strange gifts Kedtair gave her. The gifts only worked on others. She couldn't steal from herself.

Ghyldus sat with a flourish, erect and omnipotent in the heavy chair his servants had lugged from his hall in Lagdche and carried through the surf to the shore of Shande. Some aura of power lurked about it. Crafted for him, by his design, of some dark heavy wood like swamp-sodden logs, it fit his shape. Small red gemstones edged black satin cushion covers, the gem-work like bloody dew in a web, tracing outward like rays. If not for the shine of the satin or glitter of gems it appeared austere. Where the god's left shoulder rested, a groove and ledge held a small cushion. Resala's post. He expected her to stand there, subservient, hand on her master's shoulder where he could control her, the strange sense of power in the chair tingling against the skin of her arm.

Ghyldus threw a reproving glance at her. At his gesture, she bit her lip, letting Teshet support her as she returned to her station. The life in the chair trembled through her skin when she touched it. The gems winked at her, then again faded. Teshet rummaged for fabric to make a sling while Resala's broken arm hung limp at her side, throbbing. She ignored the pain. Too much went forward on the battlefield.

Now that battle neared, for the first time, she witnessed how Ghyldus used his illusions against her people. She only knew his past games by the taunts he threw at her as he described Arshal's mishaps, how he cackled his enjoyment in his manipulation of the fears of people he disdained as mere toys to conquer. Now she saw his craft and ached for the cruelty that made it.

A blast on an unfamiliar trumpet rang out. More Shandeans

poured out of the gap. Her heart pounded with hope. In that same moment Ghyldus unleashed the catapults that stood idle throughout the battle. A host of creatures his Eidhalt had lured from the stones marched out of the ground.

As the fresh troops advanced to relieve weary warriors, illusions stalked the startled Shandeans. In the same instant Resala saw them they faded as her mind dismissed them. In that heartbeat she saw a serpentine creature walking on legs like the trunks of trees. Its tail sweeping the field, its red eyes sending blinding rays that stopped the hearts of those it looked upon. Multi-headed giants wielded clubs the size of young trees, and giant wolvers larger than horses, with teeth like pitch forks, grasped their prey and tossed it aside like bales to the wagon. Giant poison snakes slithered among them, pulling down horses or striking with fatal swiftness. Even now she witnessed the horrors mirrored in faces still so distant she couldn't recognize features. Watching from the small rise the canopy perched upon, she saw Shandeans lurch from nothing, as if a force threw them, shielding their faces from empty space. Something tossed the body of the orange-clad Detarian leader aside like a sack of wheat.

At that moment, a brilliant blue flash winked from a cluster of pennants. She heard her brother's voice for the first time in years. It echoed over the din as he called his people's hearts to him. That moment, the catapults launched parts of Shandean bodies hacked to pieces on the field. In a breath of fleeting illusion before reality asserted itself, she saw disembodied hands clutch the warriors they struck. Legs tripped soldiers, marching at them in disjointed and bloody columns. Heads uttered curses from vacant and bulging eyes. Torsos writhed on the ground blocking the soldier's passage. Couldn't the soldiers see the absurdity? See the falseness through the horror of familiar features? As the Detarian leader's lips bellowed treachery from its resting place in churned mud, again her brother's voice rose. Again, blue blazed out among the approaching cluster of pennants.

She could discern features among the Shandeans now. She recognized Nali in his blue and white braid scarf. Blood coated Khoti's stellan-plated armor, his or his enemy's she couldn't tell.

But the blaze of his emerald eyes pierced her from a distance. She barely recognized Arshal. She took note of others from the Val, including Asteria. Resala remembered a delicate heir of Lharan, not this hard-eyed warrior, hair in braids and face brown and grimy, clothed in hunting cloak with a bow at her back and a sword in her hand.

They seemed unaware of Resala, intent on destroying Ghyldus's illusions, on reaching their goal. Khoti no longer led the charge. Fellow Tawnkats took his place. Instead, he rode beside Arshal, defending him, a supporting hand on his king's arm. Resala could see the healer's purposes as if a true river of strength passed between the two men. She could see the secret of Kedtair written in Nali and Khoti's faces, the purposes they served. Arshal remained asleep, his expression only the comfort of Khoti's touch as he sapped his champion's life. Resala could see the Taschian had already given much to his king. And they had yet to face Ghyldus.

"See?" Ghyldus asked, pulling Resala's attention from the battle below. The knot of flags around Arshal neared the protective guard ringing the rise supporting the canopy. All around them the Minarian army retreated from the desperate Shandeans, individual battles scattered the plain. Here the tight ring of Ghyldus's Guard held their positions. Servants prepared to whisk their god from danger at first word. No one came to pull up the stakes on the canopy or remove the chair. No one made the frenzied moves of retreat. Resala returned his obsidian gaze.

"They have come to me. What waste if I had made the effort to go to them. How amusing to watch their progress across the field. What a defeat to witness, my dear princess."

She tried to speak, to retort that for the defeated they ran quite fast in the wrong direction. She remained mute. She couldn't defeat his spell in this weakened state. She imagined herself like Verdred, another silent toy. What tortures would she use to relay her messages?

"You will be able to regale your audiences with the tale of their valiant battle to reach their doom," Ghyldus went on. "They come so recklessly to their deaths!"

His laughter fell like a drop of cold water in smoking oil. Fingers flexed and, in a moment, Verdred fell to one knee before him, head bowed, awaiting orders. Ghyldus motioned to a servant who produced a walking stick with a handle carved in the shape of the medallion with small red gems set in the head.

With another motion from Ghyldus, Verdred took up the staff and leapt upon his horse, riding to the base of the small rise. He put up his hand, palm outward. Though all around the battle raged on, an odd silence fell. The Minarians parted at the base of the rise so that only the king's guard stood between Arshal and Verdred.

Ghyldus's Malice froze as he faced the king, Khoti and Nali. She saw Verdred tense, could swear she heard his hiss of breath. She didn't dare touch his thoughts, touch the poison there, the hatred there.

"Three of you to face me!" Ghyldus laughed. "Three dead men come to face me. Why do you trouble me?" Ghyldus stood, yanking Resala forward and ignoring her silent gasp of pain. "Did you come perhaps, great warriors, to rescue the fair maiden in distress, as if you lived some childhood tale? She is content as my adoring servant. She learned well to please God, as you all will, too late. Leave us now, you children who mimic gods. Pray your punishment comes swiftly."

Arshal's gaze clung to her. She stared back, ignoring the pain, the humiliation, all of it but the look in Arshal's eyes. She saw her purpose. Already Nali struggled to avert his face from Ghyldus. She could see how the mark on his brow seared and blinded him, the spell latent in the wound, kindled. Pain pounded through the seer, Ghyldus's spell aimed at stealing away Nali's allegiance. Blood stained the concealing scarf and she felt in the Sage the fear that he'd failed. Khoti, too, appeared weary, as if the ground beneath him sapped his energy, as if he gave his entire spirit to his king, life pouring from him into Arshal, leaving nothing behind.

Arshal needed her, stood frozen in Ghyldus's spell, no, Fyraer's. Struggling to keep his gaze averted from the demon, the king failed to keep the creatures from taunting him. She could see into his mind, could track all the threads of power and enchantment that bound them. Ghyldus closed the enchantment around Arshal, the seeds of which had festered in the king so long they had become a part of him.

Resala knew herself, the thief, a fourth aberration of Kedtair of which Ghyldus remained oblivious. As a burglar in the mind, stealer of concept, impression, deceiver of muses, her role lay. Now she wouldn't merely conceal a fragment of information, or stop expression, or block a command. She must dilute, divert and steal the spells Ghyldus bent toward Arshal and Nali, the god seeming unaware of Khoti whose awakening, like hers, hadn't been foretold.

Verdred took a step back, half turning to face her as Ghyldus continued to grip her arm, the pain lost in the sense of mission she felt. Resala saw Ghyldus's Malice gazing up the slope at her with that protective stance. The light of Kedtair sinking north fell on his face, removing the shadows that hid him from her. She looked back to Arshal. Whose gray eyes filled her vision when she saw Verdred? It could be no Minarian who looked out from Verdred's helm with the intensity of Ghyldus's thralls.

"Remove this mess from my doorstep!" Ghyldus hissed.

Verdred spun and took a step. Resala's thoughts reached for Arshal, ordering him to act. In the same instant she ripped the spell from Ghyldus's control and cast her own. Instead of the three men below, the spell he aimed flowed into her. She let it fill her, let it weigh her limbs with weakness, twist her.

Instantly, Arshal lurched forward as if freed from a grip. He raised his stone as Verdred approached. Striking a chord that made the ground rumble, the blazing gem emitted a heat so intense Arshal remained mesmerized by his own power as the soil baked away to ash to open a gaping, steaming fissure at Verdred's feet. Before the ground stopped shaking, Verdred tossed Ghyldus's staff. It clattered at the feet of Arshal's mount. The horse reared as the staff slithered to life, throwing Arshal. He jumped to his feet, still seeking the breath knocked from him. As the serpentine creature escaped the shell of staff and sped for him, it blackened the ground.

"Real!" Nali gasped as his hands gripped the sides of his head. "Real," Nali repeated as he lost his grip on himself.

Arshal's stone flared again, but the flash bounded from the scaly armor the creature wore beneath the tar-like venom coating its body. It coiled to strike, its head following all movement around it, its voice a steady hiss as it writhed into position. It suddenly launched for the stunned king who thrust his sword at the creature. Severed, one half of the snake body flopped to fall on Nali's mount, which squealed a moment then fell dead. The serpent's other half flew into Arshal's face. Before his roar of pain could escape his mouth, Khoti's hands were on him. The poison remained mirrored in Khoti's features long minutes after the king recovered.

Arshal gazed at his enemy. Ghyldus's laughter licked at them like flames. Resala could see, feel and sense how the spells constricted within her brother. Doubts assailed him as the demon taunted him with failure and the deaths and debasement of all he loved. Ghyldus's laughter echoed through the king, gloating. And when the king at last sensed Resala in him, the awful revelation made his mouth fall open. She disengaged each cord of the net cast over him, speaking to him within his mind with restrained impatience. Even as she worked, even as she untangled, Ghyldus's efforts renewed, re-stringing each strand of the web as she tore it down. The godhead didn't know who he battled for control of the Shandean king. Diligent, the two warring spirits made Arshal their battleground.

As Ghyldus and Resala battled over the king, illusory creatures again attacked the ranks of Shande with no king's stone to rally to. Khoti felt an instant's panic. Nali staggered. The scarf slipped to reveal the ugly brand on him, glaring out so stark and bloody it took Khoti's breath. They failed; he knew it. Nali and Arshal slipped away from him and Khoti still hadn't dispersed the poison coursing through him. Kedtair might empower him, but Ghyldus's venom raged fierce, something the spirits couldn't whisk away. Already worn from a lifetime of battle, how long could he survive to help any of them?

He felt the familiar rage rise from the ashes of his awakening for the first time. All the lives lost, all the suffering, all the efforts came to nothing if they failed. A host of images raced through him, a panorama of bloodshed. And Ghyldus's dread warrior, a visage of evil, waited across the chasm from him, confident as he savored the king's fall. Kedtair's secret gave Khoti a control, a patience with which he had fended off his recklessness. Now fatigue loosened those fetters. Ghyldus didn't know to fear Khoti, but he would. Raging in him like Kedtair, the warrior in Khoti awoke, so consuming he couldn't breathe.

Fidra raced at the chasm and leaped, landing a pace from Verdred's mount. Both champions struck, their blows toppling one another from their mounts. They tumbled to the ground with a clatter of armor as their horses trotted out of the way, reins trailing behind them.

Reckless with Ghyldus's spell in him, Verdred regarded Khoti as if he feared no death. Khoti clashed his sword against his shield. He had never felt it like this! He needed to release the warrior in him before he burst, before it consumed him.

Verdred stared at him as the Tawnkat circled his prey. A hint of doubt emanated from the demon's dread warrior. Verdred seemed to shake off his doubts like a cloak, though his stance remained wary.

"Yes. It's champion to champion now." Khoti's grin, so cold and brutal, made even Ghyldus's Malice pause. Something possessed the Sword of Shande.

Again, Verdred seemed to hesitate as if unsure he should commence this battle. Again, he shoved the hesitation aside.

When, finally, their swords met, they anticipated one another like image and reflection, each knowing the other's movements. Skills learned from the best and practiced with relish became a death dance, neither willing to accept defeat. Though blessed by spirits' gifts, Khoti had waged a long campaign. Verdred claimed the first victory when Khoti's sword flew from his sweaty grasp.

Khoti staggered, gasping. Yet the heat in him hadn't abated. He lurched forward, as if to fall to his knees. Verdred brought his sword around at him, but Khoti sprang aside, still agile. He kicked Verdred's legs from beneath him, leaping to knock the man to the ground and jump upon his chest. Elbow pressed into Verdred's throat, Khoti struggled to free his dagger. Verdred's gaze locked on the dull brass-colored cuff on Khoti's wrist.

Verdred arched his back, throwing Khoti off balance and freeing his neck from Khoti's elbow. Verdred brought his sword up, but couldn't jab the weapon between them. Verdred managed to rip the dagger from Khoti's belt and stab at Khoti's face.

Khoti wrenched his head to the side. He planted his hands on Verdred's helm, thinking only that he wanted the fire in him to destroy his enemy. The knife dropped against the back of Khoti's legs. The man's mute mouth opened. A bellow wailed from it. Verdred spun away from Khoti's grasp, yanking the helm from his head as if expecting to find his skin afire. The only mark Khoti saw was a shawnsi birthmark mutilated by scar and callous.

"Zopher!" The name croaked out of Khoti.

A moment's hesitation clouded the other face. Gray eyes regarded Khoti, vacant but for the strange expression of fervency without meaning. Lips mouthed a name from some distant memory. Like the doubts before it, he shed them.

A shriek came from the canopy, Zopher's name wrung from Resala's lips as if torn from somewhere deep within. The princess's hand gripped the back of Ghyldus's chair like a raptor's talons, her eyes dark pits in her face.

"So, this was your lover!" Ghyldus laughed. "A deceit you orchestrated? Another spy fails. I wanted shawnsi in my ranks, molded for a purpose. And look, Witness, how he demonstrates the greater strength of the shawnsi fighter, as I promised. He destroyed the best and came back in Verdred's place—"

"I am Verdred!" the champion wailed.

"Then rid me of this rabble!"

Verdred circled Khoti. Khoti's hands went out, placating, voice a murmur as he tried to coax his old friend back within himself. Ghyldus's spell didn't fade as Khoti mumbled on about the Val, Sefresal, the Tawnkats and their friendship. No flicker of recognition crossed the shawnsi's features. Even without the dark mask Verdred could twist his face into a thing of brutality. A scar on his cheek deepened to a rift like the chasm Khoti had leaped to meet him.

Over the noise of breath and pound of blood in his ears, above Khoti's entreaties, he heard Resala's pleading cries. Ghyldus had discovered Kedtair's thief. Khoti dared glance at his king. Arshal's face remained stark, blank gaze lost to Ghyldus. While Khoti's attention turned the man who had been one of the Val's finest, who should have been mountain born, who Khoti in his compassion now hesitated to kill, took his advantage. Verdred's sword came up blazing in Kedtair's white light. Before Khoti could react, he felt the fire, the shock, as the weapon drove through his mesh tunic and on into his abdomen.

Khoti sank to his knees, stunned. Verdred spun, yanking the sword out, as Ghyldus struck Resala a blow that threw her from her feet, her mouth erupting with blood. Verdred raced to the canopy. Ghyldus's Malice reached Resala's side, bringing up the sword red with Khoti's blood to smash into the chest of his master. As the blade struck against this creature harboring Fyraer's spirit, the weapon burst into molten fragments of metal that fell in silver drops around them. Verdred fell to lay still. More harmful to Ghyldus than Verdred's sword, Khoti's blood – the spirit power that closed wounds and roused a warrior – sheathed the sword and adhered to the demon's clothing. A steam rose from Ghyldus as the blood burned holes through the satin robes and on into the skin beneath, an assault by the spirits themselves.

Khoti struggled to his feet. If he could just cross the chasm and reach Arshal, his touch might bring his king back while Verdred's attack distracted the demon. Confused, Khoti stumbled, unsure of his feet. If he could just think it through, get to Arshal, to Nali. Maybe, if his blood proved so dangerous, he could destroy the demon by bleeding to death on him. He almost laughed, a giddy feeling he knew to fear.

Resala screamed at him. He didn't understand the words. He looked uphill to find Ghyldus's fingers pointing at him, a glow of red light gathered to strike Khoti full in the chest. He flew off his feet to crash to the ground, his body quivering a moment before it lay still.

Khoti's companions stared directionless.

Resala knelt beside the black-garbed figure while the gloating godhead stared down at Nali and Arshal. Smug-smiled, Ghyldus gathered himself to destroy them all as, with a low whicker, Fidra nuzzled the fallen Sword of Shande.

25: Unraveling

As if what took place beside the billowing orange fabric of Ghyldus's canopy meant nothing beyond that moment in time and place, little changed in a war raging all over Ea. Few noted how vulnerable stood the King of Shande; nor who lay prone and who stood triumphant around the canopy. The dry hills of the Kric and the barren bluffs overlooking the sea echoed with the clank of metal on metal, the twang of bowstrings, the snap of crossbow triggers, the cries of the dying, the shriek of warriors and the squeal of horses.

While opposing forces advanced and retreated like bloody tides on the plain, in other reaches of Shande no lesser fears moved in the half-night of Kedtair. A fast rider racing west a fortnight still might find no safer place to huddle than the jagged reaches of the Kric.

Late in what should have been night the star fell north in its foreshortened path. Its eerie glow white-washed rounded stones in a stream bed now home to only a trickle of water flowing from beneath Sefresal's gates. Deep shadows clung to Sefresal itself, cast by the mountain encircling the city. Kedtair glanced off a cirque above, its rays dancing on the knife-like ridges into a sky splashed periwinkle blue with the star's setting. Below lay deepest night.

Haggard faces peered out from the rough stone battlements facing an attacking force for the third time in as many years. No defiant grins, no catcalls, no rude gestures or feats of unrivaled gall and courage did they contemplate. Mouths remained silent, expressions empty. The defenders couldn't remember past successes for the vision before them of imminent defeat.

The Tawnkat destruction of the Staph-el bridge only delayed the enemy. That fierce but small fighting unit could no longer stall an army wise to their tricks.

The Tawnkat spirit had died. Tsevon no longer leant his adamant will, nor Amhese, nor did Khoti inflame them with his reckless courage. They feared Konner and Ahrwesz dead and with them Teckhan and Gelter. Few even remained of the original Tawnkats who with Tsevon meted out the vengeance of Tasch-el. By population, few people could boast more sacrifice than the Taschians and Staphians, unless someone raised a voice for Lhata.

Forced to retreat, the Tawnkats sat out another Sefresal siege. They abandoned the rampart guarding the pass, gathering too few soldiers to man it. Refugees from the Val sought the city for protection from the natural hazards Kedtair spawned, relinquishing a haven more fortified against invasion. No one dared venture back into hiding at the Val with Kedtair shaking the ground, sending slides into valleys, collapsing caverns and ripping pathways with fissures. If the Minarians broke the siege, those once safe in the Val would die. They huddled within the walls, Steadon's command spread thin around the perimeter to protect them.

Segan peered from the battlement to survey the dusty space between the walls and the Minarian troops. His hair whipped in a hot wind exhaling up at him from below. The once close-cropped locks snapped his eyes, flicking them until they teared. Glancing along the wall, he picked out the figures of his three remaining squad leaders, the last of Tasch-el's best. Dagon, Davin and Velder appeared as scruffy as he, as if they'd lost their mountain heart with their homes. Segan knew the problem lay deeper. They assumed the four who sought Eithurdon failed. They'd heard no word, no rumor. They didn't know if their news of Ghyldus ever reached the Lharan Guard. When Konner failed to return, the mountain people looked to Segan for leadership with a sense of fatality. Segan caught himself before he cursed Khoti for abandoning them. Who knew what Tsevon's cub faced if he yet lived? Rumors of the man came to them on the east wind. The inflated legend held none of the substance of the Khoti they knew. They had to assume King Arshal's visions false.

Kedtair brought them no triumph, only more grief.

Segan studied the flicker of a shadow below. An audible sigh escaped him, drawing Geleg from his position a few paces away.

Segan nodded at the shining stones of the streambed then glanced over his shoulder at the dark windows of the city's stone houses. Geleg straightened and peered out. He grumbled a low oath. A click, almost indiscernible from the wind's movement among stone and brush, brought heads rising from slumber. Other clicks pierced the silence on the wall like the snap of sparks in a hot campfire. Men and women in the courtyards below roused themselves from naps or gulped the last swallows of broth or ale or stagnant water before grabbing weapons and filing to the battlements. Mothers left children to elders and grabbed bows from beside cradles to hurry from crowded houses. Elders drew buckets of water from the dwindling well fed by melted mountain snows, while older children scampered to attend warriors on the wall. The silent arming brought no sense of excitement, only barely subdued fear.

The star closed on the horizon, the blue of the sky deepening as the last brush of Kedtair's fingers silvered only the uppermost peaks still guarding a dusting of snow. Out of dusk shadows the Minarians crept, hugging the darkness the mountains threw at the city. But against the light stone of the stream bed a shadow passed, warning Sefresal.

Like so many times before, Minarians rushed the walls with a sudden yell, tossing up scores of ladders and hooks, striving to gain the battlement. They had yet to command surprise. Tawnkats and Guardsmen honed their senses like weapons. The enemy might have aimed to starve Sefresal out, but uncertain of the condition of the larders and unable themselves to find much to live off in the baked fields beneath Kedtair they grew impatient. A mere six hundred Guardsmen and Tawnkats, plus hundreds of elders, women and children, had held near five thousand at bay far longer than the enemy could tolerate.

Whether from weariness or just that same sense of futility with which the Tawnkats turned to Segan as interim headman, this time the defenders couldn't keep up as ladders and hooks hit the walls. Maybe the defenders hadn't noticed the advance in time. Perhaps seventeen days of siege atop weeks of skirmishes dulled their senses. In minutes Minarians held the wall.

When Kedtair at last sank, the moon rose wraith-like from an eastern haze. Bursting bright from the horizon, the moonlight iced weaponry and glazed faces as the Shandeans fell back first from the north battlements, then the south. Once again, Eithurdon's Halls, cut from the mountain's heart, became haven to retreating soldiers. Feeble sorties burst from postern doors but never returned.

As the remnants of families from the mountains, Sefresal, Sihmad Shal and Eilime gathered in the darkness of Eithurdon's Halls no hour ever felt more bleak. They could count on no help. As defenders of the march, they had failed.

Two days west as the eagle soars – a week distant on horseback in treacherous mountains – a line of warriors and pack horses scrambled from a ravine in search of cover as arrows fell from above. They unslung crossbows from their backs and in one swift pull set the trigger and shot their bolts at the attackers.

The crossbows' range and accuracy gave them the minutes they needed to escape the ambush in the open ravine and reach cover in a cluster of thick pine. A dozen remained behind in the gorge, bodies rife with black-shafted arrows.

They hadn't expected resistance so far within their own borders. Though King Keyen had thought of the outnumbered Shandeans in Sefresal, he'd waited too long. Now, the Shiadins dispatched to aid Shande hesitated, uncertain whether Minaria now moved on their homeland. They could move no farther without orders. A courier raced for King Keyen, many days distant, as Sefresal's relief settled down to hold its corner of Shiad.

In the far south, rough seas hadn't stopped Minarians determined to enter the Sea of Simiriel.

King Azren climbed the high bluffs overlooking the straits to survey the devastation of the better half of Arenh's merchant fleet now sunk in the narrows. Shikorans helped salvage what they could to open the sea lane, the vessels not designed for the pounding Simiriel and Kedtair gave them. In the east the moon rose to glint from the giant swells battering his ships. Seven Minarian vessels had beaten across the broken spines of

Arenhian craft, fighting all the way against archers and boarders. If Shikora no longer remained in Shela, Shande had better look to her back door.

He let his gaze drift northwest where his border guards battled, then northeast across Shande. He sensed the battle in Shande. His heart faltered, empty and cold. He ran a trembling hand through his hair. All of Arshal's warnings evolved like prophecy. What of his most ominous? He would die trying, the young king claimed. Standing in Azren's courtyard – hair white and waving about his face, eyes so soft and passionate – he claimed he would race to his death on an eagle's wings. Azren hoped it hadn't already come to pass. The quickness of his breath this moment, the cold chill that coursed through him as the moon rose so fierce and white while Kedtair edged away into the mists of the north made him clench his fists and pray with an intensity like none before. He sensed a distant struggle, more real and dangerous than any object tangible before him. Perhaps some battle raged in Sihmad Shal. The scene he pictured showed him a steamy plain where armies arrayed against each other with a forest of spears and banners glittering in the moonlight.

Azren turned from the north and the moon, and back to matters more his. He failed his promise to stop the Minarians from entering the Sea of Simiriel. He could only gather his forces and rush his men and the Shikorans north to the border where Minaria nipped at him.

In the vast city of Lagdche, where the departure of tens of thousands for war did not lessen the crowds, Jeret watched the death of his uprising. He delivered it, his child. He begged his father to support the crazy scheme the Tawnkats espoused. Now, hundreds of dead rebels later, the title of elected headman stripped from him, his uprising gasped its last.

Once, thousands of Pladde rallied to him. After the first casualties, many fled home, faces red, mouths silent as they shrugged off their absence and looked away, picking up lives as if never gone. The ones who remained drifted away when, one after another, raids seemed to have no effect on this giant trampling them. So long an oppression would take more than a few months or years to undo. They had grown to believe the

Hogde superior.

Even when the Pladde tallied enemy losses greater than their own, it could not hold the interest of those who expected immediate change. Jeret's support dwindled to a few hundred, then a few score.

Too much they relied on Resala to send news and directions via Teshet, never forming a network of spies or finding those Hogde sympathetic to them, nor recruiting Pladde in roles that might gain them access to weaponry, supplies, or information.

Jeret decided his rebellion failed because of him, because he let first Tsevon lead, with plans already formed, then Resala. Their rebellion existed by digesting ideas others fed it. Maybe, Jeret decided, the Pladde deserved Hogde domination if they couldn't even conduct their own revolution. Jeret discarded that musing. He had to. Accepting such an idea meant more than defeat. It meant taking the blame for wasted lives.

Finally, his scores of rebels dwindled to dozens who realized they had forgotten to make the rebellion their own. They took bold steps too late with too few. Six now languished in Lagdche's dungeons, two more left dead in a raid. With four remaining they tried once more, a last desperate move to draw a following.

Rise up when Ghyldus leaves and retake your land, they'd been told. Four men could no more comprise a rebellion than hold back an army. Even with Ghyldus gone the Pladde refused their cause. To seek sympathetic Hogde would once again turn the rebellion over to someone else. Besides, they had run out of time.

So now, on this day in the waning of Kedtair, a time they had dreamed of with the fervency of Shandeans, Jeret and his last three men watched the death of their rebellion. Who now would honor the promises made to Tsevon so long ago? Who would step forward to waylay the shipments supplying troops marching on Arenh and Shiad? Jeret didn't want to think this either, to wonder this in the last breath of his rebellion.

His eyes pressed shut, the moisture of frustration leaking at the corners as his fists clenched within their bonds. When the traps opened and the four bodies dropped with a snap to twist at the rope end, the Pladde rebellion ended without even a gasp.

Though clean and rested for the first time in months, Daris found no comfort in mended clothing and weapons honed, but no Minarian mail on which to dull them. She adjusted the lace shawl wrapping her head, holding her dark hair from the gripping west wind. Kedtair's breath blew hot in her face, but she pulled the white lace close around her to conceal the scar slashing from cheek to ear and the smaller nicks of her trade that marred her beauty. If she'd thought about the action, she would have chided herself. A Shandean warrior, a Tawnkat, what need did she have for such allure? And, certainly, the mangled arm hanging from her side was no beauty mark.

She searched the western horizon: only a line of trees and a cloud bank, black against the darkening sky as Kedtair sank. She scanned the wall's length, knowing she would find rabbit-like Laria there with her dark-eyed child on her hip. That woman didn't say what she awaited.

Daris startled when someone sat beside her on the stone bench overlooking the wall. Familiar features in a weather-worn face squinted west. Daris smiled despite her sour mood. Blue eyes twinkled at her from beneath a mop of flaming hair escaping a crocheted white snood meant to hold it in. In the last rays of Kedtair, Cookie's freckles stood out dark in a pale face.

Cookie scolded her for not resting. Daris didn't reply. Cookie's mannerisms, even her speech, made her think of Jali. If only he cooked like his mother their camp fare might have been palatable. Daris almost laughed aloud at the unkind statement on a man who saved her life and cared for her with such patience. Yet, she would make such a comment; Jali would feign hurt, then like a starving man gorging himself, come back for more.

Thinking about Jali, and knowing Cookie took care of her because of him made Daris want to laugh harder, sour pleasure escaping in a chuckle, the kind of laugh she'd used for many years to hide her true feelings. Jali always knew and fed her need to release the hurt, willingly.

"They'll be coming back a'right," Cookie soothed in her ear, adjusting a thread of hair so that the shawl covered it. Like Jali, she too seemed in tune to Daris's moods.

Daris thanked Cookie with a fleet smile then studied her

hands in her lap. Each day the hand of her wounded arm appeared smaller, the muscles dying in prelude to shrinking and shriveling until one day it would hang like a twig from her shoulder, nothing but the shape of shrunken bone. Men once fought for her, paid a month's wage for her.

With a snort to herself she considered the oddity of the soft lace around her head and shoulders. She'd tucked a trio of throwing knives in her weather-worn huntsman's belt. Her light sword hung at her side again, hours of practice allowing her to wield it one-armed with a strength that grew daily. She disdained the skirts and blouses laid out for her by servants, assigned to her, the one-time servicer. They respected her as an officer of the Sword of Shande's elite circle, as the ranking Shandean officer in this city among the hundreds of Home Guard. Yet they brought her skirts. She disdained them for the blood-stained tunic Habdelion gave her, one of her few possessions, a talisman that protected her. Much mended and patched, sleeves worn to a tatter where they reached to her elbows, passing ladies of Sihmad Shal startled at the low, loosely laced v-neck. Daris didn't care. Tawnkats had no need for fashion. Her belt hugged a lithe waist that still drew the stares of the soldiers quartered here. In idleness she practiced the art of a weapon with which she'd been born. Yet, each time she did, she imagined Jali rising to her defense and she lost interest in her game.

She forced the Home Guard officers to ignore her youth and gender. The tales of her prowess passed along by her wounded comrades helped, but the small tattoo at the base of her neck, a marker that meant more to her than any other element of her identity, gave her the greatest stature in this city. Young Daris, camp courtesan to Minarians, ranked. She slept in the king's palace and directed his city's defense. Jali would grin like a fool. Khoti would give her that special smile of pride.

She stared west for some sign of the army's return. Closing her eyes she turned her face skyward to picture her friends as she imagined they would appear riding into the final battle. Jali and Asteria flanked Khoti, Chati and Tre beside him with their swords in tandem, and then Dynresa, Cydwyn and Sedaik, all in the colors and allegiances of Shande. Suddenly her friends toppled in a splatter of blood. The last thread of her vision showed her Khoti on his knees, falling forward, eyes dull with pain as he clutched at a sword protruding from –

Her eyes flew open and she gasped. Cookie's hand gripped her shoulder. Cookie gazed out to sea. A horn rang through the courtyards of the city, a warning blast, followed by the slap of feet on stone.

"Daris!" A shout came from a man halfway to the top of the battlement. His face dripped sweat from running, almost as flushed as the maroon and gold cloak he wore. Her name always sounded odd in Oricon's thick Otayran dialect. The Captain of Farlal's forces took the last steps two at a time. He paused a moment, peering through cupped hands at the glitter of the harbor in Kedtair's failing rays. Long shadows falling on the water from western bluffs reached almost to the white pinnacle of the lighthouse.

"Ships, Minarian!" Oricon gasped when he reached her.

Daris jumped up. She almost fell as the blood rushed from her head. She shook off Cookie's supporting grasp but let Oricon guide her to view the harbor. Daris made to cup her hands around her eyes, forgetting that her right arm would not respond. He leaned closer, holding her shoulder and pointing in front of her so she could follow his gesture and hear his quiet dialect in her ear. At last, she saw the ships hugging the shoreline as they rounded the point. Distant yet, they appeared ragged and beaten by the tumultuous seas, but the wind fell in behind them. She tried to recall everything Jali told her about the Harbor, and the first battle to hold the bay.

"You can't, Daris," Cookie pleaded. "You're still not well, girl."

Daris gave the woman a dismissive gesture, thinking last moment to throw a thin smile that meant to offer both appreciation and apology. She strode away with Oricon, her stomach fluttering with anticipation. She could now test all the skills she'd learned from her mentor. Not that she wanted to face a fleet with only the aged Home Guard and a few thousand Otayrans commanded by this handsome captain so enamored of her. But she needed a remedy for an idleness more painful than wounds. It would clear her head of the constant images of her friends falling and dying.

Whatever Oricon thought of her, he didn't question her authority, though others had and would. Ignoring the proffered hand of an aide, she leaped upon her mount's back as if no injury hampered her.

She glanced up to see Laria and Cookie staring out at the Harbor from opposite ends of the wall section. As Daris, Oricon and Kelar, the Captain of the Home Guard, trotted from the gates toward the Harbor, Kedtair sank in the north. Daris turned in her saddle, waiting a moment, then nodded curtly to herself as the moon pulled away from the haze of the horizon. As memory of Kedtair's rays faded, the lunar glow fired dingy sails in Sihma Harbor, Otayran and Shandean ships swarming with activity as sailors fetched arms. Much farther into the broad bay than they had imagined, they spied the glow of sails as ten ships pressed for Sihma Harbor.

Three thousand Otayran warriors now tumbled from Harbor inns. The Home Guard numbered thousands in the region, but only a few thousand could heed a call in the city and Harbor. Many stowed craftsman's tools from the repair of the city as they readied for battle.

Pounding hooves came from behind. Daris recognized a Detarian comrade racing for them, a bandage swathing the man's leg. Daris grinned. Before he could reach her, Daris clicked her tongue against the roof of her mouth in a pattern that sent him spinning back to assemble her soldiers. Almost two hundred seriously wounded survived the two-day journey from the Etaleah Canal to the barge docks at Sihma Harbor. In the weeks since they'd arrived, many regained their health. She knew she had at least a few warriors who knew how to win.

She sensed Oricon and Kelar watching her, but ignored them. Khoti would be astride prancing Fidra where he best contemplated uneven odds. Daris merely wore a small bemused smile not quite veiled by the shawl. She knew Cookie watched from the battlement as she took the lead. Daris would be one more person for Cookie to hope on. She would wait a long time.

In all of Ea, as the last light of Kedtair mingled with the first light of a full moon, Ghyldus triumphed. In all quarters he foiled the long-laid plans of a naive people. The King's Council in the Val had dismissed suggestions the enemy might come to them on many fronts with weapons, troops and powers far superior. It never occurred to Arshal in the smoky caverns of the Val that the godhead's enchantments might ensnare him, like claws reaching from a conjuration, even at a distance. They discussed guarding all of Shande's cities, attempted it, but couldn't execute. Throughout, the errors in their plan plagued them. On this night that never came, like no other, Ghyldus had won the initiative.

While throughout Ea Ghyldus's traps closed with iron jaws, those beside the orange canopy knew if they failed now, they would have no second rebellion rising from the bones of the first. The line between success and failure appeared like a visible demarcation on the field, and they teetered close to it.

Khoti lay prone at the foot of the small rise, Fidra straddling him, still nuzzling him for some reaction. On the other side of the deep fissure the king had delved, Arshal and Nali remained locked in Ghyldus's enchantment. Behind the godhead's dark throne Resala, pale and unsteady, knelt beside the black-clad warrior, Teshet supporting her. The guilt festered in Teshet like a wound. Hope for Shande dimmed.

As Ghyldus at last turned on Arshal, arrows arced over the gaping fissure from the cluster of Shandeans battling Ghyldus's guards. Too late, Ghyldus ducked to one side. Most of the missiles bounced away from the swipe of his hand. One struck him in the eye. Distance kept it from penetrating deep as it glanced against bone and halted. The buff and pewter flights on the end quivered a moment, the small lazy 'w' marked on its shaft staring at Ghyldus's uninjured eye.

The godhead staggered from his seat. Blood welled in his eye then blazed red like the stone in his brow. The crimson light fell on Asteria who nocked another arrow. The bow fell from her grasp, clattering to the ground at her mount's feet as the arrow followed suit. Ghyldus's anger reached for her.

That moment, the god's attention still on Asteria, Tre's mount leapt the chasm. Tre scooped his fallen commander from the ground to lift him to Fidra's back. Chati circled around behind the canopy where he gestured for Teshet to lead Resala to him.

Cydwyn and Jali held Ghyldus's guards at bay as Teshet urged her mistress to rise. Resala would not leave Verdred's side. At last, Chati dashed beneath the canopy, maneuvering but a breath behind the godhead himself, and lifted Verdred to his shoulder.

Ghyldus's anger raced from him toward Asteria, slaying his own soldiers between him and his target before his weakened intent dropped Eithurdon's daughter at Dynresa's feet. He raised his hand again. Resala, regaining her wits, stole his energies into herself then fired them back at him with the fierceness of the desperate.

As Ghyldus's own weapon struck him with his own great power, Khoti's blood burning into his skin, Asteria's arrow distorting the godhead's vision, Arshal at last sagged forward as if freed from bonds holding him up. He took a deep breath, struggling to break free.

A red glow surrounded the chair Ghyldus sat upon. Arshal couldn't pull his gaze away. The gems edging the cushions blazed a fierce red, at last spitting embers at Resala as she backed from beneath the canopy. She staggered to the ground, clutching burns and her limp arm. Jali's mount carried him beneath the billowing canopy to pull her up behind him. Cydwyn grabbed Teshet by one arm. In moments, they'd crossed the fissure and disappeared among the chaos of war, leaving Ghyldus alone beneath his canopy with just the bodies of his elite and his wooden throne.

Resala forced Jali to halt and take her to a point behind Ramel. The gems on the chair flared bright like the stones of the medallion, gathering force into a stream of sparks like molten rock that jabbed from beneath the orange canopy. Resala turned the power he would aim at her back at him. The fire from the chair struck its creator full in the back, toppling him to his knees. All around battle raged. Ghyldus's guard scattered, none to see a god on his knees before a mortal king that barest moment before regathering himself.

On hands and knees, Arshal sobbed for air. So much passed in moments so instantaneous yet so clear. He heard the taunts in his head, still, though the demon attended to others. He saw Resala's danger, Khoti fallen, his long-time friend revealed as a tool of the enemy, his counselor caged by a spell cast with a brand, gasping as he, too, pulled free of the spell. Ramel hissed loud over the din, begging Nali to tell the king what he must do. Nali shook his head and continued to gasp, riveted by the same scene absorbing Arshal.

The echoes of Ghyldus's enchanting words threatened to draw tighter Arshal's bonds. Arshal's musings touched unyielding strands of the Enchanter's web.

"You thought you could face me. Fool. I master illusion and you have a pretty light in your hand," the taunt circled, spiraling around him as if to choke him with but the pull of a drawstring.

He sensed Dynresa behind him. As if from a dream he saw the arrows loosed by Dynresa and Asteria arc at Ghyldus, witnessed the godhead's wrath as Tawnkats raced to Resala's rescue.

I must do this, Arshal insisted as he fought to regain himself. I must succeed! Nali's words, uttered long ago in the wake of an osfothye dream echoed in his head: "Let the idea alone of achieving success rule your actions and you'll never succeed," Nali had told him. "Be what you are and you've succeeded. Don't let yourself stand in the way of your goals." Then the words made sense in the context of all they discussed, planned, explored of what Nali had learned from the Lierye. "It's a molding process," Nali had explained. "Your life is potter's clay, moldable into a useful thing like a bowl, or turned into a thing of art like a statue. Or it could remain uncontemplated, undiscovered, like the lump of dirt it began."

Uncontemplated, unmolded, undiscovered. The images, the concepts flitted into Arshal's mind. He remained on his hands and knees, staring into the bloody soils of Shande, unable to move and fearing the taunt of madness. Images, a world of ideas fought for mastery in his mind. Each sought a moment to reach up into his consciousness as if long submerged.

He heard Dynresa cry out and fall behind him. Remember me, think of me, and I'll be immortal, he'd told her. His life would have meaning if he achieved the secret of Kedtair. Once he'd known all he needed to, spoke of it with Dynresa ...

He wandered, fighting for the reality fleeing from him. He

stared across a vast void upon an ethereal scene, everything gone silent with Aziaris's army of winds and storms gone, Maura's symphony of waves and gulls silent. Only his mind existed, and all the fragments he must gather to understand.

Dim realization blossomed. Ghyldus did something to him that kept him from understanding. Like petals unfolding to reveal a sweet secret, he saw it all. The deceit came unveiled as far back as a restless night in Sihmad Shal when some intruder called a conjuration into his room. His enemy grew within him, fed upon him, each medallion he encountered fertilizing the seeded spell, taunting him, weakening him, drawing him into a web of threads Ghyldus sewed. When Kedtair rose, when the king had risen so weary and tortured in spirit, Ghyldus ensnared him in a trap laid in the glint of the medallion.

Ghyldus's chuckle resounded in his mind. Ghyldus turned to a king kneeling in the blood of Shande. Arshal staggered to his feet. Asteria's arrow still protruded from the godhead's eye. The demon turned to Resala again, and Arshal saw it for an instant: A storm of emotion raged in Ghyldus's face, a love and hate, obstinate warring elements within the creature strove for mastery. Hate won.

Fire gathered again in the chair. He remembered hearing Dynresa. He found her clutching a dart embedded in her shoulder. She supported Asteria who aimed another arrow at the creature, an arrow containing a small pouch of dust he knew came from Detarian. That moment, as Ghyldus's own fire swept from the chair into the god, as Asteria's dart tore from her bow, and a strangled word of command ripped from Nali, Arshal at last cast himself free.

He moaned. It all assaulted him at once: everything ever told him, all he'd known all along, all he'd learned while the enchantment festered in him, growing to a burden that almost consumed him. Ghyldus had almost mastered him the way he'd molded Zopher into a mindless repulsive servant. Arshal held back a sob. His mind hadn't been his own; he never knew to resist the assault.

Kedtair was setting.

"I master illusion," Ghyldus had taunted.

"He thrives on ambition, on fear, hatred, on your desires. You must be calm," Nali had said. Nali stood silent now, as beaten as the king. Nali didn't have the power Arshal had. Dynresa had fallen, his determination, his element of immortality. Yet Khoti chided him to discard such thoughts. Khoti fell, like the others. Zopher demanded he promise not to let Resala waste her sacrifice. Zopher fell.

"Believe it and it is, don't and it isn't." Nali said that.

Arshal tried to sort it out, his mind free to do what it should have done so long ago. Kedtair waned. If he discovered it, he might still be too late. The battle didn't end the moment he discovered himself. The moment he became one with himself, Nali had said.

Arshal straightened, studying Nali's sweaty face, then the space where Dynresa and Asteria had stood. Though somewhere on the plain armies battled, only the king, Ghyldus, Resala and Nali remained on the field. He saw no others, heard nothing but the distant purring of Maura as she urged him on, called encouragement, opened her heart, begged him look her way.

He lifted his gaze from the frozen instant of time where Detarian's powders, Nali's command and Ghyldus's own spells stunned the godhead. He wanted time to shed the enchantment, to loosen all the cords. Almost, it seemed, he could see the pattern of Resala's thoughts shaping Ghyldus's intent, stealing his power, gathering his spells like a magnet.

Dazed, he stared toward the sea and Maura's insistence. The slanting white rays of Kedtair sank into the horizon. He felt the tug of his body, the call of his mind to follow. Like the gasp of bereavement, like the lifebeat of a heart faltering in fear, Kedtair's rays polishing the clouds as it sank jolted him. In a moment, the star set, its rays only an opaque memory lingering in puffs of cloud, a slight silvering above the sea as the moon rose like a wraith from mists curling about the Kric to the east.

Arshal had fallen into that moment, an eternal instant in which all the clouds and fog parted within him to reveal the brightness of Kedtair, energy, a mix of all things, an absence of hue. He looked upon an image of all elements united, a mirror of One, the ghost of an unattainable unity.

He needed all the elements. Once he'd felt a warmth calling him in Khoti's voice; Khoti's touch brought mountain stone, pine, the damp of soil: a compassion Arshal guarded in himself. More intense in Khoti raged the warrior, the vengeful creature Arshal discovered in Hainad, the hatred alien to Terremar. Arshal controlled it.

His thoughts took him to Nali looking out over the sea, nimble fingers guiding a sail up a mast, his sage advice soothing fear with the logic of the philosopher, cooler thoughts tending an anger slower to rise, a mystery of unexpressed impression. Arshal himself grew that way. Dynresa stood opposite Nali, a taunting caprice anchored by the land as her mind raced from one rash thought to the next, as he'd once been. He pulled the threads of carelessness to him and confronted a surge of wholeness.

That instant, he knew himself and accepted those flaws from which he'd hidden.

The self-pity and self-doubt remained. And he recognized an arrogance he'd disdained, a recklessness he'd thought gone, a childishness that nearly cost him his life. That same moment he knew every hurt that never had to be, each unnecessary death. Yet the path he'd barely survived, a route the gods didn't intend, proved best. This moment he knew himself stronger and more capable than even the gods had imagined, because of the choices he'd made.

If that made the gods squirm, good.

Only mortality and the expenditure of his energy, his spirit, limited him.

Emotion wrung through him, divergent elements complimentary and contrary. Numbness penetrated him, his limbs tingling. He recognized at last the roles of his companions, and how he would need them to accomplish his purpose, and use them because despite his gifts, his body, his stamina, remained that of a mortal man.

He remembered the fog he'd once built in his mind, a task greater than his strength could control. As he thought it, fog rolled in from the sea, thick, moist, gathering its own darkness. Not even moonlight strayed on its upper layers. Ghyldus didn't create this illusion, the King of Shande did. The stone didn't restrict after all; it gave him the freedom to manage his gifts, and wield them. This, too, the gods hadn't counted upon.

He believed it; it appeared, fog, cool after Kedtair's heat. He was everything. Such an alien thought, so selfish, but he knew it. Kedtair made him one with his being, a creation and warrior of the gods, but more than Terremar. More! Terremar couldn't hate, or know recklessness. He couldn't comprehend the elements of Fyraer.

In the breath of instant when he awoke, he remained mortal; he could not alter the great magic of nature devised by One. But the power he controlled, the sheer energy that formed the essence of One, he possessed this in his measure. Stunned, he realized Nali, Khoti and Resala knew this, they no mere scholar, no mere healer/champion, and his sister no mere spy.

Arshal straightened. Other minds sought his, rebellious Maura's purring, defiant Aziaris's breath, Terremar, even, touching his heart with relief. Resala found him, and Nali, and he thought he even felt the faint groping of Khoti, struggling against death. They knew him. He brought hope. He would succeed because success came from knowing himself and he had become one.

Ghyldus stood. He cocked an eyebrow at Arshal as the fog gathered around the king, then fled from him in an intense wind that ripped the canopy from its poles, sending it tumbling and rolling off toward the sea. The poles wavered then shivered in the wind. The chair toppled and rolled, pitching into the sea. Absolute silence again surrounded them.

"Not merely the stone then," Ghyldus said as he plucked Asteria's arrow from his eye as if he pulled a stick-tight from his clothing. No mark remained to denote the wound. He tossed the arrow at Arshal, the weapon transforming into the aspect of some grotesquely misshapen bird, scales in place of feathers, red eyes peering from above a twisted beak, talons like scimitars.

Arshal ducked involuntarily. On the edge of his perception he saw Ramel's eager face, shield raised slightly against the unexpected. Nali, regaining his composure, moved closer.

"Not real," Nali reminded him in a voice grown hoarse. The Sage resettled the scarf over the bloody brand on his forehead as if rising from a tussle with his son, not a battle for his sanity.

Arshal nodded. He took a step forward, swatting his hand at the hovering bird-creature as if brushing aside a feather. A feather floated to the earth.

"You think to impress me with illusion," Ghyldus laughed with the high tone of assurance. The godhead's gaze darted to Resala who peered from behind Jali. Ghyldus raised his hand. Resala shoved Jali aside so that he fell from the horse. Before Ghyldus could strike, a blast of white shot into the godhead's face in search of the bright stone on Ghyldus's forehead.

Intent fouled, Ghyldus raised his hand defensively, reflecting Arshal's fire right back at him. Arshal shrugged it off. It wasn't real.

They joined a battle of illusion, blue gem to red. Each waiting for the other to make a fatal error, to misjudge, misstep, under-react or over-react. One with himself, Arshal was the reality that controlled illusion, the thing that made life and that which wasn't life. While that wholeness gave him great strengths, they came at a cost. Illusion required the king's own spirit to create, and he but a shadow of the true energy that fired the gods, fueled the heavens, life, the elements of nature.

The moon rose high, then the sun behind it, and Kedtair again rose. Arshal sensed only Nali beside him, tiring as he gave all the energies he could find. He couldn't draw Ghyldus off his guard; he couldn't bring the creature to misjudge him.

Day passed into a dark night. The King of Shande lost all sense of place but here, struggling on his willpower alone. In a moment when his thoughts raced in tangent, he realized he faced Fyraer, not Ghyldus. Ghyldus couldn't have aimed so fatal a blow at Resala, and Fyraer made no easy target.

He sagged as a leering, spike-toothed creature struck him full in the chest, trying to rend his heart from his flesh. He had lost his concentration, made a mistake. His enemy hesitated as if too surprised that he'd broken through to take advantage. At least two days and nights had passed since Arshal had eaten, or slept. He expended finite energy and the blood poured from the conjuration's bites.

A breath of ice blew at him from the snowpack, the cool water in the Val's lake crossed his thought, the scent of pine and wood smoke wafting to him on a fresh breeze in his lungs. The pain of the creature's attack faded. The blood ceased, the poison no longer searing. Khoti, haggard and pale, supported between

Chati and Tre grasped the king's arm with hands burning with fever. In the briefest instant, Arshal noted the blood dark and crusted on his champion's body, the distance in the fiery eyes somehow seeming even more dangerous. By whatever measure, by whatever superhuman effort, Khoti returned from the dead for him, somehow gathered the strength to fulfill his purpose, his oath. Khoti stank of death.

Arshal couldn't spare a word, a nod, not even a smile. If Khoti had the strength to seek it, he'd know his king's gratitude. Though strengthened, it wasn't much. Khoti couldn't take more poison than necessary to keep the king on his feet.

"He's tiring," Nali muttered in Arshal's ear, as weary a voice as Arshal felt. Resala stole from the demon. Khoti's blood continued to burn him. Pain twisted the demon's face.

Kedtair stood high in the north. The sun had left; the moon departed. The third day of their battle waged on. Kedtair would rise again today then be gone. Khoti gave his every ounce of strength to Arshal, gripping the king as if holding him up. Khoti's down-turned head pressed into Arshal's side as he clung to the king with both hands, eyes closed, no longer a warrior of death, but one struggling with life. Arshal felt the trickle of Khoti's strength flowing into him, finite. He sensed Resala wearying as she struggled to divert Ghyldus's intent. Nali remained beside him, the rock he leaned upon.

Arshal yanked the ground from beneath the godhead. He caught him. Ghyldus, damp with sweat, fell onto the place Khoti had bled. Ghyldus picked himself up. Khoti's blood clung to the godhead, searing and sparking, as he lifted his hands from the blood-crusted soil. Arshal thought of Resala flung aside by the demon like a child's toy, of Nali's agony, of every Shandean, any creature in Ea suffering the demon's rule, of Dynresa's shriek of pain, of his champion pouring the last of his life into his king.

A deep voice rose beside him, resonant, and of a tenor like Habdelion's great horn. Nali's throat uttered its curse, one of such proportion, of such awesome anathema to Ghyldus, to Fyraer, to whatever demon haunted the wracked body before them, attacking the creature while it weakened before their eyes. If Khoti's blood seared unearthly skin, if Arshal's illusions tired the creature, his power so intense he could shatter the bind

Fyraer had on Ea, then Nali's curse held equal power. Culled from the pages of the Lierye, recalled by long-dead Cree who remembered with chilling accuracy the banishing day when so many of the gods followed Fyraer from One, Nali repeated the curse of exile One had issued through Terremar, the words of a tongue Nali didn't know. Nali had memorized the curse at Cree's instruction, told to use it at a moment when his senses shrieked its need. Now the seer uttered the words, the very voice of the spirits within him contorting the demon's face.

A pure light fled from Arshal's palm before Ghyldus could react. The light from the stone crackled, pitching the ground, which threatened to swallow Ghyldus. No illusion, the ground fissured, rending the soil and rumbling beneath Ghyldus's feet, toppling the godhead as he struggled to strike out at Arshal. He grasped for the lip of the chasm. Arshal's palm flared again, striking the red gem in the creature's brow, shattering the stone into a million droplets of blood fleeing a wound. Arshal ignored the pain assailing him, the curse for striking such a creature. He still stood.

Ghyldus's voice ripped from him like the wail of a cyclone, the shriek of a rabbit caught in the eagle's talons. Before Arshal could send the demon into the pit he'd created, turn the creature to ash, before he could react at all, Arshal sensed the essence of pure ambition, desire, a driving force sucking at the breath, gasp out of Ghyldus. A shadow hovered a moment above them before the ground swallowed the Enchanter and sealed him within its closure.

Fyraer rose, a shadow, then became the red-orange flare of embers in a tempest, burning and singeing all that stood nearby, blackening the prairie and stone, sending horses screaming away. Glowing with an inner fire, the shadow gathered itself up as if about to strike. Arshal brought his arms together over his head. Defiant, the pure light of Arshal's palm wrapped him in an ethereal glow that hinted of a power in him unmatchable, undefeatable.

Terremar had molded a warrior that could defeat Fyraer, and by doing so, defeat them all – all of Ea, called home to One, all creation reversed.

As if with a shrug, the cloud dissipated then fled north with a laugh that echoed like the rumble of thunder against the cliffs.

Warriors across the plain faltered in their battle as the cloud fled. Some dropped arms to stare. Many Minarians surrendered in that moment as their enchantment shattered.

But as Hothur foresaw, many resettled their stances. A nation of warriors bred men who would battle to the death before accepting defeat. Some believed they deserved this conquest. Some fed on the strife that made war, life measured only by the breaths they took on a battlefield.

As the shadow departed, Arshal fell to his knees at the edge of the fissure he had first ripped in the ground, then pitched forward, slipping from Khoti's grasp. The king's mind had gone as dark as the scorched hand that dared smite Fyraer. Khoti staggered to his side. The stone lay bright in Arshal's palm, now blue, now green, now red and yellow with all the elements burning there, shifting and pulsing in the opal that had become a part of his flesh. Khoti touched the hand. A small cry escaped the Taschian. Sweat burst from his face as pain seared through him, lingered a while, then passed like the shadow of Fyraer.

"I failed," Arshal gasped, reaching for the scent of pine enveloping him. "I should have destroyed him."

"You couldn't, not without destroying everything," Nali said. "We must always hope for reconciliation. We must keep him away, drive him always toward Terremar, and hope someday he will come ready for compromise."

Arshal wasn't listening. Even Khoti's touch couldn't replace all he'd given of himself. He finally gave in to the blackness within him that even the scent of pine couldn't seem to penetrate. In moments they bore Arshal from the field, just one among many, as the battle for the soils of Shande raged on.

26: Partings and Joinings

Kedtair set for the last time.

Night fell over the battlefield as the king rested beneath pale canvas. For the first time in days, true darkness reigned and battle halted for more than an hour or so. No moon stood overhead and the sun remained long hours away.

Dazed eyes stared into the night as if the reprieve would end with the rising of one sun or another, or at least a watery moon. Only stars winked, dull and distant after so many weeks of illumination.

The battle didn't end with Ghyldus.

Throughout the dark night Maura slammed Minarian ships against the rocks. The splinter of wood became a constant accompaniment to the chorus of voices rising from the sea's surface. Those Minarians abandoning the field found safety on the decks and a wind to speed them home. Those remaining sank, jealous gods rewarding their supporters.

In the camps, an eerie silence fell as soldiers took stock of injury. An occasional voice rose in greeting to discover safe some comrade thought lost. Most spoke in whispers, barely heard above the spirits' wars upon the sea. To speak aloud would confirm the truth of all the tragedies they had seen, somehow negate the victory they claimed.

At the base of the Kric, Nali stood again on the small rise where he'd watched Khoti ride out of the dawn. Absolute weariness assailed him with more determination than any other weapon in the enemy's arsenal. An uneasy silence lulled him. Footfalls marked the camp's perimeter. Strained voices and occasional outbreaks of rebellion sounded from the enemy camp as the chain of command shuffled. Yet, despite the large force still to be faced, like others, Nali experienced a feeling of completion. Only the details of cleaning up debris after the storm remained. Yet, his idleness seemed wrong. He could think of nothing for which to prepare, no strategy to hammer out, no crisis to overcome. And he couldn't celebrate when his heart burned with his mourning for so many of the best who hadn't survived to see Arshal chase Fyraer from Ea. Hothur, body wrapped in a buff and pewter cloak, lay beside Eithurdon, whose stubbornness gave him the honor he sought, but not the breath to enjoy it. The two one-time enemies, lying side-by-side in the Lharan colors, elicited in Nali his most profound sorrow.

Marol would not return to his lifemate and sons in his lodge among the pines, but he held Arshal's standard to the last, leaning into it to hold it above the soils long after the life faded from his features. Cautious Tel would not stroll his fields picking rocks come spring while whistling a tune heard in The Old Scow Inn the night before. Sedaik, groomed to succeed his great uncle as a chief of his tribe, wouldn't pass on his father's blood. Aibak would never again hunt the border of Shiad, his purple scarf a darkening red in the fields of Shande. Ernik, who, like Azren, gave more than expected, fell in the flames of Arshal's final battle. They'd lost dozens more who had crossed Nali's path. Many still nursed injuries that might yet take them.

With a sigh, Nali admitted nothing would ever be the same. They couldn't erase the changes the war had made in all of them. His gaze flicked toward the tent where Arshal lay in death-like repose. He hadn't wakened since the battle though Khoti had called him from the brink of some darkness the healer refused to discuss or describe. The King's Champion left Arshal's side with face ashen and eyes dull, mouth twisted by whatever sour poison he'd tasted as his loyal officers supported him. Too late, he came to Eithurdon who at last breath called for Khoti. By then, Khoti stood beside the king, ending a war. Now, the Lharan Guard readied to ride for Sefresal with their fallen, and likely face battle again. Nali wondered what good these bloody troops, half their original number, might be after a breakneck ride through the barren plains.

Nali raised his head with a snap when a shadow moved in

front of him. He squinted up at a silhouette of a horse and bulky rider against the stars.

"See, he kept his promise," Cydwyn's voice came from the silhouette in a hoarse crackle.

Nali realized Cydwyn had an arm wrapped around the child's waist of a figure sitting before him while an even smaller figure perched on the pillion behind him to cling to his sword belt.

Before Nali could speak, his girls stood before him. Nali sucked in his breath. Kia's straight back, her eyes catching the glitter of campfires, knife at hip, and long hair wound in Joffan warrior braids revealed no hint of her age. Nali pulled the two girls to him, discovering something ominous in their faces.

Nali looked up at Cydwyn who inclined his head, a curt gesture. With a swift glance at Kia, he rode away.

Kia turned from her fa and pulled from his grasp. She stared into the dark after Cydwyn. She took a step, but then glanced at Rena who still hugged her father's legs as buried memories emerged. Kia plopped at her father's feet and pulled Rena into her lap, waiting patiently for Nali's questions as she stared into the night.

Khoti knelt in yet another tent. Some dark concoction of fatigue and pain threatened to engulf him. He trod a dangerous path he'd traveled before. He touched the small white scar on his forehead while Konner rubbed the palm of his hand and plucked at the scab forming there. Khoti had faltered, stumbling from the loss of blood and the poisons of his wounds. Konner had shadowed him, complaining of a stench like death. So much time had passed since Verdred's sword pierced him, the poisons had festered. Khoti's body stunk like the entrails of a dead mountbuck, days old, rummaged by scavengers. All of the plain smelled that way, rife with scavenger birds rising in angry clouds and falling single-minded behind each charge. Like the rigid bodies, Khoti had that smell. Konner had wondered aloud to him why birds hadn't already settled on the Sword of Shande. Khoti couldn't slow. He'd been a warrior. Now he must heal.

Konner toppled him with ease as Khoti left Arshal's tent. Before Khoti could wake, Konner's worn sticks echoed through the camp and he'd pressed a bloody hand and burning knife to the King's Champion. When Khoti awoke with a bellow, his flesh searing beneath a hot knife, Chati and Tre anchoring his limbs, Konner had blanched, as if facing death. Khoti merely glowered, his gaze seeming to frighten them more than ever before.

"Don't be forgetting your limits," Konner said now from beside him. "I can see you straining yourself, 'bout as sturdy as the Staph-el bridge."

Khoti gave him a mechanical nod, a distracted and dismissing gesture. He glanced up to find the constable's own eyes had shut against exhaustion.

"I'm thinking it's you who needs the rest," Khoti said. "The Guard's mustering –"

"I've got to look after you," Konner protested.

At a sign from Khoti, Chati and Tre pulled Konner to his feet. The older man cursed. Khoti only hissed at him, then turned his back. He had so little time. None could be wasted with niceties.

Tending Arshal left Khoti so dark inside even Konner's medicine couldn't help him. Fyraer's parting poison, a consuming thing that would have destroyed the king, now withered in Khoti, evil, snarling through his gut, a darkness on his soul. Khoti's wound stung as clothing brushed against the burned skin. The wound Verdred gave him would have killed him in but a few more hours without Konner's medicine. The darkness remained.

He'd gone from Arshal to Resala, setting the arm and salving injuries, not expending what little strength he had left. His mere touch comforted her. Then, he'd gone to Dynresa. The dart pierced her lung. When he left, she breathed deeply of pine-scented air. He'd moved on with a purpose, ignoring anything resembling guilt, helping all whose paths he crossed. With each touch, Khoti felt weaker, fainter, more twisted and wracked. He went to Eithurdon to find him wrapped in a shroud. Khoti would never know what words the duke meant for him. Perhaps curses? An apology? The duke left no words for Asteria.

He'd noticed her then, sitting silently in the shadows near her father's body. He could see the burns and bruises of Ghyldus's attack on her. He choked at the thought of the pain Asteria earned for following him. Her breath came harsh when he touched her. Her anger lashed at him. He'd tilted her chin, finding the sparkling eyes he'd remembered replaced by the wary gaze of a hunted creature. He'd wanted to pull her to him. He hated that expression, battle-hardened and disillusioned. He had others yet to tend.

He went then to the rows of tents where the most grievously injured lay. He found many friends who could not be saved. Others benefitted from the bit of his life he discarded with each brush of his hands.

At last, he reached a small, guarded tent. Though the last stop on his meandering journey through the camp it came first in his thoughts. Konner found him here again, begging him not waste himself on a traitor.

Alone in the tent, the sounds of camp life felt distant, removed. He studied the man in the glow filtering through the tent's sides from lantern and camp fire. He reached for the lamp he'd left outside the tent flap, bringing it in to glow upon the white walls and swell his shadow into a giant that dwarfed his patient.

He drew his fingers across the three parallel gashes on the man's forehead. Bloodshot eyes flickered open at the light striking them. A long moment passed before soft gray eyes focused on him. Then an arm flew up as if to ward off a blow.

He hid his face beneath his forearm. "Verdaen!" he gasped.

Khoti started at the name, spoken with such fervency and grief.

"I'm abomination. Join me with my name: death. I beg you."

Khoti stared at the shuddering figure he knelt beside. He could see the shoulder had broken, the skin purple and dark above the swelling. Nali told him to physically strike Ghyldus would mean death. The sword that struck down Cree had splintered, ripping the enemy with scores of tiny knives as it exploded. Yet, like Asteria, whose arrow had struck the godhead, and Arshal whose stone had struck the godhead, this man remained alive, only his shoulder and arm shattered. Khoti had struck Ghyldus with a blow even more profound. Their battle might have lasted days longer, but it ended because Khoti's blood burned. Verdred's intended death blow to Khoti may have saved them.

"Zopher –" Khoti began.

"Is dead," he stated. "He died in a reservoir above Lagdche."

"Where you got these marks?" Khoti asked, drawing his fingertips along the deep wound on the cheek. He then brushed against a scar on the shoulder. He probed, searching for knowledge from within that the prisoner didn't even know he possessed. He found a hint of something terrible and dangerous inside this man who had been so close a friend.

Dark clothing and armor gone, all that remained were the callouses he had built. The prisoner trembled at the healer's touch and Khoti felt his fear, his sense of nakedness. Khoti's call had brought him back from the brink of forgetfulness, a dark place now mirrored in his healer's face.

"You saved me once," the gray-eyed man muttered. "Let me return the favor. I wasn't worth the effort then, not to come to this. Don't try to help me. You'll only weaken yourself."

"Zopher," Khoti cut him off with just the barest whisper of his name. "You're free."

"No." He twisted away and covered his face. "You make me remember everything I –"

His breath came in a ragged gasp. Khoti could sense the last dark threads of enchantment giving way, everything he'd lived exploding into memory. "I killed hundreds, with my hands, my knife, my orders."

Gray eyes turned to the tent flap and Khoti sensed Resala behind him. He didn't look up from the eyes peeking from beneath a bare and muscular arm.

"I killed Habdelion's heir –"

"Who was a traitor."

He shook his head. "I killed Pladde, innocents! For sport! Destroyed just for the doing. I once celebrated autumn because it smelled so strong of the soil, of life that brings spring." He wiped at reddening eyes, addressing the ceiling. "Come spring, hike for days, or ride, just to see – and I stood near Saran, my father's lands, and I didn't know them. I took the lives of his subjects, my subjects. I killed an animal because it crossed my path. I ripped up a bush because it thrived. I dug up the ground because it lay smooth and mossy. I simply destroyed."

"You were under a spell," Khoti said.

"It must have been within me to do these things or I couldn't have accomplished them with such abandon. The only thing I couldn't allow hurt was Resala. I knew she hated me more than anything else. What if this brutality in me surfaces again? Khoti, we kill traitors. I beg that right."

Resala gasped.

"Zopher," Khoti began.

"Zopher died on the reservoir. Verdred –"

"Died when he struck Ghyldus with a weapon dripping my blood."

The gray eyes closed. "And you forgive me. How could I have hurt you unless the malice was in me? I deserve to die."

"It's not your choice. You'll be tried before the king and that's some time from now."

Khoti leaned back on his haunches, a weary sigh. Zopher's eyes opened to register shocked discovery that Khoti's fingers had been upon him all while they spoke.

"Pine," he muttered. "A fitting scent to cling to you." He looked up at Khoti and gasped, moisture easing his dry eyes for the first time. "What horrors have I made?"

Khoti couldn't answer. A fog in his mind at first, a curling mist shrouded detail. Then sparks flit about the edges of his vision. He felt a sudden deep sadness, weariness, all at once. He knew it came on him and with a sigh he let it take him.

The King's Champion sagged over the traitor before Resala could reach him.

The princess only glanced a moment at all that she had hated, Ghyldus's Malice remaining in his mentor's wake, a memory who had witnessed her battles, who had seen her debased. In a moment Chati and Tre rushed to Khoti's side and Resala slipped out of their way.

When the streak of dawn returned to the sky, the Lharan Guard rode away, grim. Eithurdon's horn remained silent as they pounded southwest for homes likely overrun and in ashes. Konner's parting words remained in the ears of Khoti's friends. The King's Champion refused Konner's call. The power Khoti used to close himself away exceeded Konner's skills.

"He wants his rest," Konner said. "Probably permanent. There's no use for a warrior in a world of peace. He achieved his goal. What's there to move on to?"

The Detarians, too, prepared to ride, Sedaik's remains wrapped in orange given a place of honor before his father. Perouk's words carried his deep bitterness. His only offspring, his only blood, watered soils far from his home. Nothing would grow from Sedaik's blood in the north. They made a brief salute in the direction of the tent where Khoti slept in a dark fever, bows raised, spears striking shields, the thump of fists into chests. All of Ea honored him. They turned and trotted from the fields of the north to seek homes likely ravaged while away.

Habdelion prepared to join them. He'd lost Tedwa and knew now more than he needed of Anlon's treachery and demise. He had children to find homes for and Shela to secure. Gnats alone would have to cleanse the plains of Ghyldus's refuse. Habdelion smiled only for Rena, Kia, Cydwyn and Jali who lingered beside Khoti's tent awaiting word on their mentor. Kia laughed at some aside Cydwyn made. His mouth turned in a wry twist.

Nali followed Habdelion's gaze. Kia's laughter sounded strange, too odd and shrill here on the edge of battle. Cydwyn gave her one of his spare smiles, he a youth so much older but yet a kindred spirit. When Nali looked back Habdelion and the soldiers of Tormor Wood had already fled to specks seeking to catch up with Detarian. Nali smiled after Habdelion. The man's pleasures in the children who'd come to him taught a seer a few things.

He opened his eyes at the feel of hands washing his chest in a familiar motion, tickling him as dribbles of water escaped down his sides.

Dynresa turned as if she felt his gaze upon her.

"My King," she said, inclining her head. She scrubbed at the grime of weeks of war. "I've met smiths and stokers look more regal than you." She scrubbed his elbows until the skin felt raw. "And it seems to me I've caused more harm than good." She tapped on his chest. "Do you hear me or are you off in dreamland again?"

"Still as pleasant as ever." He chuckled, then sat up and grabbed her arms.

"Seems I'm always tending you after your mishaps." She sighed. "Broken legs and dagger wounds. Now it's demon fire." She shook her head. "What next? I really don't think I want to put up with this sort of thing much longer."

He loosened his grip on her arms long enough to shift and pull her closer to him. She wrinkled her nose, gesturing at how the grime clung to him yet, his hair limp and sticking to his face, the scent of death clinging to him.

He touched her cheek. If he'd relied on himself instead of her maybe Ghyldus wouldn't have found him so easy to enchant. The thought of his enemy made his skin crawl and he shivered, feeling for a moment debased, used. Dynresa tried to make him lay back and rest, her expression suddenly concerned.

Why did the gods do this to him, twist and pervert him to their purpose, his life uprooted to serve them? He felt violated and naked as he sat there in the chill of a dawn without Kedtair, ashamed by the violation of his self. He knew the spirits in him now. He could never be the simple soul he wished to be. The extent of his power frightened him. For a moment he considered maybe Dynfearn had purposely lost himself at sea to escape the awful burden.

Arshal looked down into the stone now reflecting all the colors of the opal, all the values of the spectrum in his palm, bright and glowing. Once he had only watched one color at a time dominate the stone. The secret of awakening lay reflected in his palm for all to see. If only Cree had known.

"Ramel!" Arshal said suddenly. "Was he witness?"

Dynresa's mouth curled into the mocking sneer Arshal missed. "Ramel was there, worthless. Did he lift an arm to help? No, he was too busy being the eyes and ears of history, the unbiased witness."

"That was his purpose."

"He could have saved Ernik! Ernik fought more battles for Shande than even you. He died on foreign soil because he believed in the words you gave his king!" Dynresa trembled. "Ramel would only fight to get you there. He did nothing to help comrades when at last you faced the demon! When the demon's fire came, Ramel knew. He could have warned Ernik, who defended Marol. Instead, Ernik didn't live to see his passion proven."

Arshal pulled her to him, ignoring her resistance as he held her, her face pressed against his chest. "And you were there too, with Asteria." He reached for the shoulder he'd seen a dart pierce, but she pulled away.

"I came with Hainad." She dismissed him with a gesture as she brushed her fingers through hair loosened from her warrior braids. "I served. At least I accomplished something."

He grinned at her, forcing a sheepish smile from her. She dipped her washcloth into the bucket and slapped him with it, the water splashing into the dirt to form dark splotches of mud.

The sound of a horn brought Arshal's head up with a snap. "It continues?" His arms braced to push himself up.

"You did your part, King," she stated, wiping the sweat from his face with the wet cloth as she nudged him back down on the blanket. "The Gnats clear the battlefield. The other commands left to secure their lands."

"Except for one."

"There's not much left of Joffa." He heard none of the sourness of their earlier exchange. "And those remaining –" She looked at the ceiling and took a deep breath, giving him a shrug.

For the first time he looked at her closely. Her face held the small scars of battle now. Dark circles beneath her eyes and a thinness hinted of lingering illness, not the lithe health she'd once projected. Even her hair had lost its lustre, the aroma of cloves gone. He found an ugly scar on her arm and reached for it. She pulled away.

"Princess," he said, low and insistent. He sat up again, leaning on one elbow as he guided her face to look at him. "I've changed since I left Hainad."

"I see that."

"More than appearance."

"You aren't the self-pitying child that came to Hainad."

"That bad? And you fought for me anyway?" She merely smiled. "This power's more than I bargained for." She put her fingers to his lips and told him to be quiet and rest. The sweat had broken out on his forehead again.

"I've known Khoti for a time. I saw how the star altered –"

"Khoti?" Arshal leaned forward. How could he have not asked?

He remembered Zopher yanking a sword from Khoti's belly, the Val trickling into him as he battled Fyraer. He sank back with a groan. His hand covered his eyes as the enormity of it all swept in on him. He didn't even sense Khoti's presence, a sense he had grown used to in his battle like a part of himself missing.

"The traitor sent him into a dark fever Konner couldn't rouse him from. Only Nali and your sister keep the whole camp from hanging the prisoner before he's been tried."

From her tone, Arshal knew Dynresa numbered among them.

"Chati and Tre? Do they think that too? And Eithurdon?" Arshal asked.

She shrugged. "Chati and Tre say its weariness ailing Khoti. He's never been well since he mended Jali last year. Maybe that's it. But that man's still a traitor. And shawnsi yet, which makes it worse. Eithurdon's dead."

"Perhaps this should be discussed another time," Nali's voice stated from the tent flap, his tone hinting of command.

Just beyond Nali's silhouette Euzzeldir paced, Ramel ragged beside him.

"Zel's ready to ride and wished to take his leave," Nali said as he entered the tent.

Arshal glanced at Dynresa, but she looked out at her father.

"Zel wants a home for his people again," Nali continued. "All of Hainad came for battle. Many aren't going home again, buried as they are between Shela and here."

"You didn't tell me," Arshal said.

"The subject never arose," Dynresa returned. "I'm needed here to help tend Khoti. I'd also thought to accompany Daris and other wounded Joffans home."

Arshal ignored the small smile on Nali's dour face as he studied Dynresa. Her travels had done something to her, but he wasn't sure just what yet. They'd become different people.

"Did you chase them from the field with your tongue?" Arshal demanded suddenly.

Dynresa laughed, a gasping giggle that died away as she hid her mouth in her hand.

"Well?"

"It didn't work at Shela so I thought I'd use some other less taxing strategy."

"And what strategy is that?"

"I'm aiming to become a Tawnkat," she whispered.

Arshal leaned back, stunned by her seriousness. "The Queen of Shande a Tawnkat?"

"Queen of Shande? I recall no formal quest. Do you seek some delicate thing to grace the back of your throne, King?" Her eyes flashed, perilous. "Naturally you would want that. I went to war for you, watched my people die for you. The delicate thing you want for queen stayed in Sihmad Shal quivering her fear. If you think royal women are so delicate tell me what role your sister played? What a deadly bauble! It is such attitudes that banished Asteria and Khoti." She jumped up to leave.

Arshal's sharp word stopped her. "This time you won't run," he said, as Nali made as if to melt into the walls of the tent. Arshal's hand made a small movement and she stumbled a little, to be caught by Arshal who had reached for her.

She glared at him. "How dare you use your magic on me! You would use the magic meant to fight demons to cover your inept – "

Nali's hand came between them. "Enough! Haven't we had enough war?"

Arshal, sank back, a humming growing in his ears. Sweat broke on his face again. Dynresa reached for her cloth, still flushed with anger. Arshal flung his arm over his face. "You sacrificed for me more than I would ever ask." Dynresa pulled his arm away and pressed a hand to his hot forehead. "Would you make another sacrifice and accompany me to Sihmad Shal?"

"You make it sound so enjoyable. But Daris is in Sihmad Shal. To meet with her I have to go there anyway. I might let you ride beside me if your health improves."

Nali rolled his eyes.

Arshal smiled as Dynresa slipped from the tent to say goodbye to her father.

"Is there something sick about thinking of the heart on a battlefield?" Arshal asked Nali.

"You aren't on the battlefield anymore, King."

A wicked screech echoed up into the valleys and hills,

breaking the silence of darkness and scattering sleepy birds from peaks far distant. A yell followed, a guttural cry. The tatters of a hardened Lharan Guard raised their ragged, blood-stained standard and the outlawed beige and emerald colors of the House of Tsevon. Weary horses leaped forward at command. Those warriors whose dead mounts scattered the vast plain between the Kric and the walls of Sefresal either ran, their outrage at the sight of Minaria ravening their city returning strength to their limbs, or bounced on pillions behind friends, their bows pulled taut and ready to strike the first sign of resistance.

At the wail of Tawnkat shrieks – Konner, Ahrwesz and Teckhan at last returning home – and recognizing Kefta's fair hair and red beard blazing at the head of his command, the besieged took heart. As the Guard rode at the broken gates of Sefresal, undefended by an army not expecting challenge, the cries of Shiadin warriors broke from the cliffs above the city and from the ravines leading into the mountains. The soldiers of Shiad let their anger fall as scalers dropped from the heights into the city. Others climbed the walls in their haste, despite open gates. Arrows and bolts rained on an enemy startled from sleep.

As Kefta called out the defeat of Ghyldus over the cries of battle and as the Dyndevas notes were winded in the throatier voice of Eithurdon's horn, a sortie broke from Eithurdon's Halls and soon the Minarians raced, disheartened and stunned, from the postern doors to find the road to Staph-el.

Soldiers took chase, battling through the ruins of Tasch-el, past the Staph-el mine and at last backing the enemy up against the ruins of the Staph-el bridge. The Minarians threw themselves in the water, only a few reaching the other side for the torturous route home.

As the defeated Minarian soldiers disappeared into the mountains, Steadon stepped from the confines of Eithurdon's Halls. It wasn't lost on the besieged that Kefta and Ytri commanded, Mitte making Eithurdon's horn sing. Gelter and Aibak didn't return, nor Khoti, Chati and Tre, not even the Lady Asteria. A very small Guard returned home from war.

The sound of the brook flowing from beneath Sefresal's gates challenged the city's silence as battle moved away, becoming only the distant and indecipherable clanks and clangs and yells of war. As the bodies of Hothur and Eithurdon were borne through the gates the victory seemed hollow and the wait for Kefta's return from Staph-el too long.

The battle continued for days after the departure of the other commands. At last, the Gnats saw victory, tossing dead Minarians in the fissure Arshal first delved. The ground remained black about the tomb of Ghyldus's body and spirit, a creature who could never return to One.

They didn't linger. The van of Arshal's army sped for home. Though but remnants of Kyne's men marched with what remained of the true Harbor Gnats, they darkened the plain, stretching hours back. One lone wagon sped to keep pace with the officers riding ahead, their faces stony and silent as they crested the last rise to gaze upon the Harbor sparkling distant in the clarity of the late ripening moon.

They stared, silent, uncertain. A scurry of people moved about the waterfront and the smell of war wafted up at them again. The column moved on. Thousands of their number left for homes around Mania, more thousands to other regions along the Quelica. Many died defending that barren scrap of land known as the Kric. Still, they constituted a formidable force to face whatever foe remained.

The wagon jolted. A gasp retched from a bruised occupant.

Khoti's eyes flew open to stare at the ceiling. He'd been tending Zopher. He sat up in a swift movement, then sank back again when faintness swelled at him and sparks swirled before his eyes. He caught a glimpse of the other occupant of the wagon.

He sat up again, more slowly, and crept to his companion, each movement leaden, each muscle crying alarm.

"Zopher." Khoti removed the rag around Zopher's face to reveal his torn and bloody mouth, his dry lips cracked and swollen. Bruises masked his features, especially at his temple where the mark named him shawnsi. Hands secured behind him to a stave of the wagon, his feet hooked in a metal ring in the wagon floor, Zopher regarded him like a gray mood, sad and uncaring.

Khoti ran his fingers across the bruises in search of breaks before his patient could protest. The torn mouth opened, taking the deep breath of dawn in the Val.

"Ah, Zopher, tell me Arshal doesn't know about this."

The man snorted. "He doesn't know. Asteria tried to tell him. His officers assure him her compassion exaggerates. They say I'm fractious, my injuries self-inflicted."

Khoti sat back, letting his head drop into his hands and bringing his knees up into his chest.

"If you're so dangerous, why are you alone with me?" Khoti asked into his knees.

"They want me to witness your lingering death. They want someone here to blame when you die."

Khoti's fist slammed into the boards of the wagon.

"It's the glory of victory," the prisoner whispered.

"Zopher, I know it was the enchantment –"

"It doesn't matter! I'll be punished as I deserve and the matter will be laid to rest!"

"Ah," Khoti challenged. "But you served the aims of Shande! You should be regarded as a hero! Whatever your reasons, you delivered word of Ghyldus's destination to the right ears. And you destroyed Anlon before he could do his worst harm. You killed Verdred who truly would've been a danger unleashed –"

"I am Verdred!" he wailed. "I became what Ghyldus expected, what he created in my mind. I became his illusion and fought against my homeland, my king, my friends, my heritage and my gods. I see it so clear now, a horrible memory that won't free me. How can I live knowing the harm I brought you, dearest of friends? I didn't even know you. Images, like that cuff, tawnkats, haunted me. I taught myself to ignore them. I deserve what the people demand."

"Have you seen Resala?" Khoti demanded suddenly.

"Only the once," he mumbled. "Contempt for me kept her alive. She's seen my crimes. Teshet returned the sapphire I'd left her. The guards let me have it, punishment."

"Punishment. Is that what it meant when you sent it to her?"

Zopher shrugged and looked away.

Khoti studied the defeated man before him. He reached inside, hoping to again touch his friends through thought as he once had. But Kedtair had set. His heightened strengths remained, but the oneness of mind had gone.

"Zopher, it's you in there, my friend," Khoti stated. "It could've been any one of us who dared to race to Lagdche, hoping to make a difference. It could have been a Tawnkat, one of my parents. Even Arshal fell under Ghyldus's spell long before he ever came near the demon."

Zopher took a deep breath. "Today, you'll lay eyes on the city nearest my heart."

The flap whipped open, a guard crying out to find Zopher's mouth uncovered. The man grabbed bound hands and yanked so the prisoner's head smashed into the rear gate. Before the guard could make another move, Khoti had the guard by the collar.

"Commander! He's a danger –" the guard sputtered.

"He's my prisoner and he'll be treated as I choose!" Khoti smacked the guard across the back of his head and released him. "Tell the king and his counselor I must see them and Princess Resala, immediately. And fetch my horse." He shoved the guard out of sight beyond the canvas as the wagon bounced ever closer to Sihmad Shal.

Khoti turned his smoldering gaze on Zopher. "We're ending this nonsense. Next folk will call for Resala's banishment because she consorted with the enemy. There's many with judgments to face. Perhaps I'm held prisoner. Eithur charged me with abduction, a serious charge, and ordered my banishment. The matter will be aired in the king's court so all can gossip about our relationship and how I've made wild the duke's daughter."

"Ah, but you're a hero of this war –"

"War's over. Folks will find their morality again. They'll hate warriors, who bled for Shande, that dare to admit they killed without remorse. Good citizens will declare they know what the spirits want. Isn't that the way of wars in Otayr, Shikora, Shiad, our own history thousands of years ago? I lived beside Asteria on bloody battlefields. In a peaceful world I don't dare speak to my comrade unchaperoned. I've got the spirits in me, Zopher. People will one day claim I defied the spirits' wishes as if I didn't know what's inside me."

"Your hands burned me –"

"I healed you, Zopher. You're free of the enchantment. Now you must free yourself of guilt."

Khoti turned from him, for the first time smelling the scents of Sihma Harbor rising on the winds about him. As he waited for the Guard to return with Fidra, the rock of the wagon lulled him into an uneasy rest, propped beside Zopher.

Daris peered at the columns of troops winding down into Sihma Harbor. She marked the king in front by the circlet crown he wore. She galloped to meet them, pleased by the king's surprise when she pulled up with Oricon and Kelar shadowing her. She smiled at Dynresa and touched her own neck. A patch of Dynresa's skin bore a fresh mark, Khoti's. Daris knew the shawnsi beside the king must be his sister. Otherwise mostly Tawnkats surrounded the king, in places of honor. She noted Rena behind a dour seer with a frightening gaze. He must be Nali. Kia rode beside him, Cydwyn within reach.

Fidra pranced, but Khoti sat her pale and pained. How he'd changed! His gaze as he smiled his pride in her took her breath. Asteria rode close to him, as did Chati, Tre, and Jali. Her family had come home.

Behind her Sihma Harbor thunked with carpenters' hammers rebuilding what her stubbornness wouldn't let Minaria have. Jali merely nodded, his blue gaze darting to Oricon who hovered beside her. Thin and haggard, Jali stared ahead as the king called the column to halt.

"Jali," she whispered.

Somehow over all the noise of the Harbor and armies he heard her. He goaded his mount from ranks. Grabbing her to himself, he almost pulled her from her mount.

"You're back."

"Couldn't leave without sayin' g'bye," he said, his blue eyes so intense, so different.

"I worried after you. Only once an hour or so. I hate that." He bent to kiss her. "I never kissed a man for –"

"Good," he stated.

From beside Nali, a sturdy Harbor man cleared his throat. Jali grinned and released her. "Fa, Daris."

"You're holding up the king," Jan the Innkeeper growled.

Red-faced, Jali grinned as he returned to the ranks.

"And what did all those moon eyes get him but one kiss, anyway," Tre demanded to the chuckles of those around them.

"Clearly time to rebuild my inn," Jan told Nali. "Looks to be a fortune's worth of gossip to be had."

As Daris greeted the king she had bled for, sight unseen, she glanced at Dynresa again. The Queen of Shande a Tawnkat. How that would make the fine ladies gasp. With her wry grin in place, Daris drew her sword, deftly turning it to present the hilts to the king.

"Welcome home, Lord. The Minarians needed more than a measly ten thousand warriors to land here!"

A horn blast from Oricon cued cheers from the waterfront to the Sijway, and even far distant to the walls of Sihmad Shal. The king scanned his home. Over all hung the pall of smoke. Minarian prisoners labored to repair the charred boardwalk and docks. Ships lay askew within and outside the breakwater, many charred and broken.

While the king returned home to a victory deserving of the bunting and cheers and shrill laughter, the torches raised and flowers tossed and the festfires lit for celebration, thousands whose blood had watered the far reaches of Shande would not return home to share in it.

The harvest would be miserable, yet the scent of bruised apples teased the air, mingling with the brown must of leaf and grass passing toward autumn. Birds flocked in fields, their noisy song a symphony, not the coarse calls of the warbirds. And throughout Shande, as soldiers returned home, as fall passed on, as Shande purged itself of enemies, the country at last let out its breath.

Far south, as Evenday neared in the waning moon, remnants of the Army of Three Provinces at last bolstered the Shikorans holding Shela in a fitful stand-off for these long months. Soon the wharves of Shela would again hum with excitement, but far fewer Shelans would come out to watch the ships come in.

In the west, Sihmad Shal's exiles hesitated to leave the people who had opened their hearts to them, as many of them following the haggard Taschians and Staphians back into the mountains as prepared to take the river home to the palace city. Where Tsevon might once have disdained such outsiders, Konner and Segan and Ahrwesz accepted them in the Val with broad grins. No one would ever again walk the streets of Tasch-el, Staph-el and Lhata, unless Khoti came again, as he promised, to seek his brother Von and set him free. Beside the deep, clear lake in the Val, a place that would remain guarded and honored, remained a king and queen, and the markers of heroes such as Tsevon and Amhese. And in a special niche in the common the belongings of Peshal and Cree were kept dusted and ordered.

In the southeast, Joffans reclaimed the glassworks of Hainad from the shifting sands as tents, fewer, popped up beside the little well that served the moveable town, and Prince Euzzeldir prepared to again ride north to witness his king's second coronation, and a joining of warriors.

Far to the west, where the Sea of Tebez swallowed the sun, Minaria collapsed. No strong leader remained to lead it. When the people broke open the country's coffers, they found only the vengeance of Shande to feed the hungry.

Jan hummed as he laid another plank for his new tavern, the Harbor Gnat Inn. He glanced at his son, who bricked a fire pit for Cookie, a warrior's muscles, a warrior's features beneath that shock of red hair. Daris emitted a sour laugh when Jali nearly overturned his mortar.

Jan sat back with a sigh. Jali gave him a quizzical smile.

"We did pretty good, son. Must be our stock to come away from battle unscathed."

Jali shot a glance at Daris's withered arm. Jan cringed inside. It would likely do more harm to apologize.

"I don't know 'bout that," Jali said.

"I mean no great wounds. To come through a battle like the Kric –"

"I had my wounds."

"At the Kric?"

Cookie looked up from where she sanded shelves for her

pantry.

"Jashiho. Khoti brought me back from the dead."

"He mended a wound with that gods' magic?" Jan let out a low whistle.

Jali took a deep breath, leaning on his thighs as he stared into the firepit. "No, not just mended." He pulled the neck of his tunic aside to reveal the jagged dark mark where a Minarian had ripped his chest open. It stretched from its worst point at his shoulder and continued down at an angle to some indefinite point hidden by his clothing. Jan arched his eyebrows. Cookie turned away to stare at the pantry shelves. "He wouldn't accept me dying for him after all we'd gone through together, so instead he near died for me."

Daris reached Jali's side in two steps. She touched his cheek. "He didn't know it would hurt him." Her sourness had gone.

"He knew. He didn't tell you. I knew. I couldn't stop him."

"You kept this to yourself?" she gazed at Jali, surprised.

"If he'd a died –"

"He didn't." Daris put her arm around him.

"I wasn't worth so much as that."

"Well, you're a lousy cook, but you're a good Tawnkat. Can't ask for better. And I'm happy you're here."

Jali grinned foolishly, the pain in his expression evaporating as swiftly as it arose. "I'm glad you finally admit it."

Jan watched his son grip the Joffan woman to his heart, as if desperate, his gaze intense. What would keep idle sword arms busy when they'd finished rebuilding? When warriors became lifemates, a direction he had no doubt Daris and Jali headed, who would be the cool head in such a match? Jan flexed his hand, wondering if he himself could ever put aside the feel of a sword grip.

Nali stared out his old bedroom window onto the Harbor, which sent up a din of hammers and saws and the scent of fresh timber and mortar. He almost expected to hear Olna gasp that the hour had grown late and she must get the biscuits on.

"You sure are sour these days," Bertal's voice carried from the cottage's main room. Nali looked through the doorway to where

Kia, Rena and Bertal scrubbed burned cookpots while Cydwyn daubed holes in the cottage walls. Outside, her dark child on her hip, Laria beat rugs with a broken broom handle, passing neighbors throwing hesitant looks her way.

"I'm just me," Kia replied.

"You used to laugh," Bertal grumbled. "Now you scowl at everything like some Joffan."

Kia smiled a little. "I laugh. I think of Mam sometimes, or other things and I don't feel like laughing."

"Your golden dreams, Kia," Cydwyn reminded her. "They come true: a cottage by the sea full of laughter and the smell of bread. We're fixing up your cottage. If you want bread, you'd better make it, and in a pan better scrubbed than that." He gestured at her half-hearted work.

Kia laughed then, a sweet sound Cydwyn pulled from her like no one else could. She didn't seem so haunting when she laughed.

"I had golden dreams," Bertal said. "I wanted Fa to stop cryin' after you, and I didn't want to hide no more. Most, I wanted to just sleep in the same place every night. So, mine come out okay. Did you have a golden dream, Cyd?"

"Oh, a couple," he admitted. "One come true already. I avenged my family. We'll see about the others. There's time."

Nali had a feeling about Cydwyn's golden dream. Nali had spent his life with Olna, stealing his first kiss from her when she wasn't much older than Kia. But he and Olna were the same age. Cydwyn was a man, a warrior turning seventeen, not a boy of eleven.

"You be staying long, Cyd?" Nali asked from the doorway. Kia looked up, wary. Instinct almost moved her hand to her hip.

"Sage," Cydwyn said in greeting. He shrugged and stared at the wall he daubed. "My family's here. Nowhere else to go. I'm a Tawnkat. I'll be with Tawnkats."

"I wanna be a Tawnkat," Rena stated.

"When you get big." Kia hushed her.

Nali studied the young man who'd taken such special care of his daughters. "Then welcome home, Cyd. Think on us as family. Someday maybe I'll even let you call me Fa."

Kia reddened, smiling as she found a spot on the pan

requiring all her attention.

"Maybe someday I'll have that honor," Cyd agreed. He gazed on the back of Kia's head, then with his ghost of a smile, turned his attention to the wall.

In the king's halls, Arshal and Nali undertook the proclamations and protocol necessary to end a war and resume peaceful trade. Emissaries sailed to each nation to deliver promises of repayment and return the bodies of lost warriors who had become Shande's heroes. They issued commendations with fanfare and speeches as a sense of normalcy returned to the palace halls. Gossips again cluttered receiving rooms and children chased in the alleys.

Already the gossips buzzed about Dynresa's stay, unchaperoned by her father's house but for a warrior girl with a questionable past. They prattled loudest about the tattoo on her neck.

Since Khoti's role meant he would remain with the king, the displaced Tawnkats wandered the streets, restless behind walls that hid the plains, their dour faces clearing the way. At last, the king granted them lands northeast, toward Eithira Point. Even Resala chose to live there, near the place Aziaris had leaped to join Maura. Khoti, Chati and Tre pitched tents and marked out cottage walls, as did Jali and Daris and Cydwyn. The green hills and forested valleys of northern Kalilia felt lush in a way the mountain men might never adjust to as they raced their mounts and sparred in the crisp airs as autumn closed on them.

At last, some months after the king's return, heralds called the city to the palace. The king's long reception hall and courtyards beyond had filled to overflowing with nobles and officers in their fine gowns and livery. Even Khoti glittered in the cleaned and mended garb of the King's Champion, though he disdained the hose the noblemen wore. He'd ridden in from Eithira, Fidra prancing in the fine trappings he'd made her, his entourage of Tawnkats fierce.

Euzzeldir, Habdelion and Steadon followed Khoti into the hall, Steadon trailed by Guardsmen and scowling Tawnkats who had come to see the king's second coronation, as if the first in the

Val hadn't been ceremony enough.

As Khoti paced the hall, he had only just risen again from the ills of a long-time campaigner. In three months of rest his body still hadn't dispersed the poisons he had gathered. The reunion with Tawnkats, Guardsmen, Euzzeldir and Habdelion only added to his sense of restlessness even as he basked in their companionship. Too many were missing.

Arshal stepped from behind the dais curtain, resplendent in the garb his people had made for him, his hair combed and braided in strands of gold. The hall fell silent.

Tre touched Khoti's elbow, then guided him to his place on one side of the king. Konner watched, scowling, clearly reading the poisons and illness still in the King's Champion.

Nali entered from behind the curtain, his olive eyes glittering as Chati followed carrying the ceremonial crown in its casket. Arshal bowed to his advisor as Nali placed the crown on the king's head. Arshal straightened.

"Do the people accept this claimant to the throne?" Nali called out.

A cheer rose deafening within the hall and the courtyards outside.

Nali held up the arrow that slew King Ebon. "So ends the line of Ebon Dyndevas. And to a future, long may be the line of Arshal Dyneadon."

As the cup of wine passed along the line to the throne to Resala and at last Arshal, Khoti felt the pomp somehow cheapened that moment he'd witnessed in the Val when the King in Exile made his vow of vengeance. As if the same thought occurred to Arshal, the king hesitated, his gaze touching on all those special friends and commanders who had brought him to this place, before at last he took the cup's contents in one gulp.

"I promised in our darkest winter in the Val that I would have back this land and return my father's heart home." Arshal spoke softly at first. He straightened, his voice gaining in strength. "It took all of Ea, but Shande is ours again. Now we must rebuild these shattered lives. The Shande of old is gone. Well that it is. We lived fat and comfortable, apathetic and ignorant. We were not one people yet. We're one people now."

Nali nodded to Khoti, who knelt before his king for the second time, unbidden, as he presented his sword. Arshal rested his hand atop the Taschian's head. Khoti felt the gem and its power like a lifebeat against his scalp.

"Khoti of Tasch-el, you proved your honor and bled and battled for this land like no other soldier of Shande. The charges lodged against you prove the clash of war with the traditions of peace. I dissolve all charges and lift the banishment that keeps you from your people." He glanced up at Asteria. "And all such claims against the Lady of Sefresal are dissolved for these same reasons."

Khoti mumbled his thank yous, preparing to rise, but Arshal hadn't removed his hand. "You remain a member of my council, King's Champion and Sword of Shande. I command you form a King's Watch, patterned after the Lharan Guard. The Watch will ensure that at no time in the future will any forget why it exists. Never again will we be at a loss to defend ourselves." Arshal nodded and Khoti stood.

Arshal turned to the dour Harbor man with the scarf still bound across his brow. "I name Nali Drulson King's Counselor and Steward, the first shal to hold such post since the Making."

A rustle of voices grew as the hall's doors opened.

"Without my sister, I would have failed," Arshal continued. "And she would have failed if not for my friend Zopher don Saran." Grumbles forced Arshal to raise his voice above the clamor as a guard led Zopher, bound and in castoff clothes, before the king. "If not for Zopher, whatever his reasons, we would have failed. I know what it is to fall under such enchantment. He committed wrongs in the name of Verdred and Ghyldus. At its core, his heart remained true. I pardon his crimes." Grumbles and a buzz of fear grew in the hall. "Set him free."

His bonds loose, Zopher fell to his knees. Khoti noted how Tre had moved closer to Teshet, peered into her teary face, touched her shoulder. He wanted to grin, but the reactions to Zopher's pardon fanned an ember in his gut.

Resala went to Zopher and urged him to his feet. He flinched at her touch.

"My suitor disdains me now?" she asked in a whisper that carried to Khoti's ears. He knew she stole the pain from Zopher's memories, sensed the comfort she doled out as if a healer. As Zopher rose to his feet, she put her arm around him, eliciting several loud objections from the crowd. Khoti wanted to wipe the grumbles from their lips. His gaze brought silence to the hall.

"You can tell your children your courtship was stormy," Arshal said, though he didn't smile. "If it's your wish, I grant my blessing."

When the hall grew quiet again, Arshal again scanned the crowd. "So many Shandeans served with honor: Khoti and his Tawnkats, the battles waged by the Lharan Guard and the Army of Three Provinces, the Blood Rage of the Harbor Gnats. We must not forget. We can't go back to the soft ignorance we lived. I wield no decorative stellan sword good only for cutting butter." He drew his sword in a swift flourish, making several in the hall flinch. He raised it toward the ceiling, the bright blade glittering with the white light emanating from his palm. "And I sleep beside my armor. With Dynfearn died the fear and knowledge of war, and we forgot. I will not let us." He lowered his sword but did not sheath it. "Prince Euzzeldir granted my suit." He took a few steps toward the crowd, taking Dynresa's hand and leading her from her father's side. "The Queen of Shande will join the divergent lines of rule, just as we've joined the tribes of Shande into a nation. My lifemate will be my partner, no mere decoration at my table. Princess Dynresa fought, and bled for her king. She earned the Tawnkat mark she bears on her neck with honor. A mark even I have not earned! She will be a strong queen to help rebuild our tattered land. We will not forget."

Dynresa's eyes shone up at him. Khoti had never seen the king so regal, nor Dynresa so demure. Arshal grinned. No biting reply came, only her honored smile.

"Then the lines are joined," Nali said. "All is one." The king's gem glowed.

Only a few hours later, Khoti stood alone staring out over the city from the Tower of the Sun as the sun sank west over a homeland to which he sensed he would never return to live. He belonged to Arshal now, bound to make this land safe. He would live far from the stony castle his heart still wandered in when he slept. It made his throat constrict to think of his hunts with Konner and his fa, the flowers of spring, the soft growl of tawnkats and wolvers, wild things in a wild world.

Below him, Resala and Zopher on the parapet of a lower tower faded to a silhouette. Pariah, Dread Warrior he remained, a tool Khoti would use to build the King's Watch. Shande would not forgive Zopher. Elders threatened wayward children with a black-garbed demon come to snap their neck in the night and devour them, heart first, as Fyraer's collector of souls.

In the distance, the sea moved fitfully. He half-imagined he saw some distant beast rise above the waves to crash in a playful plume of spray.

They had vanquished the demon, but not destroyed it. Somewhere on the edge of creation the evil intent and vengeful desire simmered, awaiting only opportunity. Wherever he lurked, Fyraer could return when the awakened king had gone. Khoti felt it, knew it. He had absorbed Fyraer's dark poison, spared the king. It still gnawed him, twisted him and sapped his strength.

"Someday we'll ride to all the lands again, together," Arshal said at his elbow, startling him so that he clutched his chest. The moon popped up from behind, fat and orange like the gourds ripening in the fields. Khoti turned to find Nali accompanied the king.

Nali touched Khoti's shoulder. "Your idleness troubles you."

Khoti nodded and swept his hand toward the north, his gaze never leaving the orange glitter of the sea, lit as if by thousands of lanterns in the sparkle of the harvest moon. "I know he's waiting for our guard to slip, for some weak successor. This vigil could last eons."

"The secret will pass on," Nali assured him. "To our offspring. It'll stay alive. Perhaps your children or mine will carry on our roles, or even our grandchildren, though I hate to wish such confusion on them –"

"The demands of awakening," Arshal said, "That's probably why it faltered in the line. Then, they used the osfothye to call upon the knowledge. We forgot how to do it."

Khoti turned to stare at them. Arshal's hair absorbed the paling light of the moon as it escaped the horizon. The long blue mantle hanging from his shoulders to ward off the chill encircled him in shadow, hiding armor, sword and dagger. The war ended. Yet they stood safe within these halls in armor and armed.

He gripped the hilt of his sword in a white-knuckled grasp, his gaze again turning northward. The smiths continued to hammer out weapons. Guards and veteran warriors walked the battlements and quartered in tent towns outside the gate awaiting the construction of barracks over the charred timbers of Dlan, which in the days of Dynfearn had served the same purpose. Soon, as his Tawnkat officers took over the same roles in the King's Watch, the city would again be a fortress. No flower gardens would be replanted on the battlements in Dyneadon's day. And from the towers a new standard flapped, the lion trampling the flames, just beneath the royal blue pennants. He shivered.

Arshal's hand fell on Khoti's shoulder. "You still haven't recovered from mending me," his accusation came as a sigh. Khoti shrugged his hands away.

"Come, we've a marriage feast to attend!" Arshal clapped him on the back. "Dynresa will lash me with her Joffan tongue if I let you delay us and ruin the feast. The King and Queen of Shande certainly wouldn't want to cause any talk."

They clasped arms, smiling shyly. Without looking back at the fortified city now glowing silver-white in the moon's glow they descended from the Tower of the Sun into the hearth-warmed heart of the palace, drinking in the growing scent of the feast as it wafted through vents and passageways calling to a hunger that after so long might never be sated.

Asteria stood on the battlement, studying Laria and Nali silhouetted against the bright sparkle of the moon on the Aziaris Sea. The silent woman walked as if lost in a daze, not speaking as Nali walked beside her, carrying the dark-eyed child on his shoulders. Farther distant, she could see the brightly-lit halls and courtyards where long tables groaned with feast fare, laughing Shandeans reveling in something that had nothing to do with war.

Asteria heard a soft step behind her and instinctively tensed, crouching as she turned. Khoti emerged from the dark, the moonlight glittering from the bright garb of the King's Champion. She glanced back at Laria, as if to seek escape, from what, she didn't know. Laria and her dishonor had rounded the tower.

"You're avoiding me," Khoti stated as he leaned on the wall beside her, his emerald eyes so intense she feared losing herself in them. His voice pinched the breath from her. "I suppose you'll be going home now when Steadon departs. I've gotten used to your company."

"I am a Tawnkat," she whispered. "I do not want to become Duchess of Lharan. I gave up my castle for yours when I followed you to Mershy. I cannot turn back. I have been a Tawnkat too long and the walls of cities are no longer a comfort to me." She glanced at him, then away. "Still, I have such petty fears as being alone, without a home –"

She didn't protest when Khoti turned and pulled her against him. There seemed to be less of him, injury and the wasting poisons of past healings had left him gaunt. Her arms fit so natural around him, his touch warm. She felt the quiver in his arms like a tingle through her.

"Being a Tawnkat never stopped me from voicing petty fears to you," he muttered into her. "Let me be your home, Asteria," he said in a voice unlike the warrior that could screech with such wildcat fury. "All we've gone through – I never wanted to refuse you. It was misplaced loyalty, a boy's heart –"

"Never misplaced," she insisted into his chest. "Misunderstood, maybe. Ah, Khoti, I have nothing. I lost everything –" She looked up at him to see pain cross his face, wanting to hit herself.

"You still have me. I've nothing to go back for. My family's dead. I have an obligation to my people and to freeing Von, but I don't think I could ever be a simple Taschian again," he mumbled, looking away. "Let's not be like Maura and Aziaris, forever apart like this. I've been here all along, watching over you, failing at it, wanting to die when you bled for me."

Her fingers dug into his back. His arms seemed to absorb her, surrounding her with the aromas of pine and wood smoke, the cool damp of a tiny cave in the Val. She pressed her eyes shut, trying to remember their peace together. All the images had faces missing, Toban, Tsevon, Latra, Amhese, Tedwa, Sedaik, Ernik, Eithurdon, the images of the people grown dim with passing.

"I hate being just a fellow warrior," Khoti admitted. "I envied Jali for his giddiness over Daris. We excused him rushing to her side when she was hurt, or for him being jealous." He took a deep breath. "I wanted to kill Baynu. Not for the reasons I should've. That's why I didn't. Shela died for my jealousy. You've had more than a year to see all my faults. And there, I just admitted the worst of them."

He started to release her and turn away, but she fell against him. "We have been such fools," she said, seeing her sparkling talisman still hanging from his neck, battle long over, the pendant brighter than her eyes would ever be again.

"We've all been fools," he echoed. "Do you think we've waited a proper time now? Heard all the evils about each other?"

"I am a fallen woman. I slept in men's camps –"

"Scandalous. Remember my cave? I've built, well, Chati and Tre built me a cottage. Now I can offer you a true home."

"Some mountain boy aspires to the daughter of a duke?"

"No boy, but a man." He grinned at her a moment, before it faded as his eyes grew soft like the lush meadows around Sihmad Shal. "Be my lifemate, Asteria. Let's end this war."

She smiled at him. "The way of your people," she said softly. "The way Latra taught." She touched the fringe of the mountbuckskin tunic he'd made for her, cleaned and mended and so soft and finely sewn. Would the lost cultures of so many lands remember these best of traditions now that so many of the wise and elders were gone?

He took her hand then, and standing on the walls of Sihmad Shal, the city lain out below them, moonlight glittering from the sea, he kissed the calloused hand of a warrior.

"Welcome to Tasch-el, Lady Asteria. I am your lifemate."

Asteria woke and reached for the comforting touch that made her forget her nightmares. Khoti wasn't there. He didn't stand at the cottage window looking out over Aziaris as he often did when the moon stood high and bright, shedding a white light that reminded them of Kedtair.

She grabbed a blanket and went outside to find him sitting on the wooden steps, listening to Maura caressing the rocks far below. For a moment, she thought she caught a glimpse of some great beast far out to sea, leaping as if to reach the moon.

She set her hand on his shoulder. He rested his cheek on it.

"It goes on," she stated.

He nodded. "The poison passes, but slow. Arshal was strong enough to meet Fyraer, but not me. His poison ... sometimes I feel so dark inside."

"That woke you?"

He shook his head. "I dreamed of Shela, or Etaleah, or the Kric, some battle that roused the warrior inside." He looked up at her, eyes glittering in that way that always gave her a shiver. She glanced at the cottages of their friends scattered on this high plain and wondered if their personal warriors visited them in their sleep.

She felt the heat of the warrior pulsing through Khoti's blood. He pulled her down beside him and held her, tugging the blanket so that it covered them both. He gazed at her. The moonlight shone bright in his eyes as the scent of the Val surrounded them. Slowly his skin cooled to her touch, the darkness in him retreating. She knew it lurked in there yet, a poison he couldn't shed, so great even the spirits couldn't help him more than a little at a time.

"Someday it will end," she said.

Far out to sea, two beasts leaped and frolicked, guarding the shores of Shande.

THE END THE ENCHANTER'S WEB

Cast of Characters

In order of appearance

Ramel – Advisor to Prince Euzzeldir; Visionary.

Euzzeldir – Shawnsi. Joffan prince and provincial leader titled as a former line to the throne; father of Dynresa.

Arshaldon Dyndevas – Shawnsi. Eldest son of King Ebon and Queen Sala; King in Exile of Shande.

Cree – Advisor to the king; Arshal's tutor; Visionary; also known as Idenai; killed by Minarians in the Val.

Khoti of Tasch-el – Surviving younger son of Tsevon and Amhese; Tawnkat leader; Lieutenant in the Lharan Guard; aide to Eithurdon; healer; Headman of Tasch-el and the Independent Lharan Tribes; King's Council; King's Champion; Sword of Shande; aspiring suitor of Asteria; named Verdaen by his enemy; favorite mount: Fidra.

Habdelion – Shawnsi. Provincial leader and Duke of Mershy; brother of Queen Sala.

Nali Drulson – Fugitive from Sihma Harbor who uses aliases Nali Bertalson and Jani Hostler; derna of the First Degree (scholar); Harbor Gnat commander; King's Counselor; children: Bertal, Kia, Rena; lifemate Olna and son Nalel killed in Eilime.

Ghyldus – Takes throne of Minaria after Mol Azezial's assassination; lesser god who aids Minaria after the Great War; known for enchantments; considered an acolyte of Fyraer.

Dynresa – Shawnsi. Daughter of Euzzeldir; Princess of Joffa.

King Azren – Arenhian king, derna.

Peshaldon Dyndevas – Shawnsi. Youngest son of King Ebon and Sala; consort of Maura.

Resala Dyndevas – Shawnsi. Daughter and youngest child of King Ebon and Sala; forced to serve as consort to Ghyldus; betrothed to Zopher.

King Wyeff Shikora – King of Shikora.

Esthen -- Prince Esthenshaldon Dyndevas. Shawnsi. Second son of King Ebon and Queen Sala. A revered commander who falls in the defense of Sihmad Shal.

Eithurdon – Shawnsi. Duke of Lharan and provincial leader in exile of Kishma; brother of Steadon; father of Asteria; nephew of King Ebon.

Asteria – Shawnsi. Daughter of Eithurdon; companion of Khoti; officer in the Army of Shande; Tawnkat; favorite mount Clanna.

Verdred – "Dread warrior" King's Champion of Minaria; Ghyldus's Malice.

Zopher don Saron – Shawnsi. Son of Baron Sipheron don Saran. Suitor of Resala's and friend of Arshal. Scout leader; betrothed to Resala. Defeats an becomes Verdred.

Sedaik son of Perouk – Detarian. Labor camp internee; protégé of Khoti; leader of Detarian forces.

Tedwa – Tachi leader; uncle to Ledak.

Jan the Innkeeper – Owner of Sihma Harbor's Old Scow Inn; lifemate is Cookie; son Jali; Harbor Gnat leader.

Pedr the Drayman – Former Reve (officer of the peace) of Sihma Harbor; Harbor Gnat leader.

Loch Asmodiel – Governor of the Minarian Protectorate of Shande.

Aron Keeper – Lighthouse Keeper of Sihma Harbor; informant/traitor.

Tel – Sihma Harbor farmer; Olna's cousin; Harbor Gnat.

Cookie – Lifemate of Jan the Innkeeper and mother of Jali; Gnat cook.

Bertal Nalisson – Sihma Harbor. Son of Nali and Olna. Twin of Kia.

Konner of Tasch-el – Taschian Constable and Second to Khoti; Tawnkat; healer.

Olna Bl– Lifemate of Nali; killed by Minarians at Eilime along with infant son; mother of Bertal, Kia and Rena.

Adesia – Lifemate of Loch Asmodiel; "Matriarch" of Shande.

Laria Keeper – Eldest daughter of Aron Keeper; servant to Adesia and Loch Asmodiel.

Cydwyn Lockman – Kalilian from Etaleah. Labor camp internee; Tre's attendant, scout/courier; Tawnkat; officer in Khoti's armies.

Jali Janson – Son of Jan the Innkeeper and Cookie; labor camp internee; attendant to Khoti; Tawnkat officer and scout.

Kia Renali – Daughter of Nali and Olna; Twin of Bertal; labor camp internee; attendant to Asteria.

Rena Renali – Youngest daughter of Nali and Olna; labor camp internee.

Chati the Cooper's son – Taschian. Konner's nephew. Former attendant to Khoti; Lharan Guardsman; officer in the Army of Shande; Tawnkat.

Tre the Imager – Taschian. Khoti's former attendant; Lharan Guardsman; officer in the Army of Shande; Tawnkat.

Daris – Joffan labor camp internee and courtesan; Chati's attendant; Tawnkat officer; cousin of Dynresa.

Von – Khoti's older brother who died in raid on Tasch-el.

Baynu – King's Champion of King Wyeff Shikora.

Ledak – Tachi. Nephew of Tedwa.

Anlon of Mershy – Adopted Dasireian son of Habdelion; potential suitor of Asteria; traitor; killed by Verdred.

Kyne – Iyrafael Gnat.

Perouk – Detarian. Father of Sedaik.

Marol – Consul of Otayr. Offers refuge to noncombatants.

King Farlal – King of Otayr.

Kefta Salman – Captain of the Lharan Guard and friend of Khoti.

Hothur – Minarian; former captain of Sefresal's dungeon turned to Shande's side.

King Keyen – King of Shiad.

Jeret – Pladde resistance leader; uncle to Teshet.

Teshet – Pladde servant rescued by Amhese; handmaiden to Resala; niece of Jeret; part of Pladde resistance.

Tsevon of Tasch-el – Father of Khoti and Von and lifemate of Amhese; Former headman of Tasch-el and the Independent Lharan Tribes; Tawnkat leader; healer; sparked the Pladde rebellion; dies in exile in the Val from healing Khoti.

Amhese – Staphian. Lifemate of Tsevon and mother of Von and Khoti; assassinated Mol Azezial; dies in battle of Sefresal.

Ahrwesz – Taschian. Lifemate of Latra; Tawnkat; Cousin to Khoti.
Aibak – Shiadin border guard who arranges support for the Val.
Teckhan – Taschian. Tawnkat.
Gelter – Tawnkat.
Maura – God that rules the seas.
Aziaris – God of gardens.
Ytri – Officer in the original Lharan Guard; scout and friend of Khoti.
Geleg – Member of the original Lharan Guard, scout and friend of Khoti.
Steadon Dodfrenyen – Shawnsi. Younger brother of Eithurdon; cousin of Arshal and nephew of King Ebon.
Segan – Taschian. Tawnkat.
Habda – Shawnsi. Daughter of Habdelion.
Ernik of Ar-Tebez – King Azren's representative to Shande.
Mitte Salman – Younger brother of Kefta. Lharan Guardsman and scout.
Davin – Taschian. Tawnkat.
Velder – Tawnkat.
Dagon – Tawnkat.
Oricon – Captain of Farlal's forces in Sihmad Shal.
Kelar – Captain of Sihmad Shal's Home Guard.
Toban – Member of the original Lharan Guard; scout and friend of Khoti; executed in occupied Sefresal.
Latra – Taschian. Culture keeper; kinswoman of Tsevon and Khoti; dies in Lagdche.

TERMS

Shawnsi – descendants of unions between the gods and shals prior to the Great War. Shawnsi are largely identified by a small star-shaped birthmark on their temple.
Visionary – Term said to be reserved for the gods who remained behind after One called them home, but also a name given to the highest ranking derna
Osfothye – A plant with multiple medicinal, food and ritual purposes
Dynfearn the Lost – Historic shawnsi leader of renown from the

Great War

Verdaen – "Demon warrior" a name Minarians apply to Khoti

King's Champion – Elite warrior in service to and representing a king in battle

Sword of Shande – Commander of the armies of Shande

Eidhalt – elite warriors of Minaria

Derna – Scholars qualified to serve as advisors and cast auguries; recipients of Certificates Dernailye after many years of study; level of "degree" (first, second, etc.) suggests initial ranking of skill; singular or plural term

Pladde – Labor/oppressed caste of Minaria

Tachi – Shal tribe of Tormor Wood

Harbor Gnats – Nickname for Harbor militia

Reve – Royal appointee who serves as town leader and constable

Lierye – The official history/documentation of the land of Shande

Taschian/Staphian/Lhatan – Shal tribes of the Lharan Mountains

Second – The second in command to a Lharan tribal headman

Tawnkat – Lharan tribal resistance fighters and "soldiers" under Khoti

Hogde – Ruling/higher caste of Minaria

Sage – Term applied to high-ranking derna

Dyn Eadon – Power of Ea – title conferred on Arshal by the King of Otayr

Shal – the people of Ea who survived the Great War; creations of Terremar and his children

Stellan – A silvery metal softer than adanan mined in the mountains; often edges weaponry or is used for decorative purposes

Adanan – An extremely hard metal mined in the Lharans

DEITIES

Terremar – One of two "offspring" of One

Fyraer – One of two "offspring" of One; banished

Kedtair – Son of Terremar whose star rises every ninth year to create chaos as a sign from the gods; can mark those who will be good or evil if born during the month it's overhead.

Ghyldus – Lesser god who aids Minaria after the Great War;

known for enchantments; source of Ghyldism; becomes ruler of Minaria

Maura – Daughter of Terremar who rules the sea; creations include water, and the Merien

Aziaris – God who cared for One's gardens; breaks oath to One to serve Maura

One – The ultimate energy and fate (intent) of all that exists

Idenai – A lesser god who remained behind to become the Visionary Cree.

About the Author

A former journalist, editor, and farmer, M. Turville Heitz's short fiction appeared in anthologies and magazines before she took a break to collect a PhD and teach science and technical communications to undergrads. Her novel *Black River* was published in 2024 under the Mystique Press imprint of Crossroad Press. She lives on a defunct farm near Madison, Wisconsin where she coddles chickens and is kept by cats. She can be found on social media at MegT.bsky.social.

https://Oaklandhillsfarm.com

Other Books by M. Turville Heitz

Black River

Specters from a Dream (Book I of The Enchanter's Web)

Dread Warrior (Book II of The Enchanter's Web)

www.ingramcontent.com/pod-product-compliance
Lightning Source LLC
Chambersburg PA
CBHW022141010726
47493CB00002B/293